THE JOKER
SOLDIERS OF ANARCHY

NIKKI J SUMMERS

Copyright Material

This book is a work of fiction. Names, characters, businesses, places, events, and incidents are either the product of the author's imagination or used in a fictitious manner. Any resemblance to actual events or persons living or dead is purely coincidental.

Any trademarks, product names, or names featured are assumed to be the property of their respective owners and are used for reference only.

Copyright 2022 by Nikki J Summers.

All rights reserved. No part of this work may be reproduced, scanned, or distributed in any print or electronic form without the express, written consent of the author. A CIP record of this book is available from the British Library.

Cover Image: Chris Davis
Cover Model: Jord Liddell
Cover Designer: Lori Jackson Design
Editing/Proofreading: Lindsey Powell at Liji Editing.
Caroline Stainburn
Interior Designed and formatted by: Lou J Stock

THE JOKER

OTHER BOOKS BY NIKKI J SUMMERS

<u>Soldiers of Anarchy Series</u>
The Psycho
The Reaper

<u>Rebels of Sandland Series</u>
Renegade Hearts
Tortured Souls
Fractured Minds

<u>Stand-Alone</u>
Luca
This Cruel Love
Hurt to Love

<u>Joe and Ella Duet</u>
Obsessively Yours
Forever Mine

All available on Amazon Kindle Unlimited.
Only suitable for readers 18+ due to adult content.

THE JOKER

THE JOKER

THE JOKER

PLAYLIST

Available to download on Spotify

Darkside – Neoni
Seventeen Going Under – Sam Fender
The Kid I Used to Know – Arrested Youth
Wolf in Sheep's Clothing – Set It Off, William Beckett
Firestarter – The Prodigy
Street Fight – Adam Jensen
War – ArrDee, Aitch
Master of Puppets – Metallica
Twisted – MISSIO
Ashes – Stellar
Use Somebody – Kings of Leon
This Is Love – Air Traffic Controller
We Don't Have to Dance – Andy Black
Overwhelmed (Christian Gates Remix) – Royal & the Serpent, Christian Gates
You and I – PVRIS
Fix You – Coldplay
The Joker and The Queen (Feat. Taylor Swift) – Ed Sheeran, Taylor Swift
I Believe in a Thing Called Love – The Darkness

THE JOKER

Laugh, and the world laughs with you. Weep, and you weep alone.

ELLA WHEELER WILCOX

THE JOKER

PROLOGUE
A Message from Colton

Dear Reader,
    Let me start by saying how grateful and truly humbled I am that of all the stories out there, you decided to read mine.

Congratulations.

You have impeccable taste.

I'll try to keep things as entertaining as I can while I navigate you through the *interesting* journey that is my life. I know that, first and foremost, you're here for a little romance and perhaps a happily ever after. I want to give you that, I really do. Who knows, maybe fate has something in store for me that even I'm unaware of. Well, it wouldn't be fate if I knew, would it?

Before I start, though, I need to point out that I haven't always been the sexy, charismatic, gorgeous specimen you see on the cover of this book. It hasn't always been easy being me, it's taken a few years and life lessons to get to the point I'm at today. So, I'm going to start my story by showing you the three key moments in my life, moments that made me the person I am. I would say four, but I don't want to dwell on what happened to my mother.

Each moment has taught me something I needed to know to survive in this crazy whirlwind called my life. None of these moments are pretty. In fact, they're downright dark and disturbing at times. But I feel it's important to experience their impact on me, so you can understand where I'm coming from and get to know the real Colton. Not the one I show the world, but the one I've kept hidden.

That's right; you'll get exclusive insight into my fucked-up mind.

But I need to warn you, if you feel uncomfortable reading about child neglect, mental abuse, childhood trauma courtesy of my parent's distorted moral compass, issues around parental suicide –I don't go into detail– and scenes of a violent and sexual nature, you should turn back now. I might tell this story with a smile on my face, but my life is no laughing matter. As I outline these key moments, there will be some time jumps in the first few chapters.

Still want to find out what makes me tick?

Why, thank you for taking a chance on me!

As I said before, I am truly honoured and flattered.

So, strap yourself in. Brace yourself and get ready to be whisked back in time to experience the early life of Colton King. A boy who hadn't yet learned about the art of smiling and laughing. A youngster desperate for someone to show him the way. A lad who needed to leave his house in order to find a home.

That'll make more sense as you read, I promise.

I hope you enjoy delving into my world, the world of **The Joker**. And remember, I don't tell you what happened in my past to make you pity me. I tell you so you can understand me.

See you on the flip side.

COLTON.

16 THE JOKER

PART ONE
Lessons from the past

THE JOKER

CHAPTER ONE
The Birth of The Joker

Lesson 1: Everybody lies
Colton, Aged Five

I kept my eyes glued to my school book, sounding out the words on the page and desperately trying not to make a mistake. I wanted to impress Rosie more than anything in the world. I wanted to show her how much I'd learned since the last time she'd sat and read with me a few months ago. Getting praise wasn't something that happened to me that often, but praise from Rosie made me feel like fireworks were going off inside my belly. It was magical, and in my life, that was an emotion as rare as gold dust.

She'd already flipped the book over to look at the back before we'd started, checking what stage I was on now. Her eyes lit up like the sun I was reading about when she found out I'd skipped a whole three levels up the reading ladder since she'd last been here. The cuddle she gave me, and the warmth in her smile made me glow from the inside. I loved having Rosie around and wished she came over more often, but she only visited when she had work to do for my dad.

"B...br...igh...t, bright sun sh...sh...shone in the sk... sky."

I used my finger to focus on each word, dragging it across the page and blinking to stop the letters from dancing about. I could feel the heat from Rosie's leg radiating into me as I sat beside her, hunched over, welded to her side. Her perfume wafted over me like the flowers my mum used to keep around our house; sweet, magical, making me want to stay close and breathe her in. I wished that I could find the courage to climb into her lap. I used to sit in her lap years ago when Mum was still here, but not anymore. A lot of things had changed since Mum had gone. We didn't have flowers in our house anymore either. I knew in a moment, Rosie would be gone too, her scent lingering for a second and then disappearing.

Fleeting.

Temporary.

Like everything in my life.

"You're doing really well, Colton. You're sounding out the words so much better than you used to." Rosie leaned down, and I felt her breath tickle the hairs on my head as she whispered, "You make me so proud, little man."

That tickling sensation spread to my neck and travelled down my back in a wave of appreciative little goosebumps after hearing her say those words. I liked making her proud, and as I shivered from the affects her words and closeness had on me, she wrapped an arm around my shoulder and squeezed.

But like everything, that feeling didn't last.

Our cosy bubble was short-lived, when a saucepan clattered to the floor in the kitchen-diner where we sat, breaking through the calm like a sledgehammer to my nerves. I jumped, my heart racing as I stared across the room at Rosie's friend, Tina, who was putting away the dishes my dad had left on the draining board from the night before.

"The kid's reading a book called Sunshine and Rainbows," she hissed. "And he looks like the worlds about to end. He couldn't look more miserable if he tried." Tina spoke in a whisper, but I heard her. We both did, judging from the way Rosie's arm tensed up.

Rosie sighed next to me, pretending she didn't care about the verbal bomb her friend had just dropped. She patted my knee and told me, "Keep reading, bud. I'll be listening from the other side of the room, okay? I wanna hear about the rainbows next."

But when she stood up, I felt my stomach drop, and I didn't want to read anymore. I missed the warmth she gave me, not just from her body but from her attention. I furrowed my brow, pretending I was working out a tricky word, but I wasn't. I was homing in on the hushed conversation that Tina and Rosie were having across the kitchen. Like a strange, hissed argument conducted with gentle voices that made it look like they were sharing secrets. But the secrets they were whispering weren't theirs to tell. They were mine.

"Tina, do you have to be so vile? The kid's been through enough without you taking sly jabs." Rosie looked over her shoulder to where I was sitting, and I ducked my head, trying to appear as if I was engrossed in my reading.

"What?" Tina shrugged like she didn't get it as she forced

a frying pan into a cupboard and slammed the door shut. "I just made an observation. It's not like my sarcastic comments are the worst he's going to have to contend with. The kid's gonna have to toughen up if he wants to survive the King household."

I thought I was already doing a pretty good job of surviving the King household. I did my chores and helped my dad when he asked. What else was there? I was tough already. Tina was just mean. I wished Rosie had come on her own.

"He's five years old," Rosie stated, her fists clenched as she stood still like a statue and glared at Tina. "He's seen more shit than any of us. And I doubt Glenn is going to be winning any father of the year awards, do you?"

I didn't know there was an award.

Would Dad be mad that he wasn't going to win?

I doubted it. Not much seemed to faze my dad, apart from me. I think he found me annoying at times and wished I wasn't here. I wanted that too, sometimes. It wasn't nice feeling like an intruder in your own home.

"I don't think Glenn King even knows he's a father half the time," Tina replied, mirroring my thoughts, and I blushed. Did she know what I was thinking? "Which is all the more reason for Colton to wake up and smell the bullshit."

I sniffed quietly, but all I could smell was Rosie's perfume.

"Don't swear around him," Rosie hissed through her teeth, jabbing her finger at Tina.

"Don't *swear*?" Tina huffed out a laugh. "Because *that's* going to fuck him up?" She lowered her voice further, and with eyes narrowed on Rosie, she sneered, "Let's not forget the fact that six months ago he walked in to find his mother swinging from the rafters in her bedroom."

"Exactly." Rosie threw her arms up, then her head dropped, her chin resting on her chest as she stared blankly at the floor and added in a sad whisper, "He needs kindness. It's no wonder he doesn't smile after what he's been through. Why would he?"

"Does anyone ever smile in this house?" Tina spat back. "Apart from Glenn, when he's counting his royalties."

I had no idea what royalties were. The royal family hadn't ever been to our house, and we didn't know them.

"I feel for him." Rosie turned to glance across at me, and I felt my cheeks burn. I gripped the edges of my book in my sweaty hands and wished I could lose myself in the sunshine and rainbows on the pages, but all I saw was black and white. A life of cardboard cut-out dreams that were as flimsy as the book I was holding. My mum wasn't here anymore, and from what I could tell, you had to be ready to lose anyone at any moment because there was no promise of happiness. No forever. Life wasn't sunshine and rainbows; that was all made up, like this book. For me, life was hushed voices, secrets, and pain. Everyone left eventually. Everyone died. They'd tell you they wouldn't, but they all lied. Why smile if life gives you nothing to smile about?

Rosie picked up the cutlery and started to place it back into the drawer, and she said, "I just hope Glenn keeps the business side of things away from him for as long as possible. Otherwise, that little boy is going to grow up to become one very fucked-up man."

"Language." Tina clucked her tongue at Rosie, and Rosie rolled her eyes, jamming the drawer closed then folding her arms over her chest.

"We both know why we're here, but is it really so bad to

give the boy a bit of attention and make him feel good? Help him forget his life for a while? Every kid deserves a chance." Rosie shrugged, and then with a smile, she added, "I always wanted to be a schoolteacher. I like spending time with him."

"Don't tell Glenn." Tina smirked and waggled her eyebrows, suddenly becoming playful. "He'll have you dressed as a schoolgirl bending over for him."

Why would Rosie dress as a schoolgirl? She was an adult, and school didn't teach adults. These two had weird conversations sometimes. I didn't understand any of it.

"Like I'd tell that shithead anything," Rosie replied, just as the patio doors slid open and Kenny, one of my dad's friends, poked his head through the door and snapped, "Time's up, ladies. We need you in the summerhouse."

The summerhouse was my dad's workshop at the bottom of our garden. I wasn't allowed in there. Dad had told me he'd ground me for a month and ban all sweets in the house if I ever went inside. So, I stayed away. But I was curious about what he did in there, I couldn't lie.

Rosie and Tina sighed and walked towards the patio doors like it was the last thing they wanted to do. Almost as if their legs were made of lead. I might be a kid, but even I saw the signs.

Rosie hesitated and then came across to me and ruffled my hair. I peered up at her as she leaned towards me, then planted a kiss on the top of my head, and I took a deep breath in, savouring her for a little longer.

"Keep reading, okay? Stay here and practise. When I'm finished, I'll come back up and sign your reading record, so your teacher knows how well you did today."

I nodded, but I couldn't speak. It felt like my throat had gone all prickly.

"Whatever you do," she added. "Stay here. Don't come outside."

Another nod, but part of me didn't want to keep that promise. I wanted to know what they were going to do at the bottom of our garden in our summerhouse. Despite what I saw on their faces, I'd heard Dad tell Kenny that they were going to have some fun today.

Why was Dad having fun?

For me, fun was something that had died along with my mum, but it didn't seem to be the case for my dad. He had fun all the time when he was in his summerhouse with Kenny and whoever came around to join in. He didn't seem to feel Mum's absence as much as I did. Either that, or he was really good at hiding it. I tried to learn from him and hide my feelings better, but everyone kept saying how miserable I looked. I guess I needed to work harder, be better. I didn't want to be the lonely boy who no one wanted to be friends with.

They left the patio doors open as the three of them walked off down the garden. Biting my lip in thought, I sat and watched them, frowning hard as I tried to decide whether I should follow or not. I could sneak out. Hide around the back of the summerhouse, and maybe, if I stood on my tiptoes, I might be able to see through the windows. I felt curious, like the cat in the story my teacher read to us last week.

Before my mind could argue, my body moved, standing from the sofa and tiptoeing towards the open doors. It was a hot day, and the gentle breeze blowing through the trees seemed to beckon me on, whispering for me to come outside. I watched as the three of them disappeared through the door to the summerhouse, so I took a step into the garden. Even though it was my garden, it still felt like a step into the unknown.

The birds chirped a merry song, leaves rustled in the trees, and far away, I heard the buzz of a lawnmower, the soundtrack to spring that masked my footsteps over the grass and then along the pebbled path that led to my dad's precious workshop. I walked around the back of the wooden building, but the windows were blacked out, and when I tried to peer through the cracks, I couldn't see anything. I could hear music, though. The pounding beat made my stomach twist. It sounded like a party, and I wasn't sure how I felt about that. Without my mum, I didn't feel much like partying. Parties meant laughter and jokes, eating cakes and playing games. It didn't feel right to do that without her.

I was just thinking about how different life felt now she'd left us, scuffing my shoes on the ground and kicking pebbles as I tried to keep the tears in my eyes from falling down my cheeks. Boys don't cry. That's what my dad told me when I'd sobbed and hugged my mum as she dangled in the bedroom. Even my hugs hadn't woken her up. Maybe I should've been a better boy; then she would've stayed.

Suddenly, the door to the summerhouse swung open, and I flinched, scared that I'd been caught out sneaking around. My eyes widened as Kenny glared at me and snapped, "You were told to wait in the house."

I swallowed, not sure how to answer. Kenny might be my dad's friend, but he'd always intimidated me a little, and I didn't want to upset him.

My mouth flapped open with nothing but air escaping, and

when my dad appeared behind him, I closed my mouth and put my head down.

"The boy's curious," my dad said with cruelness in his tone. "If he wants to see what we're doing, let him in. Maybe it's time for him to learn a few life lessons."

I peered up at them through my lashes and saw Kenny's forehead crinkle as he narrowed his eyes at my dad.

"But, Glenn, he's only five. He's a kid. It'll scare the fuck out of him."

"He's *my* kid," Dad spat back. "Let him watch." Then he stormed away, shouting, "Hurry up. We've wasted enough time today and time is money. This scene needs to be done. Now."

Kenny shook his head and then glanced back at me with a look of uncertainty as I stood on the threshold of the summerhouse, shivering even though it was a warm day. He clenched his fists, and I could tell he wanted to argue, but he didn't; he knew better. No one argued with my dad. Instead, he opened the door wider and gestured for me to go inside, whispering, "Don't say I didn't warn you," to me through gritted teeth.

When I walked in, I squinted from the brightness of the lights set up in every corner, all of them focused on a gigantic bed in the middle of the room. The sheets were red and shiny, and it looked comfy, like a giant's bed. But no one ever slept here. Not my mum, my dad, or Kenny. No one.

So why *was* there a bed here?

"If you're staying, sit quietly and shut up," my dad's voice bellowed across the room. I turned my head to look at him and that's when I noticed the camera he was fiddling with, fixed to a stand at the side of the bed.

I did as I was told, sitting down on a dirty old beanbag in

the corner, making myself as small as possible. I wasn't sure I wanted to be in here anymore. The room smelled funny, and something felt off. My tummy was churning with nerves too, but despite all of that, I stayed put. If I tried to move or fuss, it'd only annoy my dad, and that was the last thing I wanted to do.

There was just Dad and Kenny in here with me, and I watched in silence as the two of them fussed over the camera and the lights. Deep down, I knew this had been a bad idea, and yet, my dad had said it was okay to stay, and Dad never really noticed me, not lately. So, I sat still and waited, the beat from the music matching the beat of my heart. Maybe my being here would please him in some way.

"Glenn, this ain't no place for a kid. This could fuck him up even more than he already is," Kenny piped up again, but Dad instantly shot him down.

"It's none of your fucking business. Just do your fucking job."

It was at that moment, that I heard a door open from the other side of the room, a door I hadn't noticed before, and Rosie stepped into the room. She was wearing a silk robe tied tightly around her, a robe that matched the covers on the bed. I didn't feel comfortable seeing Rosie like this, but I couldn't seem to make my legs move to get me out. So, I held my breath and prayed she wouldn't see me hiding in the corner.

"I told you, Glenn, I'll only do what's in my contract. You know my limits." Rosie spoke, but she didn't look at my dad; instead, she stared at the bed as she walked over to it.

"If you want to get paid, you'll stop being difficult," my dad replied. "You do the scene how I've planned it, or you can go home and forget ever being my star performer. You can forget your pay packet too."

Rosie didn't argue, and I thought from the sadness in her eyes that maybe she might cry, but she didn't. She was strong. Rosie was always strong.

"You're fucking evil," she hissed quietly under her breath, and I froze, dreading my dad's reaction.

"And you're on the clock," my dad bit back.

I'd expected him to be angrier, and his answer startled me. I looked to where Rosie stood, but I couldn't see a clock. What was he on about?

I heard more rustling and noticed Kenny start to take his clothes off. Rosie let her robe fall to the floor, and she was naked underneath. I felt embarrassed watching this, and I could tell my face was heating up, my stomach growing tight with nervous energy. I tried to swallow but my throat had gone dry. Then Kenny pulled his trousers down and climbed onto the bed behind where Rosie had crawled.

What happened next was something I'd never forget, no matter how much I wanted to. It made me sick to my stomach. Gasps, grunts, cries I didn't understand but that made me tearful and dizzy. I squeezed my eyes shut tightly and held my hands over my ears to block it out as best I could. I wished it'd stop and prayed I could wipe the images that'd already seeped into my brain, but it didn't work. I was stuck in a living nightmare.

Why did my dad let me see this? I didn't understand what was going on.

Why was Kenny hurting Rosie? She was lovely. She'd never hurt anyone, and she didn't deserve this.

Why was my dad filming it all? Telling them what to do.

And why did everything in my life suddenly feel like one

big lie?

I didn't like my dad, but until today I'd thought that I could at least trust him, but I couldn't. Rosie was being hurt, and he wasn't doing anything to help. He was making it worse. Cheering Kenny on. But then, I wasn't helping either. Did that make me a coward too?

I don't know how long I sat there, rocking back and forth on that beanbag with my hands over my ears and my eyes closed tight. Maybe the pounding in my eardrums had distracted me so much that I hadn't realised they'd all left the room. But when I reluctantly opened my eyes, after hiding in the darkness of my tormented brain for so long, I found that I was alone. All that was left were the lights, the camera, the bed, and me, clutching my schoolbook in my sweaty hands. Only the book was as crumpled as the bed before me. The pages as tattered as my heart. And all hope that I might've clung to before, the hope that maybe one day the light my mum's absence had dimmed might glow brighter again was snuffed out, courtesy of my father.

He wasn't a good man.

He'd hurt someone special to me.

But I wasn't sure I could ever see Rosie again and look her in the eye after what had happened, because I'd been bad too. I hadn't done a thing to save her, and that meant that I was no better than my father.

But one day, I would be.

One day, I'd make it all right.

I had to.

CHAPTER TWO
The Making of The Joker

Lesson 2: Smile, it fools everybody
Colton's Thirteenth Birthday

As birthdays went, it wasn't the worst one I'd ever had. I'd woken up to the smell of a fried breakfast being cooked in our kitchen, courtesy of Tina. I had new Nike trainers on my feet and a brand-new PlayStation ready to be set up in my room. Granted, I hadn't seen my dad yet, and it was almost three in the afternoon, but that didn't bother me. When he was around, I struggled to think of what to say to him.

I hated him.

I despised everything he stood for.

He was the last person I'd ever want to be around.

I much preferred being with my friends, sitting in the park

like we were now, watching some of the older kids playing football and laughing at Luke's god-awful attempt at rolling his first ever cigarette.

"It looks like the tobacco is gonna fall out, you need to roll it tighter," Tom scolded and tried to snatch the roll-up out of Luke's fingers. But Luke was too quick, and swung his arms away so Tom couldn't reach.

He smiled to himself as he rolled the papers in between his fingers, then licked along the seam to secure it in place. He was happy with the job he'd done, and no one was going to take that away from him.

"I'm no expert, but I'm pretty sure you're supposed to put a filter tip or something in the end," Jack added, frowning at the crooked roll-up like it was the last thing he wanted to try.

Luke rolled his eyes, telling us, "I'll twist the paper at the end like my dad does." Then glancing at his work, he smiled again. "I think it's a pretty good effort for my first attempt." He held the roll-up out to me, grinning with pride. "You should have the first drag, Colton. It is your birthday, after all." And the fact that he wanted to do that for me meant everything. I couldn't stop smiling, something I didn't really do all that much. I might be a ghost to my father, but my friends noticed me, and that's all that mattered.

"You wanna kill me off on my birthday," I said, my grin turning to a smirk. "Thanks, dude. I appreciate the sentiment. Why don't you drop it in some dog shit before you pass it to me and show me you really care."

Luke shrugged, ignoring my sly dig, and looking at the roll-up, he replied, "I got you a homemade gift. What more do you want? This was rolled with love."

"And sealed with your spit. I'm forever in your debt." I placed my hand over my heart, fluttering my eyelashes to mock Luke, and the others laughed.

"You can have it all. I'm not taking a drag." Tom screwed his nose up in disgust. Then he lay back on the grass, putting his hands behind his head and closing his eyes. He took a deep breath, savouring the warm summer air. I closed my eyes too as it wafted over me; clean-cut grass, the stench of stale lager from the cans that'd been left scattered about by a group of lads who'd been sitting near us a few moments ago, and dog shit that the owners couldn't be arsed to pick up.

Welcome to Brinton Manor.

What you see is what you get, and if you looked too closely, it might scar you for life.

But it was my town and I loved it.

Beauty can be found in the darkest places, and here with my friends, I'd found something special. Priceless even.

This was my home.

Days spent like this made everything seem less shitty. Being with friends and living my life the way I wanted. Watching and listening to their banter made the hairs on the back of my neck prickle with warmth. Their camaraderie created a sense of peace that I hadn't experienced for a long time, not since the days when Rosie used to come around. That feeling of quiet serenity, like a wave of comfort blanketing you and all I wanted to do was slow down time. Absorb every bit of it. Let it seep into my pores to soothe my soul. Nothing, not even Luke's awful roll-ups could bring me down today.

"Come on then, I'll take a drag," I told Luke. I wasn't that bothered about trying smoking, but it was my birthday, and I supposed this would make it memorable. Plus, he'd gone to all the effort of sneaking the stuff out of his house and bringing it here. I had to make an effort too.

Jack made a humming sound in agreement. "Count me in then. I wanna know what all the fuss is about. My dad smokes forty a day."

Tom rolled his head to the side, shielding his eyes from the glare of the sun with his hand, as he stared at us from where he lay, and asked, "Do any of you even have a lighter?"

We glanced at each other like dumbasses, expecting the other to pipe up with a yes.

"I can't be expected to think of everything," Luke snapped, dropping his hands into his lap with exasperation. He stared at the roll-up longingly, like he'd created a masterpiece that he'd never get to enjoy. "I brought the roll-up paper and tobacco. What else do you want?"

"A means to light it might be a start," Jack smirked and then huffed as he stood up, wandering over to a group of kids smoking by the swings.

"If brains were dynamite, you wouldn't have enough to blow your shitty baseball cap off," I said, laughing at Luke.

Luke just frowned and sat taller, taking his cap off his head to look at it, and whining, "This isn't shitty. Its official merchandise. Look, there's a tag inside."

Tom sat up, shaking his head as he remarked, "Because that was the most insulting thing he said to you."

But it flew over Luke's head, just like my joke had, and Luke ignored us, placing his cap back on his head and giving us a wink. "I make no apologies for my greatness."

"Or your stupidity, it would seem," I added, earning a high-five from Tom and scowl from Luke.

Two minutes later, Jack wandered back over to us, wiggling a lighter in his hand and grinning. He plonked himself down on the grass with a triumphant huff, threw the lighter into Luke's lap, and in a cocky voice, he said, "You're welcome."

Luke picked it up, and then held the roll-up in one hand and the lighter in the other, flicking with his finger to make the flame appear and hovering it over the end of the cigarette.

"Aren't you supposed to light it while it's in your mouth?" I asked, a rare smile flickering like the flame he was brandishing. "You look like you're trying to set fire to it, not smoke it."

"If you think you can do better, you have a go." Luke gave up his feeble attempt at looking like he knew what he was doing and passed everything to me.

I wiped the back of my hand over my mouth to dry my lips, then put the cigarette between them and twisted my head like I'd seen Kenny and my dad do, as I flicked the lighter and cupped my hands to ignite the end of the ciggie.

"Fuck." Jack grinned and shook his head. "How do you manage to make that look cool? I swear, Colton, you don't know how fucking cool you are."

"I was born this way." I shrugged, trying not to splutter after inhaling my first drag, and hiding the wince my face made after feeling the sharpness in my throat.

"It's the couldn't-give-a-fuck attitude," Tom added. "That's what makes him cool. That and the fact he never smiles. Girls really dig that shit."

I threw my head back and laughed. If girls liked the pissed-off vibe I carried with me like a dark cloud, they certainly didn't show it. Tom got way more attention than the rest of us, and when I said that, he looked at me like I'd gone crazy.

"They're just friends. Trust me, the girls who talk to me at school only do it to ask about you, Colton. You're an enigma. That's what Sarah Pope calls you, anyway. She's begged me for your number."

I screwed my face up at the thought of Sarah Pope sliding into my DMs. She was clingy and whiney, so not my type.

"There's a reason I'm an enigma to Sarah Pope. A bout of rabies would be more fun than a date with her. I've heard there're lemmings that jump back onto the cliff to get away from her droning voice."

"Don't worry," Tom chuckled. "I told her you're more interested in her mum."

I grabbed a handful of grass and ripped it out of the ground, throwing it into his face and telling him, "Fuck you. I'm interested in your mum, more like."

He did the same back, telling me to fuck off, and the rest joined in, telling mum jokes that, despite my family situation, I didn't mind. They knew I didn't have a mum; they also knew I didn't care about jokes like that. That's what we did, told shit jokes and took the piss out of each other. It wasn't personal. They had my back, and I had theirs. If you couldn't laugh with your mates, when could you?

We passed the cigarette around our little circle until it was almost fully smoked. Seeing as it was my birthday, Luke said I should have the last puff, so I took the ciggie from him, ready to finish it. It might be my last drag, but I doubted it'd be my last cigarette. Surprisingly, the sensation had grown on me. I kind of liked the way it made my head buzz and my mind twist.

Eager to experience the last headrush of the day, I gripped

the butt between my fingers and inhaled sharply. The heat burned my fingers and scorched my lips, but the pain wasn't unwelcome, and the buzz I felt after certainly made up for it. I'd found something else to numb the pain, which was always a good thing. Whatever helped you get through the day was a win in my book. Anything to block out the images and feelings I didn't want to acknowledge. Ever.

I squashed the butt into the grass, feeling a sense of peace wash over me. I thought this might've been my favourite birthday so far, since Mum left, that is. Savouring the numbing effects of the nicotine, I glanced off into the distance, enjoying how quiet it made my brain feel. How serene everything felt in this moment. The distant laughter of the kids, the cool rush of the breeze, the rustling trees, dogs barking, all of it was music to my ears. This was what it was all about.

But then, like a dark cloud rumbling through the skies, ready to crack a whip through my fragile peace, I heard the shouts of a familiar voice. A reminder that even though I felt content, this wasn't my life, it was all a charade. Happiness was short-lived and reality was lurking around every corner, waiting for me. Nothing lasts forever.

That deep voice bellowed from the car park behind us, a voice that stripped away my calm like a cruel hand ripping off a warm blanket. His nearness filled me with dread and made my stomach clench with unspoken fear. Fear I didn't want my friends to see. That might lead to questions, and questions would lead to lies I didn't want to tell.

"Colton! Get over here. We're leaving," my dad hollered, and it felt like every single person in this park stopped what they were doing to stare at us.

THE JOKER

My cheeks flamed with embarrassment and my heart dropped in disappointment.

Why did he have to show up here of all places?

Why couldn't I enjoy a day with my friends without him intruding?

I didn't argue, though. I knew better. If my dad wanted me to leave, I would. Nobody argued with my dad, least of all me. Plus, I didn't want him infiltrating this part of my life. Better that I left now and quickly to avoid him coming over here. I never wanted any of my friends to meet him.

"Dude, your dad wants you," Luke said, stating the obvious and I sighed.

"Party's over."

With a heavy heart and hollow legs, I lifted myself from the ground and gave each one of my friends a fist bump. "Laters," I told them, and then I left, walking slowly over to my dad's car, where he sat with the engine running. That alone gave me bad vibes, and when thoughts of why he wanted me to leave with him sprung to mind, I blocked them out. What was he up to?

My thoughts were always dark these days. They were darker the older I got, and I feared what the future held for a boy like me. A boy with a family that I wanted to keep hidden from the world. A dirty secret. There would be no happy tales and fond moments reminiscing about my childhood. The only pride I felt was that I'd survived this long. And it felt like the sand in my timer was running out. My resolve, my strength, was waning.

Dad didn't hide or feel ashamed of what he did for a living, but I did. I couldn't wait for the day when I could get some distance from him. I didn't know what my future looked like, but I knew it wasn't anything like the one my father envisaged.

One thing I was thankful for though, was my friends. They were my lifeline. I don't know what I'd do without them. They gave me moments of happiness in an otherwise miserable existence. Moments like today.

Reluctantly, I opened the car door and got in. My dad drove off before I'd even had a chance to close it or secure my seatbelt, making me squirm in my seat. He was always in a rush, oblivious to others around him. People stopped and turned to watch his Mercedes glide past, and he loved that. He lived to be worshipped. It wasn't very often a car like his drove through Brinton Manor.

It wasn't the best area, but we'd never left, no matter how much money he'd made over the years. Dad preferred to be a big fish in a little pond. He knew he could manipulate these people, and if we moved to somewhere more upmarket, he'd drown, lost in a sea of more powerful fish. He'd never let that happen. He craved control. He liked that they all knew who he was–Glenn King, or rather, the porn king as he liked to be known. A peddler of filth that I wanted no part of.

I shuffled in my seat, and he clucked his tongue.

"Stop fidgeting. You're not a little kid anymore."

"I know," I bit back, and then I asked, "Where are we going? My curfew isn't up yet. Why did I have to leave? It's my birthday for fuck's sake."

"Because I said so. And don't fucking curse at me, boy, or you'll feel the back of my hand." Dad didn't give explanations, so when he took a breath, then added, "I have one last birthday present for you." I turned to look at him, my brows hitting my hairline.

My dad didn't do anything unless it benefitted him, so where the fuck was he taking me?

"What surprise?" I narrowed my gaze at him, but he ignored me, clicking the doors locked as if he expected me to escape from a moving car.

I swallowed, my throat rough from the cigarette and my shredded nerves. Why did it feel like I'd strapped myself into a rollercoaster? And not one of those fun ones at a theme park that made your stomach role and your head spin. No. This was a rickety old death trap of a ride with rusty tracks and a harness that was threadbare and ready to snap. The kind of ride that should've been condemned years ago, just like my father. A ride that'd be the death of me.

My knee started to jiggle up and down, and Dad reached across to put his hand on it.

"Stop doing that," he chastised irritably, and I froze at the unwelcome contact. Typical. Even my jumpy knee pissed him off.

I had to admit, thinking about how much it irritated him made me want to jiggle my knee even more, but the prospect of him touching me again stopped me. The less contact we had, the better.

We drove through the downtrodden streets of Brinton Manor, where the houses looked uninhabitable, and then out into Merivale, a neighbouring town. I glanced out of the car window at the old, filthy-looking houses. Some were boarded up. Others had yellowing, dirty curtains strung up to hide whatever went on inside those crumbling walls. Kids in the street stood gawping at us as we drove past, their faces covered in mud and their threadbare clothes hanging off their scrawny frames. But given the chance, I'd have traded places with them in a heartbeat.

Theirs was filth you could see, honest. The filth sitting in this car was hidden beneath designer clothes and scowls of superiority. The worst of the worst.

I had no idea what kind of *surprise* my dad would give me here of all places, but it wasn't going to be good. I wasn't stupid, I knew he only ever brought misery my way. As he wound the car through the streets, I felt like a tight coil had been wound around my stomach, like a vice squeezing me until I felt sick with dread. Then my heart twinged as I thought about Rosie. I hadn't seen her again, not since that day all those years ago when I'd had the worst introduction into how my dad made his money. I knew she lived on a street like this in Merivale. She told me all about her neighbourhood and how lucky I was to live in one of the nicer parts of Brinton Manor. But pretty houses can hide ugly truths. We were a testament to that. And money didn't make you happy. My dad had loads of it and never cracked a smile, neither did I most of the time.

As the car slowed down, so did the beat of my heart, sending a wave of nausea through me. My palms were sweaty as I clung to the door handle, like I was clinging to a life raft. We pulled up outside a rundown terraced house and I looked up and down the street, waiting to see what would happen next. I half expected a white van to stop next to us and yank my door open then bundle me inside. Nothing was off the table at this point, and I wouldn't put anything past my father. He'd see it as character building, not giving a fuck that the character he was building was one that he'd swiped from the road to heaven and flung into the depths of hell. Feeling panicked, I glanced at the back seat in case there were ropes or something ready to restrain me, but it was empty. That didn't put my mind at rest though. He could've hidden anything anywhere in this car. I couldn't let my eyes deceive me.

"Stop looking so jumpy, boy," my dad snapped, putting the handbrake on and glowering at me.

I wanted to snap back, "What do you expect? You've brought me out here into the middle of God knows where to do what? Shoot me? Make me shoot someone? What the fuck is going on here?"

But I settled with, "Why are we here?" Although, even that had been hard to say through the golf ball sized bulge of anxiety that was lodged in my throat.

My dad cut the engine and then turned in his seat to face me with a sadistic glint in his eyes.

"Happy birthday, son." He winked, then added, "This is where you take your first step towards being a proper man." He pointed at a house we'd pulled up in front of and said, "Your present is in there. Take this time. Use it wisely." Then his head swung back towards me. "Learn." The sharpness of his stare made it feel like knives were piercing my stomach. This wasn't a treat. It was a test, at least, that's what it felt like.

Fuck.

What should I do?

Should I argue with him?

Get out the car and run away?

What if they shot at me in the street?

My mind was whirling, and I couldn't even think straight, let alone form a coherent sentence. My ability to formulate any kind of plan was non-existent. All I could seem to do was nod and try to swallow.

Breathe, Colton.

Just breathe.

I had no idea what was about to happen, but he gestured to the car door impatiently. When I looked at him, his face morphed into something evil. Demons burned in his eyes, taunting me to argue and the devil smirked back at me, begging me to put a foot wrong. If I didn't do as he said, then whatever was waiting for me in that house would be nothing compared to what I'd face in this car and at home later.

So, I opened the door, my tobacco-dried throat becoming even more scratchy as my nerves ramped up a gear.

"Number fifty-three. Go on. Grace is expecting you," he urged, shooing me with his hand. The fact he'd used a woman's name did nothing to calm the storm of panic raging through my body.

I closed the car door and forced my legs to move me towards the house. I was on automatic pilot. My body at war with my mind, and I felt like I wasn't living in my own body. I had no control. So, I stopped and took a moment, standing on the pavement outside and staring up at the house that loomed in front of me. All the curtains were drawn, and the front garden was littered with bikes, scooters, and other kid's toys. The bikes were all pink and purple with tassels on the handles, but the frames were rusty and had seen better days. The scene in front of me, one of innocent family chaos, was in stark contrast to the nightmare scenarios running through my head of what was going to happen next. How I was going to suffer.

What was I doing here?

We didn't know anyone with little girls in the family, so this was even more of a mind-fuck.

From behind, I heard the whirring sound of my dad's car

window winding down, and then his gruff voice saying, "What the fuck are you waiting for? Stop wasting time and get the fuck in there."

He wasn't speeding away, so perhaps I wasn't about to get gunned down in the street. Either that, or he was even more of a sicko than I thought, and he wanted to stay and watch.

"Is there anything I should know before I go in?" I asked, stalling for time.

"Yeah. Relax. Take that stick from your ass and grow a fucking pair." He clicked the button to raise his window again, shaking his head at me in disappointment, and that right there spurred me on. Don't ask me why, but it did. He didn't think I had it in me to face whatever was ahead, and part of me wanted to prove him wrong. The other part, wanted to bolt through the house and escape out the back. But the last thing I was going to do was let my dad think I'd bottled it.

"I can think of somewhere I'd like to shove that stick," I whispered under my breath, and on shaking legs, I pushed myself forward.

The little wooden gate at the front of the property was held up by the overgrown privet hedge on either side of it. With shaking hands, I had to lift it up to stop it from scraping along the cracked slabs of the path. Even the gate was trying to stop me from entering, and the uneven paving stones weren't much better. Navigating my way to the door was a challenge in itself.

With each step I took towards the weathered front door, with its chipped, peeling blue paint and rusty door knocker, my heart hammered in my chest.

What was all this about?

I knocked on the door and stepped back. Movement from

inside made me second guess everything, and I glanced over my shoulder to see my dad sitting back in his seat in the car, smoking a cigar like he didn't have a care in the world. I took deep breaths to try and calm my nerves, shoving my hands in my pockets to stop them from shaking.

Suddenly, the door swung open, and an older lady stared back at me.

Not what I was expecting to see at all.

She was probably around thirty-five, so not that old really. Her dark hair was pulled into a bun, but little strands had fallen out, curling and framing her smiling, kind face. She wore a lot of make-up; red lips, rosy cheeks, the sort of make-up you might see in the movies. And her clothes were sparkly; a long black skirt with moons and stars twinkling back at me, reaching right down to her bare feet and bejewelled ankles. She wore a plain black top, her shoulders bare, and I noticed she had a few tattoos; moons, stars, and was that a demon of some sort?

I shifted my focus from her body art to peer around her, expecting to see kids my own age in the house, maybe the girls whose bikes were strewn across the yard, but it was quiet inside. I guessed there was no one home, only her. I could hear the faint tinkle of music that sounded like it was coming from one of those old record players, it was crackly and old-fashioned. Not the kind of music I listened to, and definitely not party music.

"You must be Colton," she said, greeting me warmly even though I could feel my limbs freezing like icy invisible hands were trying the claim my soul. "I'm Grace. Come in. Don't be shy."

She opened the door a little wider and stepped back to give me space. It was like I'd stepped foot in a bad fairy tale, and here was the wicked witch playing the part of the kind lady, trying to tempt me to the dark side.

I nodded dumbly, mentally planning my escape or how I was going to overpower her as I walked in. As birthday gifts went, this one was shitty and really fucking weird.

I looked over my shoulder as she closed the door and put the chain across to lock us in. Red flags were fluttering all over the damn place. Sirens blaring warnings, screaming at me to get out, and as I turned my body, preparing to fight, she smiled and gestured with her arm down the hallway.

"Keep going. The living room is straight ahead," she said, like me being here was the most natural thing in the world, and for some reason, I did as I was told.

There was a sweet, smoky smell in the living room, and I noticed incense sticks burning in the far corner. Draped over the sofa was a deep-blue satin throw, and the whole moon and stars theme she seemed to love was woven into the fabric. It looked like this lady was spiritual, perhaps she really was a witch.

Was I here for a reading or a ritual?

Was this some kind of black magic?

"Take a seat. Make yourself comfortable. Can I get you a drink?" Grace smiled calmly from the doorway, her whole presence radiating a peaceful aura that made me drop into the sofa even though I didn't know what was going on. "I have lager, or whisky, if that's your thing."

I coughed, covering my mouth to hide my surprise at her offering me alcohol so freely. Was that her game? Get me drunk so she could perform her twisted shit on me? Was she a serial killer? I'd seen enough Netflix shows to know how it goes. They drug your drink then drill holes in your skull and do all sorts of weird, fucked-up shit. I wasn't a victim, never would be, and I scanned the room, searching for a weapon and a way out.

"I thought it might relax you," she elaborated, but I ignored her, too focused on what I could do to stay alive. "You don't have to drink alcohol though." She tilted her head and smiled. "I make a mean cup of tea."

"I'm fine," I snapped, fisting my hands then rubbing them on my thighs to get rid of the sweat. I needed to keep a clear head, and a good grip if I was going to fight back.

"Happy birthday, by the way," Grace added, taking a slow step into the room like a hunter approaching her prey. "Which one is it? Sweet sixteen or eighteen? Don't tell me you're twenty-one. I'd never believe it. You've got such a baby face."

I stared at her, my eyes wide, and replied, "I'm thirteen." I cleared my throat as my words came out all squeaky and unsure. I needed her to know I was the man my father had challenged me to be. I wasn't going to go down without a fight.

Instantly, Grace's face fell, and her smile evaporated as her chest started to rise and fall rapidly. She stared back at me, like I'd been dropped into her living room by Martians. The hunter didn't look so vicious anymore.

"Say that again," she asked, taking a step back, and I felt like the tables were turning in my favour.

"I'm thirteen today," I announced with more confidence than before.

"Oh my God." Grace covered her mouth, and I thought for a moment she was going to throw up, but she shook her head, closed her eyes tightly for a few seconds, then opened them, and there, in her eyes, I could see the tears she was trying to hold back.

"You're the same age as my youngest daughter." She spoke on a whisper and then she took a deep breath, threw her head back and stated, "This isn't happening. This… it's not happening."

"What's not happening?" I sat forward, willing her to shed light on what the fuck was going on.

"Do you know why your dad brought you here?" She crept over to the lone armchair across the room and sat down, wrapping her arms around herself, but it wasn't cold. It was hot and muggy in here, stifling even.

"I have no idea," I answered, then gritted my teeth. I wasn't the prey anymore. I'd got this. "He said it was my first step towards being a man or something like that." I narrowed my eyes at her. "Am I going to have to fight?"

She shook her head vehemently. "Oh my God, no. You're safe here," she spluttered, but nothing made sense.

"So, what then?" I asked with a hint of sarcasm. "Are you going to read some fucking tarot cards and tell me my future?"

She huffed out a laugh. "I wish, kid. I wish."

She bit her lip and sat in silence, staring at the dusty skirting board and frowning at it like it held all the answers.

"So, what are you going to do?" I pushed. "Why am I here?"

Her silence was deafening.

The clock on the mantlepiece ticked like a timebomb ready to obliterate my world.

Our breaths were laboured and deep as we both waited for impending doom to strike. But how it would strike was what made my heart race and my stomach twist.

A few seconds more, and then her eyes glazed over, and her face twisted and contorted with anger.

"You're here because your father is a sick, evil man."

That wasn't news to me, she'd told me fuck all. So, I stayed quiet, my pulse throbbing in my ears making it difficult to hear her whispered truths.

"You're here because I needed the money and no one in this fucking town can ever say no to the mighty Glenn King."

Again, no answers, so I waited.

She sighed, and then she hit me with the bombshell I knew was always coming my way.

"You're here because your father has paid me to have sex with you."

What.

The actual.

Fuck.

She gave a sad, low chuckle and dipped her head in shame. "He wants me to teach you how to be a man, but he's the one that needs a fucking lesson."

I could barely breath, and I turned my body away from her, unable to look at her. I gasped, pain grabbing me tightly by the throat as sickness whirled in my stomach, bile raced up my throat and threatened to spill out all over this woman's carpet. Scorching me in a way that made me want to double over.

She squeezed her eyes shut again, and more to herself than me, she whispered, "Why would he do that? What the fuck is wrong with him? You're still a fucking child, for God's sake."

"I won't do it." I shook my head, tears welling up as I felt my body launch into fight or flight mode.

Fight and flight.

I'd happily do both. There was no choice.

"You can't make me," I stated, sitting taller, tensing my muscles and preparing myself.

THE JOKER

She opened her eyes and looked over at me, a disbelieving horror painted on her face.

"I would never hurt you. I'm not a fucking paedophile. I'd rather cut my own arms off than harm a hair on your head."

I took a moment to assess my situation, and despite what she said she'd agreed to do, I believed her when she said she wouldn't hurt me. I wouldn't fully drop my guard, but she didn't come across as an immediate threat.

Despite my father bringing me here, this woman seemed to have a kindness about her, a calming aura, but I wasn't sure what to do next. I knew my dad was outside, waiting. Would he expect something from me? Details? Evidence? Was he about to charge in and stand over me while I did what he wanted?

My stomach rolled just thinking about it. I was pretty sure I was going to get my lesson in how to become a man, just not in the way he had hoped for. I had to think of a way out, and quick. There was another door just behind Grace's chair. If I could get to it fast enough, it might get me out of here.

"You don't have to look like a rabbit caught in the headlights, Colton. You're safe here with me. I promise."

I nodded but sucked my lip between my teeth and bit down so hard I could taste the blood I'd drawn. Safe was the last thing I felt when it came to my dad, and I had to do something, anything to get me out of this.

"I know you want to leave," she added. "But we have to think about this. Your dad is out there. If you walk out now, he'll know something's up. We need to come up with a plan."

"Like what?" I asked, wringing my hands in my lap.

Grace gave me a warm smile and sat forward. "He thinks he's smart, but we're going to be smarter."

"How?" I felt agitated and couldn't stop myself from rocking back and forth. I didn't care what my dad thought. I wanted out of here. "You know what'd be smart? If you let me leave from the back door and we left him out the front all night. That sounds like a solid plan to me."

"And face your father's wrath when he finds out we both went against him?" She had a point.

"So, what else do we do?"

"You do nothing," she told me. "Stay here for a while. I'll make you a sandwich and you can watch TV. That's it."

"That's it?" I spat back. "Let him think I did… stuff, and just act like that's normal?"

"What else can we do?" She shrugged sadly. "I never said it was a good plan, it's just a plan. Survival."

"Survival." I huffed. "Because he's the king and he always gets his way."

"Not always. And he hasn't got his way today, he just thinks he has." Grace kept her eyes locked on me and then, she added. "I think Bryony or Kate might have left their Nintendo DS here, you could play on that, if you want to? Or watch a bit of T.V. But you don't have to worry. Not about me or your dad. It'll all be fine. Let's put this down to a misunderstanding on our part, and a monumental fuck up on your dad's part. I think today will be a day we both want to forget."

Only, it wasn't going to be that easy for me. This was my birthday. I'd remember this for the rest of my life. The day my own father tried to sell me and ripped my soul out in return. I was getting good at lying to him, but what if he found out?

"What about my dad?" I asked, praying she'd give me some words of wisdom. Or failing that, a meteor might fall from the

THE JOKER

sky and wipe him out. I could hope, right? But as time went on, I knew the only way my father would stop, was if I stopped him.

"You don't tell your dad anything. I'm not going to breathe a word about this to anyone, and even though its playing into his sick and twisted hands, you've gotta do whatever you can to survive. It's called self-preservation, Colton, and my bet is, you haven't been doing a very good job of that lately."

I'd tried. My version of self-preservation was to make myself invisible when I was at home but avoid being in the house as much as I possibly could. Ignorance was bliss, and I was a ghost of a boy, avoiding the harsh realities of his life. I stayed quiet, out of his way, and ignored the demons that danced around him. But those parts of him, the parts that were trying to attach themselves to me like a filthy parasite, they were becoming harder and harder to fight off. The day of reckoning was fast approaching.

"Colton…" Grace's voice broke through my reverie, and I blinked up at her as she stood over me. "I don't know you, but I only have to look at you to see you've got a good heart, a pure heart. Too pure to survive a man like him for much longer. You've got to toughen up. Don't trust so easily. Don't give him anything that he doesn't deserve. I can tell you're a boy who feels things deeply, loves unapologetically; but I'm guessing that's brought you nothing but hurt so far. Am I right?"

I nodded, unable to form any words. The will to fight, that'd been keeping me going this far, was dwindling fast.

"You need to stop." She sat down carefully next to me, her body hovering on the sofa's edge. "Stop giving him power over you. Take back control. Own who you are and become someone you're proud of, someone he can't touch or hurt again."

That's what I was trying to do, but it didn't seem to be working. I lowered my head in thought, I guessed Grace realised that too. But then she hit me with the killer words. "I know what happened to your mum, and I'm sorry."

I didn't like to think about Mum, but when I did, in this moment, it felt like strips of my heart were being torn away. I couldn't breathe. There wasn't enough headspace to take that on as well.

"You need to do this for her, Colton. Be the soldier she couldn't be. Fight and stand up to him. If you don't do it now, you might never do it. Everyone knows who Glenn King is, what he stands for, but do they know Colton King? Because they should. He's going to be a better man than his father ever was. Colton King is going to be fucking amazing, excuse my language, and you, Colton, you're going to do great things. You're gonna be someone. Someone better than him. Someone that people in Brinton look up to. He's the past, and we can't change what he's done, but you're the future, and that means everything."

"But how is lying about what's happened here today fighting?" I asked, unsure about anything and everything. "If I was a real man, I'd stand up to him. Go out there and fight back."

"Fighting doesn't always happen with fists or as a show of strength." She tapped the side of her head. "Sometimes the biggest battles are up here. Be clever. Let him think he's winning but know that you hold all the cards. Knowledge is power, and he knows nothing."

I understood what she was saying to me. Some things you could bury in the sand, but not forever. Life would eventually

THE JOKER

come back to bite you in the ass, and you had to pick your battles. Today was a battle I didn't need. It didn't matter if he'd thought he'd won because I knew the truth. And that's all that mattered.

"Sometimes in life we have to learn who's gold and who's just gold-plated. And your dad out there, he's fool's gold. A shiny piece of shit that you're not going to let drag you down, are you?"

"Fuck no," I answered, feeling a trickle of power flow through me, and she smiled at my response.

"That's the spirit."

We sat in silence for a while. Me, feeling numb about what my father had tried to orchestrate today and trying to digest what Grace had said, and her, taking slow, deep breaths to calm herself. Today had been one of the worst days, and yet the things Grace had told me made me want to stand up for myself. Stop the spiral of destruction that I was destined to take. Choose a better path. Perhaps, when I looked at it a different way, this wasn't the worst birthday gift. It had certainly made me wake up to the fact that I needed to do more with my life. I needed to take better control.

"What do you want on your sandwich?" Grace asked, breaking the silence with a homely smile, and turning what was a weirdly fucked-up situation to something that resembled normality.

"Whatever you want to give me," I replied, and when she patted my knee and rose to stand, I felt a little lighter.

Today, I was thirteen years old. My dad had tried to destroy that, destroy me, but not anymore. I wasn't a kid now, and that lesson in being a man he seemed determined to give me would come, only not the way he wanted it to. It would happen on my terms.

I stayed for about an hour, playing Super Mario on her daughter's DS while some old eighties movie played in the background, but feeling like I wasn't really here. None of this felt real. Grace didn't say a lot after her initial pep talk, she just left me to it, but after a while, I felt uncomfortable and wanted to leave. I'd spent enough time in the house to make it believable. The sooner I got in the car and fed my dad some bullshit, the sooner I could get home and go to my room. Plan my next move and what I could do to escape my life.

I placed the DS on the coffee table and stood up to go, giving Grace a weak smile as I said goodbye.

"Hey." She grabbed my shoulder to stop me as I made my way into the hallway that led to the front door. I flinched at the contact, but she didn't seem to notice. "No more fake smiles, or half smiles. You give a big smile, okay? The bigger the smile, the more you'll feel it." I grinned to please her, not feeling the happiness she promised, and she stroked my cheek. "That's it. Remember, smiles are like chicken soup for the soul." I had no idea what she meant, but I nodded anyway. "See? I bet you feel better already," she remarked. "Smiles lead to laughter, and believe it or not, laughter can heal a lot of hurt. It makes you forget for a while."

"I think it'll take a lot more than a smile to forget my fucked-up family," I stated, hinting that her hallmark brand of counselling was a lost cause for someone like me.

She squeezed my shoulder in response, and added, "Maybe not, but it's worth a shot. My gran used to say, if you find yourself lost in a dark world, a simple smile can spark brightness back into your soul. And isn't life better when you're laughing?"

I gave another nod, understanding what she was getting at, but eager to get out the door.

Grace steered me forward by the shoulders and whispered in my ear, "Laughter is like the windscreen wipers on your car. It might not stop the rain from falling, but it does a damn good job of keeping you going forward… now, go. Tell him whatever you want to tell him, and then smile because you know the truth. He doesn't control you and he never will. You're your own man now, Colton."

She was right, and I walked out of that house feeling ten times taller than when I'd walked in. As I stepped closer to my dad's car, I could see that he saw it too. I hated that he thought he'd won, but then I reminded myself of Grace's words. I had to pick my battles. He only thought he'd won. He hadn't though, and he never would.

He smirked as I climbed in, and then chuckling, he said, "And now you know what it's all about." He turned to face me and added, "That was only your first lesson though, son. From here on in, you will be trained to take over my empire, whether that's in front of the camera or behind it. Either way, I want you to keep the King legacy going."

I didn't answer. I had no intention of keeping his sick legacy going or fuelling any kind of empire that he'd built on the foundation of other people's misery and tears. I was going to have my own empire. One that helped the kind of people my dad took advantage of. I would be a better man.

So, I sat up straight, stared forward, and did what Grace had told me. I smiled like the cat that'd got the fucking cream, and I made a vow to myself. A vow that I would change the course of my life from this day forward.

That smile worked, because my dad patted my knee and replied, "That's my boy," before starting the engine with a smug, self-satisfied grin on his face.

Grace was right.

Smile.

It fools them.

And my dad was the biggest fool of all.

***

Later that night, we had a visit from the local police. Some older lads at the park had jumped my friends on their way home and they wanted to question me about it. The CCTV in the park was broken and they needed help identifying who it might be. I had no idea, but knowing I hadn't been there to fight for my friends, to defend them, made me want to trawl the streets hunting down the cowardly fuckers that'd hurt them. And that night, I swore I would always put my friends first. They were the ones who stood by me. They were the ones that made my life more bearable. They meant more to me than my family.

Loyalty over blood.

Brothers in arms.

I wasn't going to take anymore bullshit. For years, I'd harboured so much anger towards my father, but no more. I had to use that anger, channel it into something worthwhile. Keeping it inside was only doing more damage, and ultimately hurting me. But things had to change. I was going to change. No more weak Colton. That was a mask I was ripping off, and I couldn't wait to replace it with something a hell of a lot more menacing.

The world wasn't ready for what I had in mind.

CHAPTER THREE
WELCOME TO MY WORLD

Lesson 3: Friends are the family you choose for yourself
Colton, Aged Seventeen

I took a swig from the hip flask full of whisky being passed around as we sat on the grass outside the church. The liquid scorched my throat as I swallowed it, but I didn't wince or let on to the others that the acquired taste Adam had talked about was still waiting to register as something enjoyable in my brain. I had to admit, though, the burn was a welcome distraction from the whirling thoughts clouding my mind, warning me what the events of this day had in store.

Today was my father's funeral. Not a particularly sad occasion and I was only here because the others had told me I should come. They thought it'd give me closure. Honestly, I didn't need closure; I'd already got the outcome I wanted. He was gone. Burning in hell for all I cared, but I humoured them anyway and decided to view this as a final purge. A chance to expel the last hold my father had on me in this life. By tonight, there would be nothing left of Glenn King's legacy. Only me. And I wasn't his legacy; I was his nemesis.

My life had altered immeasurably since that day four years ago, when I'd sat in Brinton Park smoking my first ciggie with my friends, existing in a daze to try and block out the reality of what being Glenn King's son actually meant.

The name King was like a dark, dirty cloud, a black stain on the town of Brinton Manor, but I was determined to change that. I wanted to create my own legacy, something I could be proud of.

His legacy?

I wanted no part of it.

I despised it, and I despised him too.

It had taken me a while to get where I was today. My transformation wasn't easy, and it'd hurt when my old friends drifted away. After being jumped in the park that night on my thirteenth birthday, Tom's parents moved from Brinton Manor to Sandland, and Tom changed schools. They wanted better for him, and apparently, that meant finding new friends and staying away from us, or rather, me.

It didn't take long for Jack and Luke's parents to go the same way. I guess they finally realised what the consequences of their kids being associated with a King were. My father made money by using people and selling sex, and misery followed wherever he went. A misery I'd put to bed when I'd slipped a little too much Fentanyl into his coffee and the fucker had finally croaked it. A thirteen-year-old Colton wouldn't have had the nerve to do something so fucking brave. But after meeting Grace, and having my eyes opened to what would happen to me if I didn't take control, namely being another one of my father's sexploits, I grew a pair. I became the man I needed to be to put right some of the wrongs that'd been done over the years.

But his death was only the beginning. I knew there were other ghosts I had to deal with. Demons that still lingered from a past I refused to take with me into the future. Never look back; that's what I continued to tell myself on days when I felt the weight of guilt from what my father had done, and why I didn't speak up or try to stop it. Never look back and live without regret. I lost three friends because of my father. I lost a hell of a lot more if I really thought about it. But in return, after embracing the anger and twisting it into something I could truly master, I gained four brothers. Brothers who would stand shoulder-to-shoulder with me, no matter what. They already had, we did it for each other, and their loyalty was something I'd never had to question, despite my last name being King.

Four years ago, I decided to change. I was tired of trying to fit into a world that didn't fit me. The proverbial square peg in a round hole.

Four years ago, my school decided it could no longer cope with a degenerate like me, who disrupted learning, questioned authority and stood up for himself.

Four years ago, I was sent to a pupil referral unit as a way for the system to look like they were doing something to help me rehabilitate back into a society that was beyond fucked. And that's where I found my people. My brothers. Boys who were the same as me.

Their backgrounds weren't identical to mine. They'd lived in financially poorer families; some with one parent, others with none, as they bounced from one foster home to another. But none of them could boast that their father was the king of porn. Why would they want to? It wasn't exactly a badge of honour you'd want to wear with pride.

However, despite the slight differences in our histories, our moral compass, code of ethics and what we stood for were so aligned, so in sync, we were like five parts of one perfect machine. Trundling down an unknown road together, taking a common path to our own righteousness. A path only we could comprehend.

I glanced around our circle of five as we sat on the grass outside the church. We looked like a budget version of the cast of Reservoir Dogs; all dressed in our black suits, white shirts and black ties. Well, that was their look. I'd paired my suit with a white T-shirt that announced in black letters across the front, *'Do I look like I give a fuck?'*

I liked it.

I thought it fit the vibe of the day to a tee.

Plus, it acted as a repellent. Anyone who wanted to come over and give me their fake condolences would take one look at my statement T-shirt and stay the fuck away.

Job done.

"So, question time," I announced, smirking as I looked at each of my friends in turn. "If you had to be a character from Reservoir Dogs, who would you be? I mean, we do look like a pretty decent Brinton Manor version of those motherfuckers right now, don't you think?" I looked down at my suit and let the pride I felt in my choice of shirt buzz through me.

Adam rolled his eyes, but from the sneaky smile he tried to suppress, I could tell he liked this game, and was thinking about his answer, making sure he got it right. Adam didn't like getting things wrong. Ever.

"I reckon I'd be Mr White," I stated. "Harvey Keitel, the main motherfucker. I'd be the one they all showed up for, because let's face it, if he wasn't in the movie, Tarantino would've bombed out."

"He also gets shot at the end," Will added drily, like I didn't know what I was fucking talking about.

"Mate, they all get shot in the end, but Mr White... he's a moral guy, you know? He protects the ones that get wounded. He makes sacrifices." I shrugged and turned to face Adam, thumbing at him as I said, "We all know Adam here would be Mr Blonde, Vic Vega. He was an impulsive psycho too, who acted first and thought later. That sums you up to a tee, Ad."

I placed my hands behind me on the grass and waited for his snarky response. Adam Noble *was* a psycho, but he was our psycho, and like Madsen in the film, he'd stop at nothing to get what he wanted. I liked his style. He was someone I always looked up to. I'd never tell him that, though. His head was big enough.

"Can't say that I disagree with you." Adam nodded to himself thoughtfully. "That warehouse scene after the robbery is one of my favourite movie scenes ever. And I do have a clown to the left..." He stared at Will and then thumbed at me before adding, "And a Joker to my right."

"Nice." Tyler huffed out a smile at Adam's attempt at humour in paraphrasing the song lyrics from that scene. He wasn't far wrong, though. Will was a clown and liked messing around as much as I did, but there was only room for one joker. I was just about to tell Adam to leave the humour to the professionals when Devon piped up.

"Did you know they filmed that scene in a disused mortuary?" Devon had pockets of knowledge that seemed to stem from nowhere. Kind of fitting that as our reaper, with an obsession for all things death and destruction, he'd know a fact like that. "And Tim Roth's apartment scenes were filmed in the rooms upstairs. I love that idea, work and play all in one place. We should do that one day."

"What? Buy a mortuary and then kidnap a cop, tie him to a chair and cut his ear off?" I laughed.

Devon scowled. "I meant find a base. A place we can call our own."

"Where everybody knows your name," I sang, making light of something, which below the surface, was actually pretty depressing. You see, Devon had a point. None of us felt like we had a place we could call home. Not one we felt truly comfortable in, anyway. We were like nomads searching for something, but we didn't know what. We had each other, now we needed a base. A bat cave, if you will. So, in all honesty, Devon was right on the money.

"Where *no one* knows our name more like," Devon replied, giving me a knowing look. "Somewhere we can be ourselves."

Which loosely translated to somewhere we could go crazy and fuck shit up without getting caught.

You see, lately, we'd been doing some pretty fucked-up stuff to people we thought deserved it. People from our past. We were like Batman, going all vigilante, only without the billionaire budget and self-righteousness. We called ourselves the Brinton

Soldiers or Soldiers of Anarchy because that's what we were; street soldiers creating anarchy for those that deserved our wrath. Plus, we liked feeling part of a gang. Finally belonging.

Adam looked pensive as he took the hip flask and swigged a mouthful. I could see the cogs turning in his brain. When he said, "I think you might be onto something," I knew Devon's suggestion would eventually become more than an idea. When Adam got something in his head, he went for it. He was a go-getter. Obsessively so. Nothing could stop him when he was focused on a goal.

"Anyway, back to my question." I swung around to face Tyler. "So, Adam is Mr Blonde, the psycho. I'm the main man, Mr White, with all the star quality. Who would you be?" I loved winding up Adam, but Tyler was a good target too. He was strait-laced, if you put the thieving and hacking to one side.

"I reckon he'd be Mr Orange, Tim Roth," Will said, narrowing his eyes at Tyler, like he was picturing him in the role.

"Fuck off. He's the undercover cop. I'm no rat." Tyler's face screwed up as he showed us how offended he was by the comparison.

"No, you're not a rat, but if anyone can go undercover, it's you, with all the technical shit you love messing with. And didn't he get away with the diamonds in the end? See? He's a thief like you are." Will laughed and Tyler frowned, snatching the hip flask from Adam and throwing his head back as he took a huge gulp of whisky.

"You've got it wrong," Devon piped up. "It was Mr Pink who was the last man standing. He took the diamonds."

"You'd be Mr Pink," I told Devon.

THE JOKER

"No, I wouldn't."

"Yes, you would. He's logical, a little neurotic like you, and he doesn't let his feelings get in the way of his work. Isn't that what any reaper would aspire to?" I could tell Devon didn't know which statement to unpick first, judging from the look of extreme concentration on his face. Would it be the neurotic dig, the cold and calculatedness, or something else entirely?

"He refuses to tip the waitress at the beginning. I'm not a tight cunt like him." Yep, there it was. Devon's unique quality to see and interpret what no one else could.

We knew way too much about the film, and I threw my head back and laughed at how serious this conversation had become. But my smile soon faded when the boys turned their heads in the direction of the low rumbling sound of the engine pulling into the church driveway. The black hearse crept slowly down the path, my eyes following as it pulled up in front of the church doors. Death had arrived, and I was ready to face it. But I had no fear, only relief.

"Looks like it's showtime," I said, pulling myself up to standing and taking the hip flask from Adam to put into my pocket. He didn't argue. He knew as well as I did, I'd need it to get through the service with all the fake grief and phoney tears.

The other guys stood up too, brushing the grass and dirt from the ground off their trousers. Then we started to walk towards the entrance to the church, with long slow strides, standing side by side. I couldn't help but hum the Reservoir Dogs walking scene music, *Little Green Bag*, as I put my dark sunglasses on and stood tall and proud. The last King standing, that was me, and it felt fucking awesome.

I was having the last laugh.

"You know…" Devon leaned his head to the side as I hummed, and in response to the cool soundtrack we were walking to, he said, "They actually stole the idea of the colour character names from the nineteen seventy-four movie, *The Taking of Pelham One Two Three*."

I shook my head, smiling at the fact that Devon had the power to pull me out of the impending funk my father's phoney cortege was pulling me into. "Devon, your knowledge of useless facts never ceases to amaze me. You're gonna rock some lucky girl's world one day with your huge… encyclopaedic brain."

"We can't all exude big dick energy like you, Colton." He nudged me playfully with his elbow as his footsteps kept in time with mine. "Better to have a big brain," he whispered to himself.

"Said no girl ever," I volleyed back, and earned a chuckle from Will.

"I'll let you have the last word, seeing as it's such a shitty day for you," Devon replied, thinking he was being graceful with his response.

"I always have the last word." I winked and stuffed my hands into my pockets. I'd certainly had the last word where my father was concerned. No one fucks with this King. Not ever.

We stopped just as the funeral directors took the coffin from the back of the hearse. Kenny was right in there, acting as chief pallbearer, but I wanted no part of it. I wasn't about to carry that man on my shoulders. I'd carried enough of his crap over the years, and the sooner they buried him, forgot about him, and this day was done, the better.

"Why did you opt for a burial? Why didn't you have him cremated?" Will asked as we all stood back, letting them walk ahead with the coffin into the church.

"He'd already stipulated what he wanted in his will," I explained. Not that I was bothered about following any protocol, but it was set up, and I couldn't be arsed to argue the toss when push came to shove. "But trust me," I added with a sly grin. "There will be a cremation. That comes later tonight."

I saw Adam frown and then give me a look that said, 'Whatever you need, brother, I'm there.'

Devon must've felt the same because he patted me on the shoulder.

"That's something I have to do alone though," I told them, and they all nodded with support.

They got it.

They knew some things I had to do for myself, and tonight was one of those things. I'd let them help me with the other 'fuck you' I had planned for today, but tonight was just for me.

Thinking of that first 'fuck you', I couldn't help but smirk to myself at what I'd hidden around the back of the church, ready for when the gravediggers had done their shit. That's when I felt the warmth of a stare and I looked up to find two pairs of familiar, kind eyes blinking right back at me. I hadn't expected a big turnout for today, and there were only a handful of my father's lackeys dotted around, but the last two people I'd ever expected to see here were Rosie and Grace, smiling at me like it was some long-overdue reunion. To be honest, I never expected to see either of them again, let alone at my father's funeral. Why had they bothered coming here?

Rosie moved first, grabbing me in a bear hug and then sighed. "It's so good to see you, Colton. You look so grown up."

I wanted to give her a sarcastic response about how I'd only been five years old the last time I'd seen her, but the little boy that lingered inside me still had too much respect for her, and I didn't want to be rude, so I settled on, "That's because I am, Rosie." And I stood there and let her squeeze me like her life depended on it as my arms hung at my sides and I stood rooted to the spot.

After what felt like forever, Rosie pulled back, and then Grace stepped up, running her hand down the lapel of my jacket, and with a glint in her eye she said, "Nice T-shirt."

I broadened my shoulders and smoothed my hands down the front of the lettering, telling them, "Hey, if I'm gonna go down, I'm going down in style."

"That's what I like to hear," Grace replied. "Looks like you took my advice. Sometimes you've just gotta give the world the middle finger."

"Oh, I gave it more than a middle finger," I said, leaning down to whisper in her ear.

She frowned but didn't push me on it. Not that I'd admit to anything. My father overdosed on Fentanyl because he was a narcissist who thought he knew better than the doctors about what the correct dosage was. That was my story, and I was sticking to it. If I were going to do time, it wouldn't be for that low-life piece of shit. I had thought of other ways to make him suffer, and God knows he deserved a shitty ending, but I had to weigh up the pros and cons. If he'd disappeared, his face would've ended up all over the media. The last thing that fucker needed was more notoriety. Torture him and leave him for the authorities to find and he'd become a martyr. Remembered for the way he died and not the slow death he instigated in others. All his sins would've been swept under the carpet in favour of mourning his loss and berating the cruel way he'd been taken from the world. Death had a way of distorting the truth, and I didn't want that to be the case here.

"You found your freedom. I'm so pleased for you," Grace said. "I always thought you were too handsome to walk with your head down like you used to. You need to let the world see that gorgeous, smiling face. It's your time now." She grinned at me, and I gave her a wink.

"As lovely as it is to see you both, I have to ask, why are you here? I thought this'd be the last place you'd want to be."

They gave each other a knowing look, then turned to me.

"We came to pay our respects… to you," Rosie said, reaching out to squeeze my bicep in some strange show of solidarity. "Not that we needed to worry." She gestured to my brothers, that stood to the side of me. "I can see you're doing just fine. I'm glad he didn't manage to drag you down to the gutter with him." She turned to Grace and added, "See, sis, today is a good day for a funeral."

"Sis?" I frowned, looking from one to the other. "You two are sisters?"

"Rosie is my little sister," Grace informed me, threading her arm through Rosie's. "And if you ever need anything, anything at all, just call. We're always here for you, Colton."

They nodded in agreement, and then with wistful expressions they said their goodbyes.

I suppose my father had been good for something. He showed me there were still decent people left in the world, and Rosie and Grace were two of the best. They hadn't let life, or their shitty circumstances and what they had to do for a living get them down. One day, I'd pay them back for what my father took from them. And I was hoping that day would come sooner rather than later.

"It's showtime," Adam announced. The dry sarcasm dripping from his tone broke through my daydream, and I nodded, heading into the church with my hands in my pockets, ready to get it over with.

Showtime indeed.

I was about to put on the performance of a lifetime.

***

A few hours later, once the hangers-on had headed to the wake I had no intention of attending, and the gravediggers had clocked off for the night, I got ready to play my next card.

"This is fucking genius, mate." Will laughed as he picked up one side of the sign, and I grabbed the other. "I fucking love when you do crazy shit like this."

Devon had his mallet in his hand ready. Tyler held his camera, eager to record it all for prosperity. And Adam? He was keeping look out. The CCTV cameras had been spray-painted over, but you could never be too careful. And if a security guard or anyone else confronted us, Adam was only too eager to defend and attack. He knew I wanted to do this, and he wouldn't let anything stand in my way. He had my back, as always.

We carried the sign over to the mound of dirt where my father now resided. With Will's help, I lifted it up and speared it into the ground. The hate that I'd carried for so many years seemed pointless now, when I looked back. And standing here, in the middle of the graveyard with my brothers, looking at what we'd done, I couldn't help but hold my stomach as I laughed.

Will held the middle of the signpost in place as Adam and

Tyler helped Devon by giving him a knee-up so he could pound his mallet on the wood at the top and secure it properly into the ground. Then Tyler stood back, videoing the end result.

And me?

I just could not stop laughing.

God, I wished my father could see me now. I really fucking hoped he was peering up at this from the hell he was enslaved in. Even in death, I could make him look like a fucking jerk. I loved it.

"Soul for rent!" Tyler called out, reading the sign we'd put into the burial plot. "But I thought that fucker had no soul. Why did you choose this sign?"

"That's the whole fucking point," I blurted out, my sides hurting from laughing so hard. "This…" I gestured to the sign with my arms outstretched as Tyler filmed me. "It's his plea to the world. Take my soul, 'cos I sure as fuck don't deserve it. In fact, I'm pretty sure he sold it to the devil years ago. I hope they leave this post in the ground forever. I love making him look like a prick even though he's dead."

"He doesn't need your help to look like a prick, he did that all on his own," Adam stated.

He knew what my father had put me through, what he'd put everyone through. He knew every sordid, filthy story I had to tell. They all did. And like soldiers in arms, they stood by me, supported me, letting me get my crazy out in any way I wanted to, because they knew that's how I coped. Sometimes, crazy is the only way. Crazy is the best way, if you asked me.

"He doesn't," I concurred, letting my arms fall to my sides. "But until I'm satisfied, I'm going to piss all over his memory and make sure everyone in this town knows that I might be the joker, but *he* was the fucking joke."

I threw my head back and sucked in a breath of the cold night air, exhilaration washing over me. "Feels good, doesn't it?" I called out into the night. Then I lowered my gaze to look at my brothers. "It feels good to know we have control. We're all kings here. We can do anything we want to. This is our town."

"Amen to that," Adam replied, and the others hummed their agreement.

"So, are you finished for tonight? Ready for a pint down the pub?" Will asked, but I shook my head.

"Not tonight. I have one more mark of disrespect that I need to pay, and this one is all on me."

I patted each one of them on the shoulder as I started to walk away. "Fellas, it's been… memorable, as always. Feel free to take a piss on his grave before you leave." And with that, I walked away, knowing that this was the last time I'd ever set foot in this graveyard.

CHAPTER FOUR
The Rise of the Soldiers

Lesson 4: Sometimes a lie is better than the truth
Colton, later that night

With a lighter step and a smug smile, I headed back to the house my father owned. It wasn't my home, and I'd never call it that. It hadn't been home since the day he'd pushed my mother to the brink of insanity and made her take her own life. It held no warmth for me, and I wanted no part of it after finding out how my father had funded his lifestyle. I knew a lot of what he videoed had been non-consensual, and I was not okay with that. He deserved everything he had coming to him, and I had no doubt he'd be getting royally fucked by karma in the depths of depravity that was his damned eternity.

I opened the door to the house, grabbing the remote control

for the music system my father had paid ridiculous money to have piped throughout the house. I had to have some theme music playing when I gave my final performance. Then, I headed straight through to the back garden. I had no intention of staying here within these four walls. Will had already said there was a bed for me at the flat he shared with his mum and little brother, and after tonight, that's where I planned to go. But as light as I felt, knowing my future was in my hands now, I still had one thing I needed to get done, one lingering fester that was gnawing away inside of me.

The summerhouse.

I stood in the middle of the lawn and looked down at the wooden monstrosity that'd held so many sordid secrets within its walls for so many years. A building full of lies and deceit, hurt and humiliation. I once overheard my father telling Kenny the humiliation scenes were his best sellers. The pain and tears on the faces of the men and women that he'd tricked into partaking in his more twisted, sick performances made him more money than anything else. He didn't care about the scars he'd left behind. Like I said, he had no soul. He'd sold it to the devil because he knew he'd have no use for it.

I'd left a petrol can on the patio ready for tonight. I knew I'd want to do this after the funeral. He'd had his burial, now it was time for me to initiate the cremation. I reached down and picked the can up, walking slowly down to the summerhouse with determination. Once there, I pushed the door open, but I didn't look too closely at anything inside. I didn't care for the set-up he had down here. Why would I? He'd made it look like a bedroom, but it was, for all intents and purposes, a torture chamber.

"My only regret," I huffed as I started to paint the walls and floor in petrol. "Is that I waited so long to do this. That, and the fact you're not getting burned alive in here too. It's what you deserved."

I stood back, so the petrol didn't splash me, and emptied the can, dripping the last dregs in a trail towards the door. Then, I threw the can into the middle of the room and took a packet of cigarettes from my back pocket, pulled one out and sparked it up with my lighter. I took a long slow drag, feeling wicked retribution trickle through my veins.

"Ashes to ashes, motherfucker. Burn in hell," I said with a grin to the ghost of my father. Then I threw my lighter down to the ground and walked backwards to the safety of the lawn, away from the flames that began to crawl and lick across the floor. Flames that grew wilder, angrier as they curled around the furniture and up the walls. The linen on the bed went up like hellfire, and I folded my arms, standing proudly as I watched it all burn to nothing. I took another drag of my cigarette and closed my eyes as the nicotine soothed my soul and the crackle of the fire warmed my heart. The pride that washed over me for what I'd done, how I'd created some recompense for the lives he'd destroyed, made me shiver, and I turned to face the house, lifting the remote control to start the song I'd set up to play, *Firestarter* by The Prodigy. Keith Flint would be fucking proud of me tonight. Even I was proud of me.

The flames grew higher, and my excitement levels hit fever pitch as I sat on the patio in a deckchair, enjoying the view. Firestarter played out on a loop, and I lit up a second cigarette, oblivious to anything else other than the elation running through me. Eventually, the sounds of sirens broke through my euphoria and a group of firemen burst through the side gate into the back garden, shouting instructions to each other, ready to fight the fire. I gave them a grin and waved from my deckchair then sat back, watching them get to work.

"Glad you could join me, fellas," I shouted across, but they didn't hear me over the noise of the music, the fire, and the heavy helmets they wore. They soon got to work dousing the fire, but the summerhouse was obliterated. It was nothing but a dripping, smouldering skeleton of what it once was. Black, empty and ugly, just like my dad's heart. I wouldn't have had it any other way.

Once the flames were out, they came over to question me, asking what had happened. I did a good job of acting dumb, despite the cheeky way I'd greeted them when they'd charged in here, along with the music I was playing that I'd since turned off. I guessed their helmets and adrenaline had blocked that out. Either that or they didn't want to acknowledge what they feared might be true.

I told them I'd come home to find the summerhouse on fire. I hadn't seen anyone. It was as much a shock to me as it was to them. 'Why would anyone do this?' I'd cried in mock anger. 'And on the day of my father's funeral.' The fact that I'd dropped that nugget, about it being my father's funeral, bought me a degree of sympathy and they eased off the questioning pretty soon after.

In their opinion, it was kids messing about. I shook my head in disgust and said, "I don't know what this world is coming to."

They were way too easy to manipulate, which worked out well for me.

One of them patted my shoulder and told me, "It's a shame

more youngsters can't take a leaf out of your book, son. Your mum must be so proud." He looked up at the house like he expected to see my mother at the window.

I didn't correct him on the reality of my situation. I let him think what he wanted. I couldn't give a fuck. Then he sighed and said, "Take good care of her... and yourself. I'm sorry you had to go through this, today of all days."

"It's a burden I bear willingly," I added, wishing they'd fuck off so I could pack my bags and be gone.

The fireman gave a sad, pitying smile, and then, taking a step back, he said, "We'll be in touch." And with that, they left, and I used that silent, solitary moment to take one last look at the wreckage of the garden and my life.

"You always had to have the last word," I said to my father. "But not this time. Not anymore. You're nothing now. A nobody. The only King this town will ever remember is me. I'm going to make damn sure of that. You made my childhood a misery, but now I'm having the last laugh. I always will."

***

That night, and every night after, I stayed with Will and his family. They welcomed me with open arms and made me feel like an honorary member of the Stokes family. The police and fire department recorded the fire as arson, but their enquiries soon fizzled out. It was just another headache in a long line of cases that plagued our town. No one had been hurt, and no one was making waves about it, so it was soon brushed under the carpet.

As for my father's estate, that was put into the guardianship of an aunt I barely knew, for her to oversee until I was eighteen years old, but as luck would have it, I turned eighteen a few weeks after his death.

Perfect timing.

I didn't hesitate to put the house on the market, and when it sold, I split the proceeds between every man and woman my father had taken from, including Tina, Rosie, and Grace. I hoped that it'd help to make their life easier, and as far as I was concerned, it was their money anyway. It was the least I could do.

Last I heard, Kenny had sloped off to Spain to live his life in hiding. I did consider going after him, but honestly, I couldn't be bothered. Maybe one day I'd track him down, but for now, I had bigger fish to fry and better things to do with my time.

I thought I'd gotten everything under control, until one morning, I had another call from my father's solicitors, telling me there were offshore accounts and savings that needed signing over to me.

Fuck.

I didn't want it.

I wasn't interested in his filthy money, and when I attended the solicitor's offices to sign all the necessary papers, I fully intended to donate it all to charity or send another lump sum to all the recipients of the house sale. But something stopped me that day. A voice in my head told me to hang fire, and I'm glad I did, because there was something close to my heart that I decided to use the money on during a cold and wet Friday evening in Brinton Manor.

***

"Who was the first person you ever killed?" Will asked as we all stood huddled under the shitty underpass in our manor.

It was almost midnight, and the streetlights were flickering on and off, as if they didn't want to see what Brinton looked like at this time of night. Couldn't say I blamed them. Where we stood, sheltered from the elements, it was dirty, covered in crap graffiti and stunk of piss. Empty cans and rubbish littered the floor. The buildings that surrounded us were mostly abandoned with broken windows and crumbling brickwork. Footfall here was scarce, mainly because the people of Brinton wanted to stay away from us. Most of them knew this was our spot, the perfect place to see who was coming into our town and who we needed to watch. Plus, we had a stellar reputation for taking no shit. No one crossed the soldiers and lived to tell the tale.

Adam rubbed his hands together, blew into them to heat them up, and shuffled on his feet to try and stay warm. Then he said, "My foster father," and kept his eyes trained in the distance, looking for trouble. We knew that look. It meant he didn't want to talk about it, and we knew better than to push him.

Tyler was the next one to speak, ignoring Adam's admission like it was nothing. "For me, it'd be Devon's stepdad's friend. Ray, was it?"

Will nodded, his eyes going bright as he said, "That was mine too. It felt pretty damn good that day."

"He wasn't my stepfather," Devon added matter of fact, not a hint of emotion in his tone. "He never married my mum." He shrugged. "He was nothing to me. And my first kill? It was him. Vinnie." His voice soon changed when he spoke his name, venom dripping from his tongue as his eyes turned a shade darker.

"We're the best fucking vigilantes," I stated, trying to lighten the mood. "Like superheroes, only not, we're the antiheroes. No one fucks with us. I fucking love it."

Adam ignored me, taking a step forward to stand directly underneath the dim streetlamp to make his presence known to a group of men passing by in the street. They took one look at him and crossed the road. They knew the score. Avoid the soldiers at all costs.

"We might be decent vigilantes," Adam huffed. "But it doesn't pay well." He turned to stare at us, folding his arms over his chest and giving us a pointed glare. "I don't know about you, but I don't plan on standing on these streets for the rest of my life. We need a better plan. We need to do better, be better. Those boys over in Sandland, the ones who call themselves the Renaissance men, they make a fortune every weekend putting on illegal parties. Brandon Mathers kills it with his bare-knuckle boxing, and the gambling scams they have going on make them a shitload of money. They charge a fee for entry, and they pay fuck all for the gig, zero overheads. We should be more like them."

"You want to put on illegal parties?" Devon asked, his face forming a frown that reflected our own confusion.

"No. We can do better than that. But we need a base first. Premises of our own where we can run something no one around here has ever seen before. Our own club, but better than anything the Sandland boys could pull together. Something for the people of Brinton. Something that's ours."

Adam's eyes glazed over, and I could tell he was thinking, dreaming big, planning for a future that we could all be proud of. That was Adam; always pushing, finding the next thing to excite him.

"And how do you suggest we fund something like that?" Tyler asked, ever the realist.

"Well, I don't fucking know yet, do I?" Adam snapped, the anger at being challenged burning on his face. "I don't have all the answers, but I'll find a way. I always find a way."

"I told you, super-antiheroes. That's the answer. Only, we should choose our masks wisely. We don't want to end up like Bane. I mean, how the fuck does that guy eat anything? He must be fucking starving," I joked, earning a laugh from Will and Tyler. But Adam didn't see the funny side. To him, our future was no laughing matter.

"You either die a hero or you live long enough to become the villain," Devon said, going all philosophical on us. "I think we've all lived through enough shit to know which ones we are now."

"Even villains deserve some recognition," Tyler replied, mirroring what we all felt. We believed there was a fine line between right and wrong; good and bad. And when you looked closely, who were the real heroes and villains in this life? Because the heroes of the people weren't always the ones that were hailed as such in the media. "I like Adam's idea," he reiterated, rubbing his jaw in thought. "We just need to find a way to fund it. We need a better income. We're not going to get there through petty theft and the odd backhander."

Adam, Devon, and Tyler started to talk about ways they could make more money. Will stood to side of me, half listening and half playing on his phone, and me, I already had the answer, but I wasn't about to show them my cards yet. It wasn't that simple.

"Maybe we could pimp Will out? He's the prettiest one here. Boys, girls, I don't think he'd be fussy," I suggested as a joke, trying to break through the seriousness stifling the air.

Will laughed, but Adam stopped talking and glared at me. "If you put half as much effort into helping as you do joking around, we'd be fucking millionaires."

"Millionaires? I'm fucking priceless. There is no number you can put on perfection like this," I said, gesturing up and down my body, so they knew I meant the outside package as well.

They all groaned, and I knew it pissed Adam off to think I wasn't taking this seriously, but I was. I just didn't want them to know that. Adam was one of my best friends. I'd do anything for him. But sometimes, it was easier to be the drifter and not take life too seriously. Or at least project that to the outside world. Adam took life too seriously. But that was something I'd never do again. If you couldn't laugh about something, then what was the point?

"Knowledge is power," I stated, getting on my proverbial soap box. "And power breeds corruption. So, let's study hard and become the best at being evil."

"Dude, that sounds really fucking awesome." Will laughed. "I have no idea what it means, but I like it."

"You'll need to grow up first before you start working at that level," Adam chided, lifting his chin to challenge me.

"I know," I replied with a smile. "I've got a hell of a lot of growing up to do. I realised that the other day when I was in my blanket fort."

Will chuckled, Tyler grinned and shook his head, but Adam

and Devon rolled their eyes and turned away. They obviously weren't in the mood for a bit of mindless banter.

"Thank you very much. I'm here all week," I said taking a bow.

***

Later that night, when I got back to Will's and had a quiet moment to myself, I put my plan into action. I set up a fake email account, and I sent an email to Adam, telling him I was a victim of a well-known burglar from our town. A burglar that I knew had recently come out of prison and was bragging to anyone that'd listen that his time inside was a breeze, his stretch too short, and he couldn't wait to get back to thieving again. Only thing was, unlike our thief, Tyler, he robbed from the poor to make himself rich. He was a perfect target, and we'd already said we wanted to pay him a little visit. Now, I could set those wheels in motion and make it pay for us, all courtesy of the ill-gotten gains of my sperm donor.

> *To: ANoblePsycho@ftmail.com*
> *From: BillFinger@talkmail.com*
> *Message: I need your help.*
>
> Dear Mr Noble,
> I have a problem, and a close friend told me this is something your vigilante group may be able to help me with.
> A few months ago, our home was broken into by a local man called Phil Tuckett. He stole a lot of

sentimental family treasures; my father's war medals, jewellery left to me by my grandmother, silver photo frames that contained the only pictures we ever took of the baby we never got to hold in our arms. Our rainbow baby, my wife calls her. This has truly broken her.

But it's not about what he stole, it's the sleepless nights he's given us. The fact that my wife can't go to bed unless we've checked the doors and windows a dozen times. That she's scared to be in the house on her own after dark. He has stolen our peace and robbed us of peace of mind. We never feel safe or relaxed in our own home anymore. It doesn't feel the same.

So, I'm asking if you'd be willing to pay this man a visit. Give him a taste of his own medicine and show him that victims won't stay victims forever. I'm willing to pay for your time. I understand there are five of you altogether, so I'm willing to start negotiations at five thousand pounds.

I await your response, but I hope that you hear my plea and help me.

Please.

I don't know what else to do.

I am desperate.

Regards,

Bill

I was impressed with my skills of storytelling and persuasion, and I felt sure that Adam would take the bait. The fact that I'd used the name of the creator of The Joker from the DC Comics was the icing on the cake too. I had Bob Kane and Jerry Robinson, the other two creators, in mind, ready to use for the next fake emails I was going to send. My father had left money behind, and now I knew what I wanted to use it for. I was going to clean his dirty money the best way, the soldier way, using it to pay for jobs we would normally do for free.

Why not?

If I'd offered the money outright to the lads, they wouldn't have taken it. But this way, they earned the cash and kept their pride intact. That was something I knew was important to all of them, especially Adam.

***

The next day, Adam showed us the email. He wasn't keen. He said he didn't feel right about taking an honest man's money to do a job we would be doing anyway. But I argued the case. I reminded him this person had reached out to us. They wanted to pay because they wanted the job doing properly and they knew we were the best. That we needed the money if we were ever going to get off the streets of Brinton and into our own place, a business we could run. I told him it was pay for work we were damn good at, and he'd be a fool to look a gift horse like this in the mouth. Will agreed. Tyler wasn't sure, and Devon, as usual, was siding with whatever Adam wanted to do. So, we put it to a vote, and after I put my hand up to confirm I was in, Will did too, and Tyler reluctantly followed suit.

"Well, I guess the majority wins," Adam announced, and he raised his hand, which encouraged Devon to do the same. "We won't negotiate, though. Five grand is more than enough. Let's not take the piss."

The others agreed, and I smiled, satisfied in the knowledge I was doing something to help my brothers. Something I wouldn't ever tell a soul; I'd take it to my grave. The Soldiers of Anarchy were on the way up, and this was just the beginning.

***

After that first hit, I set up a few more. I'd heard on the grapevine my old school friend, Tom, had entered the police service, and after a few secret meetings, he fed me some names I could use. People who had lied and cheated their way out of the system and were walking free, even though they were as guilty as hell.

The law could be manipulated, there were loopholes for everything if you had enough money to pay a decent lawyer. But as far as we were concerned, there were no loopholes. If we found out you were guilty, we made you pay. Revenge is never pretty, but when it's done cleverly and meticulously, it can be a thing of fucking beauty.

Eventually, word got around there was a paid service in Brinton Manor. A service for the people.

Justice in its truest form.

We grew as a unit, became tighter, stronger. We created our own bat signal to cash in on a business that was booming. Tyler set up an email for us to receive work, and soon we started to get emails I hadn't initiated. I never let on I was writing the earlier ones or sending the money, but I was sure Tyler might've had his suspicions. He was into computers and all that shit, and maybe he'd matched the IP address to my laptop.

I don't know.

But sometimes, he'd give me a strange look or frown at me when the others weren't looking. If he had guessed though, he never let on. Like me, he knew Adam had pride in what we did, and he'd never want to upset the status quo.

Our savings grew, and my father's money turned from ill-gotten gains to divine retribution. It also made up a large percentage of the money we used, years later, to buy the lease on a building we wanted to acquire for our club venture.

The old asylum in Sandland.

It was a huge gothic building that stood on the outskirts of Sandland and Brinton Manor, looking deceptively dark and menacing to passers-by. A little like us when we'd stood on the street corners.

It was perfect.

Sure, it needed a bit of work, but we didn't mind putting in some hard graft to get it to where we needed it to be. And putting the building work to one side, it was a prime piece of real estate.

Hauntingly enticing.

Unique.

The outside walls hinted at the danger and temptation that lay within. Like a beacon to anyone with a darker side they wanted to explore, the asylum was made for people that liked to play in the shadows, people like us.

Buying that place had been made even sweeter by the fact that the boys from Sandland, the Renaissance men, had wanted it. But we rocked up and stole that place right out from under their noses. No one was going to stop us or stand in our way. We were ready to turn the asylum into our sanctuary. Ready to show the world what the soldiers of Brinton Manor were capable of.

Life was ours for the taking.

No looking back.

No regrets.

All who come here abandon all fear, because when the soldiers were in attendance, all bets were off.

THE JOKER

PART TWO
Welcome to my world

THE JOKER

CHAPTER FIVE
Colton

Present Day

A sea of people stood around me, moving to the thumping beat of the DJ's music. Some wore tight little dresses, suits, designer clothes that made them feel a kinship to the social media idols they worshipped. Others let their true personalities shine through with their own individual style. Ripped jeans, band T-shirts, and black eyeliner were their two-finger salute to a world of conformity. We didn't discriminate at The Sanctuary and there was no dress code at the door. As long as you weren't totally obscene or offensive, it was all good. Everyone was welcome here, from the flashy crowd to the outcasts, and we liked those best; after all, we were outcasts too.

The strobe lights bounced over the crowd, and the electricity it created, along with the vibe from the people here, gave me a real buzz. The music, the party atmosphere, the knowledge that all of this was ours was fucking phenomenal. Even though I was on duty on the ground floor tonight, I threw my arms in the air and hollered as the bassline dropped and the crowd went wild.

Sunday night wasn't our busiest night, but tonight it was buzzing. I fucking loved it. I let my head go a little, moving to the beat of the music, and a few girls close by reached out to me, touching my arm and trying to get me to dance with them. I gave them my wicked smile and a wink, but after a few cheeky moves to keep them happy, I walked away. It was a fine line you had to walk, knowing when to turn the charm on and off. I loved women's company, and I loved keeping the guests happy, but I wasn't a fucking plaything, despite the reputation I knew I had. I liked to party, I loved a good time, but on my terms.

I pushed my way through to the side of the dance floor, then made my way around the periphery of the room, watching, assessing, listening. A group of men gathered at the foot of the stairs where Gaz, our head of security and right-hand man, was stationed. They looked lairy and I had a feeling they might be about to start some shit, so I headed over there.

"I'm not saying it's a bad club," some drunk guy in a grey suit said, slurring his words and sloshing the beer around as he held court with his mates. "But the owners? The fucking soldiers of crap or whatever they like to call themselves... I can't stand them. They think they're all badass motherfuckers but I'm telling you–" He pointed at each of his friends and swayed on his unsteady feet, blinking as he tried to clear his blurry vision. "They're just a bunch of jumped-up fucking cunts. Wankers, the lot of them."

They hadn't seen me loitering behind them. I knew, because they all fucking laughed, but I laughed louder, and that's what made them all turn around and then pale at my presence.

I took a step closer, so I was in the middle of their circle, and I frowned at the drunken shithead that thought he could say what he wanted just because he'd had a drink and felt brave.

"Got a problem, mate?" I asked, tilting my head and waiting to see how he'd play this. "Is there something you want to share with me?"

His eyes glazed over, and I could see the dilemma playing out across his face as he debated his options. Back down, and he'd look like an idiot in front of his mates. Stand up to me, and he'd find out exactly how much of a cunt I really was. He went for a middle-of-the-road option, which only pissed me off more because it showed he had no backbone.

"I'm not trying to start trouble; I just don't get why you're a big deal."

"Nobody said we're a big fucking deal." I gritted my teeth and took a step into his personal space; my nose inches from his as his so-called friends started to back away. "But I'll tell you what I did hear, I heard you call me and my friends cunts and wankers. So, I'm going to ask you this, what the fuck do you think gives you the right to walk into our club, our fucking property, and talk shit about us?"

He swallowed, but in his drunken state, he couldn't devise a worthy response; all he could do was give me a fake-ass grin, so I went in harder.

"Why are you smiling? Having a face like yours is nothing to smile about."

There was a low rumble amongst his friends as they

recognised what was about to go down, but I wasn't letting up. I was on a roll.

"This is our home." I gestured around me. "As well as our business, you sorry sack of shit. Do you see me strolling into your house and calling your family a bunch of tight-ass motherfuckers? Which I bet they are, by the way, judging from the cheap aftershave and crap haircut you've got." I stepped back to make a show of looking him up and down. "And the less said about your suit, the better. There're corpses that'd refuse to be buried in that polyester piece of crap." I folded my arms over my chest as I felt myself falling into a rhythm. "We've built this place from nothing. We came from nothing. What have you ever done? Oh…" I tapped my finger on my chin and pretended to think. But I didn't need to think about what I said to this guy. It all came naturally. "That's right, you came here, even though you thought we were cunts, and you spent your money at our bar, drinking our beer, lining our pockets and chatting shit. That's what you've done. And then, you've stood up here and disrespected me and my friends, as if that's part of the package deal. Do you think because you've paid to get in here, you can do whatever the fuck you want?"

He opened his mouth to respond, but I didn't give him chance. My craziness had taken over, and I wouldn't stop until I'd annihilated him.

Reaching forward, I grabbed his tie and yanked him down from the high horse he seemed to think he deserved to be on, dragging him to the staircase and then pulling him up the steps behind me.

His friends didn't try to stop me; instead, they scattered like rats from a sinking ship, not wanting to be a part of this man's impending doom. Even his taste in mates was shit. They wouldn't stand by him. They preferred to save themselves.

"I'm going to show you something, Clive," I told him as I led him up the stairs.

"My name's Alex," he spluttered as the tie I was dragging him along by constricted around his neck.

"Good for you, Clive. Anyway, as I was saying, I'm going to show you something. Something that maybe one day, you can aspire to, if you ever open a club of your own, that is. I'm going to give you a lesson."

I turned to face him as I yanked him up the last few steps, and he followed like my fucking lap dog, albeit a reluctant, pissed-off one. "That is what you want, isn't it, Clive? To be better than a bunch of jumped-up wankers like us. So let me give you the grand tour. Make sure you get the full soldiers of crap experience."

Gaz touched my arm as we reached the first floor and asked, "Is everything okay, Colton?" with a look of concern on his face.

I turned to face Clive, who I'd never give the respect to call Alex, and I smiled, patting his cheek as I replied, "We're perfect. I'm just going to show my good friend Clive here what we do at The Sanctuary." I hushed my voice and added, "Show him what the soldiers are really all about."

Clive swallowed.

Gaz nodded in recognition and turned back to his job, overseeing the patrons and making sure shit didn't pop off.

And me?

I stood staring down the corridor at the doors that led off it, wondering which one I'd throw Clive into. It would be like throwing a pitiful animal into a lion's den, only this wasn't a scary place, it was fucking awesome.

The mood on the first floor differed from the party atmosphere we'd left behind. It was chilled with a hint of sensual, seductive anticipation for the delights that waited behind each door. But for Clive, the anticipation was more a dread, judging from the heavy panting and the look of horror in his eyes.

I was still holding his tie like a leash, and I mused out loud, "Now, which one do I show you? The dark room? How many people does it take to change a lightbulb in the dark room, Clive?"

Clive just shook his head, staring at me like I'd gone insane.

"None, Clive. Fucking zero, because it doesn't have any lightbulbs, you dick. It's a fucking dark room." I rolled my eyes and added. "How many egomaniacs like you does it take to change a lightbulb?"

"What?" Clive narrowed his eyes in confusion, there were clearly no lightbulbs switched on in his brain right now. He looked like he didn't know where the fuck he was.

"One, Clive. One. Just you, holding the lightbulb while the rest of the world revolves around you. Isn't that right?" The spaced-out look on his face made me laugh. "Or are you going to argue with me?"

"I need to find my friends," Clive replied, trying to shake me off, but I turned my smile to psycho, making sure he knew I wasn't fucking about.

"You're going nowhere, mate."

I carried on pulling him down the darkened corridor, past the closed doors that held so much promise as he tried to argue for his release.

"We could try the voyeur room. That's always a fan

favourite. But what if, by some awful twist of fate, I put you in the wrong part of the room and you had to put on a show for them?" I gave an exaggerated gasp. "I hope you've got your best underwear on, Clive."

Clive's eyes went wide, and his mouth fell open like the dumb idiot he was. His pitiful begging and wittering suddenly replaced with shock.

"The toy rooms are fun," I said, ignoring his paralysis and yanking him down the corridor. "In fact, all our themed rooms are the fucking bomb." I knew exactly where I was headed, but I was having fun winding him up, letting him know what kind of club we'd created and how far off the mark he really was in his character assassination of us. If anyone was a loser here, it was him.

I noticed Tyler standing at the other end of the corridor, his head jerking back when he saw me, as if to say, 'What the fuck are you doing dragging some random dude around?'

Educating, Tyler, my friend. Educating the ignorant masses.

In a last-ditch attempt to maintain some degree of dignity, Clive pulled back and hissed, "Where the fuck are you taking me, you psycho freak?"

I tutted and shook my head. This guy was a walking disaster, and he needed to learn to quit while he was ahead.

"Psycho? I think you've got the wrong soldier, mate. I'm not the psycho. Not that much, anyway."

I yanked harder on his tie, and even though he was mumbling, he acquiesced, letting me lead him to the door I considered one of my favourites. Not that I liked to discriminate. They were all fucking awesome.

I pulled him through into the communal room, and once

inside, he soon shut up.

This room was one of the larger ones on this floor, and the subdued red lighting gave it a forbidden aura. One that made your body hum with seductive warmth, mirroring the crimson hue that enveloped you. Like you were hidden in the shadows, but you could still watch the scenes playing out around you. Forbidden desires brought to life, and whether you wanted to watch or participate, it was all good. There was no judgement here. It was the communal room, after all, so anything was possible, and nothing was off-limits.

The walls were black, just like the beds in the middle of the room. And around the perimeter, people stood watching the scenes playing out before their eyes. The rule was no touching unless you were invited. No playing unless you were given permission from the other players. Consent was a big thing for me, for all of us, that made this club what it was.

Some might look at what my father had done for a living and question why I agreed to something like this. He'd sold sex, so why was I? But it wasn't the same, not in my eyes. We sold a dream, bringing like-minded people together. This club empowered its patrons, let them explore in a safe environment. My father was about ridicule and exploitation. We were the complete opposite.

The people currently living out their fantasies on the beds in the middle of the room were the ones that held all the power. Nothing happened unless they wanted it to. Everything was consensual. We rigorously vetted our members and made sure everything was done safely and with respect. But it was fun. It was a fucking head trip. I loved our club and all that we stood for. That's why I couldn't let little shits like Clive, or anyone else who might come along, get away with acting like cunts under our roof.

I felt Clive stiffen besides me. He didn't need to be reminded to stay back. He was already rooted to the floor. I nudged him and pointed at a couple, ensuring he was focused on a man and woman in the far corner. There was a reason I brought him in here, and it wasn't for him to get a kick. He needed teaching a lesson.

The woman was naked and sprawled on her back with her legs open. The guy was on his front, nestled between her legs and eating her pussy with slow sensual licks. She arched her back and closed her eyes, her mouth falling open as she mewled out in appreciation. Then he began sucking on her clit, forcing her to gaze down at him and grab his hair in her fist to guide him the way she wanted him. The movement of his head as he slowly devoured her was so fucking sexy, I could feel myself responding to it, even with Clive, the fucking knob stood next to me.

"Still think we're losers?" I asked on a whisper, but I wasn't expecting a response, and I didn't get one.

I watched as the woman's head fell to the side, and she spotted a shirtless guy in a worn pair of jeans leaning against the wall. She must've called him over, because the next thing I knew, he was unbuttoning his jeans and sliding them off, along with his boxers, and then he crawled over the bed towards her. With his upper body caging hers in, he leaned down to kiss her, then reared back, bracing one hand on the bed frame above her head as he stroked his dick with the other. He rubbed the head of his dick against her lips before pushing slowly into her mouth. The woman lay back with her head tilted slightly to take him down her throat as her legs quivered while the other guy sucked on her clit, bringing her to orgasm.

Two men were pleasuring her, enjoying her, and this was only one of the scenes playing out in front of us. Clive was breathing heavier now, and when the guy we were watching pulled his dick out of her mouth and growled, "You love being watched, don't you? You love showing everyone you're our filthy little slut."

I heard Clive groan too, and I knew it was time to wrap this up.

I turned to face him, spoiling his view of the show and slapping my hand on his shoulder as I said, "Time's up. Show's over. And now, so are you."

He frowned, not quite getting what I was hinting at. He must've forgotten what had happened only moments ago or why he was in here, and he smiled and asked, "Where do I sign up for this?"

This guy was un-fucking-believable. As I ushered him out of the room, he was craning his neck over my shoulder to try and get a glimpse of what he'd never see again.

"Sign up? Are you fucking joking? You can kiss my ass, *mate*. That's the last time you ever see anything like that in my club."

I closed the door behind me and pushed him back into the corridor.

"What's up there?" he asked, pointing at the staircase to the second floor, his eyes wide like a bloody kid in a sweet shop.

"Our living quarters, not that it's any of your business." I shoved him forward. "It'll be the stairway to hell for you if you ever tried to go up there."

I could see Gaz watching from his place by the stairs and I jerked my head, giving him the okay to come over.

"Clive," I said smiling, despite the fact I was about to kick his ass to the kerb. "I would say it's been a pleasure to meet you, but it really hasn't. In fact, I hope I never see your smug face ever again."

Clive began to splutter over his response, telling me he was sorry and begging for a second chance. "I only said what I did downstairs to look hard in front of my mates. I didn't really mean it. I'm sorry."

"So, you're an asshole and a liar?" I tutted. "I hate liars the most. If you say something, you should own it. Even if it's bullshit." I pushed my face into his. "Own your bullshit, Clive."

"My name's Alex," he repeated, like I gave a fuck.

"I couldn't give a rat's ass what your name is. You've seen what you're missing, you know what we stand for, so now, all that's left is for you to fuck off."

Gaz was standing next to me, holding his radio, ready to call for extra security.

"Throw him out the back door," I instructed Gaz. "And make sure he's never allowed in again. He's barred. Blacklisted. We have a no cunts rule here, and he's a grade A cunt."

Gaz grabbed Clive's arm in a harsh grip as he radioed for security, and Clive thrashed against him, arguing, "I didn't fucking do anything. Get your fucking hands off me."

I grabbed Clive's tie in my fist one last time and yanked his face to mine. I could feel the anger burning in my eyes as I spat out my response.

"You called me a wanker. You should be thanking your lucky stars that all I'm doing is throwing you out. Catch me on a bad day, and I'd slice your fingers off. I'd make sure you never wank again, mate, let alone call me one. Am I making myself clear?"

I opened my eyes wider, waiting for him to reply. He nodded, so I added, "Your shitty behaviour has really fucked up my night. You need to work on your people skills, Clive, and be thankful it was me who heard you and not one of the others. Oh, and feel free to tell your friends that the soldiers don't fuck about. We are fucking awesome and so is our club. But you? You're a dickhead, aren't you?"

Clive just stared at me, so I repeated, "You're a dickhead…" And I nodded my head, waiting for it. "Say it, Clive…"

Clive finally cottoned on and repeated like a dumbass, "I'm a dickhead."

"Good. I'm glad there's something we agree on." I turned to Gaz and the two security guys that were standing ready. "Take out the trash," I ordered and walked away with as much swagger as I could as Gaz and the security bustled Clive down the stairs towards the rear exit.

I leaned over the balcony, feeling smug as I watched the revellers below and felt Tyler come to stand next to me.

"Was that really necessary?" he asked.

I glanced to the side and gave him a smile.

"No one comes into our club and disses us. You know that. He forgot and needed a reminder." I gazed back at the sea of people down below. "Doesn't hurt to remind some of them down there as well. Respect is a two-way street. If you come into our home and disrespect us, expect the same back."

"By taking them into the communal room?" Tyler asked, arching his brow.

"By showing them what they're missing out on, and what we're capable of." I cocked my head to the side to lean closer to Tyler, and added, "It could've been worse, could've been the chapel and an introduction to Devon's armoury."

Tyler knew I was right. The asylum chapel that was attached to this club was full to the brim of every weapon known to man, courtesy of our Reaper and weapon enthusiast, Devon.

"Remind me to bring up the problem of customer relations in the next meeting," Tyler said, then his mouth curled into the smile he'd tried to fight down.

"Remind me to give a fuck when you do," I replied.

I glanced back out over the sea of people below us, and there, standing stock-still in the middle of a heaving dance floor, was a girl staring right back up at me.

She was surrounded by dancers, but she didn't move a muscle; she didn't care about what was happening around her, her focus was solely on me. When she saw that I'd noticed her, the hint of a smile graced her full lips. This girl was stunning, with a mass of brown curls cascading over her shoulders and a perfect, beautiful face that seemed to hold a million secrets behind her delicate smile. It wasn't unusual for girls to hit on us at the club, but with our connected gazes, I couldn't work out if this girl wanted to fuck me or gut me; cut out my spleen and wear it as a souvenir.

Was it twisted that I liked that about her?

One look and I wanted to know more. But as the lights in the club dimmed for a second, then the strobe lights took over, she disappeared, and I never saw her again.

CHAPTER SIX
Colton

"I can't believe that guy was stupid enough to let himself get dragged around like that."

I walked into the living room the next morning to find Will and Tyler huddled together at the table, watching CCTV footage from the club. The pair of them were glued to the screen like my run-in with Clive from the night before was the latest Netflix sensation.

"And I can't believe it took him so long to throw the fucker out." Tyler thumbed at me and then focused on the screen, laughing as he watched the part where Gaz yanked him down the stairs.

"That was the highlight of my night." I nodded at the laptop as I grabbed a mug to make myself a coffee. "I hope you got my good side."

"You don't have a good side. Just a twisted, crazy one."

Tyler gave me the side-eye, then smirked to himself, and I just laughed.

"My crazy side is my good side. Anyway, he was lucky. There was no bloodshed. I didn't fuck him up, just fucked around."

I leaned against the kitchen counter, sipping my coffee as I watched them pour over the footage. Will kept rewinding the part where Clive got his marching orders. That was his favourite part.

"His face," Will chuckled. "He looks petrified, and you've done fuck all. Imagine if he really fucked up and you gave him the chapel tour."

"I wish he had done more, given me a reason to wipe the smugness out of him. He was a spineless wanker."

"One look at Devon's katana sword and he'd shit his pants." Will laughed.

"I wouldn't waste the katana on him. A good aim with a throwing knife right between his eyes would be enough." I pulled a carving knife from the knife block and took aim, throwing it into the wall opposite. "Bullseye."

Just then, Leah, Devon's girlfriend, and Liv, Adam's wife, walked in. I would say they had shitty timing, but they'd managed to avoid the knife throwing, so it wasn't all bad.

Liv took one look at the knife stuck in the wall, then the laptop screen and stated, "If that's how you're getting your kicks these days, Colton, you really need to get a life. Or a hobby. Or a girlfriend even." She shrugged and went over to the corner of the room to pick up Tyson's food bowl.

I huffed on a smile.

"I have a life. My hobby is fucking shit up with these guys.

But a girlfriend?" I shook my head. "Not gonna happen. Why deprive the rest of the female population?" I gestured up and down my body. "Perfection like this can't be chained down or locked away. That'd be a travesty. And besides, I'm too much for one girl to handle."

"I'd agree with that," Liv whispered, raising her brow at me as she spooned dog food into the bowl. "How could one girl be expected to cope with an ego your size?"

"It's not the size of my ego that'd impress her." I waggled my brow.

"You do know, when you say shit like that you give off small dick energy." Liv walked back to the corner to put the bowl down, just as Tyson, our Rottweiler, bounded into the room, sniffing out his breakfast and knocking into half the furniture as he went for it.

"Only insecure men with tiny dicks would let that faze them. Me? I have no issues."

"You have more issues than Vogue," Tyler quipped. "Even your issues have issues," he chuckled under his breath, just as Adam and Devon stalked through the door.

I didn't get chance to argue back, but it didn't bother me.

"Can we cut the crap and focus?" Adam snapped, taking a seat at the table. "We have work to do."

"I'm always focused," I replied, giving Leah a wink and hiding my smile behind my coffee mug. But when Adam started talking, I shifted into business mode. We did indeed have work to do.

"We got an email late last night about a new target," Adam told us. "Some guy called Derek Headley who's out on parole. He murdered a guy in a drunken fight over a game of snooker, did five years for it. But since getting out, he's been taunting the victim's family; threatening them. They want us to pay him a visit. Give him a little scare, and if needs be, put him out of his misery. The last time he made a nuisance of himself, he waited outside the local high school, then followed the victim's thirteen-year-old son home, shouting abuse at him."

"Sounds like he needs shutting up for good." I rubbed my hands together. These hits were my favourite, showing some cocky twat he couldn't get away with bullshit like that. Who taunts a kid outside their school, for fuck's sake?

"We'll pay him a visit first," Adam replied, keeping his head while I fantasised about the other guy losing theirs. "Let's see how the land lies. If we take him in, we take him in. But let's play it by ear."

By taking him in, Adam meant bringing him to our warehouse. Some targets we liked to taunt with text messages and threats, making them jump through hoops with tasks we called our game of consequences. Those were usually marks that we could use and manipulate. People that weren't an immediate threat to the public. But for guys like this, we acted accordingly. If he needed to be taken off the streets to spend a few days chained up in our warehouse while he thought about his crimes before we served him his retribution, then so be it. There was no one-size-fits-all when it came to vigilante work. That's what made it so exciting. Every job was unique. We loved working at the club, we were proud of what we'd created. But our soldier work? That was what we lived for.

***

We loaded up the van with a few of our chosen weapons and got in; Adam driving, Devon in the passenger seat, and Tyler, Will, and I in the back as we drove to the address we'd been given.

Eventually, we came to a stop outside a shitty rundown cottage on the outskirts of town. I say cottage, but it wasn't some pretty, thatched thing. It looked more like a barn, although that'd be an insult to animals. Even they had standards, and this guy clearly didn't. Most of the windows had newspaper taped up to hide the occupants from the outside world. The small garden at the front was overgrown with weeds. So much so, that you could barely make out the path that led to the rickety old wooden front door.

We climbed out of the van, and the noise of kids shouting as they played on the grass opposite, pulled my attention from the shitty building we were here to visit. I turned to see a group of lads who couldn't have been more than eight or nine years old, kicking a football around. When one of them saw me, he stuck two fingers up, and his friends decided to do the same, thinking they were cool.

"Great neighbourhood they've got here," I announced to the others, flipping the bird back to the kids then standing still and glaring at them, giving them a twisted, menacing half-grimace, half-grin.

"They're just kids. Ignore them," Adam snapped, sliding the doors to the van closed and marching towards the cottage with purpose. But I was enjoying goading them. I saw it as character building, for them of course.

Some kid ran over to the ones who were jeering and began nudging them, saying something with a look of concern on his face. He must've known who we were and was warning his friends to knock it off because seconds later, they all scattered and ran away. A few glanced back at us to make sure we weren't following. A couple felt lucky and told us to fuck off, so they looked hard in front of their mates as they ran to hide. But most gave an 'Oh shit' as they scarpered. It didn't matter where we were in Brinton, someone had always heard of us. Our reputation proceeded us.

"Leaving so soon?" I called out, but Devon grabbed my arm and pulled my focus back to the matter at hand.

"Save it for inside," he told me, and I smiled in agreement.

"I always have more to give, don't worry about that."

We pushed our way through the broken gate that led into the guy's front yard. Black bags full of rubbish littered the outside area. Some of the bags had torn open, and paper and other crap billowed out, scattering on the wind or getting caught in the overgrown hedge that lined the front of the property. I guess it was the perfect addition to his home, a decoration of filth.

I kicked a broken tile out of the way, and when I glanced up, I noticed the roof matched the rest of the house. Numerous tiles were missing, most lying broken on the ground around the building. Testament to how much this man valued his place here in Brinton Manor. His home was a piece of shit, and so was he.

"Nice to see he cleaned up for us," I said, picking my way across the path towards the front door.

"Stay quiet," Adam barked, giving me a wicked stare over his shoulder. "We don't want him bolting out the back door."

"I'll go around the back with Tyler," Devon said quietly. "Cover all bases. We can't let this fucker get away."

The others nodded, and Tyler and Devon picked their way

around the side of the cottage. Adam, Will, and I stayed by the front door, ready to bust it open. We were raring to go. But as luck would have it, we didn't need to do any busting. When Adam pushed the handle down, it opened freely.

The door gave a bit of resistance as he pried it open, and we heard the crinkling sound of old newspapers and letters that'd been posted through the letterbox as they got stuck underneath. When he eventually got it open wide enough for us to get through, Adam stepped into the hallway first, but he screwed his nose up and put his arm over his face right away. Following him, we immediately understood why. The house stunk of unwashed filth, stale cooking, dirty shit, and something else, something metallic... blood.

"I think we need to put our masks on now, don't you?" I coughed, taking my balaclava from my back pocket as the others followed suit. We pulled them over our heads to give us some respite from the stench, but it didn't help that much. The filth was seeping into our pores; it was so pungent.

The inside of the cottage mirrored the expectations we'd built from seeing the outside. Peering around us, we could see how neglected the place was. The walls were bare, no wallpaper, just crumbling plaster with years of filth and grease that trickled down like brown and yellow tears.

"I think this guy could use my artistic skills," I joked, as Adam and I stepped on something that snapped and crunched. "This shithole makes our warehouse look like Buckingham Palace."

Looking above my head, I saw the single lightbulb that hung from the ceiling was broken. That break was obviously a new occurrence, seeing as it was the glass from that bulb that was now crunching into the stained, threadbare carpet under our feet. Like footsteps in fresh snow, no one else had taken this route since that'd smashed.

I felt a chill run down my spine, and I smiled. I loved that feeling. The feeling that something epic was about to go down. But when I heard Adam say, "What the fuck?" I knew the chill I felt this time wasn't a good one.

We entered the living room at the same time as Tyler and Devon came in from the back; and what we saw made all of us fall silent.

The metallic smell was stronger in here, and when we looked at Derek, who sat slumped in a chair against the far wall, we could see why.

His bloated head was hanging forward, chin against his chest, and a red scarf hung around his neck from where he'd obviously been choked. Both of his arms were tied to the chair with his palms facing up. Cuts from each wrist had dripped onto the carpet that was now stained dark brown, and the wounds on his wrists were congealed into a mess of flesh, muscle, and bone. His legs were tied together by the ankles. He was fully restrained. He had no chance. And if we weren't standing here seeing this for the first time, we'd have thought this was our work. But it wasn't, and what also gave us chills was the graffiti that was sprayed above his head onto the old plaster in the living room. Graffiti that was left like a calling card for whoever found him, to let them know who had done this.

Two words.

The Masters.

"Who the fuck are The Masters?" Will uttered the question on all our lips, screwing his face up and stepping forward to take a closer look at the artwork. But he soon had to take a step back when the stench from the guy's body became overpowering.

"Fuck me." Tyler glanced around, taking it all in and then added, "Whoever they are, they must have a fucking death wish, coming into our manor."

"And crazy fuckers with a death wish are our forte," I replied. The prospect of finding these fuckers sent a thrill through my veins and gave me a head trip. I liked a twisted challenge.

"Get a photo," Adam stated, ignoring us and stalking over to the chair to take a closer look at the body.

"How long do you think he's been dead?" I asked, cocking my head to the side and squinting in concentration as I watched Adam poke and prod the guy.

"Rigor mortis has set in his face and limbs, so definitely over six hours," he informed us as he did his checks. "But less than a day I'd say. Whoever did this probably struck in the early hours."

Tyler lifted his phone to take a photo of Derek, and Adam scolded, "Not a photo of him, you prick. The graffiti." Then he shook his head. "For fuck's sake. I couldn't give a fuck about him. Someone beat us to this kill, and I want to know who. This is our manor. If there's another gang coming into our town, trying to get one over on us, I want to know who they are, and that–" He pointed at the graffiti. "–Is how we find them."

None of us had ever heard of The Masters. We'd never seen anything like this graffiti before. Tall, colourful letters taunted us from the wall. Bold, like the people that'd come here before us. But we'd find them, and when we did, we'd make sure to tell them they had no business here in Brinton. Brinton Manor already had an elite group of vigilantes. There wasn't room for anyone else. Besides, if we'd done this kill, it'd be cleaned up and forgotten about already. These guys were shoddy and thoughtless in their approach. They wouldn't last long.

"I'll call Gaz. Get him to clean up this mess," Adam said, taking his phone out as he stomped towards the door.

Gaz was our clean-up guy as well as head of security at The Sanctuary. He was an all-round dogsbody. A wannabe soldier. But he didn't quite meet the standard, not that we'd ever tell him. If we said jump, he'd ask how high, and we needed him. Someone had to do the dirtier work that we didn't have time for.

"The Masters are anything but fucking masters. They're amateurs," Adam said, sneering as he tapped away on his phone and stared at the graffiti from the back door. "They leave their shit for others to find. They're sloppy and we can't afford to have sloppy work in our manor. Not when it's this kind of work."

"Maybe they wanted us to find it?" Will added, and Adam rolled his eyes.

"Of course they wanted us to find it. Us, or the police. But whatever their game is, we aren't playing. No one gets the better of us."

"Maybe we need to take a closer look around," I said, walking over to the back window to peer out onto the backyard. "You never know, they might have left something else."

But they hadn't. The only clue to who had done this was painted on the wall. Whoever they were, they'd probably taken the back door out of here, and apart from a random footprint in the dirt, a size five or six trainer that was too small to be Devon or Tyler's from earlier, there was nothing. Hell, that footprint could've belonged to anyone. A random kid collecting their lost football from the garden for all we knew.

"Maybe it was the victim's family? The thirteen-year-old lad, perhaps?" Tyler mused as he took a photo of the footprint as we all stood around it in the backyard.

"Why bother emailing us then?" Will answered, then added, "My gut says it's not the family. This is something else entirely. These *Masters* are trying to look professional, even though they're not. They're taunting us, I reckon."

"I agree," Adam stated. "And whoever they are, we'll find them. Once we get our hands on them, they'll wish they'd never heard of Brinton fucking Manor."

I watched as the others walked away down the yard, but I didn't follow. Not yet. I had to leave a calling card of my own, even if it was only going to be seen by Gaz and the clean-up crew. I couldn't help myself.

Calling out, "I'll be there in a minute," I walked back into the house and saw a cup filled with sharpie pens on a table, next to Derek's landline, and I picked up a red and black one. Strolling over to the graffiti, like I didn't have a care in the world, I leaned over Derek and gave an ironic, "Excuse me, mate." Like he was going to protest about me being in his personal space. Then I reached up and crossed out the 's' from Masters and added 'baters' onto the end with the black sharpie.

I heard a chuckle from behind, and I turned to see Will standing in the doorway watching me.

"The Master-baters. I like it." He nodded his head in approval and then walked away.

I stepped back to admire my handiwork.

"You might think you're *The Masters*," I whispered to no one except Derek. "But I'm a king, and no one sits on the throne that I made for me and my friends. It's ours."

116 **THE JOKER**

I pocketed the black sharpie, then leant down to Derek and yanked his head back. With his head slumped forward like it had been, and his long greasy hair covering his face, we hadn't seen the other message they'd left for us. The word 'We' was written on one eyelid, and 'See U' on the other.

"We see you. Clever," I whispered to myself. Then, ignoring what the implications of that message were, I took the black sharpie out again, and ran it over the words, changing them to nothing but a smudge so Gaz and the clean-up crew wouldn't see.

I'd tell the others what I'd found a bit later, but for now, I wanted to do things my way. Create my own masterpiece. After decorating his eyes, I drew crosses on his cheeks with the red sharpie. Then I took my knife out and pressed it into his mouth, pushing into the soft flesh as I cut into his cheeks and gave him what I liked to call the Brinton smile. Slicing a curve into the edges of his mouth, I gave him a smile to wear for eternity. A clown of my own making, but less Coco and more John Wayne Gacy.

"Not so serious now, hey." I wiped my blade on his shoulder and stood back to admire my work. "You just made your victims very happy today, Derek," I said, patting his cheek. "Wear that smile with pride… in hell."

I stood tall, happy that the scene was arranged just the way I liked it. The calling card was exactly as it should be, a two-finger salute to anyone who dared to challenge the soldiers. And the dead guy was perfect, an idiotic grin carved onto his face, making him look like the fool he'd always been in this life.

And the extra message they'd left us?

That was buried just like they'd be when we caught up with

them.

We always had the last word; the last laugh. No one would ever take that away from us. Ever.

CHAPTER SEVEN
Colton

There was barely any talk on the way home. Even my one-liners were met with feeble laughter no one felt. The mood was off, and it was all because of The Masters. Their spray-painted calling card was mocking us. Their disrespect taunted us. The fact that we didn't have a clue who they were was the worst part of all. Nothing happened in this town unless we knew about it.

Until now.

When we got back to The Sanctuary, we all headed to the living room with our heads down. Our early euphoria that proceeded a kill was long gone. That hit was ours, and The Masters, whoever they were, had taken it away. If they were trying to sabotage our business, the business I'd made my life's mission to get off the ground, then my crazy side was about to ramp up a gear. The Masters had better be ready when we came calling. They needed teaching a lesson in vigilante manners and fucking etiquette. Don't fuck with the soldiers, especially this one. Find your own damn hunting ground.

"Why do you all look like it's the end of the world?" Liv asked, sitting forward on the sofa and turning the TV off, ready to give us her undivided attention.

"We had a job. Some fuckers beat us to it," I informed her, sitting between her and Leah on the sofa. Adam scowled at my choice of seat and stalked across the room to tower over me and state, "Move," so he could sit next to her. I shuffled along, giving him a tiny space, making it a cosy sofa for the four of us.

"What do you mean, someone beat you to it?" Liv frowned and leaned forward to address me, but Adam was the one who answered her.

"When we got there, someone had already taken him out."

"Who?"

"We don't know, but they left a pretty impressive calling card behind to piss us off."

That sparked Liv's interest even more. "What sort of calling card?"

"Graffiti. On the wall. It said, *The Masters*," Tyler told her, pulling his phone out of his pocket and getting the photo up to show her. "Don't scroll through the photos though," he added with a panicked expression on his face.

"Why? Have you got nudes on there?" I joked.

"No. But I've got photos of the dead body and I'm guessing she doesn't want to see that."

Liv ignored us, choosing to study the photo and enlarge it so she could see if there was anything else hidden in the graffiti.

"I have no idea who The Masters are." She lifted the phone

up so Leah could see it too and asked, "Do you?"

"No," Leah replied. "But with a name like that, it sounds like they mean business."

"It sounds like they're begging for a war," Adam added angrily, a look of disgust on his face as he glanced at the photo in question. Then he took the phone out of Liv's hand, clicked off the photo and threw it back to Tyler.

"A *war*?" Liv turned to face him with a look of exasperation, her eyes wide and her brows raised. "Why would they want a war if they're doing the same thing you are? Surely, they're helping the cause. Cleaning up the streets too."

"By making us look like fools who can't do the job properly?" Adam snapped, and Liv gave him a pointed stare that told him he'd better drop the attitude. "This is our town." He carried on, preaching to the converted. "If they want to clean up the streets, they can do it somewhere else."

"There's only room for five bad asses," I exclaimed, trying to break the tension in the air, and Leah gave a low chuckle, but the rest of the room continued to brood silently as we sat and thought about what our next move would be.

"The Soldiers and The Masters. I think it's got a nice ring to it," Liv announced, but there would be no soldiers and masters, that was something we all agreed on. We didn't do collaborations.

"The Soldiers run Brinton," Adam stated. "If The Masters want notoriety, they've got to earn it, and on their own turf, not ours."

Liv worried her lip between her teeth before asking her next question. She knew she was treading a fine line. "Do you want me to ask Finn about this?"

THE JOKER

Finn, meaning Finn Knowles, one of the renaissance rebels of Sandland. A group of men we despised, but Liv had grown up with them, being from the wealthier part of Sandland herself. The thing was, we had history with Knowles. A dark and not altogether positive history, so we doubted he'd do anything to help us. But Knowles was dating Liv's best friend, so if it was for her, he might just help and give her some information about who we were dealing with.

"It's worth a shot," Tyler replied on a shrug.

"Finn knows a lot of the local graffiti artists. If The Masters have tagged anything else around here, he'll know about it," she added. "Can you send that photo to my phone? There might be something on there that he recognises, a style maybe, or something we're missing. I can show him and see what he thinks."

Tyler nodded and tapped away, sending the image across to her.

"Show him, but don't tell him it's for us," Adam explained. "We don't want him to make up some shit to throw us off the scent."

"Finn wouldn't do that, but okay, I won't say anything."

I had to agree with Liv. We might not be on Finn Knowles's Christmas card list, but the guy was as straight as they came. He wouldn't mess around. And speaking of messing around, I felt that now was the perfect time to tell them about the other message I'd discovered.

"I think now might be a good time to tell you that I found something else at the scene," I announced, making them all stop and glare at me with accusatory stares.

"What the fuck are you talking about, Colton?" Adam

snapped.

"When you all left." I shrugged like it was nothing, even though I knew it was. "I stayed behind to do a little… rearranging."

"Oh, for fuck's sake!" Adam threw his head back and let out an exasperated breath. "What did you do?"

"Nothing. But when I moved his head back, I saw they'd left a message for us on his eyelids."

"Jesus," Adam cursed, scrubbing his hands over his face.

"Why didn't you call us back?" Devon questioned, raising his eyebrows at me and growing red in the face.

"What message?" Will asked with slightly less animosity than the others.

"Did you get a picture of it?" Tyler growled, and I knew I'd fucked up big time, but what was done was done. All I could do now was fill them in and move forward.

"I don't know why I didn't call you back, I just didn't. It was a shit call to make. I know that now and I'm sorry. And no, I didn't get a photo either. I scrubbed the message out so Gaz and the clean-up crew wouldn't see it, but it said, 'We see U'. On his eyelids. Written in red pen."

The disappointment I felt from each one of them as they sighed and groaned at my fuck-up permeated through me. I didn't like letting them down, and today, I'd done just that. It was a dick move.

"These Masters are trying to play us at our own game, leaving cryptic shit to fuck with our heads." Adam leant forward with his hands fisted together, his head down as he thought about our next move. Seconds later, he lifted his eyes to look at us and said, "From now on, if anyone notices anything out of the ordinary, you log it. Tell the rest of us." He turned to face me. "No more secrets or hiding things. We work stronger when we work together."

"Damn right we do," Tyler added.

"Total transparency," Adam stated, his glare becoming sterner, more pointed. "Agreed?"

"Agreed," we all stated in unison.

"And in my defence…" I went to try and explain my part in the supposed cover-up, but Adam butted in.

"You have no defence. From now on, you share everything."

I didn't argue. I knew I'd messed up in more ways than one. All that was left to do now was to track these Masters down by any means necessary.

CHAPTER EIGHT
Colton

We See U.

It was a bold statement to make, considering who they were dealing with.

Adam had spent months watching and stalking Liv into becoming his. Leah had watched Devon for almost ten years before stepping out of the shadows to make her move. And Devon? Let's just say, watching was his favourite thing. So, the fact that someone out there was leaving taunting messages was either brave or incredibly stupid. My money was on stupid.

Over the next few days, we all remained hyper aware of our surroundings, attuned to everything, but nothing stood out. No creepy girls staring at us at the club, well, no more than usual. No weird sensations that gave us prickles on the backs of our necks when we were out. Nothing raised our concern, and we found ourselves becoming complacent, figuring the whole thing had been a one-off, or a misunderstanding, maybe.

Were the messages really meant for us?

Tyler had gone online, researching local graffiti tags and tapping into every record he could find for The Masters, but he got nowhere. Discreetly, we questioned our trusted contacts, asking if they'd heard if anything was going down that we needed to know about, but there was nothing.

As for Finn Knowles, he still hadn't gotten back to Liv, and we weren't hopeful of a result there. It was starting to feel like the whole sorry mess was something we'd have to put to bed and move on from. Perhaps we'd never find the answers we were looking for. Could be, The Masters had performed their one and only triumph.

Only time would tell.

***

When we got our next email, asking for help with a situation the local police had fucked up, we didn't hesitate to take it. It was time to sharpen our focus. Work needed to be done. We had to utilise our time and resources in the correct way, not chasing ghost vigilantes who shouldn't have even registered on our radar.

There was a guy called Chris Borne, who hadn't long moved to Brinton Manor. The email stated he was on the sex offenders register for downloading stuff he really fucking shouldn't have; sick, twisted, worse category shit. The type you didn't even want to think about, let alone talk about. The email told us that he'd started hanging around a local nursery and that needed taking care of. A man like him had no place loitering there, even thinking about it gave us the creeps. We knew he was up to no good. And a hit like him? That was right up our street.

We knew this wasn't going to be a game of consequences, taunt and terrorise job. This guy needed our immediate attention, and so we decided to prep the warehouse, ready for a new visitor, or rather victim, to take up residence. You couldn't take any chances with a guy like Borne. If he got wind that we were on to him, he'd bolt, and we couldn't risk him doing a runner, not when he had form. He needed putting down.

I helped Devon load up the van with knives, swords, drills, hammers, anything we could use to inflict some justice on the sick pervert. We also packed rope and duct tape so we could properly restrain him. We'd done some recon and he wasn't a big guy, but you never knew how much fight they'd have in them. Sometimes, the bigger ones went down easier than the scrawny ones. It certainly kept us on our toes though. We had to be ready for anything.

"It's a good day to fuck shit up," I said, standing next to the van and breathing in the cool autumn air. That buzz I always got on a job was thrumming through my veins and I smiled, thankful this was what I did for a living. Life was good. Not for Derek or Chris, but it certainly was for us.

"It's always a good day to take out a fucker like Borne," Devon added. "Have you got your playlist ready?"

"Of course." I took my phone out of my pocket and tapped into Spotify.

I loved music. In the early days, when my dad was the bane of my life, I'd used it to block out all the bad thoughts he'd planted into my brain like the devil's seed. It worked for a while. Music had helped to transport me away to another world; a kinder, safer world. Now, I used it to lift me, spur me on, make me feel all the emotions I wanted to feel as we carried out our revenge. Revenge that we gave to others who'd been let down by a system that was broken. To some people we might've come across as the sickos for what we did, how we took pride in torturing others, but we were far from broken. As a unit, we were complete, and nobody would ever stand in the way of us serving justice where it was needed. Bringing retribution, the only way we knew how, with our tools, weapons, and fists.

We all climbed into the van and Adam drove us to the place where this Borne fucker lived. I sat in the passenger seat this time and put some music on to get us psyched up and ready. *Master of Puppets* by Metallica blasted out, and I started to rock out, letting it take me away to another world, one where we were invincible. The guitar riff made me feel like a fucking God, and I was revelling in it.

"Do we have to listen to a song about fucking masters?" Adam moaned, acting his usual, cheerful self.

"It's a classic," I replied proudly. "Don't diss Metallica or we're going to have a bigger problem than Chris Borne today."

He huffed but chose to ignore me.

"According to my recon, he'll probably be in bed when we get there," Adam carried on, turning the music down and making my back go up. Metallica didn't work as well on a lower volume, and I didn't like being muted. "He doesn't leave the house before midday, so we'll take him by surprise, knock the fucker out, tie him up, and get him to the warehouse ready for a day he deserves."

"I like your plan." I grinned, shaking off my irritation and turning the music back up. Adam shook his head. He liked to get into the zone by planning and playing it out in his mind, but I did it with kick-ass tunes.

Minutes later, we pulled into a quieter street in the town. Adam turned the music off so as not to alert anyone to our presence. Chris Borne lived in a neat looking, newly built, mid-terrace house. From what we could see, his neighbours took pride in their homes and had tidy front yards with the odd, well-tended hanging basket at the door. When we pulled up at the kerb outside his house, the road was virtually empty, and from the open window, I could hear the birds chirping in the trees that lined the street.

"Are we leading him out the front?" I asked, trying to figure out why we'd stopped here.

"No, but I wanted to check out the front first." Adam stared at the house then used the van's mirrors to check the road behind us. "I'll park around the back. The fences should give us some privacy, but from what I've heard from the locals, they'll happily turn a blind eye if they see us with him. They just want rid."

We drove slowly down the road and turned into the alleyway at the back of the houses. It was narrower down here, but more secluded. Perfect for what we needed to do. Adam pulled up beside a fence that looked shabbier than the rest and shut the engine off.

"Let's do this," he said, opening the van door and knocking on the side to tell the others to get out.

I stepped out of the van onto the cobbled path, and when I felt a twisting, burn inside, I looked up, then down the alley to where a bus stop was situated on the opposite side of the road.

THE JOKER

There, standing alone at the stop but staring right at me, was a girl. The wind blew her thick brown curls into her face, but she didn't shake it off or take her eyes off me. Her stare was like arrows penetrating through my soul and I felt something twist inside. I was getting bad vibes from her. She wasn't watching, she was studying. I stayed silent for moment, wracking my brain, until suddenly, it all clicked into place. I'd seen this girl before, and when recognition hit me, she smiled as if she knew what I was thinking.

"Get your balaclava on, mate." I heard Tyler's voice echo through the fog in my brain.

"I know her," I said, ignoring him and pointing down the alley.

Tyler huffed. "So, you recognise a girl in Brinton Manor. Big deal. That's hardly front-page news, Colton. I'd be more shocked if you didn't know her."

"I don't mean like that," I snapped, shaking my head and feeling a ripple of irritation run through me. "I meant I saw her a while ago at the club, staring at me just like she is now."

At that moment, Adam came to stand at the side of me. "Do you think she's going to be a problem?" he asked.

"I don't know. But you said to log anything that didn't feel right, and her…" I gritted my teeth and folded my arms over my chest, matching her stare with one of my own. "She's setting off every alarm bell in my head."

"Well, let's go and talk to her." Adam strode forward with purpose, but luck wasn't on our side. That second, a bus pulled up in front of the stop, and moments later, as it pulled away, she was gone.

"Shall we follow the bus?" Tyler asked, looking between

Adam and me.

Adam took a moment to collect his thoughts, sighed, then said, "No. Let's stick to the plan for today. But if you see that girl again–" He pointed to the vacant spot where she'd stood. "–Make sure she doesn't get away. It could be nothing, but we don't know for sure. Let's not take anything for granted."

I agreed, and even though my mind was slightly scrambled trying to figure out who that girl was and why she seemed to affect me, I shrugged it off, ready to focus on the task in hand. I turned to see Devon clinging onto some rope and duct tape, waiting for the show to start. Tyler held up the hammer I hadn't noticed in his hand, swaying it through the air, and then Will smirked at me, brandishing an impressive hunting knife.

"Don't I get a toy?" I asked, feeling my already racing heart start to hike from the adrenaline kicking in.

"You can startle him with your wit," Adam joked, grabbing two baseball bats from the back of the van, then slamming the side door shut. "Or better yet, just keep your mouth shut and do your job."

He threw a bat over to me and I caught it.

"Fuck this shit," I replied, passing the bat to Will and snatching the hunting knife.

I followed Adam's surly ass to the back gate, ready to fuck shit up. Lucky for us, it wasn't locked, and we walked right through and up the garden path towards Chris Borne's back door. Tyler stepped forward, ready to smash the glass with his hammer, but when Adam tried the handle, it opened.

"People in Brinton Manor really need to start locking their doors. You never know what kind of scumbag might be lurking on the other side," I said sarcastically, pushing through to get into the house.

The door led into a small kitchen. The sink was piled high with dirty dishes, and the table still had half a plate of fish and chips on it, probably left over from the night before. "Good to see he chose something traditional for his last meal." I nodded at the plate, then traced Adam's footsteps through to the hallway and up the stairs.

Walking up to the next floor, the air became stale and dust particles danced in front of our eyes as we glanced around at the closed doors on the landing.

"Which one do you think is his bedroom?" I whispered, trying to decide which one to stand by. "Shall we take a door each? It could be fun, like a sick killer gameshow. Winner gets first strike."

"It's that one," Adam stated plainly, pointing to a door on our left and totally pissing all over my fun. "But feel free to browse the other rooms later if that's how you wanna get your kicks."

I shrugged, letting Adam move past me to get to the door. I knew he liked to be the first one in during situations like this, and it really didn't bother me. I was quite happy to be his wingman. The Robin to his Batman, the Goose to his Maverick, the Cagney to his Lacey, the... shit, I lost focus for a second and almost fell into the back of Adam as he stopped in the doorway, his feet rooted to the ground.

"Motherfuckers," he growled, and when I took a step around him to see what he was seeing, I understood why.

The naked body of what I assume used to be Chris Borne was lying on the bed. His wrists and ankles were bound with cable ties, and his face was covered with a clear plastic bag that'd been secured around the neck with tape to suffocate him. We were too late, but what made that fact even more bitter was what was on the wall above the bed.

Graffiti.

Freshly painted graffiti, with the words *The Masters* staring right back at us, taunting us.

"This has got to be a fucking joke," I said, my mouth hanging open in shock at the sheer audacity of these fuckers.

The others filed into the room behind me, and we stood in stunned silence for a few seconds, taking it all in.

"Once was rude, but twice is a fucking liberty. They're targeting us." Tyler took his phone out and photographed the evidence.

"No shit, Sherlock," I replied, staring at the scene, still struggling to comprehend what was happening.

"Do you know what pisses me off, aside from the obvious?" Will said, walking over to the side of the bed to stare down at a pitiful Chris Borne. "They don't even attempt to clean up this shit. They're rookies."

"No, they're not." Adam took a step closer to the wall with the graffiti on it and peered closely. "They knew we'd be here, and they want us to see it. They don't want to clean up because they want us to know they're trying to beat us, or just plain piss us off." He frowned and leaned a little closer and then said, "Fuck the patriarchy."

"It's not really the time to be going all feminist on us." I smirked. "We have our own shit to deal with. Save that for when you're at home with Liv."

"Look at it." Adam wasn't impressed, and he stabbed his finger towards a part of the graffiti. "That's what it says here.

You can barely see it, but it's there. Fuck the patriarchy."

I leaned over his shoulder, and sure enough, in small writing on the wall, that's what it said.

"So, this was probably done by *women*?" Will asked, clearly not believing what he was saying.

But Adam wasn't fazed by that thought. "Women with a grudge," he added plainly. "Women who're watching us."

"I'm insulted," Tyler said, looking affronted as his lips thinned and his eyes narrowed to glare at the graffiti. "We're not the fucking patriarchy, and if they think we are they need to check themselves. Men can be fucked over by the patriarchy too."

"Maybe it wasn't a message to us?" Will questioned, but Adam disagreed.

"Oh, it was meant for us. Who else was going to find this?" Adam spun around to face me. "That girl you saw at the end of the alleyway, the one from the club, she has to have something to do with this."

"We should've ambushed her then," I snapped, feeling the pressure get to me. "Taken her to the warehouse and made her talk." I didn't like feeling blindsided. I needed to do something to centre myself.

"She's in on this," he added, nodding surely to himself. "That's why she was here today. She wanted to watch it all play out."

"She's one of those murderers that comes back to the scene of the crime to relive it," Tyler chipped in.

"If it is her," I replied. "I highly doubt she's working alone. Look at the guy." I gestured to the dead guy on the bed. "And think about the last one we found. Do you really think one girl could do all that?"

"One, a group, I don't care," Adam stated. "But she's definitely involved, and the next time she rears her head, I want to know about it."

I had my suspicions too, and that girl with the curly brown hair and eyes that pinned me like she was spearing me with a bloody javelin, was sat right at the top of my list. But why was she doing this? What the fuck was her problem?

"I agree with you," Tyler said. "But let's address the elephant in the room here… what exactly has Colton done to piss this girl off? Because he's the one she seems to be watching. That, and the fact she's leaving dead guys for us to find. It's all fucking creepy. So, what is it, Colton? Did you sleep with her and forget to call her back? Or is she Catwoman? Leaving fucked-up gifts on your doorstep to say thank you."

I wasn't the worst looking guy, but even I drew the line at that kind of obsession. Who goes that far to impress someone? Or piss them off, even? Apart from Adam, that is. I have to admit, I did like the Catwoman idea, though.

"Before I saw her in the club that night, I'd never seen her before," I told them. "Whatever her fucking problem is, it's nothing to do with me."

"But it is though, isn't it?" Tyler reiterated. "Because if this carries on, our business is fucked. You should go through the CCTV when we get back. I'll help you. If we can find her and track her down, we can get some answers. I need to secure our emails too. It's obvious our systems have been hacked. I need to do some damage control."

"Do you really think our emails have been hacked?" Will asked dumbly.

"How else do you think they intercepted our jobs? It won't happen again, though."

I stood staring at the graffiti as Adam made a call to Gaz for clean-up and Tyler started tapping away on his phone, setting things in place.

Fuck the patriarchy.

I agreed with them.

But if they thought we were their target to fight, they'd got us all wrong. Making an enemy of us was going to be the biggest mistake The Masters had ever made, and let's face it, they'd made a lot.

"They might think they've got the upper hand," I said, looming over the body. "But let's have the last laugh." I looked over at Devon in the corner. "Come on, you like creating art. What shall we do to put our stamp on this?"

"Its artistic retribution, not pointless mutilation that I'm good at," Devon stated.

"What's the difference?" I shrugged. "This fucker deserved both. The Masters did the first part, now let's finish the job how it should be done."

I leaned over, taking the hunting knife and pushing it into his left eye socket, through the plastic and into the soft flesh, spearing his eyeball as it squelched and crunched under my blade, then I twisted and scooped, slowly gouging it out.

"You won't ever look at that filth you downloaded again, will you? Sick fuck." I did the same to the right eye, smiling as blood oozed out of his head, and the eyeball, along with the optic nerve and other gunky shit, rolled over his cheek to settle on the bed.

Will stepped forward, but he threw the bat down and took

an ice pick from his jacket pocket and started stabbing furiously at the guy's legs.

"He won't ever loiter around a nursery again either," he gasped, jabbing hole after hole into the leg muscle and occasionally hitting bone and getting the pick jammed.

I glanced across to Adam.

"Wanna have a turn?" I asked, but Adam shrugged and folded his arms.

"Have at it," he said, happy to watch us expel our anger.

We stabbed, gouged, and sliced away to try and feed our fury. It wasn't the same as making a kill, but it helped to quench our thirst. Finally, I took the hunting knife and carved a smiling face into his stomach.

"What's that for?" Tyler asked, frowning and cocking his head to the side as he studied my handiwork.

"Because I always like to leave work with a smile," I replied, grinning, and then I stood back. "So much better." I nodded, and then I turned and walked away.

Fuck the Patriarchy.

Fuck The Masters.

And fuck anyone who tried to get in our way.

This was our town.

Our rules.

All who fuck up here will live in eternal fear.

I shot down the stairs and marched out of the house, slamming the door behind me. Demons that I didn't want to acknowledge called out my name, taunting and tempting me to lose my shit. But I stopped, bent over with my hands on my knees, and took a few deep, calming breaths. I would take back control.

Be ready, Masters, because we're coming for you next, and when we do, we won't be taking any prisoners.

CHAPTER NINE
Colton

The clean-up was underway, and after today, no one would ever guess that The Masters, or anyone else had ever set foot in that house. But we couldn't deny that our heads were left reeling from what we'd seen. This life had prepared us for gangs of vicious men; men from the worst walks of life, drugs, violence, all that shit. It hadn't prepared us for women with a grudge who wanted to take our place and paint us as something that we didn't believe we were; men who abused their power, belittled women, and made them feel inferior. All the women in our lives had been treated a certain way; respectfully always, cheekily sometimes, but we knew their worth. We weren't the patriarchy The Masters thought we were. We never would be.

When we marched back into the main hall of The Sanctuary, Liv was standing over by the bar, helping with a stock take, and when she saw us, she called us over.

"Take a break, Joel," she told our head barman.

Joel smiled and nodded, taking the kitchen towel from his shoulder and laying it on the bar.

"I'll be back in fifteen, but text me if you need me sooner."

Joel walked away and Liv sat down at a table close to the bar, gesturing for us to sit with her.

"Bad day?" she asked.

"You could say that," Adam replied, taking the chair closest to her and putting his arm around her. "The Masters struck again. It's the second time they've taken our kill, but it'll be the last."

"It wasn't all that bad," I joked. "We managed to have a bit of fun when we found him." I was making light of the situation, even though it was really fucking grating on me, but that was something I'd never admit to.

"Fun for you," Adam snapped. "Me? I had the overwhelming urge to burn the whole fucking town to the ground and smoke these fuckers out."

"I don't think you'll need to go that far, babe," Liv interjected, patting his thigh.

"Have you got something for us?" Adam asked.

"I sure do. Finn finally got back to me about the graffiti. He wasn't sure at first. He said it looked familiar, but he had to do a bit of research, ask around, and eventually he managed to get a name."

Our ears perked up, and we sat forward, eager to hear what she'd say next.

"Good, because I'm ready for some payback. Teach these fuckers a lesson they won't forget." Adam dropped his head and folded his arms over his chest, readying himself to hear the bombshell Liv was about to drop.

"I think you'll need to calm it down for this one, babe." Liv tapped his knee, then gave his thigh a squeeze. "Finn said the artist is called Shelley Masters. She's not from Brinton, she lives in Merivale."

"Shelley Masters." Adam shook his head and then added, "Did he only give you one name? Because it's fairly obvious, if it's her, she isn't doing this alone."

"That's all he had." She sighed, clearly disappointed that she couldn't tell us more. "But I'm sure Tyler can look into who her friends are, or you perhaps, with your love of stalking." She smirked, but Adam clearly wasn't in the mood, judging by the way he clenched his jaw.

"Get an address," Adam barked at Tyler. "And then we'll pay this Shelley Masters a little visit. She might want to fuck the patriarchy, but nobody fucks with us."

I noticed Liv bite her lip, anxiously, then staring from Adam to the rest of us, she said, "You all take your job seriously and you're proud of what you do. I get that, but just remember a lot of people in this town are proud of you too. Me included." She leant towards Adam and placed a kiss on his cheek. "Get the answers you need, but don't let this derail you. No one has heart for this town more than you. Stay true to yourselves."

"Oh, we will. Mark my words." Adam stood up and then leaned down to kiss Liv on the lips.

The rest of us stood too, mentally preparing ourselves for another job, but instead of making a kill, we were about to make a statement.

***

Once we knew she came from Merivale, it didn't take long for Tyler to get an address and send the details to Adam. That afternoon, we climbed back into the van, me riding in the front with Adam, and the others in the back. Only this time, I didn't play any music. I needed the quiet to think and focus.

"I think it might be best if you let me do the talking when we get there," Adam announced as he pulled away and drove down the road.

"No offence, mate," I shot back. "But talking isn't your strong point. Maybe leave it to one of us."

I saw his jaw tense as I spoke, but he knew I made sense. He didn't answer though, just grunted and continued driving as the Sat Nav gave him instructions to get to our destination. Brinton streets turned into Merivale lanes, and eventually, after driving in tension-filled silence, we pulled into a familiar road, a road I recognised from years ago. Chills ran down my spine, but I played it cool. It could just be a coincidence.

Adam slowed down to look at the house numbers, then when he said, "We're looking for number fifty-three." My stomach dropped out.

I felt sick.

Fuck.

Fifty-three was the number I really didn't want him to say.

That was a house I'd entered as a pitiful, weak thirteen-year-old, and left as a boy determined to right his father's wrongs. A house that belonged to a woman I owed a hell of a lot to, after the way she'd made me look at things and the kindness she'd shown me all those years ago. An hour or so of my life that changed everything. That woke me from a coma I'd lived in since my mother's death. There was a reason I had the word Gemini tattooed on my left shoulder. I'd always felt like I led a double life, had a foot in two worlds but couldn't reconcile to them both. A life of contradictions, and I was two people; the Colton the world needed me to be, and the one I tried to suppress because his hang-ups and insecurities weren't worth shit. But now, I had a feeling those worlds were about to collide. Spectacularly.

I knew Grace would hate us barging in and causing trouble, and I prayed that maybe this wouldn't play out as my sick mind was imagining. Perhaps she'd moved away, used the money from my father's estate to get out of this slum, to a place where she could find peace. After all, her name wasn't Masters. I was pretty sure her surname was Haughton. But what did I know? Pigs might fly past and shit all over the windscreen. I was guessing that option sounded more realistic.

I debated whether to front it out, act like I didn't know who could be living there and stand with my brothers as we carried out our unique form of *enquiries*, but when Adam reached into the glove box and pulled out a knife, my stomach rolled over. I knew I couldn't do it. I had to say something. The war I felt inside was churning me up, and that wasn't something I was used to feeling.

On the one hand, I wanted to go nuclear. Show Shelley Masters she'd picked the wrong men to fuck with. She was trying to destroy everything we'd built, and I wouldn't stand for it. But I also had respect for Grace. I had to stay calm, work out what was happening and play it differently, if this was still her house. I needed to be respectful. It was the least she deserved after the chaos my family had brought to her door over the years, her and her sister, Rosie.

"I know who might live here," I blurted out. "This used to be Grace's house. I think it still is." I could feel my heart pounding, and I tried to steady my breaths and keep a cool, level head.

"Grace who?" Adam asked, frowning and staring at the house then back at me.

"Grace Haughton. She knew my father. She worked for him." Adam knew what my dad did for a living, so he nodded and stayed quiet, letting me explain myself further. "I think I should go in alone."

I was being honest.

This wasn't a time for joking.

I guessed that Shelley could be Grace's daughter, and I needed to tread carefully. I was starting to piece the puzzle together and everything came back to the same conclusion. If this was linked to Grace, then it was clear Shelley held a grudge against me because of my father. She blamed me for what had happened to her mum and aunt, and wanted revenge. I couldn't say I blamed her. But one thing I was sure of, Grace didn't deserve to have five irate soldiers standing on her doorstep, looking like they were about to tear the place apart. Better that she got one, calmer soldier.

Me.

Adam sighed, ran his hands over his face and then said, "I trust you, mate. If you want to go in alone, then do it. I can't say I'm happy about it, but I get it. But remember, we have no idea what might happen inside that house or what she could use against you. Like you say, Grace might not even live there anymore. And let's not forget, The Masters isn't one girl. The others could be in there too. Keep your guard up." He turned to face me and added, "And trust me, the minute I see or hear anything that sets me off, I'll be bulldozing right through that front door and doing things my way. Are we clear?"

"I'd expect nothing less."

I pushed the door to the van open and got out, leaving Adam to sit and chew on his lip as he no doubt questioned why he'd given me free rein to do this on my own. Soldiers always stood together. Hurt one, hurt all. But here I was going rogue.

I heard the others call out questions from the back, but I left that for Adam to deal with and turned, heading to the gate that led to Grace's house.

I pushed the little wooden gate open and stepped into the front yard that looked much neater than it had years ago. Bikes and scooters had been replaced with colourful pot plants and flowers. A black wrought iron bench sat directly under the front window, and the old, worn-out blue front door had been replaced by a neat, white one with trellising arched around it, full of dark green twisting vines.

I rang the doorbell and took a step back, smiling when I saw the doormat that said, Forget about the dog, beware of the daughters. So, there was more than one master here. This could get interesting.

The door swung open, and I looked up into blue-grey eyes that'd held so much warmth and comfort towards me the last time I'd seen them. My earlier suspicions had been right. This was Grace's home.

"Oh my God! Colton!" She gasped and stepped over the threshold to come towards me and pull me into a hug. "What are you doing here? It's so lovely to see you. Is everything okay? You were the last person I expected to see at my door today.

How are you?" Her words and questions came tumbling out like she was nervous, and I grinned, trying to put her at ease.

"I'm good, Grace. I was just driving through the neighbourhood, and I thought I'd stop by and see how one of my favourite ladies is getting on. Can I come in?"

Grace cocked her head at me and gave a pointed stare that told me she didn't buy my bullshit answer. But the smile that followed said she didn't care.

"Hmmm, why don't I believe that? The last time you were at my door, Colton King, you were thirteen years old. And as lovely as it was to meet you back then, I don't think you'd have chosen my house as your ideal birthday venue. Am I right?"

"You're always right, Grace." I gave her a playful wink that I didn't feel, and played it cool. "But can't a guy catch up with an old friend without there being an ulterior motive?"

Grace's frown softened and she linked her arm through mine as she led me inside. "I don't know what you're up to, but you've always been able to charm the birds from the trees with that smile of yours. And I'll always have time for you, to let you charm me too."

She closed the door behind me and gestured for me to follow her down the hallway. "Do you want a cup of tea or coffee? Maybe something stronger? I think I have a bottle of whisky somewhere. I don't tend to drink much these days, but I like to keep something for surprise guests."

"I'll have a coffee, black, two sugars," I replied and followed Grace into the kitchen. I glanced into the living room as we passed it, but no one was there, and the house sounded quiet, so I guessed she was on her own. "How have you been keeping, Grace? You look as stunning as ever. Not a day over thirty."

"Oh, get off," she slapped my arm playfully. "I look every one of my forty-five years, and I'm proud of it too." She smiled to herself as she flipped the kettle switch and started to spoon coffee granules into two mugs. "Life's been kind to me in recent years, or rather, people I knew from a former life have been kind. Thank you for the money, Colton. I really didn't expect that, but you made such a difference in our lives. I was struggling to make ends meet when that cheque from your dad's estate came through. I'll never be able to thank you enough. But I need to ask…" She swivelled around to face me. "Why did you give it all away?"

I shrugged like it was nothing, because to me, it was. I never wanted his money. I never wanted anything from him. But today, I needed answers. And I was hoping I could steer Grace in that direction.

"I wouldn't take a dime from that man. You earned his money, you deserved it, not me. I'd rather make my own way in this world. I'm just glad it could help you and your daughters." I cocked my brow, waiting for her to respond and tell me something about those daughters.

Grace's cheeks glowed, and her face warmed as she said, "You've grown into a fine young man, Colton. I always knew you would."

And yet, here I was, ready to ambush whoever else lived here and remind them why they'd monumentally fucked up, poking their stick into the hive of an angry group of motherfuckers. Not so honourable when you scratched the surface, I guessed. I wasn't here to play nice.

She turned her back to me and started making the coffees, so I thought I'd push harder. That was what I was here for, after all.

"Do you live here alone, Grace?"

I knew she didn't.

"No." She smiled as she stirred the drinks. "My eldest, Kate, has her own place, she lives on her own. But I've still got Bryony and Shelley here with me."

Bullseye.

Hello, Shelley Masters.

So, there were three sisters, three possible Masters at play, along with whoever else they'd roped into their little fucked-up scheme.

"Wow. Three younger versions of you. I bet you get a lot of visitors."

Who else comes around here plotting to fuck us over? Tell me, Grace.

"Oh no," she chuckled to herself. "My girls keep themselves to themselves. Kate's always been independent. Ten years old, and she was racing home from school to peel the potatoes and get the dinner started for me. She was always a massive help. A second mother to the other two. As for Bryony, my middle girl, she's always been happier living in her own little world–"

"And your youngest?" I butted in, eager for her to get to the good part.

"Shelley?" She sighed. "She's... complicated. A loner. She's a lot like Bryony, but her world just seems–"

"What?" I pressed.

"Darker."

And there it was.

She was a dark loner, intent on causing havoc. But that was going to stop. Today.

"You know," Grace continued. "After we got your money–"

"It wasn't *my* money."

"Oh, you know what I mean, the King money, I went back to college and studied English Literature. Growing up, Rosie and I always wanted to be teachers. Rosie wanted to teach the little ones, but I wanted to work with older kids. Because of that money, I was able to put myself through university, and now I'm an English lecturer at the local college. Rosie teaches year one at Sandland Primary. It all worked out as it should." She beamed at me as if she meant it'd worked out okay for me too, and then a dreamy expression washed over her face. "I've always been obsessed with the romantic poets. That's why I gave my girls the names I did. Kate after Keats, Bryony for Lord Byron, and then there's my youngest, Shelley. I don't think I need to explain that one."

I loved that her life had changed so drastically, and she was realising her true passion after being under my father's grubby thumb for far too long. But reminiscing wasn't what I was here for. I wanted to be polite, but I also needed answers.

"You rebel, Grace. Do they have a cool surname too?"

I knew it was Masters, but I wanted her to confirm it, anyway.

Grace's expression dimmed slightly. "They took their dad's surname, Masters. But I wish I'd gone with my head instead of my heart and registered them as Haughton when they were born. I never did marry their father, and after all the shit he put us through, he doesn't deserve any recognition."

So, there was a lot of anger stewing in this household. Grace and her girls really had been shit on by the men in their life, by all accounts. And here I was about to do the very same thing.

THE JOKER

The kettle clicked off as it came to the boil, and Grace began to pour the water into the mugs.

"Are you expecting them home anytime soon?" I asked, trying to appear curious yet unaffected as I casually leaned against the countertop.

"Bryony's at work until later tonight," she informed me. "She's a tattoo artist. Really talented too. All my girls are artistic. Kate's a sculptor, and Shelley's in art school. She paints. They get their flare for the arts from me."

And then, as if she'd summoned the she-devil herself, I heard the front door close, followed by gentle footsteps down the hallway. When the door to the kitchen finally swung open, a voice that hissed venom from behind me said, "What the fuck is *he* doing here?" And I felt myself prickle with excitement. Things were about to get interesting.

I spun around, painting on the cheesiest grin I could, ready to meet one of Grace's daughters for the first time. My grin spread wider when I saw which daughter was standing in the doorway, gripping the frame like she wanted to tear it apart and breathing heavily through her nostrils in anger.

My curly-haired, sexy as fuck stalker.

"Shelley, don't be so rude!" Grace reprimanded, but she ignored her mum, choosing to glare daggers at me like she expected her stare to obliterate me to kingdom come.

"It's okay, Grace," I said by way of an apology. "Shelley has been caught off-guard. She didn't expect anyone to be here. It's all good." I shrugged, keeping a calm composure. I was ninety-nine percent sure she hated me, and one hundred percent positive that I didn't give a fuck. It was fun to rile her up, though.

Her responding huff only made me more determined to

irritate and agitate her, get her alone and show her who was the boss here. Because it certainly wasn't her, even though she seemed to think her snarling affected me. I was the master at remaining unaffected. I'd honed that skill years ago.

"Nothing about you being in my kitchen is good," Shelley spat back, and Grace slammed the kitchen cabinet shut in an angry response to her daughter.

"Shelley, do you have any idea what this man has done—"

I knew what was coming, and I had no intention of letting Grace air that little nugget. I'd made it quite clear in the stipulations when I sent the money that under no circumstances was my name to be attached to any of it. Grace was about to disclose it, though, and that was the last thing I wanted.

"Now, now," I butted in, giving Grace a gentle but pointed stare. "No need to fall out over me, ladies." Shelley gave another huff of displeasure at my display of cocky, self-assuredness that earned her another scowl from her mum.

"You're always welcome in my house," Grace replied, keeping her stern glare on her daughter. "And Shelley, if you've got nothing nice to say, then just… go in the other room out of the way."

Shelley smirked, and while she folded her arms slowly, and cocked her head at me, she announced, "I'm going nowhere. If anyone's going to leave, it'll be him." She nodded her head in my direction and I smiled wide.

I was going to enjoy taking this girl down. How I'd do it was still up for debate, but it'd happen. If she was a man, storming onto our territory and taking what was ours, it'd be an easy fix. Violence. But this was something else entirely. I could never be aggressive to a woman, no matter what they'd done.

But how do you fight someone like her, and warn them off without coming off as a sexist prick?

Answer is, you don't.

You find other ways to get them to back off. We had to tread lightly, be smarter, because the one thing we all agreed on was we weren't violent to women. Ever. But that wasn't to say I couldn't scare her off, make her second guess whatever fucked-up plan she'd cooked up to shit all over our business.

"I don't want to make anyone uncomfortable." I held my hands up and made a point of stepping cautiously towards the door, showing I was ready to leave, and I felt some remorse at disturbing their peace. I didn't. I also didn't care if Shelley felt rattled. There was more where that came from. I was only just beginning.

"You're not," Grace replied, but the look on Shelley's face said it all. She wanted me to disappear in a ball of flames. Too bad her run of getting what she wanted was about to end.

"If I startled you, I do apologise," I addressed Shelley. "My name's Colton, by the way. I'm sorry I didn't formally introduce myself from the start. I'm an old friend of your mum's"

"I know exactly who *you* are. And, old friend?" She huffed sarcastically. "Yeah, right."

She shook her head, gritting her teeth and clenching her jaw in defiance.

I couldn't deny, looking at her now, up-close, Shelley Masters was a cute little thing; fiery and full of venom that bore into me from the heat of her wicked stare, but she couldn't have been more than five foot two or three. She was the epitome of a pocket rocket, and I liked that. She made something inside me stir. A hatred for the threat she posed to us, coupled with intrigue. She was a girl who'd done unspeakable things, just like me, but why? Why was she taking our hits and putting herself in the firing line? What made her want to rise-up the way she had? What was the fucking deal here? Because I could accept the hatred for what my father had done, but me? Grace accepted me. She held no ill will towards me, which was clear as day as we stood in this kitchen. But apparently, to Shelley Masters, that meant fuck all.

"And on that note, I'll say my goodbyes." I placed a peck on Grace's cheek and headed to the door where Shelley stood guard, putting swagger into my step just to piss her off.

I had no intention of leaving quite yet, but I knew I had to get Shelley on her own to say what I'd come here to say, and adding a hint of arrogance to my departure would goad her into falling head-first into my trap. Once I walked out of the kitchen, I knew she'd follow me to warn me off. I was the spider, and she was my fly. This shit was too easy.

"I'll see you around, Grace, Shelley." I dipped my head and then strolled through the doorway, heading towards the front door. But then the sound of a door slamming shut and feet stomping behind me made me stop and smile a self-satisfied smile.

I knew she'd take the bait.

"Don't ever come here again. Don't come anywhere near us." Shelley cursed behind me in the darkened hallway. "I know why you turned up today, but you don't scare me. Your intimidation won't work."

I spun around to face her, my smile turning wicked as my eyes lasered onto hers. She came to stand right in front of me and tilted her head up to glare back at me. The fact that there was so much anger and fight radiating from her did something to me. I was a sucker for a feisty woman, and she was the feistiest I'd ever met.

"And why did I come here?" I asked, goading her. Using a flippant response to tease her into fighting back.

Come on, Shelley, hit me with everything you've got.

She took a few deep breaths, her mass of brown curls framing a red, furious face. Cat-like eyes bore into me like she wanted to claw out my soul as she contemplated her response. Her little upturned nose flared in repulsion. She had the face of an angel that'd fallen right from heaven and bypassed all the bullshit to land in my lap in hell. If she thought she hated me now, she was in for a surprise. She'd seen nothing yet.

"We're one step ahead of you." She spoke with so much confidence I almost felt sorry for her. No one was one step ahead of us. "And mark my words, when me and my sisters are done, you'll be finished."

That was the first answer I'd wanted, to know they were all in on it. Now, I needed to push further.

"Three Masters." I raised my brows and shook my head. "Do you really think you're a match for five soldiers?" I wanted her to crack, tell me who else was involved in this. I was manipulating her into telling me all her sordid little truths.

"Three's the magic number." She smiled smugly back at me. "We don't need anything else. We have righteousness on our side. We're here to make sure you never hurt anyone again."

I knew she wanted to ruin our business, but her comment about me not hurting anyone pissed me off. We were righteous. We gave a voice to the silenced. It wasn't mindless violence, well not all the time. It was retribution. Justice. This woman was getting under my skin, and I had to stop her.

"You don't have to like me, sweetheart." I grinned. "And I don't have to give a fuck."

She scoffed, and sneered back at me.

"I'm sorry that your terrible attitude and awful existence caused me to act out of character. You should really work on that."

This girl was something else, and despite her wicked tongue, I was beginning to enjoy this. Maybe her getting under my skin wasn't so bad, after all. Seems it brought out the masochist in me.

So, I ignored her threats and stepped to her, and despite her defiance, she stepped back, stopping when her back hit the wall.

Interesting.

She had a weakness, and I'd just found it.

She didn't like me being close.

But just as I thought I'd gotten the upper hand, I felt something sharp dig into my side. Looking down, I saw a small flick knife, and I chuckled.

"That's cute. Are you flirting with me?" I glanced from the knife to her face, and gave her a sly wink.

"I'd rather flirt with a viper," she spat back, pushing the knife in a little further.

I bit my lip and chuckled again, shaking my head regretfully.

"I'll bite back sharper than a viper, baby. Do you really think pulling a knife on me is going to make me back down?" I pushed my face closer towards hers. "Do you think you're scaring me right now?"

"I think you have more dick in your personality than you do in your pants." She lifted her chin, defiantly. "Maybe I should aim my knife there?"

I gave another low chuckle. This girl's banter was giving me life. This shit was what I lived for.

"Now I know you're really flirting with me. You're interested in what's in my pants, and I'd be more than happy to show you."

She flared her nostrils in disgust.

"If you want to toy with me, I'll be your toy. Just call me Annabelle." She cocked her head, smirked, and pushed the knife even further into my side, making me tense my muscles.

I shook my head with a smile and whispered, "We both know cutting me is the last thing you're going to do here, in your mother's hallway, *Annabelle*." I grimaced for effect and added, "Stain the carpet? And risk Grace coming out to see me bleeding out on the floor? I don't know what would be worse. But that's a moot point." I leant forward, so I was speaking right in her face. "It's not going to happen. You don't have what it takes."

I knew she did.

I'd seen the evidence myself, but I was never a guy that'd back down from confrontation.

Suddenly, I grabbed her wrist, yanking the knife from my side to place it on my neck, right over my pulse, and she let me, her eyes narrowing as she looked at where I held it in place.

"If you're going to threaten someone, at least make it believable. Down there you might pierce a vital organ, maybe an artery if you get lucky, but I doubt it. Chances are I'd get a nasty cut, there'd be a bit of bleeding, and I'd live to tell people what I did to get revenge. But here?" I moved her hand to tap the knife against my neck. "If you cut my neck right here, I'll bleed out in minutes." I pushed her hand forward, forcing her knife harder against my skin, and I grinned as I felt the sharpness of it penetrating me, the sweet trickle of blood rolling down to dampen the edge of my T-shirt. "If you're going to use your weapon, use it properly. Make it count."

"You're a fucking psycho," she snarled, snatching her hand and the knife away and glancing down the hallway to where her mother was. "You're fucking crazy, but don't think for a moment I won't fight back. I might not do it here because you're right, why subject my mum to that? But when the time is right, I will use this on you." She brandished the knife in my face.

"I'll look forward to it," I replied. "Just make sure you don't bring a knife to a gun fight."

She didn't like that I was belittling her, insinuating that she might not bring it when the day came.

"I know you don't fight fair, but I'm ready for anything," she spat.

"Oh, I fight fair, I just don't take any bullshit."

I snatched the knife from her hand and closed it, twisting it between my fingers before placing the blunt end of the handle onto her neck and sliding it down towards her chest. Her arm shot up to stop my trail from going any further and she ripped the knife out of my hands in disgust, sliding it back into the pocket of her jeans.

Feeling the adrenaline pump through me, spurring me on to push her further, I stepped into her, pinning her back to the wall.

"Do you really think you can walk into our town, disrespect us and get away with it? Because you won't." I leaned forward, my face so close to hers that I could feel her warm, minty breath on my face. "You're not as clever as you think you are," I hissed, my body flush against hers as I spoke calmly. "You're not one step ahead, you're not even on the same level as us." I reached up and ran one of her brown curls through my fingers, feeding off the hatred that flowed from her. She panted out her breaths, keeping her venomous glare fixed on me. "It's cute that you think you affect us." I released the curl then placed my hands flat on the wall either side of her head. "That you think you have any control here. But you don't." I pushed forward into her mass of soft curly hair, inhaling the scent of vanilla as I whispered into her ear, "You need to remember who you're talking to. Respect is earned, never given."

"I don't want your respect," she hissed, lifting her chin up and turning her face until her nose was grazing mine, her lips so close I had to fight the urge to move an inch and kiss her, or bite her, either one would work for me. But the scorching fire that her defiance seemed to spark inside me burned differently when she added, "Why would I have respect for a man who shows none for any woman he's ever met?"

I pulled away slightly, waiting for her to elaborate, because I knew she would. She couldn't help herself.

"What?" she teased in a playful voice. "You think people around here don't know about you?" She pushed her body into mine now, trying to show me that she couldn't be intimidated. But her cute little display of defiance had the opposite effect; it fucking turned me on. "Do you think that *I* don't know about you?" A few seconds passed, seconds that beat in time to the drum of my heart. A beat that I felt sure she could hear resounding in my ears, because to me, it was deafening. "Everyone knows about you, Colton King. The Joker. And the biggest liar in Brinton Manor, because what you stand for is a far cry from the man you really are."

I gritted my teeth, holding myself back from reacting, because that's what she wanted, and I wasn't about to play into her hands and dance like the fucking puppet she thought I was. Instead, I reminded myself that she knew jack shit and I didn't have to prove myself to anyone. She was goading me, and I needed to turn the tables and take back control. A real joker didn't let anyone get the better of him, and I was as real as they came.

"You know fuck all about me or what I stand for." I crowded her petite frame with my own to overpower her, unnerve her, make her feel the weight of my presence. "You, *little girl*, need to stay out of things that don't concern you. Take this as a warning."

"Call me little girl again and I'll knee you in the fucking balls." She raised herself up on her tiptoes as she spoke. "I can do anything you can. Haven't I already proven that with the last few gifts I left you? Don't fucking patronise me, and don't underestimate me, or you'll be getting more than a warning."

She put her hands flat against my chest and pushed. Her effort wasn't enough to make me stumble, but I moved back slightly. "And I might not know everything about you," she added. "But I know enough. You're a joke, and I won't be scared off. We'll do what we set out to do, and by the end of it, everyone will see you for the loser you really are."

Game on, sweetheart.

"You're playing with fire, *little girl*." My grin widened as I tried to provoke her, reusing the nickname she hated. "You're batting with the big boys, but the problem is, you don't have the skills to pull it off. All big words, but your actions are sloppy. You're making mistakes and leaving us to pick up the pieces.

We could've nailed your asses with the first hit. You left a fucking calling card with your name on, for fuck's sake. You're no match for us, but by all means, keep telling yourself that you are. That's the real fucking joke here."

She didn't falter, instead she crossed her arms over her chest and said, "But we are on your radar, though, aren't we? Otherwise, why are you here? And why didn't you nail our asses that first time, or the second? Are you waiting for the third or fourth? Or are you scared you'll be exposed as a bunch of frauds who were bested by a group of girls?"

I was enjoying arguing with her too much.

Bested by a group of girls?

Bring it all on.

I fucking loved the challenge.

"We didn't shit on you, because we're not rats. But we don't stand for bullshit either. Brinton is our manor. We control the streets. You want to run Merivale? Be our guests. But stay away from our town. Stay out of our business and stay out of Brinton Manor." I gave her a smirk, and a wink then stepped back. "If you pull a stunt like that again, you won't like the results."

"Is that a threat or an invitation?" she purred, leaning to the side, propped up against the wall we'd just been against, giving me a provocative look. Fuck, this woman knew how to play me, and I fucking loved it.

"Take it any way you want, sweetheart, but be prepared for the consequences."

She threw her head back and laughed.

"You know…" She glanced at her nails nonchalantly, like this discussion meant nothing. "I googled who gives a fuck and I'm pretty sure my face didn't come up on the search results."

Then a wicked smile crept over her face. "You should be the one preparing for the consequences. Karma's a bitch… and she's standing right in front of you."

I'd never met anyone like her, and after today, I was glad she'd fallen into my life. Finally, there was a girl willing to hold her own and stand against me.

"Don't invite the devil to dance if you can't handle the steps." I stood firm, watching the way her pupils dilated as I spoke. The way her breathing altered when I took a step towards her; her neck movement as she swallowed. All subtle tells that she was more affected than she wanted to let on. I thought making a kill was the most fun I'd ever had but sparring with her was a pretty close second.

"Karma *is* a bitch, so watch your back, Shelley." I grinned, and in a low voice, I whispered, "I did a google search of my own, and it told me a King always comes out on top. Kings are born to greatness. Masters? They're just students who hit a lucky break and made it to the next rung of the ladder, but they'll never reach my level. All masters fail eventually."

And with that, I opened the front door and walked out. I didn't want to give her the opportunity to argue back. Shelley Masters was like me; she always wanted to have the last word. But she wouldn't get it, not today.

I stalked back to the van, getting in and slamming the door shut as Adam burned the side of my face with his stare.

"What happened?" he asked, gripping the steering wheel in a vice-like grip.

"They won't stop. They think they're better than us."

"Then let's go back in there and remind them they're not."

I shook my head.

"We need to play this differently."

Adam sighed and dipped his head in thought.

I didn't want to underestimate Shelley, or her sisters. I knew my visit today would spur them on. There'd be comeback. I'd be disappointed if there wasn't. She played the part of a formidable opponent and I wanted to see that in action. This game of chess was only just getting started.

"Well, if they won't stay out of Brinton," Adam announced. "Maybe we need to give them a reminder of why it's not the place for them. Show them what happens to outsiders."

I nodded in response, but my mind wasn't in the moment. It was back in a dark hallway, arguing with a feisty brunette who had me twisted up in the best way.

My gut told me life was about to get interesting, and I was here for it. Every twisted, crazy, insane minute.

Game on.

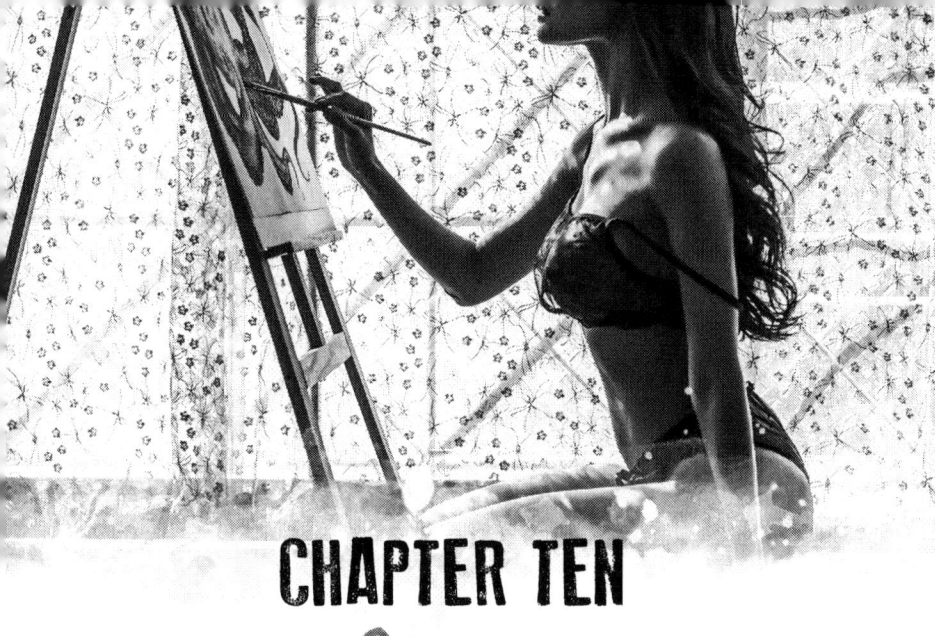

CHAPTER TEN
Shelley

I should've known a man like him would have the audacity to show up on our doorstep. I wasn't surprised in the slightest. Although, why my mother was giving him the time of day was beyond me. I thought she had more about her than that, in fact, I knew she did. So maybe Colton King was more cunning than I'd originally thought.

Despite keeping her past from us, we knew about it, and we knew he was involved. So her weird act with Colton today had to be just that, an act, because the alternative didn't make sense.

When Bryony walked through the door a few hours later, I shot up from my spot on the sofa and charged into the hallway, grabbing her by the arm before she'd even had a chance to take her coat off.

"Hold up. Where's the fire?" she complained, trying to pull away from me as I steered her to the stairs before Mum saw her.

I needed to fill her in on developments without any distractions.

"The fire? *That* showed up three hours ago, chatting to Mum in the kitchen. You know, the one that comes in the form of a traitorous soldier," I hissed so that Mum wouldn't hear, but Bryony would sense my pissed-off vibe.

"Oh shit, seriously?" She sounded disappointed as she walked up the stairs beside me, staring at the side of my face to try and gauge my reaction.

"Would I joke about a joker like him?" I huffed at myself for using his ridiculous self-given nickname.

"I wish I'd been here. What did he say?"

"He tried to intimidate me, but it didn't work. He thinks he can play games, but we'll play them better. One visit, where he growls and threatens me isn't going to change a damn thing. If anything, it's only made me more determined to stick to our plan and see it through to the bitter end. After what he's done, we need payback."

Bryony nodded in agreement as we entered my room, and I closed the door behind me to give us more privacy.

"Have you had any more emails?" I asked, and Bryony pulled her phone from her pocket and sighed.

"Nothing since the last one, thank God. To be honest, I don't know how long we're going to be able to hold him off. It's all going to come to a head soon, and when it does, we'll make sure everyone knows exactly what Colton fucking King is. If we go down, we'll take him with us. He won't get away with this." Bryony shook her phone as she spoke. Both of us contemplating the fucked-up messages that we'd kept hidden on there. Messages we were ready to bury once we'd dealt with the person who'd sent them.

This was a game of chess, and today we'd both made our next move. What Colton failed to remember though, was a queen has more power than the king in chess. We would take him down.

"That's a problem for another day," I stated. "For now, we need to keep chipping away at him. We're obviously getting to him if he's taken to showing up on our doorstep."

Bryony bit her lip and leant her head to the side, her long black hair falling into her face before she sighed and scooped it up into a ponytail, tying it with the tie she always kept on her wrist.

"What was he like up close? Are those blue eyes as intoxicating as everyone in Brinton says they are?"

I rolled my eyes and ignored her, but she wouldn't let it go. Bryony might argue and fight like me, but her glasses weren't as darkly tinted as mine. She saw the world with hope. I saw hopelessness.

"You know," she carried on. "I've heard a girl can get lost in those eyes. Did he have any effect on you at all? Come on, Shelley. You can't deny he's your type. Tall, dark and deranged. Did he chip through any of that armour as he was growling demands at you?"

"He made me want to punch the wall, and his face, and not in that order. He's smug, self-centred, and arrogant. There's nothing remotely attractive about him as far as I'm concerned. Why would I want anything to do with a guy like him?"

"Because you like danger?"

I ignored her and turned on my TV to distract myself from her insinuations and my racing mind. Still, I felt irritated and agitated, so I threw the remote control onto the bed and glared back at her. "It'll be a cold day in hell before I ever let Colton King have any kind of effect on me. My type? Let's not forget what he's done. My type is loyal and trustworthy. Two things he'll never be."

"Sounds like he's getting to you more than you realise," she whispered to herself as her phone chimed an alert.

"And it sounds like you've been reading too many dark romance novels. There's not going to be a happily ever after here, Bryony. Just an ending. A brutal one."

I'd never admit he was getting to me, because I'd never admit defeat. He'd wronged this family and retribution was needed. Seeing him suffer was all I was interested in.

"Bingo." Bryony smirked. "We have another hit on the soldier email. Time to sharpen our tools. Looks like our next job has come in sooner than we realised."

CHAPTER ELEVEN
Colton

We didn't hang around. Shit needed to be dealt with, and we wanted The Masters gone. So, we wasted no time planting a fake job in our inbox, knowing they'd take the bait; they couldn't help themselves. We'd set everything up to take place in a squalid flat in an abandoned block in Brinton. Gaz was sent to watch the girls and let us know if they made any movements earlier than we expected, and we sat and waited. Planning and counting down the hours until we could put this whole farce to bed and get on with our real work.

For me, I wanted answers, proper answers. Yes, I was a King, and my father had been a complete shit to their mum and aunt, but I knew it went further than that. I knew there was something else behind their thirst for vengeance, and being the nosy fucker that I was, I wouldn't stop until I found out what it was.

"Do you really think they'll buy into the whole Alan Bell, wife beater story we planted?" Will asked as we made our way up the concrete staircase that'd lead us to the floor we'd assigned for our confrontation tonight.

The walls were plastered in pointless graffiti, and when we turned into the dark, narrow corridor that led to flat thirty-five, the graffiti mixed with filth made it feel like you were walking into your own nightmare or horror movie. It was a shithole by anyone's standards.

"Will they believe that someone actually lives here would be a better question," Tyler replied, keeping his hands stuffed into the pockets of his jeans as we picked over the rubbish and used needles that littered the floor.

"There's so much crime and vandalism in this building," I said, shaking my head in disgust. "That's wrong on so many… *levels*."

"Very funny." Adam rolled his eyes at my lame joke and then got straight back to business. "If they don't show, we'll try again." He stopped outside number thirty-five and opened the door.

"Damn right we will," I said, following Adam inside, and glancing around at the set-up we had in place.

"Do you think you can stay quiet long enough for this stakeout to work?" he asked me.

I put my finger on my lips, but I couldn't help myself. "If a mime artist gets arrested, do the police still tell him he has the right to remain silent?"

Will laughed and did a few mimes in front of us. He got me.

"Why don't you shut up and you might find out?" Adam

growled, pushing past us and walking further into the room to do his checks.

I shrugged on a laugh. "I tried to start a professional hide and seek team once. It didn't work out. Turns out, good players are hard to find."

Even Tyler laughed at that one.

"You'll be hard to find if you don't start taking this seriously," Adam spat.

I stayed quiet.

There was a first time for everything.

But Adam was wrong on one account. He didn't realise how seriously I took this. I wasn't playing about because I was being flippant. I did it to distract myself from the voices in my head. It was my way of coping. I took this as seriously as the rest of them, I just had a different way of showing it.

It was difficult to see clearly in the dim, empty flat. The only light came from the streetlamps outside and the moon that reflected off the chipped plaster and wooden floorboards. But that didn't matter, there was only one focal point in the room, and that was a chair bolted down in the middle of the floor. In it, sat a dummy chained up and wearing a blue boiler suit with a Michael Myers mask on. Something to make the girls think they'd found their mark as they walked in. It wouldn't trick them for long, but it'd buy us enough time to shut the door on our honey trap and lock them in.

Along the back wall, hidden behind the door, out of plain sight, we had a table full of instruments. Weapons we had no intention of using. Their only purpose was to look menacing, like fake Michael in his chair. Tonight was a reminder, a final warning that this was going to stop. There would be no bloodshed. But pride? Honour? That was on the line, and we weren't going to lose any of it.

Adam's phone chimed with an incoming message, and after reading, he told us Gaz had said they were on the move. We stood against the wall and pulled our balaclavas over our heads.

Silently we waited, our breaths mingled with the sound of police sirens wailing in the distance, and the biting wind blowing through the boarded-up windows. Eventually, we heard the thud of footsteps on the concrete staircase in the distance, and then those thuds grew louder as they ascended the hallway. Any second now, and that door would fly open. The way my heart raced and my stomach flipped, I could barely contain my excitement.

There was a low hum of whispered voices outside the door, and then boom, the door flew open, hitting the plaster to the side of us, and three dark figures barrelled into the room, holding up weapons and shouting, "Don't fucking move. Stay where you are."

As one of them approached Michael Myers, kicking out at the plastic leg of the dummy, Adam, who was the closest to the door, slammed it shut and stood in front of it. His tall, wide frame towered over them, blocking any exit they might attempt to make. The girl who'd kicked out dropped her arms to the side and cursed, "What the fuck?" While the other two spun around to face us, their eyes widening for a split second before narrowing with pure hatred and hellfire.

The kung fu sister turned last, and barely hanging onto her sanity, she hissed, "Is this a fucking joke?"

Shelley had been the last to enter the room, and since turning around, she hadn't taken her eyes off me. If looks could kill, I would have died and been reincarnated a dozen times with how much fury she was throwing my way.

I loved it.

So, I smiled at her, and then moved my attention to Little Miss High-kick and asked, "Do you think we're fucking joking? This is the last time you ever step foot in this town."

The other sister huffed and looked at Shelley for confirmation as she stated, "This was a set-up."

But Shelley didn't like to admit defeat. She would never admit she was wrong. "It was indeed," she said, shifting her gaze from her sister to me. "And now we've got you where we want you, we can outline our terms and let you know exactly how this is going to go."

She was unbelievable. Trapped in front of us without a leg to stand on, and yet she was still claiming to have the upper hand. It felt kind of fucked up that this shit was turning me on. I'd never met anyone like her before.

"No one dictates anything to us," Adam snapped through gritted teeth.

"You need to show some manners," Devon added, taking a step forward to stand in solidarity with Adam.

"You're not welcome here, and you will stop whatever fucking game you're playing," Tyler chipped in, his chin lifting in defiance.

"Time to fuck off home to Merivale," Will sneered.

And me?

I didn't say a word.

My smirk and the laughter that I held in my eyes were enough.

"Haven't you got anything to say?" Shelley asked. "Seeing

as you're the reason we're all here."

I rubbed my chin, pretending to look perplexed as I replied, "And why is that exactly? Can I speak freely?" I held my arms up at my sides in question. "Because I'm guessing you all know my history with your family. But tell me, please, because there's something I'm struggling with here."

"And what exactly are you struggling with?" The kick-happy sister asked. "The fact that you're a liar? A coward? A poor excuse for a human being?"

"Let him speak, Kate," Shelley said, putting her hand up. "I want to watch him dig his own grave."

"Be very careful what you say." Adam's dark, low voice bellowed through the grim stand-off. "We don't take kindly to attacks of any kind on one of our brothers. If you come for one of us, you come for all. When we're under fire, that's when we come out fighting the hardest."

I took a few breaths to let Adam's words sink in before I used my own.

"I can accept the fact you hate me, hate my family name, and despise what my father did. But those were wrongs that I put to bed a long time ago."

"How so?" the middle one, who I assumed was Bryony, asked.

"I don't think we need to go into detail about what my father did. He was a depraved sicko who fed off everyone around him, me included. He used men and women for his own gains, and as far as the evidence that he videoed, I took care of what I could. I destroyed it. I'm not saying there isn't crap still circulating out there, I couldn't destroy what was out of my hands, but I took my responsibility to obliterate his legacy seriously. I shut him down."

I didn't want to go into any more detail than that. I didn't feel I had to. My father's movies were on the market, out there for public consumption, and there was nothing I could do to alter that fact. But anything I could do to halt his business from my end, I'd done. There were no more original film rolls or images, no summerhouse. What more did they want from me? I'd already given blood. My father's.

"But you didn't destroy it all, though, did you?" I could see the rise and fall of Shelley's chest as she spoke through the anger that fuelled her.

"Let's get one thing straight," I said, breaking character and letting the heat of the moment get to me. "I was five years old when I found out what my father did for a living. At thirteen, I found out how fucked-up he really was, and from that day on, I did everything in my power to stop him. If you want to spend the rest of your life crucifying me for something he did, something I brought to an end, then go right ahead. See where it gets you. But if you think this shitty vendetta you've started is going to make any difference or make you feel better about what happened to your mum or Rosie, then let me tell you, it won't."

"Shitty vendetta?" Shelley's eyes burned with fire. We both stood facing each other, barely registering anyone else in the room. I could see her hands shaking by her sides, and I knew she was ready to explode. "You're really good at playing the victim, Colton, but we know you for what you are." She stepped toward me, her hands fisting as she braced herself. "You might be able to pull the wool over our mum's eyes, but we know."

"You know what?" I snapped, feeling my sanity slowly ebbing away.

"Show him, Bryony." The eldest, Kate, spoke up, and we both turned to look their way.

Bryony pulled her phone from her pocket and began to tap on the screen. "We know this is you, Colton, because it couldn't be anyone else. The things you've said about our mum and Rosie, the videos you sent, private videos that wouldn't be in the public domain, it could only come from your dad's private collection."

My brothers looked as confused as I felt. Nothing she was saying was making any sense.

"What things?" Adam asked as I stood there dumbfounded for the first time in my life. "Can someone spell this out for us? We prefer to make the riddles, not solve them."

All three sisters moved to stand shoulder to shoulder, looking down at the phone as Bryony spoke.

"A few weeks ago, we received an email telling us if we didn't pay fifty grand, someone was going to leak unseen footage of our mum and Rosie in one of Glenn King's special films. They threatened to send it to their workplaces and destroy their lives if we didn't comply. There was enough images and footage for us to take it seriously. Backstage stuff that showed it'd come from King himself, only he's dead, right? So, who else had access to that shit? You. No one else. And before you ask, we did our homework, checked the IP for the email. We aren't stupid, but you covered your tracks. But know this… we won't pay. And we'd never tell Mum and Rosie what you're trying to do. As far as we're concerned, that part of their lives is over, and we'd never rake up that crap and cause them any pain. So, here we are, teaching you a lesson, Mr King. You can't fuck with The Masters and expect to get away with it. You're the one that's going to pay."

To say I was gobsmacked was an understatement. I needed to take a second to try and gather my thoughts.

They were being blackmailed, and they thought it was me?

"I've done fuck all," I blurted out, looking to my brothers in bewilderment, and then, seeing the fury on their faces, my own began to rise to the surface. "I've paid my dues for what he did. The sins of my father fell well and truly onto my shoulders, and I took it, I dealt with it. But not this time." I shook my head and made sure they could see that I meant it. I wasn't fucking about. "I'm not paying for this one."

"Let us see the emails." Tyler stepped forward, and Bryony hesitated, then held her phone out, letting him scroll through, so I stepped forward too. I needed to see this for myself.

> Pay up, bitches, or I'll make your lives a misery.
> You've got thirty days to wire the funds.
> Don't test me or I will make sure this goes viral.

The messages were all in the same vein. This person wanted money, they were threatening all sorts to expose Grace and Rosie. And from the wording they used, I knew exactly who it was.

"You said you didn't want to involve your mum, didn't want to upset her, but one look at those emails and she'd have told you who sent them, and it wasn't me."

The room was silent as everyone waited for my next words.

"There's only one person who had access to those sorts of videos and images." I bit my lip and shook my head in disappointment. "You really didn't do your homework, did you, girls?"

"If you're going to say Kenny Byers," Kate stated. "Then

don't. We already looked into him, and he died a few months after your father."

"Really?" I shot back. "Because the last I heard, he was living under the name Oscar Gold somewhere on the Costa Del Sol."

Silence.

I guessed they wouldn't take my word for it, so I took my phone out and clicked on the last image I'd been sent of Kenny, from the private investigator I'd paid to track his movements. I didn't check on him regularly, but I liked to know where he was, so I paid the guy to give me yearly updates. That way, I could make sure he never darkened my doorstep. But maybe I needed to increase my checks. I hadn't foreseen Kenny making a comeback like this.

Shelley snatched my phone and held it up so her sisters could see.

"It looks like him."

"That's because it is him." I rubbed my hands over my face in exasperation, and then took my phone back, and as my fingers brushed Shelley's, I felt something spark in my fingertips.

"I think you need to get onto your guy," Tyler stated. "I don't think Kenny wants to stay hidden anymore. He's made a bold move, and from what you've told us about him, Colton, I don't think he'll stop." Tyler turned to address Bryony. "Let me have a closer look at the emails, see if there's something I can find." He then glanced back at the rest of us. "Two gangs are better than one, right?" He turned back to glare at the girls. "Not that you deserve our help after what you've done."

"We don't need your help," Shelley spat, but Bryony piped up, "Let's not be a dick about it. If they know something, let's use them."

We didn't argue. Tyler wanted to see if there was something they'd missed that he could find; that's what he loved to do. But it didn't change the fact that these girls had overstepped the mark. We weren't about to buddy up with them anytime soon, and I knew they felt the same way.

"You might not have sent the emails, but don't think this changes anything," Shelley hissed, as the rest of the group migrated to the window to pour over the emails and discuss their next steps. "I still hate you."

"The feeling's mutual," I spat back, and even though my mind was screaming at me to walk away, show her I was unaffected, my body didn't listen. It moved closer, brushing against her, and making my damn heart race at the feel of her near me. It was as if I wanted to torture myself by dancing closer to the fire. Burning from the heat. This girl hated me, and yet, I couldn't seem to take my eyes off her. Like a magnet, she drew me near.

When I first met her mum, Grace, I'd always thought she might be some kind of white witch. But Shelley? She was all dark, stormy vibes of fury and hate. A whirlwind of destruction and danger that called out to me. I'd always been that kid who ran out into the rainstorm, chasing the lightning as others turned away. And she was the perfect storm. From the thunder of her presence to the lightning of her words, her actions, her whole being. She set me on fire, made me feel alive, woke up parts of me that I'd buried years ago. She made me feel, and no one had done that. Ever.

CHAPTER TWELVE
Shelley

I should've trusted my instincts when we first set foot in this shithole. Something felt off the minute we got here, but I kept quiet, fought the nagging doubts eating away at me. I won't make that mistake again. Bursting through that door and seeing what lay on the other side for us pissed me off even more. How fucking dare he.

I always knew Colton King was a shady motherfucker, but I'd underestimated him. After his surprise visit to our house a few days ago, I thought I'd bought us more time, but no. He must've gone back to his soldiers that same day and set up this trap.

Anger turned to fury when he warned us to stay away from his town like he owned the place. So, I did what I do best, and I turned the tables on him, made him think that we knew what was going on, that we were still in control. I told him we'd got him right where we wanted him, and now, he had to listen to our terms. I was getting tired of dancing around the issue. He needed to be called out for the blackmail. The fact that we were on the back foot was a moot point. Tonight, we were going to put a stop to this, put a stop to him and his narcissistic bullshit. But when we stood there and played our ace, spelling it out for the rest of the soldiers, his reaction knocked me for six.

I wanted to doubt him, but he was so adamant when he shouted, "I've done fuck all," that I had to stop myself from backing down. I knew a liar when I saw one, and Colton King wasn't lying. We'd thought we had it all figured out, and yet we'd gotten it so wrong. I couldn't ever admit that, though. Knowing he was innocent this time didn't alter the fact that his dad was who he was. And yes, the sins of the father shouldn't fall on his shoulders, but my stubborn ass couldn't seem to let go of the vengeance that'd kept me going for so long. If Colton were on fire, I wouldn't spit on him.

"I still hate you," I seethed, wishing it'd been different. If I was honest, I wanted him to be guilty. It'd certainly make life easier for me. Hate I could cope with, but the way he was making me feel right now was a whole other ball game, and it was one I couldn't get my head around. I didn't like it.

"The feeling's mutual," he growled back at me, but the way he moved his body closer to mine told me a different story.

The others were gathered in the corner, pouring over the emails on Bryony's phone and making a plan of action, but all I could focus on was how unnerved I felt having Colton standing so close to me. I tried to stare him down, but his eyes were too intense, so I focused on the tattoos that decorated his neck. There were the letters G-E-M on the left-hand side that disappeared under his T-shirt, and I guessed it was probably Gemma, an old girlfriend, or perhaps a current one? Why did the thought of that make my stomach turn?

"Everything bad that's happened to my family is because of you," I said, as a way to punish him for the way I was feeling; unsettled, nervous, and out of sorts.

Heat coursed through me as he stared me down and gave me that bloody smirk of his. Except this time, it made my stomach flip, which pissed me off even more.

I wasn't one of those women who couldn't control their damn emotions around a man. I prided myself on always being in control. But the fact he was stealing that away from me made me want to lash out.

"What do you want?" He cocked his head to the side. "Blood? You want me to bleed out in front of you? Would that make you happy?"

"It'd be a start."

He bent forward to whisper in my ear. I hated him doing that, his breath tickling my neck, making my skin bristle and my heart race.

"I know your type," he said, making my back straighten in protest. "You'll never be satisfied. I could burn the world down for you and you'd ask why I'd left the ashes."

"I'd ask why you bothered at all because I want nothing from you," I replied, trying to pull away from him, but my body didn't seem to be working in time with my brain and I stayed still, trying to regulate my breathing.

He turned to look me in the eyes, and I swallowed slowly, carefully, desperate not to show he was getting to me as he towered over me.

"I'd never do anything to hurt Grace or Rosie. So, that means I wouldn't hurt you… not unless you asked me to." And there was that smirk again. Only this time, I wanted to wipe it off his face.

"Just being in your presence is painful enough."

He huffed, but he didn't move away. I think he was enjoying our little standoff.

Maybe I was too.

"And yet you seem to be drawn to me. I saw you watching me in the club, in the street, even now, you can't take your eyes off me."

"Because I don't trust you. Keep your friends close and your enemies even closer. Never take your eyes off the ball. If I see a snake, I'm going to watch it's every move. And that's what you are, Colton, a snake. You can play the saviour to my mother all you like, but that's not what you are to me."

"And what am I to you?" he asked, pressing every one of my buttons.

"The bane of my life."

"Wrong DC character, sweetheart. I'm The Joker."

"Cut the crap, Colton. I've done my homework. I know exactly what you are, and your fake charm won't work on me."

"Who said I was faking?"

I heard movement from the corner of the room, and Bryony said, "I can't believe I'm going to say this, but we're heading back to The Sanctuary to see if their computers are better than ours at tracking this fucker. Strike while the iron's hot, right?"

Neither Colton nor I acknowledged them, we just stood glaring at each other as one of the soldiers added, "I guess we'll leave you to the staring contest and meet you outside when whatever this is, is all over."

The slam of the door echoed through the room, letting us know we were alone. That, and the ragged breaths we were both panting out. The moonlight reflected off his face, and I could see he was unsure, trying to decide what his next move would be. Then, that wicked veil of intent fell over him and he pushed forward, making me step backwards until my back met the cold, hard wall behind me. His body was so close to mine, caging me in but not pressing against me, and something inside me wanted that, wanted to feel the hardness of his body. If I wanted to, I could have pushed him off, but I was hypnotised. Held captive by his presence. I wanted to know what he'd do next.

He closed his eyes for a split second, then leaned into me again and whispered, "You are the most infuriating, annoying woman I've ever met. You walk into a room, and I can't even think straight. You make me want to punch the fucking wall, and I've always said, I'm a lover not a fighter."

"Yeah, right," I scoffed, but he carried on.

"Why is that? Why do you have this effect on me?"

I closed my eyes and breathed in his masculine scent as I told him, "One look at you and I grind my teeth so hard its painful. You're cocky, full of shit, and if you were the last man on earth, I'd rather jump off the closest cliff than spend a minute longer than I had to in your presence. You make my skin crawl."

He pressed a little closer to me, and I could feel the hardness in his jeans as he replied, "Some people come into our lives as a blessing, but you? You're a fucking curse. Even the devil himself will be begging for a break when you land in hell."

"Now I know why you've never settled down," I shot back. "No woman could put up with you for long. You're so in love with yourself there isn't room for anyone else. But maybe that's a good thing. God forbid one woman should get lumbered with your ego for the rest of her life."

He threw his head back and laughed, then settled back into the crook of my neck, where he growled, "And any man that gets saddled with you better be ready to give up his balls. I bet you'd carry them around in your purse. Use them for satanic rituals and shit like that."

I turned my head towards him. "Any man I'm with better have a set of balls, because I don't play with little boys–" I was about to elaborate, and say some shit about him being a boy, but I didn't get chance. He crashed his lips to mine, grabbing the back of my neck and fusing our mouths together. My mind left my body, and against every nerve and fibre of my being, I responded, closing my eyes as I got lost in him. Teeth clashed as we moved against each other in a fumbled, clumsy mess. His tongue tangled with mine, the taste of him sending me into a spiral of despair.

I hated him, but he felt so good.

I wanted to push him away, but pull him closer–push myself into him and feel more, so much more.

He kissed me like he hated me, like he wanted to bruise me, but I loved it.

I kissed him like I was giving him a taste of what he'd never get, all the time knowing I couldn't get enough.

This kiss was passion and hate, fire and fury. I gripped the front of his T-shirt in my fists as he carried on his assault, tasting me, teasing me. He pushed his hips to mine, showing me the affect I was having on him. No words were needed, I could feel it all. This kiss felt like he was claiming me. And then, he took my bottom lip between his teeth and bit down, pulling away and letting go as I sighed gently and slowly opened my eyes to find him staring at me like he couldn't quite believe what he'd done.

"I didn't know whether to kiss or bite you, so I went with both." His voice was gravelly, low and seductive. Half of me wanted to pull him back to me for a repeat performance, and the other said I should slap him to retain my dignity.

"I hope you enjoyed it," I replied, using a finger to wipe the corner of my mouth. "Because that's the last time you'll ever kiss me."

He pushed his forehead against mine, and I couldn't stop a gasp from breaking free.

"It won't be the last time," he said with wicked authority. "But next time, I'll be better prepared."

I opened my mouth to give a sarcastic response, but he turned and walked away, leaving me standing in the dark, feeling like I'd been hit by a ten-tonne truck. A few seconds passed and the door creaked open again.

"Are you coming," he asked with a sly sneer. "Or are you going to stay there in the dark replaying the best kiss you've ever had?"

And just like that, my walls snapped firmly back into place.

"If that was the best you've got, you need to keep practising." I pushed off the wall and stalked over to the doorway where he stood. "You're supposed to sweep a girl off her feet, not paralyse her with fear and disgust."

And with that, I walked away. A little shred of dignity intact, but my heart well and truly at war with my head.

Keep practising?
What the fuck, Shelley?

I swallowed and tried to get the image of him kissing any other girl out of my head, because if anything was making my heart rate spike right now, it was that.

CHAPTER THIRTEEN
Colton

She never came back to The Sanctuary, none of her sisters did. I guessed after our encounter in the flat, she'd talked them out of it, deciding to give me a wide berth. But out of sight wasn't out of mind as far as I was concerned. I couldn't get the damn woman out of my head. It had to be some sort of witchcraft. No woman had ever had a choke hold on me like she did. And because of that, I wanted to go out of my way to provoke her and piss her off. She was a little hellion, and I was in the mood to play in hell.

As Tyler had promised, we looked into the emails to see if they'd missed anything. I had to admit, Kenny was going in hard, threatening to obliterate the family with his evidence. The man must've been desperate, reading the things he said to them, the way he villainised Grace and Rosie. Yet, he'd instigated every dirty, seedy thing that'd happened, along with my father, and it made me furious and thirsty for revenge. We hadn't wanted to help the sisters at first after the shit they'd pulled, and from what we'd seen, they could look after themselves, but we weren't assholes. Kenny was a loose end I should've taken care of years ago. I had to take some responsibility for him still being out there, causing the kind of havoc he was.

I had my private investigator check out Kenny's whereabouts, and sure enough, a few days later, I got a call to say he was back in the U.K. I assumed he'd blown through his savings and the small amount he'd managed to cream off the top of my father's estate before he left, and that's why he was back, using whatever tools he had in his arsenal to make a quick buck. He wanted the girls to pay up, that's why he hadn't sent the videos and photos out like he'd threatened. That was his only ace, and he couldn't afford to play it. He needed that money.

I kept my PI on the case to try and track down his exact location. I felt sure that if he'd crawled back into Brinton, we'd know about it from one of our sources, but that didn't mean he wasn't skulking close by in Sandland or Merivale. That thought created a nauseous dread to flood the pit of my stomach. It was why I was currently leaning against a building on the campus of Shelley's art college, waiting to catch a glimpse of her today, so I could tell her what we'd found out. That, and it gave me another excuse to annoy her, and then stand back and watch my handiwork as she blew up all because of me.

Twenty minutes later, an influx of students spilled out of one of the buildings across from where I stood. I straightened, pushing off the wall and scanning the crowds to catch sight of her. When I saw a mass of brown curls, I felt a heat burn in my chest.

There she was.

But then I watched her turn and smile at a guy walking next to her, and that heat turned to something else entirely.

"You know, in his day, he was seen as quite the radical," I heard the guy say in a boring, monotone voice as I drew near.

"I don't care who you are or what you think of Rodin," Shelley replied, acting all innocent, like she hadn't left real life artwork of her own all over Brinton. "If you walk past *The Thinker* or *The Kiss*, you're going to stop and look."

"I'd stop and look," I butted in, positioning myself close to Shelley's side and giving the guy next to her a discreet warning stare over her shoulder. "The kiss? That sounds like my kind of art."

"What are you doing here?" Shelley snapped. She was pissed, and began walking at a faster pace; like that'd stop me.

"Can't a guy pay a visit to a friend these days?" I increased my own pace, and she stopped, turning to glare at me.

She was holding a large black art folder and her knuckles were white from gripping the handle so tightly. It was the cutest thing I'd seen; cuter than the last time she'd lost her shit with me.

The guy stopped too and held his hand out as if I was going to shake it.

"I'm Eric. Pleased to meet you. Are you a fan of Rodin's work?"

"Never met the guy, and you can leave now. I've got it from here," I snapped, my mouth twitching as it fought between a sarcastic smile and a grimace of hate.

Eric faltered, his arm going limp like he couldn't decide whether to pull away or try again.

"Don't be so fucking rude," Shelley blasted, and turning her back on me, she said, "Come on, Eric. Let's go."

Eric's eyes flickered from her to me and back again. He dipped his head, and then pushed his glasses up his nose nervously. "I have a class to get to. But I'll see you tomorrow, Shelley." He peered over her shoulder to where I stood with my eyes burning holes into his soul. "Or maybe not. I'm kind of busy with finals." And with that, he scurried away like the rat he was.

Shelley gave an over-exaggerated sigh and spun around to face me.

"What the fuck do you want, King? Isn't it bad enough that I have to deal with you over the blackmail stuff? Are you intent on infiltrating every part of my life now and making everything miserable?"

"On the contrary, I'm a ray of fucking sunshine when you get to know me. I'm that friend you can always call on if you ever need to hide a dead body, and we all know you're not the best at covering your tracks. But remember, if you disrespect me or my brothers, I know how to hide a dead body."

She sneered at me, her nose wrinkling in disgust. "I don't want to get to know you. I know enough."

Her cheeks were flushed, and her eyes burned with anger. We both took a second, taking slow deep breaths as we stared at each other. The pavement we were standing on was quieter now as people scattered about, going to their next lecture or wherever they needed to be. I leant my head down so that my forehead was almost touching hers, and on a whisper, I replied, "I beg to differ." I nodded in the direction that Eric had left. "And if he's the standard that I've got to aspire to, I don't think there's going to be any problems, do you?"

My question, along with the cock of my head, and my grin was like a red rag to a bull.

"Eric is a sweetheart," she replied, glaring at me with contempt. "He's more man than you'll ever be. And the last time I checked, he's one hundred percent gay. In fact, he'll probably ask me for your number the next time I see him, and part of me wishes I hadn't told you that. It's fun seeing your ridiculous alpha bullshit, but I figure Eric deserves fair representation. He's a good friend, and he doesn't deserve to have you snarling at him."

"I don't snarl, I smoulder."

She bit her lip and shook her head as she huffed and tried not to smile.

"And I wouldn't blame him," I added. "I am a bit of a catch."

"Oh, my fucking God." She started to walk away. "You really love yourself. But then, I suppose someone has to."

She strode purposefully along the street, keeping her head forward and her chin high. I kept in step with her, and from the corner of my eye, I noticed that we were dressed similar, like mirror images, yin and yang. Both wearing tight black skinny jeans, black T-shirt and black boots. Both of us fighting a war in our heads. The only difference was I was smiling, and she was scowling.

"Can I see your artwork?" I asked, gesturing to the folder in her hand.

"Over my dead body."

"You know that can be arranged, but I'd rather you showed me without the theatrics."

She huffed again. Something she seemed to like to do a lot

around me.

"The day I show you my artwork will be a cold day in hell."

"I'll get the ice-pops ready then." A few more steps in silence and then I added, "I've seen your artwork already, anyway. Two and three dimensional. You should spend a day with Devon. He always calls our line of work his art."

She came to a stop and turned to me, her jaw tense before she spoke.

"Apart from the tag I left on the wall, that wasn't art, it was a fucking necessity. Cleaning up the filth and pissing you off at the same time." She cocked her head, and then tapped her finger on her bottom lip. "I suppose, in a way, that's an artform in itself. An art that creates drama. Has anyone ever told you you're a drama queen?"

"I'd prefer drama king, but whatever floats your boat, sweetheart."

Her nostrils flared. I loved how sexy she looked when she was angry.

"Cut the crap, Colton. Why are you here?"

She wanted to cut the crap, so I did.

"I came to let you know Kenny is back in the U.K."

She rolled her eyes and clucked her tongue at me.

"Well, that's not news. Don't you have anything better to tell me?"

I thought about hitting her with a one-liner, maybe a few stupid facts, but I went with the truth.

"I've got my men on the case. They're trying to track down his exact location, but I wanted to warn you. He could be anywhere."

"And you think I need protecting? Thanks, but if I needed

help from a man, you'd be the last one I'd come to."

I shook my head in mock regret.

"God forbid anyone ever suggests that Shelley Masters needs help. I've seen you in action and I know you can take care of yourself. Your stalking and IT skills could use some work though."

That sneer of hers became more menacing. I loved it.

"Let's not forget the fact that my family wouldn't be going through this right now if it wasn't for you and your dad."

That one hit me in the gut, but I didn't show it.

"And that's why I'm here now," I said, as if that made up for it all, and I moved closer to her, wanting to unnerve her. "So, don't bite my head off for keeping you informed. Isn't that what you wanted us to do?"

"There is such a thing as emails and text messages."

I laughed.

"You'd need to unblock my number for that."

I hadn't tried texting, but I assumed she'd blocked me in every way possible, and her smirk of a reaction confirmed that I was right.

I spotted a pen in the inside pocket of her bag that was slung over her shoulder, and I reached in to grab it. Then, I took her arm by the wrist and lifted it, twisting to expose the underside. I kept her wrist in my hand and pulled the pen lid off with my teeth. Then I began to write my mobile phone number on the inside of her arm.

"What are you doing?" she asked, but she didn't pull away.

"Making sure you have my number, so you can message me if you need anything."

I knew she had my number saved somewhere, but this

wasn't about the phone number, I was making a statement. It was also a good excuse to touch her again. Maybe the fact that she wasn't pulling away meant she liked it a little bit too, not that she'd ever admit it.

"I don't need your number. I'm sure you'll be lurking somewhere in the shadows if I ever want something."

"Isn't lurking in the shadows your trick?" I'd finished writing the number, but I couldn't seem to let go of her.

"I thought you said my stalking skills could use some work?" She turned her head to glare at me, and I pulled back slightly, looking from her eyes to her lips.

"Doesn't mean I want you to stop." I licked my lips, waiting to see how she'd react.

Her pupils dilated as she opened her mouth to reply, then closed it. She opened it again, then just gasped. I took that as my cue to make another move. So, I leant forward, brushing my lips over hers with a ghost of a touch before switching it up and planting a kiss on her cheek. Thing was, the minute I drew closer to her, she'd closed her eyes. But feeling my kiss on her cheek made her eyes spring open, and another breathier gasp escaped those full pink lips of hers.

"Why did you do that?" She touched her lips, and then frowned at me as I rocked back and forth on my heels and smirked.

"You said I needed practise. The last time I kissed you, I went all in and bombed out, so I figured I had to start simple and work my way up to the big stuff."

Her brows knitted together as she took a step away from me.

"Don't use me, Colton. I'm not your plaything, so don't make fun of me."

"Who says I'm playing?" I tried to give her my earnest expression, but it wasn't something I was used to, and I think it backfired.

"And don't patronise me," she hissed. "Don't follow me. And don't think for a second that I want your attention or your *practise*. I'll tolerate you while we find this Kenny guy, but anything else? Forget it."

She spun around and marched away from me. Her shoulders were tense, and I could tell she wanted to make a statement with her grand exit. But I couldn't let her have the last word.

"You know," I shouted out from the spot where I stood. "There is such a thing as protesting too much. And I hear there's a fine line between love and hate. Wanna walk that line with me?"

Her responding middle finger that she put into the air, without turning around or breaking her stride, made me throw my head back and laugh.

Seems we both got the last word after all.

We were a match made in heaven.

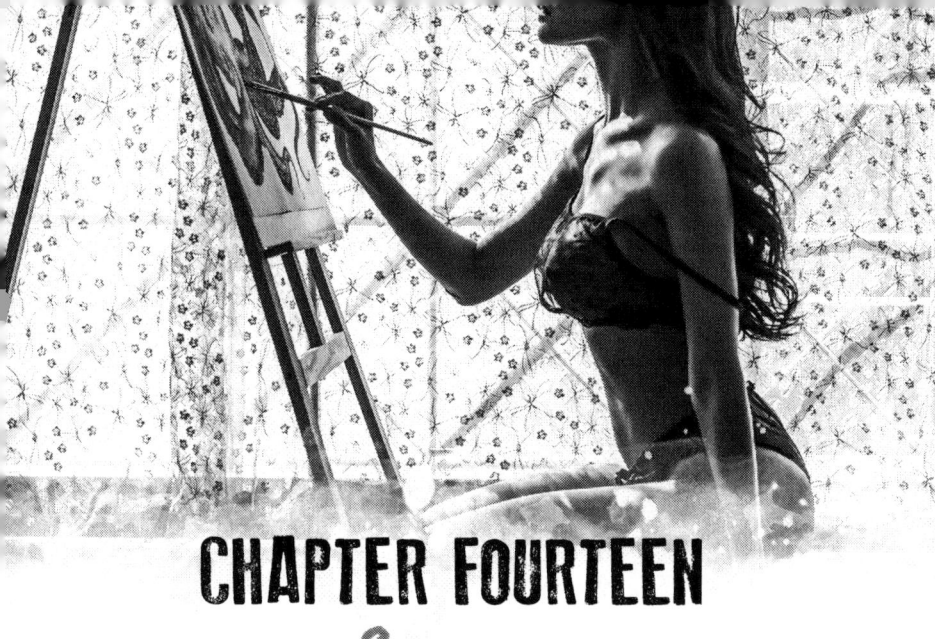

CHAPTER FOURTEEN
Shelley

I'd barely gotten through the front door when I was jumped on by Bryony and Kate. My wits weren't as sharp as they usually were, and I was blaming a dark haired, tattooed annoyance for that. All the way home, I was stuck in my head, thinking, 'Why didn't I walk away sooner? Why was I letting him get to me? Why didn't he practise his flirting on Gemma, seeing as she was tattooed on his shoulder for everyone to see?' An irrational thought, I know. I didn't care. He could tattoo the female population of Brinton Manor on his body, and it'd mean nothing. It wouldn't.

He needed to leave me alone, and I needed to remember who he was, and what he'd done to my family. Okay, not directly, but he was a King, and that wasn't a good thing as far as I was concerned. But the other half of me was antsy and anxious. Colton hadn't really been in the wrong, coming to tell me what was going on. Kenny could be around the next corner, watching where I was going, ready to plan his attack.

I'd been so focused on Colton and Kenny, I hadn't noticed my two sisters at my front door, ready to grab me.

"No time for chit chat, we need to go," Kate said, steering me backwards and out of the door, only giving me a second to put my art folder against the wall in the hallway before she shoved me out.

"What is that on your arm?" Bryony lifted my arm up as we bustled down the path, and found Colton's scrawled numbers etched onto my skin.

"It's nothing." I scowled and pulled away, dropping my arm to my side. I'd made no effort to try and rub it off since he'd done it. What was wrong with me? "It's just a phone number for one of my college friends."

Bryony didn't push it and Kate was too focused on getting into the car to care.

"Where are we going?" I asked, taking the back seat, while Bryony rode shotgun.

"We've been summoned by the mighty soldiers," Bryony said, turning around in her seat. "They didn't sound happy–"

"When are they ever?" Kate butted in.

"And they want us to meet them now," Bryony added. "Because whatever's gone down can't wait, apparently. That's as far as I got before they put the phone down."

"And of course, when they say jump, we ask how high from now on," Kate retorted with a sarcastic bitterness to her voice.

"No," Bryony snipped. "I thought about telling them to take a hike, but I figured we'd hear them out. They did say they were going to help us with our problem."

"They are the problem." Kate sped off, gripping the steering wheel and giving me a pointed glare in the rear-view mirror.

"It's probably to tell us that Kenny Byers is back in the U.K.," I announced, staring out of the window and trying not to count my unlucky blessings that I was about to go toe-to-toe with Colton again for the second time in one day.

"We already know that. Wait, did you speak to one of them today?" Bryony asked, turning her head to face me again.

I shrugged, staying quiet, because I didn't want to rake over my encounter with Colton. That was a conversation for another time.

"Whatever it is," Kate interjected, thankfully taking the heat off me. "We may as well hear them out. We've come this far."

Moments later, we pulled up to The Sanctuary, and as we did, we noticed the door open, and Adam and Devon came strolling out. They'd been waiting for us.

"Oh look, the welcoming committee," Kate said drily as she parked close by and turned the engine off.

We got out and then walked side by side towards the door they were standing next to with their arms folded, like a pair of demonic doormen.

"Nice of you to invite us," Bryony stated as we walked past them and headed into the building.

"Nice of you to bother turning up," Adam replied.

The door slammed shut behind us, bathing us all in darkness as we made our way down the corridor towards the main hall of the club. Devon and Adam's footsteps echoed behind us as they followed, like we were part of their death march.

"What is this all about?" I asked, craning my neck to glance behind me. "We already know Byers is back in the country, you

THE JOKER

don't need to drag us all the way here for that."

"Oh, it's better than that." Adam gave a sadistic smile as he spoke, and when we entered the main room of the club and saw the rest of the soldiers, along with a few of their club security, all gathered around a table with a laptop, he added, "Your game is up."

"What game?" Kate spat, like a rabid animal ready to launch an attack.

"You thought you were smart, didn't you?" Devon sneered. "Letting us believe you'd pack in the vigilante shit and stay out of Brinton. Focus on the blackmail and leave us to do our job." Devon was making no sense, but the other soldiers seemed to know exactly what he was on about, and when I chanced a look Colton's way, I saw that he was staring straight at me and shaking his head. He was as pissed off as the rest of them.

"We love a riddle, but yours are shit. Just speak in plain English and tell us what's going on," I said, losing what little patience I had.

"We can do better than that." Colton stood, hovering over the laptop with both of his hands laid flat on the table, then he gestured for us to come closer. "We can show you."

The three of us walked over to stand by the table to see whatever it was they wanted to show us. When Colton clicked the laptop to life, a photograph of a guy chained to some kind of dentist's chair, with half of his face hanging off, glowed back at us. His chest had been cut open, and his intestines were spilling out onto the floor. His wrists were slit, and his legs were covered in gashes and slices that'd been taken out of his flesh. As murder scenes went, it was messy, chaotic, and brutal.

"What the fuck is this?" I asked, pointing to the laptop and screwing my face up in disgust at whatever sick game they were trying to play.

"You tell us," Tyler replied, folding his arms, and each of them stayed still, waiting for a response. When they didn't get one, Tyler added, "A friend of ours in the force notified us of this hit today. They thought it was one of ours, only it isn't, is it? It's yours."

"Are you fucking joking?" I couldn't believe what I was hearing, and neither could my sisters, judging from their groans of annoyance.

"Do we look like we're joking?" Adam bit back.

I leaned forward to get a better look at the scene pictured in front of me.

"There isn't even a graffiti tag." I pointed to the empty space on the wall behind the guy in the photo, but that didn't mean shit to these soldiers.

"So, you decided not to make it obvious this time." Devon shrugged. "Doesn't mean it wasn't you."

"We don't even know who that guy is," Bryony said with exasperation.

"She does." Colton pointed right at me, and I glared back at him. What the fuck was his problem?

"I have no fucking clue who that is," I replied, keeping my eyes on him, hoping he could feel the burn of hatred that I was throwing his way. I couldn't give a fuck what the soldiers thought of us, but I wouldn't stand to be called a liar.

Colton sat back down like he was on a bloody holiday, his legs splayed out and his hands behind his head. He was loving this, whatever *this* was.

"That right there is, or rather was, Alex Cross. Clive to his friends."

I was still none the wiser, but I let Colton ramble on.

"He came to the club a few weeks ago, spouted his mouth off, made a few enemies, and then I made sure he was escorted from the premises."

"What has that got to do with us?" Kate asked.

"She was here that night." He nodded my way. "She saw it all." He pointed to the middle of the room. "Standing right there on the dance floor. She watched me have him thrown out. Turns out, Alex Cross was as easy with his fists as he was with his mouth. My friend Tom, the policeman–" He looked at me as he said that, as if it had an impact. "–He said the guy had form. He was the perfect target for us. Only we didn't get that job… you did. And we don't take kindly to anyone who makes a deal with us then tries to make us look like fucking fools."

"We didn't do it." Kate stepped forward, as if she was moving to protect me. "I don't give a fuck what you think or what Shelley saw that night, we weren't involved in that." She gestured to the laptop.

"Well, if you didn't do it, who did?" Colton replied. "Are you saying there's another vigilante group on the go? A trio of terror gangs in Brinton Manor? Or a lone wolf maybe?"

"That's not our problem," I stated.

"It is if we don't believe you." Adam moved to stand next to where Colton sat. "We're making it your problem."

"And we're not taking your bait." Bryony moved to stand with me and Kate. "If you don't believe us, that's your problem, not ours. We know we didn't do it, so maybe, instead of standing here arguing, your time would be better spent finding out who really did it, because it looks like you've got a killer on your hands. And a killer that the soldiers don't know about in Brinton Manor?" She shook her head and whistled. "That's going to make you look even weaker than you already are."

The soldiers glared at us like they were ready to explode, and we stood shoulder-to-shoulder, happy to let them. But it was Will who eventually stepped forward to break the deadlock.

"I believe them," he stated. "Why would they deny it? It doesn't make sense. The other hits, they wanted us to know about. Why would this be different?"

"Finally! A man that speaks sense," I said, narrowing my eyes on the one that grated on my soul.

"Sometimes." Colton smirked back at me.

"And they do need our help," Tyler reluctantly chipped in.

"We don't need shit from you," Kate barked, but I held my hand up.

"We aren't getting anywhere here. Obviously, we all have our issues going on right now. Let's try and focus on what we can salvage, before someone tries to kill someone else today."

Tyler began mumbling something about IP trackers and computer facial recognition, which went over my head. Bryony was nodding in agreement, adding in her own computer jargon as Kate hummed in support.

After a few minutes of crossed conversations and chaotic discussions, my sisters announced that they'd be happy to look at the evidence Tyler had collected so far. The group all made their way towards the stairs, but an arm reached out to grab me and pull me back.

"We'll be up in a minute," Colton called out as he held me in place, his front to my back, but no one replied. They hadn't even noticed we weren't following.

"There's a few more photos... want to take a look?" he whispered into my ear.

"You might be into horror porn, Colton, but dead guys don't do it for me."

"But you've got such a good eye for details." His words sent a shiver down my spine as the tickle of his breath wafted over my prickled skin. "I'm guessing you were the one that left the message on that guy Derek's eyes; you know, *we see you*."

I was, but I wouldn't admit that.

"And let's not forget the hidden messages in your artwork. Fuck the patriarchy."

Again, another one of my ideas, but I was staying quiet.

"Look." He pointed at the screen as we stood next to the table. "Do you see anything?" He stayed behind me but reached around to click onto another image. It was much the same as before and I had no intention of scrutinising it to help him. But moments later, he rested his chin on my shoulder like a fucking dog, and in a low voice, he asked, "What do you see, sweetheart?"

On instinct, I wriggled my shoulders to get him away from me and when he moved back, I turned to face him, ready to stand my ground. "One, I'm not your sweetheart. And two, I see nothing."

"Is me being near clouding your spidey-senses? Are you missing what's right in front of you?" he teased.

"What, that you're annoying and about three seconds away from having my elbow shoved into your ribs? Count yourself lucky it isn't my knife. I know how much you like to play with that."

"No, buttercup." His change of nickname made me tense.

"The message on his arm."

Colton brushed past me, making the hairs on my arm stand on end, and then he leaned down and clicked the mouse pad, zooming into the photo. And there, on the guy's arms were the words, 'This one's for you'.

"Whoever did this, they did it as a gift." He turned, giving me a heated stare. "Did you leave another gift for me, Catwoman?"

I reared back, my nose screwed up in disgust as I said, "One, I'm not playing the Catwoman to your Joker in this fucked-up little scenario. And two, we both know who likes to write on people's arms." I held up my own, that was still inked with his scrawl from earlier, as evidence. "Are you sure you didn't do this yourself?" I gestured to the laptop. "Something to impress the boys? Turn them against us and make yourself look good."

"I don't need to kill some fucker to look good, I always look good." He took hold of my arm and lifted it to look at his handiwork. "You didn't wash it off. I think you like me more than you want to admit."

The way he smirked a self-righteous, smug grin made me yank my arm away.

"I didn't have time. But I'll be washing it off later without writing your number down. Don't flatter yourself. I'll use the scrubbing brush, so it comes off quicker." I was losing patience fast. "Why did you drag us all the way here? You saw me today; you know that hit wasn't ours. Why am I even here?"

He took a step towards me. "Maybe I missed you."

"You saw me hours ago. Don't bullshit me."

Another step, and he was right in my space, his face close to mine. "Maybe I didn't get to say everything I wanted to say before."

"You did nothing but talk. What more is there to say?"

He reached up and ran his thumb along my bottom lip.

"Maybe I wanted another chance to practise my skills."

I wasn't going to let his gentle touch or his twisted words lull me into anything, so I moved my head and kept my walls in place.

"Why don't you practise with Gemma?" The words came out before I could stop them, and internally, I cursed myself for sounding like a jealous idiot.

I didn't even care, but I was acting like I did, and that pissed me off.

"Who the fuck is Gemma?" His screwed-up face was a picture of confusion, laced with a hint of patronising bewilderment.

I nodded to his shoulder. "The girl who's name you've got tattooed on you."

He jerked his head back and I wasn't sure if he'd laugh at me, but when he pulled his T-shirt down from the neck and said, "What? This?" pointing at the word, I felt like a prize dick.

There, in grey italic lettering, was the word 'Gemini'.

"Why would you have Gemini tattooed on you?" I asked, trying to hide my embarrassment.

"It's my sign. You know, the twins. Split personality. Two sides of the same coin. That's me. You never know which one you're going to get, but it keeps things interesting."

"Both sides are insane."

"How do you know you've seen both sides?" His eyes darkened, and then that cocky face of his glowed with pride. "You thought it was a woman's name?" He shook his head, then cocked his brow at me. "Were you jealous, Miss Masters?"

"I wasn't jealous. I felt sorry for her."

He didn't believe me, and his arrogance told me as much. Mind you; I wasn't convinced either. I was coming off as jealous, and I needed to have a word with myself and calm the fuck down.

"If you think I'd be stupid enough to have a woman's name tattooed on my body, then you don't know me as well as you think you do."

I was going to reply that I didn't know him and didn't want to, but when he turned and pointed to his butt, I shut my mouth, stunned into silence, waiting to hear what was coming next.

"I might consider getting 'Shelley Masters can kiss my ass' here though. Do you think that'd work?" He slapped his ass cheek for effect, and I felt my hackles rise.

"Do whatever you want with your body, but keep me out of it."

I turned to leave, but when I felt him reach for my arm to pull me back again, I stopped.

"I quite like this little game we're playing," he whispered in my ear.

"And I've told you, I won't play them anymore. Back off."

"Maybe you just don't like the rules? If that's the case, change them. I like a woman who can keep me on my toes."

I spun around to face him. "Colton, you and I seem to be drawn together, unfortunately, and there's fuck all I can do about it. I'm willing to work with you to help stop this motherfucker from destroying my family, after all, you do have intimate knowledge of our blackmailer, and part of me still blames you for bringing him to our door. But don't kid yourself into thinking it'll be anything else. It's business. That's it."

"Have you ever heard the saying; I think the lady does

protest too much?"

"My mum would have a field day with your lack of English grammar, but that's not even my main problem with what you just said." I took a step towards him, making sure I had his full focus. "Listen to me. I'll tolerate you, but this game you think we're playing? It's over."

He rubbed his chin in thought and then bent down and kissed my forehead.

If I'd thought he was an enigma before, then he'd turned into a total maelstrom of confusion now.

What the hell was that for?

"It was nice seeing you, Shelley," he said and turned to walk away from me, taking a seat in front of the laptop and tapping away as if nothing had happened.

I stood there dumbfounded, feeling like I should say something else, but not having the first clue as to what. So slowly, I turned and headed in the direction that my sisters had taken. As I did, I heard him mutter to himself.

"You're right on one thing, though. We are drawn together. And the sooner you admit why, the better."

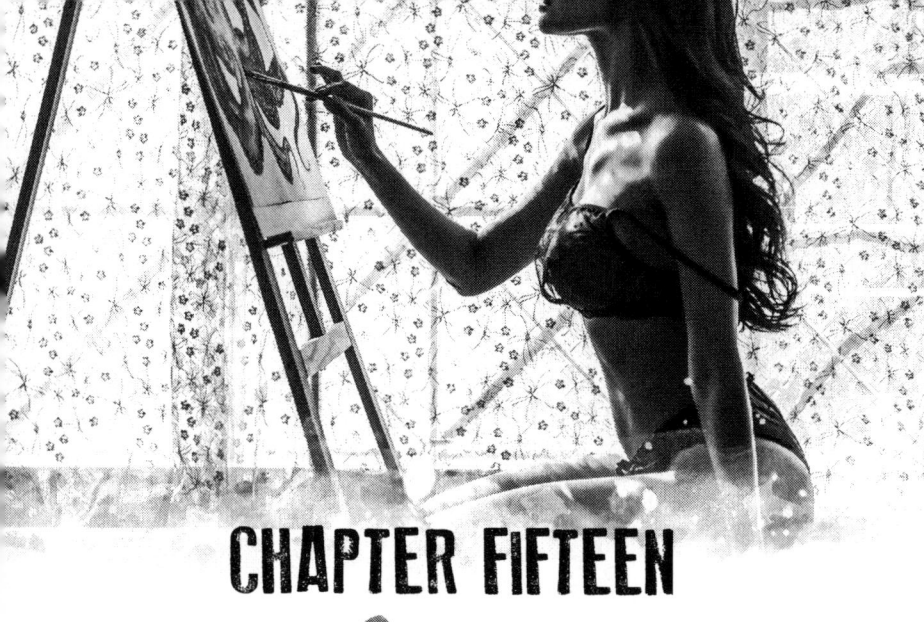

CHAPTER FIFTEEN
Shelley

To: BMasters@worldmail.com
From: oldfriend@email.com
Subject: Tick Tock

I've been a patient man, but time is running out. You have forty-eight hours to wire the money to me. Otherwise, this gets sent to everyone. Will your mum and aunt like going viral? I think you'll admit, we definitely filmed their good side.

Attachment 1
Attachment 2

We knew it was only a matter of time before he reared his ugly head again. When Bryony showed me the latest email, I wanted to call his bluff and tell him to shove his threats up his ass. But our loyalty won out and held us back from answering the way we wanted to. We couldn't even bring ourselves to open the attachments. Some things don't need to be seen, and that was one of them.

So, we did what we'd set out to do when the soldiers offered their help. We took it. Which in itself was a big thing for us because we didn't like being reliant on anyone. After a few exchanged emails, we decided to hang fire on replying to Byers. The Soldiers told us they had a lead on a place he'd been spotted recently, and the thought of confronting him there was far more appealing than sending a pointless email. Reluctantly, they gave us the address and we agreed, with their assistance, to check it out. Apparently, staking it out on our own wasn't an option, but we weren't stupid. Eight bodies, eight pairs of eyes, and two kickass groups of maniacs were better than one. Who'd have thought the Soldiers and Masters would ever be working side-by-side. Byers wasn't going to know what'd hit him.

***

The next day, we drove to the address on the outskirts of Sandland, ready to stake it out in the hope that Byers would show up. When we turned into the rundown estate and then onto the road in question, we could see why he was so desperate for money. The place was a shithole, and the houses here looked more like crack dens. We decided to park around the corner, not wanting to draw attention to ourselves, but when the back door of the car opened, we knew our cover was blown. Only, the person who got in and sat next to me in the back of the car, grinning like he was on a day trip to a theme park, was Colton.

"You could have texted your whereabouts," Bryony said, twisting in her seat to scowl at him.

He didn't care, though. He loved the attention.

"She's still got my number blocked." He thumbed at me, and then in a low voice, he said, "Still can't trust yourself around me, can you?"

"I can't trust that I won't gut you like a fish for pissing me off."

"I love it when you talk dirty."

I pulled my knife from my pocket and held it in my hand to show him. "Someone once told me if I use this, I need to make it count. I know where I need to aim to make it hurt." I glanced at his crotch to hit the message home but suddenly found myself blushing.

What the fuck was wrong with me?

He must've picked up on it because he chuckled and replied, "If you want to see what I'm packing, you only have to ask. No threats needed."

"The only thing I want to see is you squirm when I–"

"Children, please," Kate butted in. "We have a job to do. Can we focus on that?"

With him sitting so close to me, I couldn't focus on anything, but Colton snapped straight to business and leaned forward to tell us, "We've set up a lookout to cover every angle. Tyler is round the back, Will is stationed across the street, Adam has the left side neighbour's house and Devon is on the right."

"So, what are we here for, decoration?" Kate hit back.

"You're here to help. Tyler could use someone where he is."

"I'll join Tyler," Kate stated abruptly, ready to get started.

"Will's covering a pretty broad area too," he added.

"I'm on it," Bryony replied.

That left Colton and me.

"What are you doing?" I asked, expecting some crazy, stupid response.

"I'm going inside."

Trust him to give me an answer that'd have me on board in a nanosecond.

"Then so am I."

He cocked his brow in surprise.

"Don't get your hopes up, Romeo. I want to be at the heart of this thing. You tagging along is just the icing on the shit heap."

"Glad I can be of assistance."

My sisters had long since disappeared, taking up their posts to watch the house for any sign of Byers. We had our weapons and wits about us, and we prayed we wouldn't have to wait long to test them out.

"We've watched the house for a few hours, and we don't think anyone's inside, but we need to be prepared to fight in case we're wrong." Colton must've thought this was my first rodeo.

"I know how this goes. I'm not a newbie," I spat back.

"Just giving you a heads up. I could've been an asshole and sent you in blind."

"Why change the habit of a lifetime?" He frowned, so I added, "You're always an asshole."

"You love it."

I decided not to engage in his brand of crazy. There was a job that we needed to get done, and that's what I was here for.

The house we were staking out had all the curtains closed,

and the garden was surrounded by tall fir trees, which worked in our favour; as it gave us the privacy we needed to poke around without being watched. Seems we weren't the only ones who'd been nosing around though, because the wood on the frame of the front door looked damaged like it'd been forced open before.

Colton reached into his jacket and pulled out a hammer, then gouging into the wood, he managed to force the door open without much effort. Glancing behind us to check no one had seen, we both ducked inside, and I closed the door behind us, locking us in to whatever our fate may be. Colton glanced at me over his shoulder and held his finger up to his lips to let me know I needed to be quiet. I glowered back at him. I wasn't an idiot.

The downstairs was dark and musty, and none of the rooms had doors, but we still stepped cautiously to each one ready to face whatever was there. The house was silent though, and all we found in the rooms were floorboards scattered with empty beer cans, cigarette butts, and old food cartons. Taking the stairs, it wasn't much better up there. Dirty mattresses sat on the floor of the three bedrooms, and the bathroom was so disgusting it didn't deserve to hold the name. You'd leave it feeling dirtier than when you entered.

Once we knew we were alone, Colton's shoulders relaxed, and he wandered into the front bedroom, kicking the litter from the floor out of the way and standing at the window. He moved the curtain slightly, so he could get a better look outside, and then turning to me, he said, "It's a little rough around the edges, but I think if we put the work in, give it a lick of paint, we could make it work for us."

"This house is my idea of hell and being here with you only

heightens that."

He looked me up and down and added, "I like your T-shirt."

I was wearing a black T-shirt with a skeletal hand giving the finger and the words 'fuck you and have a nice day' written across it. I'd worn it on purpose.

"I think I have one similar," he remarked.

"I wore it just for you."

"Nice to know you think of me when you're getting ready in the morning."

He had an irritating knack of turning anything I said into something that amused him.

"Thinking about torture and murder is always a good start to any day, don't you think?" I replied, trying to turn the tables.

"But you still thought of me, however you sugar-coat it."

I had to stifle a smile at his attempt to sweet-talk me.

"So how long are we going to have to wait here until he shows? What did your guy tell you?" I was trying to bring the conversation back to something I felt comfortable with.

"He said he'd been seen around here. That he might've stayed here a few times. We'll wait for a while, see what happens, then check in with the others." He glanced to the side where I'd come to stand and peer out of the window, and reaching up, he took a lock of my hair in his fingers, wrapping my curl around it and smiling.

"Can you not touch me, please." I tried to pull away, but something inside was stopping me. I liked how he stroked my hair and looked at it like it was the greatest thing he'd ever seen.

"You know," he mused, biting his lip. "I don't think I can." He side-stepped until he was standing right in front of me and whispered, "I love your hair."

Words eluded me, and my breaths were coming in short sharp gasps that I tried to hide.

"Do I need to remind you about my newly acquired knife skills?" I stared at him from under my lashes, my heart racing with anticipation.

"Do your worst," he replied, moving closer to me, his lips an inch from mine. "I'd die a happy man."

And then he crushed his lips to mine, stealing my breath and injecting my body with the kind of adrenaline that made my toes curl. I gripped the front of his T-shirt like I was hanging on for dear life, my lips moving against his, and my mind shutting down. I didn't want to hear any internal arguments; all I wanted to do was feel.

His tongue swept into my mouth, sliding against mine, curling and caressing until I couldn't breathe.

This was the kiss to which every other kiss would always fail to live up to.

This was the kiss I'd never forget because, unlike the one he'd given me before, I was all in.

I groaned and felt my body melt into him as he kissed me, tasted me, and then when he groaned too, I moved my hands to grip the back of his head.

This was utter madness, but I was too far gone to overthink it.

Gently, he pulled away and pressed his forehead to mine. Slowly, I opened my eyes to find him staring at me, not a hint of humour in his eyes, only lust and something else I couldn't quite figure out. Admiration maybe? Need? Want? Whatever it was, I felt it too.

"Was that better?" he asked.

I couldn't find the words to reply.

"I like practising with you," he added. "Maybe we need to try that again."

I wasn't going to argue, and when he started to kiss me again, I opened up to him, taking everything he gave, as I raked my fingernails through his hair and then across his neck. The way he moaned showed how much he liked that, so I retraced my track, trailing over his skin until he pushed his lips against mine harder, kissed me with more depth, and then, he reached down to grab my ass and squeeze. Then, those hands took the backs of my thighs and lifted me.

I straddled him, wrapping my legs around his waist as he pinned me to the wall. He ground his hips into me, to show me exactly how much he was enjoying our momentary truce. I reciprocated, moving my hips in time with his. All rational thought had flown out the window. What the fuck were we doing? We were supposed to be watching and waiting for a motherfucking blackmailing piece of scum, and yet we couldn't stop ourselves or pull away.

His kisses were sparking a fire of electrical fever through me. My knees were weak, my body craving his touch. The wetness pooling between my legs made me squirm with need. But his moans and groans were what affected me the most. I loved that I was having this effect on him.

He kissed a trail down my jaw, then my neck, and I held onto him, tilting my head to give him better access. My legs clamped tightly around him, pulling him to me. My eyes were closed, revelling in the sensations he was eliciting from my body, when suddenly, I heard someone clearing their throat behind us.

My eyes snapped open, and I let my legs fall and drop to

the floor as I pushed him away. He was reluctant to stop. I don't think he'd even heard my sister, Bryony, clearing her throat, but when he saw my look of terror peering over his shoulder, he pulled away and turned around.

"Sorry to interrupt whatever *that* was." Bryony gestured to the two of us. "But we're gonna call it a day."

"We've only just got here," I said breathlessly, my mind a whirl of confusion.

"I know. But Adam spoke to a few of the neighbours, and they said no one has been at the house for a few days now. He showed them a photo of Byers and they hadn't seen him either. We could be here for hours for nothing. So, we've decided to take a different approach."

"What different approach?" I could feel myself growing agitated. The spell Colton had put me under was slowly breaking and I didn't like it.

"We're going to email him. Get him to meet us. Draw the rat out on our terms, so to speak."

I had to admit that did make more sense, and Colton nodded and hummed his agreement.

"Sounds like a better plan," he interjected. "Although, I will miss this."

"What? The stake out? Or eating my sister's face?" Bryony laughed wickedly. "I'm guessing you haven't swept the house for any clues?" She gave me a sly wink and added. "Too busy sweeping my sister off her feet, hey? And on that note, I'll leave you two lovebirds alone. Although birds of prey would probably be a more accurate description after what I just saw." She turned to leave. "Will and I will give this place the once over. Wouldn't want to disturb you two."

THE JOKER

I stood for a moment, watching her walk away, gathering my thoughts and regulating my breathing.

"You shouldn't have done that," I snapped, staring absent-mindedly at the floor as I touched my lips, and replayed the moment over and over in my head.

"I think that's exactly what I should've done." He took my chin between his thumb and forefinger and tilted my head so that I was looking at him. "And I'll do it again. Only next time, we won't get disturbed."

"There won't be a next time." I broke free of his grasp and walked with determination towards the door to follow my sister.

"There's always a next time with us, haven't you noticed that yet?"

***

Later that night, when we eventually pulled up in our street, we got out of the car and noticed something stuck to the front of our door.

"What the fuck is that?" Bryony asked as we walked down the path.

There was a white envelope taped to the door, and she pulled it off, twisted it in her hand, and then opened it. Inside were three photographs, images we couldn't ignore like the attachments sent with the email. This was another threat from Byers, and he was showing us how dark his threat really went, because we'd have rather died than let our mum see these. Thank God we'd come home when we did.

"Is there a note?" I asked, taking the envelope from her.

I checked but it was empty.

Bryony turned the photos over, and on the back of one was a scrawled message.

You think you can beat me? I hope you enjoyed your little stakeout today. But next time, you'll need to try harder. I can't be caught that easily.

CHAPTER SIXTEEN
Colton

It was a stupid plan. Hiding out at a place where he'd been spotted a handful of times and might never show again. A fool's errand by anyone's standards. But I'd been the one to suggest it because it felt like a good way to pull her over to my dark side again. The others didn't agree, but they humoured me. I think they were cottoning on to the fact that I had an ulterior motive.

This girl had a hold on me like nothing I'd ever experienced before. The more she pushed me away, the more I wanted her. Thing was, her version of pushing me away was confusing as hell because when she wrapped her legs around me and kissed me back, making those soft little moans, it sure felt like a pull and not a push. She wanted me; she just didn't want to admit she did. That wasn't something I was used to dealing with when it came to women, but it certainly made things interesting. Shelley

Masters was accomplishing something that no woman had ever done before. She had captured my interest, beguiled me, and I couldn't stop thinking about her.

***

A few days later, I was back at the art college where she studied. It was bustling with students, but it didn't take long for me to ask around and find out where she was. A group of girls pointed to a building on the edge of the campus where we stood and told me she was in the studios. It was a large glass building, and when I walked through into the lobby adorned with colourful paintings and sculptures, the security guard at the desk called me over to check me out.

"Can I help you?"

I didn't want to get on his bad side, so I used my posh voice. "I'm here to see Shelley Masters. She's in one of the studios."

He tapped away at his computer and then looked up at me over his glasses.

"And you are?"

"I'm her brother." I figured potential fuck buddy wouldn't go down well.

I thought he'd tell me to do one, judging from the silence that ensued, but after a while, he said, "She's in studio twelve." He stood up from behind his desk, and leaning forward; he pointed towards some double doors on the left. "Through those doors, straight down the corridor, and it's at the bottom on the right. Sign in here." He pushed a signing-in book towards me, and I signed, C Masters. Then smiling, I pushed away from the desk and headed to the doors. That'd been easier than I thought.

THE JOKER

I strolled down the quiet corridor with my hands in the pockets of my jeans, glancing at each numbered door as I got closer to where I wanted to be. Once I came to stand outside the door to studio twelve, I could hear the faint sound of music and singing. Moving my head to listen at the door, I heard Kings of Leon's *Use Somebody* blasting out. I hoped she was here alone. Otherwise, I would have to become even more of an asshole to get rid of whoever might be in there with her.

I turned the door handle and walked in, relieved to find her alone. The smell of the paint, the sound of her voice and mere sight of her made the butterflies in my stomach multiply and scatter. She didn't notice me at first, and for a moment, I was able to watch her in all her glory. Barefoot and dressed in an oversized white button-down shirt with paint splattered down the front. She wore her hair in a ponytail that almost couldn't contain all the curls. She puffed a few loose strands out of her face as she concentrated on the canvas in front of her and sang along to the song. I couldn't see what she was working on, but the way she bit her lip, cocked her head to the side, and gave delicate strokes with her brush showed how hard she was working. Seeing the concentration on her face made the hairs on the back of my neck stand on end. I could've watched her all day, but when she caught sight of me, she stopped, and her face went from a sublime, serene picture of happiness to confusion and then distrust.

"What are you doing here?" She put her brush down, and marched over to the radio to turn it down. "This is my workspace, Colton. You can't just barge in here."

"Who's barging?" I held my hands up in defence.

"I'm busy," she snapped. "I only have a few months left

to complete this piece for my final collection, and I don't have time for your bullshit."

"What final collection?"

She appeared to blush as she told me, "I'm showing my work at a gallery opening as part of my finals. Not that it's any of your business."

"What are you working on?" I stepped forward, hoping to catch a glimpse of what was on the canvas, but her eyes widened in fear, and she grabbed a sheet from the side and threw it over her work so I couldn't see it.

"Its private. I don't like sharing my work."

"You'll have to share it eventually, or are the visitors to the gallery expected to wear masks?" I smirked. "Sounds like my kind of gallery if they do."

"I'll be ready by then." She huffed. "For now, it's for my eyes only."

I stepped forward and noticed papers on the table beside me. The word Gemini caught my eye, and I picked some of the pages up to see what she'd been googling and printing off.

"You like my sign?" I quirked my brow at her, and she stalked over to me and ripped the papers out of my hand.

"I got inspiration is all. I'm doing a zodiac inspired piece. Don't flatter yourself."

"A piece inspired by me. How could I not be flattered?"

I held her gaze, neither of us willing to break the spell or look away. My heart was pounding, and I reached up to brush the delicate paint flecks on her cheeks, but as I did, the door flung open, and she took a step back.

"Eric, I forgot you were coming." She acted like I wasn't here and peered over my shoulder towards the door.

THE JOKER

I turned to see Eric, the friend I'd met the last time I saw her on campus, standing in the doorway holding two polystyrene coffee cups and grinning like he'd caught us naked.

"I got waylaid. Looks like I came at the right time though." He walked over to Shelley, and passed her one of the cups which she instantly discarded on the table, but he never took his eyes off me. "I'm Eric." He thrust his free arm out. "I never got chance to formally introduce myself last time... well, I did, but we seemed to get off on the wrong foot." I stared down at his hand then back up at him. "Shelley's told me all about you."

"I highly doubt that," I replied drily, ignoring his offered handshake.

"Play nicely, boys," Shelley interjected, but even though I knew Eric was gay, I still felt protective. He was here to take her attention away, and I didn't like that.

"I always play nice. You know me," Eric replied, placing his coffee cup on the table, then folding his arms over his chest, he looked me up and down. "You know, with all those tattoos, you're like a walking work of art." He laughed at his feeble joke.

I didn't.

Neither did Shelley.

"Have you ever thought about doing some live modelling? I'd love to sketch you."

"I can't say it's ever crossed my mind."

He bit his lip, and after a moment's thought, he added, "Models like you are really in demand these days. You have that unique look. Striking."

"I've been called many things in my time, but never striking," I replied. "Maybe you should think outside the box, pin me to the wall at your next art showing."

"Don't tempt me," Eric muttered, pushing his glasses up his nose with a suggestive twinkle in his eyes, and I threw my head back and laughed. This guy was growing on me. I liked his cheekiness. He was barking up the wrong tree, but I admired his sass.

"Okay. Thanks for dropping by, Eric. I'll call you later." Shelley bustled forward, nudging Eric towards the door as he called out his goodbyes over her shoulder. I guess she was more jealous than I was in this instance, which made me smile.

When she shut the door behind him, she leaned against it and closed her eyes, letting out a deep breath.

I expected her to come to her senses and tell me to leave too, but she didn't.

"Why are you here?" she whispered.

I wasn't entirely sure why myself. If I thought about it, I did look like a creeper. A little bit desperate, but maybe not totally hopeless, judging from the small sparkle I saw in her eyes as she looked at me from across the studio.

"I came to invite you to our Halloween night at the club." A lame response, but it was partly true. I wanted her there this year, and I had plans.

"You could've sent a text to invite us. You didn't need to show up here... *uninvited*."

"But where's the fun in that? And besides, you still haven't unblocked my number." I tried not to show that her keeping me blocked pissed me off by giving her a cute, lopsided grin. But she avoided looking directly at me and stalked over to where her paints and brushes were and started fussing over them. An avoidance tactic if ever I saw one.

"Poor Shelley," I mused. "Blocks me on everything but I still manage to appear in her dreams."

"Don't flatter yourself." She scoffed. "I'm not some weak, love-struck little girl. I'm just as strong as you, I can do whatever you can… I have done what you do," she said through her clenched jaw, referencing her talents for the vigilante life.

"You didn't do it as well as me though, did you?"

"Yes, we did." Her cheeks reddened as her hands fisted at her sides.

"Just think how fucking awesome it'd be if we did that together." I stepped towards her, and she scowled to show her distaste at the idea.

"There's only one collaboration with you that I'm interested in, and that's getting rid of Byers. You can forget anything else, and if you ever need to speak to me in the future, don't. Speak to Kate or Bryony."

I know that I told myself I liked the push and pull, but the push was starting to grate on me. I needed the pull from her to kick in before I did something crazy.

"But I'm not interested in getting to know Bryony or Kate."

"And what made you think coming here to see me was a good idea?"

Yeah, that something crazy inside me was about to go off, and I was here for it. She turned slowly as I walked over to where she stood. Her eyes were defiant, but the closer I got, the more she seemed to soften. When I came to stand right in front of her, she stepped back, leaning against the wall.

"It's fancy dress," I added, then took the collar of her white shirt in between my thumb and forefinger and felt the soft cotton between my fingers as I lost myself to the dirty thoughts swirling through my mind. "But I wouldn't complain if you turned up in this. You could come as the tortured artist." I leaned further into her and whispered, "I like seeing you like this... vulnerable."

She didn't speak, just took slow deep breaths as she looked at me, anticipating my next move.

"It suits you," I carried on, letting my fingers trail from the collar down to the first button, skimming my fingers delicately over the top of her chest, and feeling the goosebumps I left in my wake. "And I like pushing you out of your comfort zone. You're beautiful when you fight me, but you're fucking stunning when you submit."

I flicked the top button open, exposing the top of her chest, and I could just make out the pale blue lace underneath. She watched my fingers, her breaths becoming more ragged now as I slid my fingers under the cotton for a brief second before moving to the next button, then the next.

"Blue is my favourite colour," I said, coming to the last button, and then pushing the shirt open.

Her chest heaved as she took deep breaths, her taut stomach looking so fucking delicious, I wanted to get on my knees and taste her skin, feel her softness. But it was the tiny blue G-string that had my full attention, that and what lay underneath. I put my finger under her chin and forced her head up, so she was looking in my eyes.

"You're unbelievable," I whispered, my lips ghosting a kiss over hers before pulling back slightly so I could drink her in. She was perfect, and I stroked my finger down her neck, over her tits, taking a little more time there and brushing my thumb over her hardened nipples. But I wanted to feel all of her and take my time doing it. My hand grazed her stomach, and I felt her muscles tense, but the shallow breaths and sighs she gave told me she wanted this too.

We both stared with our foreheads almost touching, watching my hand trail down to her G-string, and I let the tips of my fingers dip slightly below the waistband, fighting the urge to pull and rip. I had to do this slowly. I noticed her eyes close, and I asked, "Can I touch you?"

She didn't reply, but I felt the nod of her head.

Gently, painfully slowly, I ran my fingers over the front of her underwear, and she shifted her legs slightly to accommodate me. I could feel her wetness through the lace, her heat burning from my touch, and I felt my dick straining in my jeans as I thought about being inside her; feeling her wrapped around me, squeezing me. Slow and deep or fast and brutally hard, I didn't care. I wanted it every way I could get it with her.

"You're so wet." My voice was gravelly, and I knew I was moments away from taking this to the next level. "So ready for me."

My hand was between her legs, my fingers aching to explore. I pushed the tip of my finger under the lace and ran it along the seam of her pussy, and she sighed. In long, slow strokes, I felt what I was doing to her, how wet she was, how much she wanted this. She rested her head on my shoulder as I pushed a little deeper, and then stroked up towards her clit. And as I began to circle, using my fingers to open her up to me, losing myself in the softness of her, she whispered, "Fuck, yes," and then…

Bang.

I was startled and my body jolted at the noise. Shelley yelped, and coming to her senses, she pushed me away. When I turned to see what'd made the noise, the guy from the front desk was standing in the doorway, glaring at us.

"Closing in ten minutes, Shelley," he barked, looking between us and giving me the evil eye. "You need to clear out. I wouldn't want to lock you and your–" he looked at me like I was a piece of filth. "–*brother* here into the building for the night."

For the first time, I saw Shelley truly blush, and she cleared her throat before spluttering, "He's not my brother. We were just… It's not…"

He held his hand up.

"No need to explain. I've seen it all." And with that, he turned around and walked away, leaving the door wide open.

Fucker.

Shelley's back went up, and she wrapped her shirt tightly around herself as she stomped over to the table to gather her zodiac research papers.

"You need to leave, and *that*… whatever that was, never happened."

I was tired of her bullshit and done with her telling me it wouldn't happen again, it was a mistake, and all that crap.

"It did happen, and it'll happen again." I waited for her to argue, but she didn't. She focused on the table, probably willing me to leave, but I wouldn't. Not until I'd had my say. "But next time, and I mean it this time, I won't get interrupted." She gave a huff, but I wanted to make myself clear. "And even if we do get interrupted, I won't stop."

I headed for the door and gave her one last parting shot. "I'll see you next Saturday, at the Halloween night. I can't wait to see what you wear for me."

She didn't like that and spun around, protesting that

THE JOKER

whatever she wore was for her and not me, but I smiled and walked away. I couldn't care less what she wore, but it was nice to know that she was going to come after all.

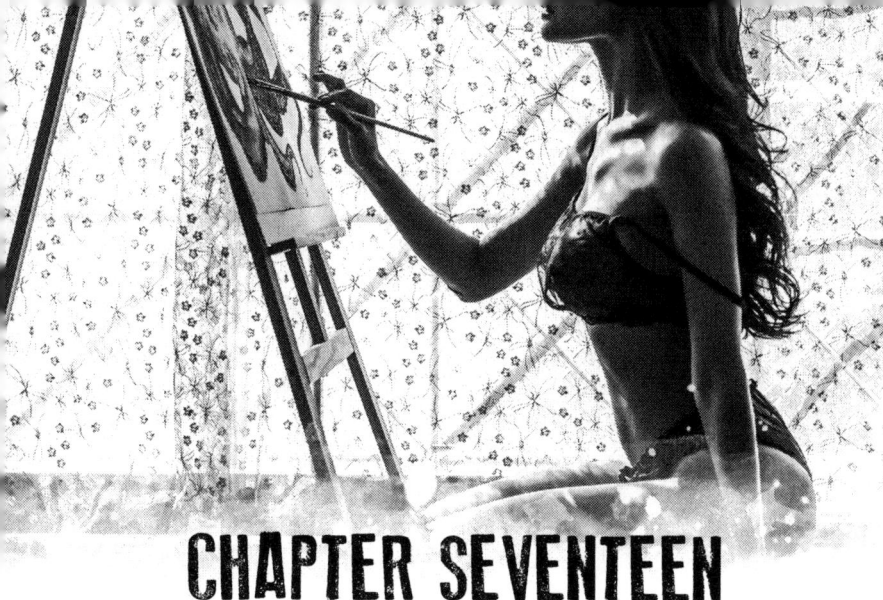

CHAPTER SEVENTEEN
Shelley

Why did I keep giving in to him?

Why did I let him play me like this?

I felt pissed and had to remind myself not to take it out on my art supplies as I cleaned and tidied away in the studio. It was getting dark outside, and I needed to get home and vent to someone about my nemesis because he was starting to get to me in a way no one else ever had.

Once I'd packed everything away, pulled my clothes out of my bag, and put my jeans and t-shirt back on, I hung my painting shirt up and picked up my art folder, heading for the door. I took one last glance around, then turned the light off, dreading the walk of shame through the foyer. But I needn't have worried. When I got down there, the guard wasn't manning the desk. With relief, I strode purposefully out of the door and into the dark, crisp evening.

There were a few students dotted around campus as I made my way across the courtyard. I kept my head down and focused on walking briskly and getting home as fast as I could. The light chatter from the people around me soon faded away, and all I could hear was the faint thrum of traffic in the distance and the wind rustling through the trees. This part of Merivale was quiet and deserted most nights, because it wasn't the best area, and most people avoided it. But for me, it was the quickest way home.

I debated putting my AirPods in and listening to some music but thought better of it. It was always best to keep your wits about you in this neighbourhood, and I'm glad I did because a few seconds later, I heard footsteps behind me. I didn't think anything of it at first. The footsteps were far enough away that I didn't panic, but as I increased my pace, so did they.

I turned my head to see if I could see anyone following me, but the street was dark, and no one was there. But as I faced forward and began to walk quicker, I could hear those footsteps again, a stark reminder that I wasn't alone.

Someone was preying on me, but I wasn't prey. I never would be.

Feeling my fight and anger surge within me, I stopped and turned around, putting my hand into my jeans to grab the handle of my knife.

"Hello?" I called out down the dark street to nothing but the cold night air. "Is anyone there?"

Silence.

I stood for a moment and waited, but nothing caught my eye, so I turned and started walking again, and there it was, those bloody footsteps.

I spun around, pulling the knife out of my pocket and I held it up in front of me.

"This isn't funny. I know someone's there. Is that you, Colton?"

I knew even before I'd said his name, that as twisted as Colton could be, this wasn't his style. It wasn't him.

"If you think you're scaring me, you're wrong. You should be the one who's scared. I know how to use my knife. Keep following me and you'll find out. Go on, try me."

I waited, but no one spoke.

"Byers," I added, my voice dripping with venom, "I'd love nothing more than to carve my revenge into your skin and then carve out your heart. So please, take another step and grant me my wish."

Again, silence.

Whoever was there knew I meant business, and I would never be a victim.

"Come out from the shadows," I dared them. "Face me. Be a real man." But who was I kidding? Whoever this was, they weren't a real man. They preferred to hide in the dark, murky corners of a deserted street. Or behind their computer screen.

"You're a dead man walking." I smiled as I spoke. "Follow me home, trace every step I take, I don't care. I'll happily lure you into my trap."

I took a moment to wait, then, keeping the knife in my hand, I turned and walked away.

No one followed me.

No one dared.

They knew I meant what I said.

Taunt me, tease me all you want, but I'm not weak, and I would have the last laugh.

CHAPTER EIGHTEEN
Colton

When I got back to The Sanctuary, I found everyone in the bar, and it looked like a meeting was about to go down. Jake was busy doing a stocktake, but everyone else was sitting around a table a little way off. The laptop was set up, and judging from their faces, they weren't happy.

"Let me guess," I said, parking myself on a chair next to Will. "You found out what I'm wearing to Halloween night, and you're all pissed because your outfits are shit compared to mine?"

A huff came from someone around the table and Tyler replied, "You're going as The Joker, like you do every year. Why would that bother us?"

"Ah! But which Joker? I could be political and go for the Joaquin Phoenix version or do one for the kids and channel my inner Cesar Romero. Maybe even go old school with a touch of the Jack Nicholson–"

"We couldn't give a shit which Joker you go as." Devon interrupted. "They're all the same."

I shook my head and gave him a pitying look at his sweeping misstatement.

"No two Jokers are ever the same. I could write a thesis on the merits of each one, and they all bring something uniquely twisted to the table. But this year, I thought I'd go for the Jared Leto style. Ledger is my favourite, but I wanted to try a different approach."

"We didn't ask," Adam deadpanned.

"You didn't have to. I'm an open book."

"As long as you don't copy his method acting and start sending us weird shit, we couldn't give a fuck," Devon added, then gesturing to the laptop, he said, "Can we get back to business now?"

I watched as Devon clicked onto images and angled the screen so I could get a better look. "Tom sent us these a few hours ago. There's been another one."

The photos showed a guy strapped to a bed; only the straps weren't doing a great job at holding him down, seeing as his hands and feet had been hacked off. The ligature that was still draped around his neck, and the way his face was swollen and purple showed he'd been strangled first before any of the other shit had taken place. He was lying in a standard bedroom that any guy our age would have, but his shirt lay open and carved into his chest with a knife were the words, *You're welcome.*

"Another message," I remarked, leaning forward to check the photos for other clues.

"Do you recognise him?" Adam asked, clicking to enlarge the frame so I could get a better look at his face.

"That's…" I pointed at the screen, trying to filter through the Rolodex in my brain for a name. "Ralf? Rory?"

"Ross Peterson," Devon stated helpfully, and it all came flooding back.

"Ross! That's the one. Thought it'd be a good idea to steal workmen's tools from their vans outside here, so I dragged him in and taught him a lesson."

"Looks like someone didn't think that lesson worked so took it upon themselves to right that wrong," Will informed us.

We hadn't had anything to do with Ross since that day. We didn't think he was a risk. Sure, he was a chancer, a petty crook who needed putting straight. But if crossing our path was what'd gotten him killed, then it was a fucking high price to pay in my opinion.

"How do you know this is linked to us?" I asked. It was good of Tom to send it to us. As a policeman, he was putting himself on the line, breaking protocol, and every rule in the handbook by colluding with us like this, but Tom was my old school friend, and I knew he always had my back.

"We don't," Adam replied. "But it's too much of a coincidence that the last two murders in Brinton were men who'd pissed us off."

"Most of the fuckers that live in Brinton piss us off. What's so special about them?" I asked.

The room was silent for a while, and then Tyler said, "We need to face the fact that this could be the work of The Masters."

I shook my head vehemently. Shelley and her sisters could be shady like us, but this wasn't them. I'd stake my life on it.

"There's no graffiti," I argued. "Nothing to tie them to this."

"They hate us. They might be working with us for the time being, but they want to bring us down. What better way than to pull some bullshit like this? How do we know they haven't planted our DNA at the scene. We can't rule anything out."

"I can. I know it's not them." I was going to die on this hill, and I didn't give a fuck. I might not be Shelley's favourite person, but she'd never do anything like this. I was sure of it.

The others started to grumble and argue the pros and cons, and conversations turned into a noise where no one was being heard.

"Okay!" Adam cut through the din, bringing the attention back to him. "Let's put a pin in The Masters for a moment. The messages on both of the bodies, Alex and Ross, were clearly meant as some kind of thank you. Both men had a run in with you, Colton. So, let's take another route. Kenny Byers."

"What about him?" I hated that man, and I still cursed the day I let him walk free.

"Well, we know he's back in the country. He's got zero morals, and maybe he thinks he owes you and wants to make amends the only way he knows how. The way he knows you'll appreciate. By killing random dudes that've pissed you off."

"That does make sense," Will chipped in.

It didn't to me.

"The last thing Byers would do is a favour for me." I felt my jaw tighten as I gritted my teeth. Even the thought of that man made me feel feral.

"We can't rule it out, though." Adam looked at each of us in turn, and in a low voice he added, "We need to keep this under wraps for as long as we can. Tom said the police are keeping it out of the press because they don't want to cause panic. If anyone finds out there's a serial killer in Brinton, it wouldn't be good."

"Understatement of the century, but I get your point." Adam didn't like my blasé attitude, but I shrugged it off.

"Having a serial killer in our town is going to make our lives a fucking nightmare," Devon stated. "But at least we know to be on our guard. If they're targeting our enemies, maybe we'd better make a list."

"Have you got all fucking year?" I replied sarcastically, rolling my eyes. "The world and his wife hate us; we've collected so many enemies we make comic book villains look like the good guy. And you want to make a list? It'd be easier to write down who does like us."

"Do you have any better ideas?" Devon spat, angry that I'd challenged him.

"Yeah. Let's find Byers and rule him out first. The sisters are setting up a meeting. When they do, we'll be there." The others nodded in agreement at my suggestion. "Let's be proactive not reactive. We still control Brinton Manor, despite what some weird-ass killer on the block might think."

"For the first time ever, I'm going to say, I think what Colton says makes sense," Adam said in support.

"Thank you, my friend."

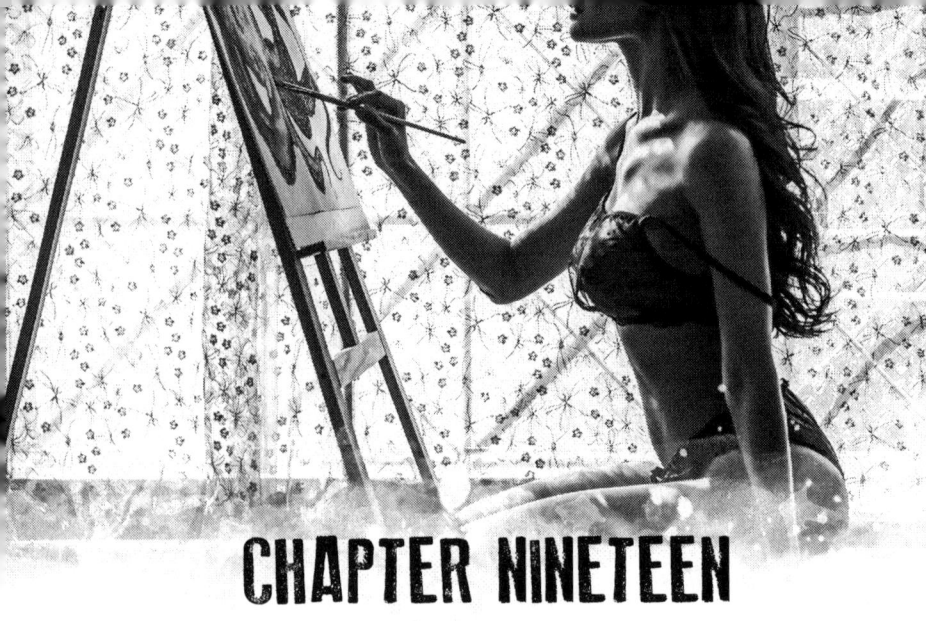

CHAPTER NINETEEN
Shelley

"He won't take the bait," Bryony informed me as she put the finishing touches to her Halloween costume for the soldiers' party tonight.

"Then make the bait more enticing," I told her, feeling increasingly irritated that this Kenny Byers crap was still hanging over our heads. After being followed home the other night, I was ready to put this bullshit to bed.

"I'm trying to think of another angle," she whined. "Asking to see him in person is pointless, he's not stupid. He knows everything is done online and he doesn't care. He just wants his money. He won't fall into our trap."

What she said was true; apart from one thing, Byers was old school, and no one was more important in his life than him.

"We need to think more like him," I replied, mentally trying to list all the things we knew about him, but there wasn't much to go on. "We know he's desperate for money, he likes sex, and has no morals." I counted each one off on my fingers.

"I don't think offering ourselves up for sex with him is going to do the trick."

I had my lightbulb moment.

"It might. Maybe we could tell him we've got a business plan of our own. Something that'll make King's empire look like an amateur outfit and we need his help. Three sisters who want to make porn but don't know how to get it off the ground… that'll get his sick and twisted heart singing. Money, sex, and misogyny all rolled into one. How could he resist becoming a part of that? Let him think he's doing us a favour, meeting us to offer his extensive expertise in the area. The guy has an overinflated ego, and we need to play on that."

"But he knows we hate what we found out about Mum and Rosie. Why would he believe that we'd be up for doing the same?"

"Because he's a narcissist, and if we butter him up, he'll believe anything. It's worth a shot, right? Nothing else has worked so far. I'm not sending that man a dime, and we need to coax him out of his hiding hole. It's the only way we'll get pay back. Our family deserves this."

I was hellbent on making this man pay, not only for the blackmail but for the years of abuse my mum and aunt had endured. Glenn King and anyone who worked for him were fair game. Nothing was off the table.

"Speaking of what we deserve, I hope you're going to have some fun tonight." Bryony gave me a pointed stare.

"I'm getting dressed up, aren't I? I'm forcing myself to go

to this thing. What else do you want from me?"

Bryony sighed and sank down onto my bed.

"I've seen the way you and Colton look at each other when you're together." She smirked and added, "I've seen the way you act around each other too. Don't deny it. You like him, and you can't help yourself when he's around."

I tensed, feeling myself morph into defence mode.

"I hate him."

"Hate fucks can work too, sometimes they're even better."

"I'm not going to hate fuck him," I argued, but my heart skipped a beat thinking about what that meant.

"Listen–" She tapped the space on the bed at the side of her for me to sit down. "–I know you find it hard to open up to people. Dad leaving affected you more than any of us. But you can't spend the rest of your life closed off from the world. Sometimes, you have to take a chance. You're happier with a knife or a hammer in your hand making enemies than you are trying to find happiness for yourself."

"I don't *make* enemies, I end them." I knew I was avoiding the subject.

"And since we started our crusade, I've loved it too. Who wouldn't want to show a mean motherfucker what us women can do? I think Kate might be a bit power hungry with it all, she's obsessed, but that's beside the point… I know that gives you something, but it's not enough. You need more in your life. Colton can be a cocky little shit sometimes, but maybe he could be the one to give you more. Let's face it, he's hot and he's made it perfectly clear he's interested in you, so what's the big deal? I say have a bit of fun with him. A girl has needs too."

"Needs that I'm quite happy to fulfil with a battery-operated boyfriend, thank you very much."

"But can a battery-operated dick tell you what a good girl you are and spank your ass as it pulls your hair?"

I had no words.

Well, I did, but using them would've exposed me, and I wasn't ready for that.

But when I stopped and really thought about it, did I still hate Colton? I found him irritating, self-centred, and he had way too much self-esteem, but hate? Was I learning to tolerate him?

"I have way too much on my plate. I can't deal with any more complications."

Bryony laughed and shook her head. "Colton is the least complicated person I've ever met. I'm pretty sure he'd agree to be your fuck buddy without any drama. He doesn't look high maintenance."

I don't know why, but that statement bugged me. Colton took the piss out of himself, and he'd probably be the first to say those things too. But hearing them from someone else, even if it was my sister, didn't sit well with me.

Fuck.

Was I offended on his behalf?

I was so screwed.

I didn't want to talk about Colton's low-maintenance, careless lifestyle, so I forced a change of subject.

"Not that I don't love your costume, but why did you decide to go as the little mermaid?" I asked her.

"Nice swerve off topic," she chastised, then flicked the hair of her red wig, and replied, "Isn't it obvious? All guys want to score with the mermaid. I think it's the whole tail and where's the vagina that draws them in."

It was my turn to shake my head.

"We need to get back out there and do more badass shit. You're forgetting who you are."

"Killers can be sexy too," she purred back, stroking her fake hair to one side and winking at me. "And don't think you're off the hook. I'm on a mission to get you out there, dating."

"Promise me you won't wink like that again tonight."

Bryony cackled, and gesturing to my outfit, she said, "Do you think he'll be pissed at what you're wearing?"

"I hope so." I couldn't stop myself from smiling smugly. "Winding up Colton King has become one of my favourite things to do."

"Try winding him up in other ways. That might be even better."

"Let's solve our Byers problem first. We don't need to invite any more complications into our lives."

I concentrated on braiding my hair as Bryony began tapping away on her phone. I had to admit one thing though, I couldn't wait to see his face when he saw me.

To: oldfriend@email.com
From: BMasters@worldmail.com

Subject: A New Proposal

I told you in our last email that we wouldn't pay your ransom, but I think I might have found a solution that suits all of us. You have something we want, but we have something that I think you'll be very interested in.

In exchange for the raw copies of the videos, we'd like to propose a business deal. We know who you are, and we know what you do. You know the sex industry and we want to break into it. We're three sisters who'll do whatever it takes. Together, I think we could take the adult entertainment industry by storm and we're willing to offer you a percentage of our earnings. With your expertise, we would make a killing.

If you agree to meet with us, we can discuss the logistics, percentages, everything that this could entail.
This is an opportunity you don't want to miss.

B Masters.

***

To: BMasters@worldmail.com
From: oldfriend@email.com
Subject: RE: A New Proposal

Do you think I was born yesterday? You drag your feet and mess me about over this and now you expect me to believe you want to buy my business skills?
You have one more week, and if the money isn't in my account by then, your family will be ruined.

Tick Tock.

***

To: oldfriend@email.com
From: BMasters@worldmail.com
Subject: Think smart

You're turning down a lucrative, life changing offer? And for what? To make a quick grab for cash?

Think smart.

Look at what we're offering you. We don't like the way our mum and aunt were taken advantage of, but our business model is different. Don't you want to be a part of something that could be incredibly lucrative? You were kings in the industry, back in the day. But with The Masters, you could be a God.

***

To: BMasters@worldmail.com
From: oldfriend@email.com
Subject: I'm listening

Email me your business plan.
Once I've read it, I'll be in touch.

CHAPTER TWENTY
COLTON

"Nice to see you're keeping up your Halloween tradition," Liv said as she waltzed into the living room, looking like a blow-up doll.

"It'll always be the Joker," I replied, glancing down at my white shirt that was open to showcase my tattoos. I had the untied bowtie and the braces on my black trousers to mirror the Leto look. The green hair was the icing on the cake. That, and the white face paint. "Who else would I be? And I see you've come as the blow-up doll Adam divorced after he met you."

"I'm Malibu Barbie," she stated, and I couldn't hold in my excitement.

"Please tell me Adam is Ken. That would make my fucking night."

"I tried." She laughed. "But he flat out refused. His outfit is

THE JOKER 245

much more… Adam."

Will flounced in, wearing nothing but a pair of red swimming shorts, and holding a red rescue buoy. "Baywatch!" he announced proudly and went to the fridge to get a cold beer. Neither of us answered because what the fuck do you say to that?

Tyler was next to grace our presence, and he wore the scowl to match his outfit. "Nobody fucks with Tommy Shelby," he said in a Birmingham accent, taking the pocket watch out of his waistcoat and adding, "I think the show's about to start, lads. Let's show these fuckers how it's done, the Shelby way." Then he pointed at Liv, Will, and me in turn. "Now remember you lot, no fucking fighting!"

"Why?" I goaded. "Because we can. And you know, if we can, then you can bet we fucking do," I replied, paraphrasing the great man himself.

"Who's fighting?" asked Devon, entering the room with Leah May right behind him. The perfect Sally to his Jack Skellington.

"Who *won't* be fighting if it kicks off?" I replied. "A computer beat me at chess once, but it was no match for me at kickboxing." I did a stylish kung fu kick to finish off my joke, waiting for a laugh. I didn't get one. "Fuck me, people. Lighten up. It's a party!"

"You know it's heaving with people down there," Liv stated, ignoring my attempts at humour and bouncing up and down on the balls of her feet. She was full of nervous energy. "I've seen about twelve Harley Quinns already." She waggled her eyebrows at me, but I shrugged.

"I think Colton's waiting to see what his favourite brunette shows up as. Probably the girl from *The Ring* if I know Shelley." Tyler laughed to himself.

"Or Wednesday Adams," Will chipped in.

"Oh, *now* you're all comedians." I rolled my eyes. "She wouldn't be that predictable," I told them, then smirking, I added. "But she would make an awesome Cousin It."

"A girl who speaks gibberish and can't see your cocky face. She'd be perfect for you." Liv cackled.

"She might not show up at all." It was a throwaway comment from Tyler, but my stomach twisted all the same.

"Well, let's get going and find out." I slapped my palms together, then rubbed my hands, and it was at that exact moment that Adam walked through the door, dressed head to toe in black leather.

"Holy fuck, dude. Have you come as the gimp from Pulp Fiction?" I could not stop laughing.

"Fuck off," Adam spat. "I'm Pinhead."

"You can say that again." I had to hold my sides, they hurt so much from laughing.

"From Hellraiser," Adam argued. "You know, Pinhead. The hell priest."

Tyler pulled his phone out of his pocket to google it, and when he started to read the description, I could not control myself.

"Pinhead is the main character in the Hellraiser movies. Also known as the hell priest. He is a cenobite in the order of the gash."

"I bet he fucking is. Order of the gash. Priceless." Adam wasn't impressed I was taking the piss, and I did feel a little sorry for him. He'd made an effort, making it look like he had pins in his face. But when a moment like this comes your way, an opportunity to take the piss, you grab it with both hands.

"I hope Liv's acupuncture kit helps with your stress. You might need it after tonight." I chuckled.

Liv tried to mask her grin and she pushed Adam's chest, forcing him to turn back around. "Come on, Pinhead, let's go. There's booze to be drunk and fun to be had," she said in her sing-song voice, and we all followed.

Pinhead.

I was going to enjoy calling him that all night.

I had a feeling this was going to be a night to remember.

I let the others walk ahead, hanging back because I wanted to take my time scanning the room below over the balcony on the first floor. Liv was right, the amount of Harley Quinns was fucking ridiculous, and a few noticed me looking down and waved, giving me a look that told me they were mine tonight if I wanted. But I didn't wave back. I wanted to find her, not a cheap replacement.

The place was packed, and the strobe lights made it difficult to focus. But then, as if some weird force was in play, I saw her, and the rest of the room fell away.

I couldn't see anyone but her.

She was standing to the side of the dance floor, her eyes darting about like she'd lost something or someone. The rare vulnerability she had in that moment made something in my chest constrict, and I took a second to compose myself. And then, when her eyes lifted and she caught sight of me standing at the top of the staircase, that look changed to one that showed she'd found what she was looking for.

Me.

Knowing that made the hairs on the back of my neck stand to attention. Warmth spread through me like hot treacle; gooey and sweet, and so not my usual style. This woman was turning me into a sap, but I was helpless to stop it. In a room full of fake Harleys and harlots, she was all I wanted.

I took each step of the staircase slowly, keeping my eyes on her as she walked towards me with the same curious intensity.

"You came." It wasn't my finest moment or my greatest choice of words, but it was all I could muster as I came to stand in front of her.

"Bryony insisted," she replied nonchalantly, like her being here meant nothing. We both knew that was a lie. This was a huge step for her. "Jared Leto's Joker," she said, checking me out.

I held my arms out. "That's me, the clown prince, or should I say, the clown king of crime. The Jester of genocide."

She glanced behind her at the heaving dance floor, and over the beat of the music, she asked, "Are you disappointed that I didn't come as Harley Quinn or Catwoman?"

"Are you fucking joking?" I laughed, looking her up and down, appreciation making me grow hot under the collar. "People seem to forget that Joker treated Harley like shit sometimes. And one thing I'd never accuse you of is being predictable."

From her black thigh-high boots to her leather skin-tight body and black mask, she was fucking perfect.

"Before you ask, I'm the Batman. Not Batgirl, or Batwoman. Batman." She peered down her front and said, "See? No tits, just a six pack."

"I really hope that's not true when the suit comes off," I

joked, and she rolled her eyes and scoffed at me.

"You're such a..."

"Red-blooded male? Human?"

"I was going to say chauvinist pig, but whatever."

We stood in silence for a moment regarding each other. She'd plaited her hair so she could wear the mask more comfortably, and I reached forward and picked it up, stroking my fingers along the silky twists. "I like the plait, but I like it when you wear your hair down. I love the wild look."

I'd said the wrong thing again, and she pulled her plait from my grasp.

"I dressed for me tonight."

I knew that was a lie. She'd picked that outfit for a reason, and that reason was me. But I held my tongue, fighting the urge to give her another sarcastic or flirty comment that would go down like a lead balloon. Instead, I decided to talk about something I knew–Joker.

"You know, you picked the perfect outfit."

"How so?" She tilted her head to the side, challenging me.

"Joker might like Harley Quinn, but it's the Batman he lives for. Without Batman, there is no Joker. Without Joker, there's no Batman. Everything Joker does is to force Batman to become a better, stronger version of himself. They're the yin and yang of the comic book world. I'm not saying it isn't a complicated relationship..." She huffed her agreement, but I carried on. "Joker is flawed, but so is Batman. He might be a superhero, but he has no actual superpowers, and that makes him more vulnerable, more human." I took a step towards her. "When you look closer, Batman and Joker are eerily similar, and yet, they're poles apart. Rivals that're two sides of the same coin, sublime symmetry." And then I shrugged. "Everyone knows that."

"I didn't know that." Her eyes were wide, and the way they shined back at me made my heart twist. That wall she always kept in place when she was around me was crumbling, I could tell, and I didn't want to waste a moment longer in case it shot back up again.

"We've set up a fairground outside. Do you want to come and see? We've got a Joker's Fun House."

"Okay," she said, her voice breathless, softer than before. "Lead the way."

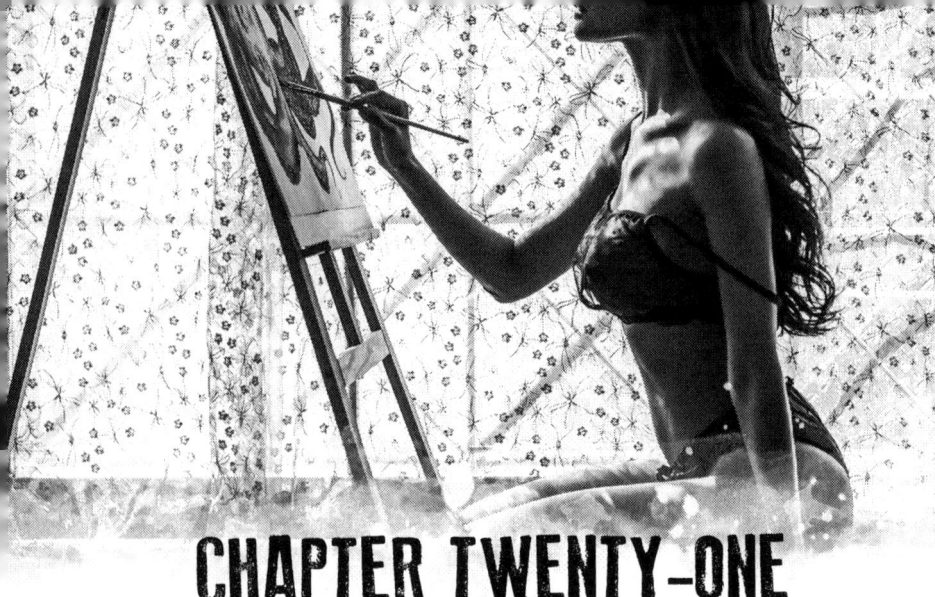

CHAPTER TWENTY-ONE
Shelley

Mesmerising.

Magnetic.

Hypnotic.

All words I never thought I'd use to describe Colton King, and yet, when he caught my eye on the stairs and walked down to meet me, that's what I felt. It was like the whole room fell silent, and all that mattered, all that existed was him. I noticed a few girls and guys gazing up at him as he descended the stairs, desperate to catch his eye, but he didn't notice them. He kept his gaze on me, and that gaze was like nothing I'd ever felt before.

When Colton looked at you, you felt special, beyond special. And tonight, I was the lucky one. It was like he was the sun, moon, and all the stars lighting up the darkness of my life. I hadn't felt that in a long time, not since my father had left.

Being near Colton, holding his attention was pure magic. He had the power to make you feel better about yourself, just by being nearby. But that was what scared me the most.

How would I survive when he walked away? I knew what it was like to lose that light, and the thought of going through a loss like that again terrified me.

But as I stood watching him walk towards me, I remembered Bryony's words.

Have fun.

Live a little.

Be happy.

I hadn't been happy for a long time, and maybe I did need to let go. Feel the sun's warmth on my face, even if it was for a short while. Fleeting sun was better than eternal darkness.

I tried to keep my walls in place for as long as possible, even though they were flimsy and cracked. But when he started to talk about Batman and Joker with such honesty and passion, I saw a glimpse to another side of him. A deeper, more meaningful side. One I didn't know existed. We all wear masks in our lives, something we can hide behind that helps us cope and protects us from the harsh realities of life. But maybe his whole life had been lived behind a mask. Perhaps mine had too. Could we be more alike than I'd ever realised?

He invited me outside to see the funfair, and I followed him through the dark. I'd have followed him anywhere. I felt powerless to stop the pull he had on me.

The club was heaving with wall-to-wall partygoers, making it hard to move easily as we pushed our way through, but he made sure I was near, never letting me out of his sight. My stomach twisted as I noticed people around him drink him in with their sultry stares, and it made me feel jealous. In this moment, he was mine, not theirs. But he didn't notice them. He had one goal, to get me outside to the fairground.

Once we stepped outside and the cool night air washed over us, I breathed in, glad to be out of the crowds. Then I saw all the lights, the colour, everything that was set up out here, and my eyes didn't know where to look first. The field at the back of The Sanctuary was alive with laughter, music, and people.

There was a coconut shy, and other stalls with revellers crowded around, cheering on whoever was playing, hoping to win one of the cuddly toys that hung on display. The smell of popcorn, burger vans, and doughnuts wafting through the air made me hungry and nostalgic. There were carnival rides and squeals of delight coming from every corner. I couldn't deny it; the soldiers knew how to throw a party.

Colton was standing next to me, giving me time to take it all in.

"Do you like it?" he asked as if my approval meant something to him.

"I love it." I gasped, my eyes darting from one attraction to the next.

I felt him reach for my hand, and I let him, too dazed to pull away or argue like I normally would. I was tired of fighting whatever this was.

Holding my hand in his, he led me down the field, pointing things out as we went. We walked past the big wheel, and he asked, "We could go on there later. Have you seen the movie Fear?"

I shook my head to answer no, peering up in wonder, lost for words.

"It's not a rollercoaster, but I'm sure I can make it work."

He sounded so mischievous, and I knew there was a hidden meaning in what he was saying, and for once, it didn't irritate me.

Tonight, I wanted to be a different Shelley. The old Shelley. Being out here with the magic and wonder, it made me feel things. Things I wanted to lose myself in.

We stopped in front of a building with a massive clown face. The eyes lit up to entice us in, and the gaping mouth acted as the entrance. Above it was the words, 'The Joker's Fun House'.

"Do you trust me?" he asked, leaning close to my ear and making my skin prickle.

"No," I answered. "But I'll go in anyway."

"Good answer."

I loved the way his eyes twinkled as he spoke. Forbidden promises reflecting back at me. It made my heart race and my stomach flip.

As we walked through, I gazed up at the smiling face we were stepping under. Cackling laughter played through the speakers and dry ice drifted across the floor to add to the eerie effect of it all. And in that moment, I realised that I did trust him. I wouldn't have come here if I didn't.

"Is this a ride?" I asked, not sure what to expect.

"It's a walk-through experience," he replied. "Full of tricks and surprises." And on a whisper, he added, "It'll bend your mind in the best way."

Those goosebumps that hadn't disappeared since I got here multiplied. I had a feeling I wasn't going to leave this Fun House in the same way I'd entered.

The first part of the experience was a shrinking corridor

that tricked you into thinking the walls were getting smaller. A little bit Alice in Wonderland meets Charlie and the Chocolate Factory, only bathed in The Joker's favourite shades of purple on the wooden panelled walls. As we went further down the corridor, the cackling laughter followed us. Everything here was an optical illusion, just like him. Once you moved forward, you couldn't go back, and nothing felt the same, but you couldn't stop. You wanted to find out what was coming next, what lay at the end.

"Batman and Joker, walking hand in hand. Bet no one expected to see that tonight," he said, and I peered down at our joined hands.

"Are you going soft on me?" I whispered back.

His eyes glittered with wicked intent as he said, "If I thought that was what you wanted, then yes, I would." He stopped and turned to face me, lowering his head into the crook of my neck. "But I don't think that's what you want."

I swallowed, feeling him everywhere, from the prickle of my skin to the pounding of my heart. The flutter in my stomach to the warmth in my veins. No one had ever made me feel this way before. I was drowning in Colton King, and I never wanted to come up for air.

He moved to look me in the eyes, as if he was speaking right to my soul, telling me the words I'd always dreamt of hearing. "You're the kind of girl that wants... no, *needs* a man to work for it. Make the effort. Because in the end, you are worth it. You've fought for everything in your life, you want someone who's going to fight for you. Fight with you. To show you the kind of strength that proves he's in it for the long haul. You need a man that'll stick around, not a boy who runs. Someone who can handle the heat. And you know what? I've lived my whole life in the flames of hell."

My throat was dry, my pulse racing as I tried to calm my nerves. "Where did all that come from?"

"I know you, Shelley Masters." The warmth of his voice matched the heat I felt in my heart. "I see you for who you really are. You push people away, because in the long run, it's better that way. It saves you the heartache when they eventually leave. But not everyone leaves. Not if you give them a chance."

He sauntered ahead, like he hadn't just dropped a bomb on me. I took a few deep breaths, my head telling me to call him out for his bullshit psychoanalysis, but my heart was in total meltdown, wondering when he'd become the guy that finally saw the truth. I was selective with who I let in, because after watching the one person I idolised walk away and never return, I'd always felt that I had to.

Was Colton about to become the one to break the fucked-up cycle?

"Everyone leaves eventually," I said, waiting to see what he'd say.

He stopped in his tracks and spun around to face me.

"What are you so scared of?" He took long, slow strides towards me and frowned, reached up with his thumb and forefinger, and tilted my chin so he could stare down at me. "You can kill a man, but you can't trust one?"

"Trust is earned."

His eyes burned, and I watched his Adam's apple bob as he gruffly replied, "Haven't I earned it?"

The intensity of his stare made me nervous, and I stepped back, then walking forward to go through the door to the next part of The Joker journey, I called out, "You're getting there." It was all part of the game, toying with him, but I wasn't as confident in my response as I usually was. The rules of the game had changed.

"Oh, I'll get there," I heard him mutter under his breath. "You can count on it."

We came into another corridor filled with gold-framed cartoon paintings of the villains from the DC world that he loved so much. Each one with eyes that followed you wherever you went. The lights above us flickered, giving it a haunted house feel, and the misty smoke followed us, curling around our feet as we delved further into Joker's den.

"Why the Joker?" I asked, running my fingers along the walls as I strolled past each image. "Why is everything such a joke to you?"

He didn't answer right away, and I thought maybe he was ignoring me, or he'd make some sarcastic comment eventually. When I reached the end of the hallway, I stopped and turned to find him standing at the other end with his arms folded tightly over his chest, his face twisted in what looked like confusion. The deep lines on his forehead told me he wasn't sure what he should say.

"Be honest with me," I encouraged, and he sighed.

Then he walked over to where I stood.

"A wise person once told me it's better to laugh at the world. It's a cruel place, and if you show weakness, they'll eat you alive." He let his arms fall to his sides. "Laugh and the world laughs with you. But if you cry–" He shook his head and breathed sharply through his teeth. "–The sharks will come circling. They can smell fear and sadness as well as they smell blood, and they feed off it. They fed off me once, but never again."

"You play a role?"

"Don't we all play a role in life? The dutiful daughter. The helpful friend. The attentive niece. The supportive sister." He stopped right in front of me, gave my plait a gentle tug and whispered, "The vengeful vigilante."

I lifted my chin defiantly. "I like my roles."

"I like them too, but what about a role that's just for you?" His words breathed gentle promises to me, and I closed my eyes, savouring his closeness. "Don't you want that? Don't you want to feel something else? Something forbidden? Something that makes you feel good."

I could barely breathe, and slowly, I tilted my head, waiting for that first brush of his lips, feeling the gentle tickle of his breath so close to mine, and then, it was gone.

"There's more to see," he said over his shoulder as he walked off like he didn't just have me in the palm of his hands; his for the taking. "Come on. I want to show you the hall of mirrors."

And like Alice down the rabbit hole, I followed.

How could I not?

As we entered the hall of mirrors, you could hear the echo of other people's screams of laughter reverberating around us as they made their way through the maze of mayhem. On instinct, I put my arms out in front of me and felt my way through. Ahead, I could see Colton's reflection, a glimpse of different aspects, different angles of him. Each mirror showing that he was focused solely on me and wearing a massive grin on his face. My head started to pound as my mind played tricks. I thought I didn't mind being teased like this, that it wouldn't affect me, but it did. He was everywhere and nowhere, and I didn't like it.

THE JOKER

Which Colton was real?

Where was he?

Why was I so frustrated that I couldn't get to him?

I pushed ahead, reaching out to touch him, only to slap my palms on a cold, hard mirror. I heard him laugh, and so I turned, grabbing for him again, but the cool glass of another mirror was all I got.

"Where are you?" I called out, feeling anxiety surge through me.

"I'm right here," he replied, and I spun around, lifting my arms to touch him where he stood, but it still wasn't him, only a reflection.

It was starting to feel like a sick joke. I could see him, but I couldn't get to him. He was there, but was he really? I didn't like the way this illusion was playing with my mind, and then my heart stuttered in my chest as it all changed.

"Stop panicking. I'm right here," he muttered in a low, sultry voice, and I felt the warmth of his arms wrapping around my waist from behind. "I'm always here," he whispered, and then I felt him pull me backwards.

There was a click, and all of a sudden, we weren't in the hall of mirrors anymore; we were in a dark corridor. The glow of a single red light on the ceiling was the only light we could see.

"Where are we?" I asked, my breath coming in rapid pants as I looked up and down the corridor to find it deserted.

Everything felt eerie and forbidden, and I sensed a war of emotions building inside me, telling me I wasn't safe. I needed to get out. But he was still holding me from behind, and without thinking, I reached down to thread my fingers through his. I liked the comfort he gave me. With him, the fear became something else. A risky fear that I craved. I wanted to experience everything with him. Why follow him down the rabbit hole if you aren't willing to open your mind to what lies ahead?

"We're in the backstage area," he whispered. "The escape exit, if you like. Don't worry, no one comes back here. No one can see us."

"What about the red light?" I gestured to what I thought was a camera of some kind.

"It's just the emergency light. Nothing else."

I heard a scream and moved my head in the direction it came from.

"No one can hear us either. They're too busy finding their way out of the maze. Having their own fun." His voice was so close, his lips grazing the shell of my ear. "Their screams will mask our own."

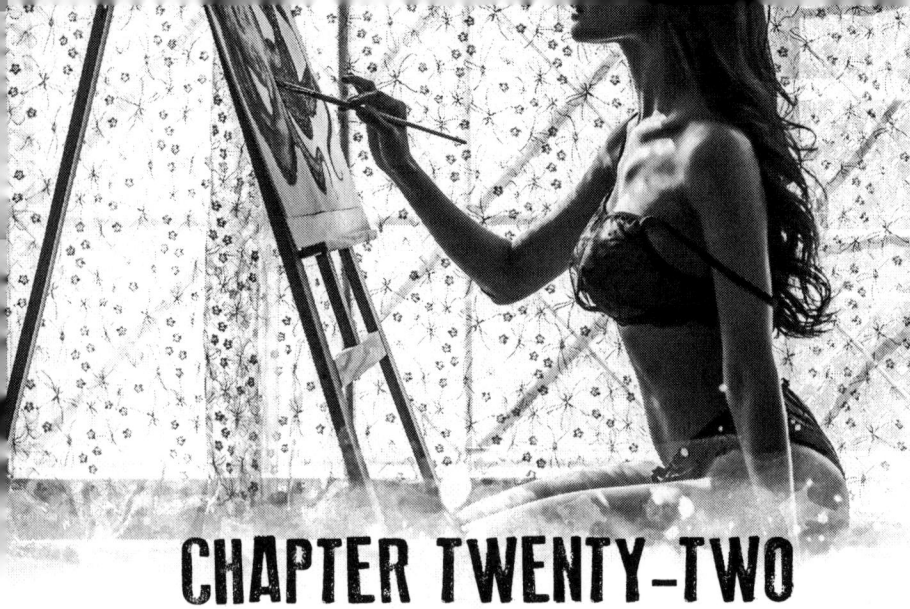

CHAPTER TWENTY-TWO
Shelley

The way his words made my stomach flip had me craving more. The feel of his arms around me, hugging me from behind, was too much but not enough. Was I really going to do this? Could I ever stop it?

"I need to hear your words." Colton's gravelly voice whispered in my ear, "Do you trust me?"

I leant back into him, my face turning to seek him out. "Yes."

He held me tighter and asked, "Do you want me?"

I'd never wanted anyone in my whole damn life more than I wanted him in that moment.

"Yes." I took a moment, and clinging to the last little bit of pride I had, I said, "I still hate you, though."

"That's okay." I could hear the playfulness in his voice.

"You don't have to like me to fuck me."

"Don't keep me waiting then."

I wanted to drown myself in everything he made me feel. Switch off from the world and join him in that space between make-believe and utter euphoria. Live for just a moment in a bubble where only he and I existed.

He nuzzled into my neck, peppering kiss along my jaw, across the shell of my ear, and I sighed, closing my eyes to savour the feeling of the delicious shiver that washed over me.

"I want you, Shelley Masters. I want to worship every gorgeous inch of you."

I pushed myself backwards into his body, showing that I wanted that too, and then he laughed.

"As much as I love your outfit, I have no fucking idea how I'm supposed to get into it. Why do you always have to make things awkward for me?"

I gave a low chuckle. He was right. It wasn't the easiest suit to slip in and out of. "Because I like making you work for it, remember?"

I took the mask off and unclipped the cape, throwing them both to the floor. Then over my shoulder, I told him, "There are poppers at the bottom of the body suit." I could've popped them open myself, but I wanted his fingers on me.

"Will you keep the boots on? I fucking love the boots," he growled.

"Hell yes," I gasped, desperate for his touch.

His lips trailed kisses down my neck as he reached from my waist down to the poppers between my legs. I was so hungry with anticipation that I almost couldn't stand it.

"Please," I begged, pushing my hips back into him as I held

onto the wall in front of me.

"So needy. I always knew you'd beg for it."

"I'll make you beg next," I warned him.

He yanked the poppers open with force.

"No underwear. I like it. Then his fingers ghosted over where I desperately needed them, tracing a delicate pattern on the inside of my thighs. All the time, I was squirming in his grasp, aching for more.

When his fingers finally touched my pussy for the first time, I let out a seductive moan, loving how he slid the tips of his fingers up and down. The way he groaned when he found out how wet I was for him made me pulse with need. His fingers stroked then circled my clit, and I rotated my hips slowly, gently, chasing the high he was about to give me.

"I love how wet you are." His voice in my ear sent shivers down my spine. "I need to taste you. Keep your hands on the wall and bend over." He commanded.

I did as he asked, but when he pushed down on my back to get me to the angle he wanted me, that pulse between my legs turned into delicious sparks. "Don't keep me waiting," I begged, opening my legs a little more.

"As if I would."

I could feel him moving behind me, kneeling, and then he pushed the material of the body suit up, giving him full access. My ass was on display, my pussy throbbing with need, and then, when I felt the first flick of his tongue feather across my clit, I cried out.

He used his hands to pull my ass apart, and I bent down further, crazy desperation burning inside me. He buried his face between my legs, his tongue lapping at my centre. Tasting me as he moaned his appreciation. Every lick made me cry out. My hips pushed back into his face wanting more, more friction, more movement.

"Fucking delicious," he growled, and then his tongue flickered over my clit again before he clamped his mouth over me, sucking me, coaxing an orgasm out of me. His fingers circled my pussy as he lapped at my clit, and then he pushed one inside, stroking my walls.

"Oh fuck, yes," I cried, my legs shaking as I clung onto the wall. "More, harder."

He slid his finger out, then I felt the stretch as he pushed inside again, two fingers this time, pumping into me, fucking me as I rocked back and forth on this hand.

"Soak my fingers," he moaned. "Then come on my tongue. Give me everything you've got."

"Oh, God, yes." I let him finger fuck me roughly as I rocked in time with his sharp thrusts. And when I was close, I cried out, "Fuck, Colton, I'm gonna come."

A few more pumps of his hand and then he pulled away, switching back to his mouth. His face pressed deep into my pussy, but I didn't care. I ground against him like my fucking life depended on it, out of my mind, trying to reach that high. And then, I came. An explosion erupted inside my pussy, my walls clenching as my clit throbbed hard and warm liquid oozed out of me. My legs were shaking and my body tingling. I'd never come so hard in my life. I panted, rocking on his tongue to milk every last sensation out of him.

"Fuck." He gasped, pulling away, then I felt him gently kiss my pussy before he slapped the side of my ass. "You taste like fucking heaven."

I couldn't speak, all I could do was pant.

"I'm so fucking hard, I really need to fuck you now." I felt him lift slowly behind me, and with care, he reached out to take hold of my arms and pull me up to stand. I was a pool of lust, melting on the floor right there in front of him, and yet, I wanted more. I needed it.

I turned and put my hand around his neck, pulling him to me to kiss him. As our tongues teased and tangled together, I could taste myself on him. It made my desire spiral again, and as he ground his jeans against my naked pussy, I felt myself turn feral, grabbing his bottom lip between my teeth and pulling.

"If you're going to fuck me, fuck me hard," I growled at him, and his eyes lit up.

"It's the only way I know how, sweetheart," he replied with a devilish smirk.

I reached down to pull the buttons of his jeans open and slid one hand inside to feel him.

"Holy fuck." I was not prepared for what I felt, and as he smirked, I looked down and pulled his jeans and boxers over his hips and thighs to see what I'd just felt.

"Do you like it?" he asked smugly.

"Colton. You have a bionic penis." I half gasped, half chuckled.

"It's a Jacob's ladder, baby. Stairway to heaven."

I didn't doubt him for a second.

"I've never seen one before, but why doesn't it surprise me?" The smile on my face grew as I thought about what it meant for me.

"I did think about getting a tattoo here," he said, stroking his fingers below his navel. "Ribbed for your pleasure."

"Oh God, please don't." I shook my head. I was ridiculously turned on, and yet he still had the power to infuriate me. I ran my fingers along each metal bar on his dick, right up to the tip and then took him in my hand and pumped up and down with slow strokes.

"You can be a little rougher," he said, his eyes penetrating mine as his hips pushed forward. "Grip me harder, I don't bite."

So, I did what he asked, pumping his dick until he gasped. "Okay, we don't want this to be over too soon." He pulled his hips back, releasing himself from my grasp. "Do you want me to fuck you from behind?" he asked, stroking himself with his eyes hooded and his breaths slow and deep.

I had to admit, that idea was so fucking tempting, but I shook my head. "I want to see your face when you come."

His head fell back, and he groaned. "Fuuuuck. How did I manage to find a girl so fucking perfect for me?" Then he snapped his head back, and that smile that used to spark the fire of fury inside me ignited me in a different way. I wanted to rock his world.

He took a step towards me, pinning me to the wall and rested his forehead against mine. "Whatever happens next, I want you to know, I will never forget tonight."

"Neither will I." I sighed, growing needier by the second.

Then he squatted slightly, grabbing the backs of my thighs to lift me. I smashed my lips to his, my arms wrapped around his neck as he reached down with his hand to position himself at my entrance. As he slid inside me painfully slowly, I felt each piercing rubbing against my sensitive skin. It was the best feeling ever, to be stretched and massaged in a way I'd never experienced before. I knew I would never recover from this.

When he was fully inside me, I felt him twitch and throb. This was going to be fast and hard, and I couldn't wait.

I clung onto his shoulders as he growled, "Hold on, baby. I'm going to fuck you so hard I want the whole club to hear you screaming."

And then he pulled out and slammed back into me, ramming me against the plaster as he thrust into me harder and harder. Our hips ground together as he pounded into me. The piercings hitting my G-spot at the perfect angle as his pelvic bone hit my clit and made me cry out in ecstasy.

"Say my name," he demanded as he powered each thrust into me. "Say my fucking name."

"Colton." I gasped.

"Whose pussy is this?"

"Yours."

I clung to him, crying out as the next orgasm hit me, and when my walls contracted and gripped him, he growled and slowed down a little, savouring the way my pussy was milking him.

Wave after wave of pleasure, and then he started to pick up the pace again. Our bodies moulded together as he fucked me. Our combined moans filled the air around us. His hips were relentless as he thrust harder and harder.

"You feel so fucking good," he cried as he pushed into me, and then he stopped, holding himself still, filling me completely.

He started to roll his hips, rotating and rubbing me, circling from the inside. I'd never felt anything like it. It drove me crazy. The piercings and the way they grazed my walls was unbelievable. I could barely breathe. The sensation of his hips fused so close to mine; I couldn't get enough.

"Oh yes, don't stop," I cried, moving against him to match his rhythm.

"I want to mark you," he groaned. "Make you feel my cock for days. Do you like that?" He kept rolling his hips. "Do you like the way I'm fucking you?"

"I love it," I moaned, and then, out of nowhere, another orgasm exploded. "Fuuuck." I felt my legs weaken, and I dug my nails into him as my body shook.

Colton gasped as he held me up, his head buried in my neck and his cock stretching, filling me in the most mind-blowing way. When he started to thrust into me harder again, I clung to him.

"I'm so close," he groaned, his hands kneading my ass as he held me in place.

A few more thrusts and I felt him thicken, and he let out the sexiest moan I'd ever heard as he came hard inside me. His hips slowed and he kept his head buried deep in my neck, gasping, "You're fucking amazing. So fucking amazing."

We stayed pinned together for as long as we could, holding each other against the wall, hidden from the world, coming down from the incredible high that'd had us spiralling in some hedonistic euphoria. A heaven that was all ours.

But in reality, could we ever recover after what we'd just done?

Lines had been crossed. Words had been spoken. And feelings? I was too scared to admit to myself what it all meant. But I knew after tonight, things would never be the same again.

Colton rested his forehead against mine, and in a low voice, he whispered, "I think this could be the start of something."

I didn't know what to say, so I replied, "That was something, all right. I think we've just detonated an atomic bomb that's gonna rip through both our lives."

His eyes shone wickedly as he said, "Don't you know, there's beauty in destruction."

And before I could stop myself, I blurted out, "And pain."

He cocked his head, studying me carefully before he said, "There's pleasure in pain."

I sighed.

"Do you have an answer for everything?"

He smirked, and what he said next made my whole body spark to life.

"I *am* the answer to everything."

PART THREE
And then, there was you.

CHAPTER TWENTY-THREE
Colton

The morning after Halloween

"That's one Halloween I won't forget in a hurry." Will shook his head regretfully. "I mean, she was dressed as a fucking mermaid, for Christ's sake, and I was a lifeguard. I thought it was the perfect opportunity."

It was a Halloween I'd never forget either. In fact, I'd been playing it over in my head on repeat since it'd happened. After everything, I'd asked Shelley to stay, but she'd refused. I wasn't surprised. She obviously wanted a one-night thing, and usually, that's what I preferred too, but not this time. This time, I felt different. I was curious about where this could go. She'd talked about bombs and destruction, and yet, when she'd walked away, getting into an Uber with her irate, dripping wet sister, I felt like I was the one doing damage control, and not because of Will's monumental fuck-up. It was damage control for myself, because watching her leave hurt, and that'd never happened to me before. I knew I wanted more than one night, and it felt strange, wanting something and not getting it. Like the roles had reversed. I wanted to open up and find out more about her, but I wasn't sure she wanted the same thing, because she was as closed off as they came.

"How was I to know she couldn't swim?" Will's whining broke through my daydream, and I watched as he picked up a hammer and smacked it against the chapel's brick wall in anger, putting a dent in Devon's treasured sanctuary. "I fucked it up before it'd even started."

"There's better things than the fucking wall to take your anger out on in here, mate," I told him.

Will, Tyler, and me had drawn the short straw. We were on morning duty, tidying loose ends from the night before while Devon and Adam slept off their hangovers. One of those loose ends was currently strapped to a chair in the chapel. He'd been here all night. After trying to steal money from one of the stalls, we'd brought him in here to teach him a lesson, and the first lesson had been patience. We'd left him alone for twelve hours while we got some sleep. We were in no hurry. We'd get to him when we were good and ready.

"You never know," Tyler said, picking a scalpel from Devon's collection. "She could be playing hard to get."

"He picked her up and threw her into the fucking duck pond at the bottom of the field. That doesn't exactly scream romantic come-on, does it?" I laughed. "But if hard to get means drowning in filthy pond scum and then screaming obscenities at you as she storms out, then yeah, she nailed it."

"It was a joke." Will stormed over to the guy shackled to our chair, watching us like he was at a fucking tennis match, and smacked the hammer off the chair frame, making the guy scream and jolt like he'd been given an electric shock.

"If you'd dunked one of us, it'd be a good joke," I said. "But come on, mate. She was at a party, she'd gotten all dressed up, and you threw her in the fucking water. Even I wouldn't go that far."

"It made her notice him." Tyler shrugged.

"It made her hate him," I replied.

"Maybe you could send something to apologise," the tied-up dude chipped in.

"Who the fuck asked you?" I snapped back, giving him an evil glare.

"I was drunk," Will moaned. "And I figured a bit of role-play would be a laugh." He screwed his face up and threw his head back on a sigh.

"You need some tips on how to role-play with women, mate. The first floor would've been better for that, not the fucking duck pond." I smirked, taking a baseball bat and stepping towards our restrained guest.

"Speaking of role-play," Tyler interjected as he tapped the scalpel, checking its sharpness. "How did it go between you and Batgirl?"

"She was Batman, not Batgirl," I replied, feeling irritated.

"She was fucking hot, is what she was." He grinned and waggled his brows, and in that moment, I wanted to smack him in the face for talking about her. For noticing she was hot. I didn't have a jealous bone in my body, so what the fuck was

THE JOKER

that about?

"We made progress," I said to shut him up, surprised that for once, I didn't want to discuss my sex life. Usually, Will would've called me out on it and pushed for more, but he was so lost in his head, stressing over his fuck-up with Bryony, he wasn't even listening.

"The Joker scored with Batman." Tyler laughed.

"I've read fan-fiction about those two hooking up," chained up guy said, and I lost it.

"Put some fucking tape over his mouth. I don't want to hear another fucking word from him." I pointed at him, striding over to where he sat and glared right in his face. "And count yourself lucky its only tape. If you'd done more than thieving, I'd be cutting your tongue out."

Will slapped some duct tape over his mouth as he thrashed in the chair and shook his head in protest.

"Bet you wish you'd kept your thieving hands to yourself now, don't you, Mark?" Tyler jeered at him.

"Mark? That's his name?" Tyler nodded at me, and I turned to glare down at him. "There're brainless dickheads, and then there's you, Mark. The idiot who thought it'd be a good idea to come to a soldiers' party and steal from them." I tutted and slowly shook my head. "Bad move, Mark. Very bad."

Tyler came to stand next to me, then leaned down and pushed the scalpel against Mark's forehead. "Shall I carve the word twat right here on your forehead?" he asked.

Mark shook his head, giving muffled cries from behind the duct tape, tears streaming down his face.

"I think Will needs to break his thieving fingers with his hammer," I sneered and swung my bat through the air. "While I knock some sense into him."

"I'm not a flowers kind of guy, but do you think I should send some?" Will asked, frowning in confusion, totally oblivious to where he was and what we'd just said.

"I think you need to get your head on straight and stop obsessing over a bloody woman," Tyler spat back. "Even Adam wasn't this bad. He never let anything get in the way of his soldier work."

"I'm not obsessing," Will argued.

"Good." Tyler nodded and smiled. "Then use the hammer and lose the guilt. It's done. Get over it."

Will lifted the hammer and Mark yanked on his restraints, screwing his eyes closed as he waited for that first strike, but just as he was about to hit, Will stopped and announced, "I should go and apologise in person. That'd be better than flowers, don't you think?"

"For fuck's sake!" Tyler ran his hands through his hair and gripped hard. "Am I the only one taking this seriously?"

"I'm serious," I replied, lifting my bat and whacking it into Mark's legs, making him cry out and jerk in pain. Then, focusing on Will, I said, "You need to use those four beautiful words every woman wants to hear… 'Sorry I fucked up'. Isn't that right, Mark?" I gave him another whack and grinned as he writhed in pain.

"You're right. I'll do that." Will stared blankly from us to the door, then threw the hammer onto the table and walked away.

"Where's he going?" Tyler groaned, gesturing to the empty doorway.

"Does it matter?" I shrugged. "Let's get this over with. We've all got things to do, and I'm sure Mark doesn't want to be here any longer than he has to."

Mark nodded furiously; his eyes wide with fear. In a few hours, it'd all be over. We wouldn't kill him; we'd just mess him up enough to know he couldn't fuck us over. Then we'd send him on his way so he could tell the rest of Brinton what he'd learned.

I think we'd all learned a lesson this Halloween. Will realised you couldn't treat a woman like one of your mates, if you wanted her to actually like you. Tyler learned that sometimes it's hard to focus when other things are playing on your mind; we're not all machines. Devon and Adam learned that whisky chasers would be the death of them.

And me?

I learned that maybe I wasn't the player I thought I was. There was a heart in there somewhere, and slowly but surely, it was starting to warm towards a girl who seemed to mirror the coldness I used to feel. I never thought I'd want to be with someone or have a relationship. But since meeting her, that idea didn't seem so bad. After living my life one day, one hit at a time, I was excited for the future.

CHAPTER TWENTY-FOUR
Shelley

I'd be the first to admit I wasn't the most chilled person, but since our night together, I'd reached a whole new level of stress that I didn't know was possible. Warring thoughts circled through my brain constantly, questioning anything and everything.

Shit, I'd overstepped the mark.

Had I done the right thing hooking up with him?

Why had we gotten involved with them in the first place? We hated them, and I knew we could sort the blackmail out ourselves; we didn't need help. Or maybe we did?

What was I thinking, making it more complicated than it already was? I hated complications.

I was starting to piss myself off, and I knew the next time I saw him, I'd do everything I could to keep my game face on. I was a strong woman. It was just one night. A bit of fun. Nothing needed to change.

But I felt different.

I had changed.

Because of him.

I heard my mum shout her goodbyes from downstairs, and I called out my own as I lay wallowing in a bath full of bubbles and my ridiculous overanalysing.

The front door slammed shut, and I closed my eyes, letting the warm water soothe me, getting lost in the bliss of nothingness. But when the gentle, crackling sound of the bubbles popping and my deep breaths were interrupted by the creak of the bathroom door, my eyes shot open, and I tensed.

I was alone.

So, who the fuck was opening the door? Because it wasn't the fucking wind.

I had nothing in here I could use as a weapon, and my adrenaline spiked through the roof as my heart pounded. I grabbed the edge of the bathtub, readying myself to haul ass out of there and fight. When I whipped my head to the side, I let out a startled yelp as I saw a grinning Colton standing in the doorway.

"What the fuck are you doing here?" I said, startled.

He glanced down at the bubbles that hid my naked body, then back at me, and took a step into the bathroom, closing the door behind him.

"How did you get in?" I snapped, pushing him to answer me. I had visions of him climbing through a window or scaling the side of the house. I wouldn't put anything past Colton. He was a liability on a good day.

"Your mum let me in," he answered casually, and I narrowed my gaze at him.

"Why?"

"Because she trusts me, and she knows I'm not a deranged psycho."

"You mean she doesn't know *yet* that you're a deranged psycho."

"Ouch." He pressed his hands over his heart. "That hurts, Shelley. I might be a little crazy, but full-on psycho? Nah. I leave that to Adam." He shook his head, grinning as if I'd said the most ridiculous thing, and took another step closer to where I lay. "But if I was a psychopath, I would've bypassed the door and come in through the window."

I glanced at the open bathroom window, and as if he could hear my thoughts, he said, "I did think about it, actually. It seemed like a cool way to surprise you until I thought it might be someone else in here. So, I guess that makes me part psycho. The thought was there, but the final execution had more finesse."

"If you call tricking my mum into letting you come in here, finesse," I replied with a hint of sarcasm.

He came to stand at the side of the bath, then crouched down, so we were face to face. His cool, minty breath fanned across my face, and I held my breath, waiting to see what he'd do or say next.

"There were no tricks for your mum," he said on a whisper, licking his lips and glancing down at the bubbles again. Then looking back at me, he added, "I've saved those for you."

"Why are you here?" I asked again, sounding exasperated, even though I felt anything but with my heart thumping an erratic, expectant beat.

THE JOKER 283

The sparkle in his eyes made my toes curl, and the way I lay there, vulnerable and naked as he kneeled, fully clothed, felt forbidden, exciting, like he could do whatever he wanted, and I'd be powerless. I kind of liked it.

"I like sex," he stated without a hint of shame, only a prideful smile. "And you're the only person on this planet that I want to have sex with."

I spluttered through my answer. "Wow! You really know how to sweet-talk a girl. Am I supposed to be flattered by that?"

He lifted his arm, dipping his fingers into the bubbles and swirling them around the surface. "Let me rephrase that," he said softly. "I don't want anyone else. I only want you."

"Is this your way of saying you want to be exclusive?" I asked, trying to sound calm as my chest pounded and my body tingled from his closeness.

"I'm not asking–" His eyes darkened as they bored into mine, his fingers dancing across the surface of the water. "–I'm telling. I've had a taste and I want more. I know you do too. Don't lie. You can't help yourself around me."

I huffed, smiling at his cheek and shaking my head at his nerve. "We had one night. It's very presumptuous of you to think that means you can stake your claim."

"I staked my claim well before that night. You did too. Don't think I didn't notice how jealous you got when Eric flirted with me." He sighed, his fingers tracing a delicious stroke up the side of my arm to my shoulder. "And you can argue all you like; you know it's true."

I wanted to argue, but all I could do was hold my breath as his fingers marked a delicate line from my shoulder to my neck and then my jaw. Then he used his thumb and forefinger to tilt my head to the side, and he leaned forward and kissed me. He might be a cocky, confident shit sometimes, but he was right. I couldn't help myself around him.

I closed my eyes, letting the softness of his lips and the feel of his desire take me away. He always tasted so good, and I opened up to him, tangling my tongue with his, taking what I wanted.

He teased me, sliding his tongue over mine, making my body crave more as he let out soft, gentle moans that drove me crazy. I moaned too, to let him know I felt the same way. Deep down, I did want more. So much more. When he pulled back, I gave a soft cry. I wasn't ready to feel the loss. I didn't want this to end. He placed his forehead against mine, and I watched as his gaze fell from my eyes to the water below.

"No need to ask if you're wet for me," he whispered, with a twinkle in his eyes.

He moved back slightly and rolled his sleeves up, making the butterflies in my stomach erupt with excitement. I knew what was coming and I wanted it so badly.

He placed one arm behind my head on the edge of the bath and put his face close to mine. His breaths were ragged, warming my neck and sending goosebumps through my body. I heard the trickling sound of the water as he used his other hand to reach for me, his fingers gently stroking the wetness of my chest before he dipped them under the water. I sighed and arched my back as he took my breast in his hand and massaged hard, making me moan breathlessly. I edged into his hand as he tweaked my nipple, rolling and twisting it between his fingers.

"Do you like that?" he asked, knowing full well from the reaction he was getting that I did.

I nodded, a breathy 'yes' spilling from my mouth, and he moved to the other side, kneading and groping, watching his hands as he bit his lip and breathed a little deeper. Seeing his large, warm, tattooed hand take what he wanted, play with me in such a commanding way, made me wanton with desire. I started to squirm, and he chuckled.

"So eager. I'll take care of you, baby, don't worry. I've got you."

I turned to give him a pointed stare.

"It isn't like you to be so… gentle." I held his gaze, my eyes begging him to unleash that hungry beast I'd seen on Halloween, and he smirked back at me, letting his smile spread wider across his face. I knew then what I'd done. I'd given him permission to be as rough with me as he wanted. That thought made my butterflies turn to sparks of electricity, firing me up inside.

"I like to mix it up a little, but it's good to know you can handle me," he replied, and his hands moved with determination down my body, skimming over my stomach, and then sliding between my legs. "Open your legs wide for me," he commanded. "I want to finger fuck you the way you deserve."

I did as he asked, letting my knees rest on either side of the bathtub, watching his arm disappear in the bubbles. When he touched me, running his fingers up and down, and circling my clit, I let out a throaty groan and lifted my hips. I loved how he played with me, always so needy and a little rough, like he couldn't hold himself back.

He slipped a finger inside and began stroking me, his thumb circling my clit as my hips rotated slowly to create the perfect tempo. He kept his face close to mine, watching every expression I made, drinking in every sound. He was feeding off my reaction. Getting off on what he was doing to me, and so was I. I couldn't get enough.

"That's it," he encouraged, as I rolled my hips and clung to the bathtub. "Ride my hand. Fuck my fingers." His whispered words were my undoing, adding to the burning need clawing inside me. "I want you to come hard for me. Show me what I do to you. Come on my hand, Shelley, like a good girl. My good girl."

"Yes," I cried, throwing my head back, losing myself down the spiralling swirl of ecstasy that he was sending me.

He pulled his finger out, then pushed back in, adding more than one this time, and the sublime way that he stretched me made me groan. "Yes. More. Harder." My hips rocked against the palm of his hand, seeking the friction I so desperately needed. I wanted to come. I had to come. The build was too much and not enough all at once.

The water was lapping and spilling over the side of the bath as I held onto the edges and thrust my hips. His fingers were pumping hard into me, his thumb rubbing the sweetest sensations, and I needed more; so much more.

"Fuck, Colton. Fuck me," I cried, and kneeling up a little taller over the bath, he went to town, thrusting his fingers harder, faster, pushing me up the bathtub as he roughly forced the orgasm out of me.

"That's it, close your eyes and feel me inside you." He groaned; his face so close to mine. "I can't wait to fuck you with my cock after this. I'm so goddamn hard, Shelley. I'm going to fuck you until you scream. Fill you so full of my come. I'm gonna own every beautiful fucking inch of you."

I loved his dirty talk. And with every filthy promise and

firm thrust, he sent me further and further over the edge. Over and over, he filled me with his fingers, curling them inside and teasing me to the brink. Hard thrusts that had me begging for release.

"Please," I cried. "I'm so close."

He wasn't cruel, he knew what he needed to do, and he did it perfectly, rubbing me and telling me filthy things to make me come.

"After this, I'm going to take you to the bedroom, bend you over, and taste this pretty little pussy until you scream. I'll lick from your pussy to your ass. Would you like that? My tongue in your ass?"

I couldn't speak, but his dirty words were spurring me on.

"I'll do anything you want me to," he rasped. "And when you're crying, begging for more, I'm going to fuck your tight little pussy hard from behind and watch that sexy ass move for me. Do you want me to play in your asshole, Shelley? Work you with my fingers as I fuck you with my cock?"

The thought of him doing that had me buckling underneath him. My head fell back, and my mouth hung open as I cried out my orgasm. My walls squeezed his fingers, and my legs shook as my back arched in ecstasy. Wave after wave of pure bliss washed over me and I never wanted to come back from it.

"That's it, beautiful," he moaned. "Use me any way you need." He pulled me closer as his fingers continued to pull every ounce of my orgasm from me. "You're fucking beautiful when you come."

I lay with my head back, letting the pulse and sparks subside. And then, I relaxed back into the bath with a contented sigh. I couldn't stop smiling, and when I turned to look at him, he had the exact same expression on his face.

"Thank you," I said.

"It's all part of the service," he replied, winking as he pulled his fingers from me. "But don't get too relaxed. I haven't finished with you yet. Weren't you listening to what I just said?"

He stood up, and then with the smuggest grin, he reached down and put his arms under me, pulling me out of the bath and into his arms.

"Colton! I'm all wet." I laughed.

"Of course you are, you're with me. I always make you wet."

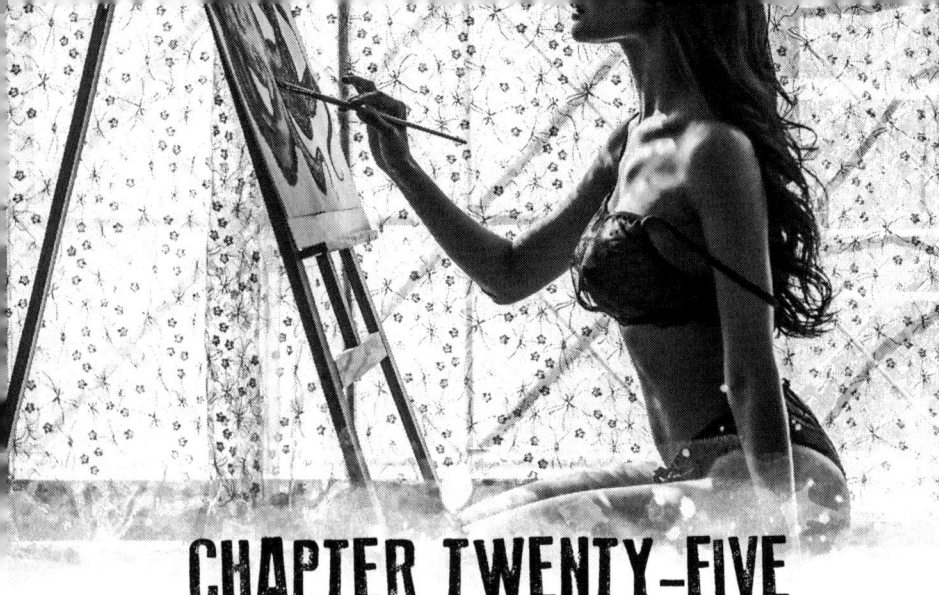

CHAPTER TWENTY-FIVE
Shelley

He carried me, dripping wet, into my bedroom and threw me down on my bed. I crawled up the mattress, keeping my eyes on him as he pulled his shirt over the back of his head and off.

"Knock, knock," he said, smirking as he took slow steps towards me.

"Who's there?" I asked, playing along as I writhed on top of the covers.

"Holden."

"Holden, who?"

"Hold on tight, baby. I'm about to fuck the soul right out of you, and make you come all over my cock."

Holy shit.

He said he'd having me begging and he was right, I was.

THE JOKER

"Don't keep me waiting then, *soldier*."

With the devil burning back at me in his eyes, he popped the buttons of his jeans open and then pulled his trousers and boxers down. He was hard, and he took his dick in his hand and gave it a few pumps as he said, "On all fours, ass up."

I licked my lips, wondering what it'd feel like to have those piercings on my tongue. To taste and tease him, flickering over every one of those piercings until it drove him wild.

"Keep licking those lips like that and I'll put them to good use."

"Promises, promises," I taunted back, and he chuckled.

"I keep my promises."

He walked over to the edge of the bed with his dick in his hand. I knelt on the mattress, and with my eyes on him, I leaned forward and gave the tip of his cock a slow, long lick.

"That's it, baby," he rasped. "Don't be shy. Do whatever makes you feel good."

I pushed his hand away from the base of his cock and replaced it with my own, moving my legs so I was sitting on the edge of the bed. I swirled my tongue around the head, tasting his sweet precum as he moaned and took a handful of my hair to guide me onto him. My hand pumped the base as I sucked him into my mouth. It was intoxicating hearing him hiss as I pushed him to the back of my throat. But I wanted to explore. I didn't want this to be over yet. So, I pulled back, and with my tongue on the base of his cock, I started to lick around and across each piercing, working my way up the ladder, familiarising myself with how he felt. I watched his face to see what he liked, and when I licked and sucked the final piercing at the top, he let out a throaty groan that told me I'd hit the jackpot. I used my tongue to flick, tease, and rub him there the way he liked. I could feel his dick twitch and throb as I worked him with my tongue and mouth. His hips rocked into me, and then, he gasped, "I'm close. I need to come in your throat."

I took him into my mouth, pushing him back down my throat, swallowing and tightening around him. He grabbed my head, angling me and fucking my face.

"Fuck, Shelley. You're going to make me come so hard," he growled.

Hearing him say that, I realised I wanted to watch him come. So slowly, I pulled back and took his cock in my hand, pumping him as I opened my mouth and gazed up at him.

"Holy fuck." He gasped, realising what I wanted, and then he came in white hot spurts that coated my tongue. The way his eyes burned as he watched himself come in my mouth, the fire that smouldered as I let him do it and then swallowed it was electric. In a way, I felt proud for pleasing him.

He reached down to brush the wetness from my chin and smiled at me like I was his whole fucking world. That smile did things to me. I'd suck his cock every day if it meant I got that smile from him.

"You're such a good girl." He sighed. "You suck my cock so well, baby." I blinked back at him, loving the praise. Who knew I'd like that? He'd certainly unlocked something in me. "Now it's my turn." He winked. "Get on all fours, just like I asked."

"Yes, sir," I teased and was rewarded with another wink.

I climbed back onto the bed and held onto the bedframe as I knelt on all fours. The bed dipped as he climbed on behind me.

"You'll need to hold onto that," he said, his warm breath teasing the backs of my legs. "When I fuck you, the bed frame is going to be the only thing keeping you up."

He yanked my legs apart at the knees, and slapped the side of my ass. Then he gripped my ass in both hands and spread my cheeks so that he could see everything. "So, fucking beautiful. You're perfect, Shelley. So pretty."

He didn't waste time, and when I felt his tongue lick my clit, along my pussy and then up to my ass, I let out a ragged cry. No one had ever done the things that he was doing to me. But I liked how forbidden it felt. His tongue circling places, probing, eliciting the most erotic feelings.

His fingers slid along my pussy, circling my clit as his tongue continued its assault on my senses. I clung onto the headboard and pushed back into him, wanting more. The roughness of his tongue, the way he lapped and flicked in the most delicious way was too much. I couldn't take it, and my hips moved back into him, riding his face. The next orgasm hit me out of nowhere. I didn't know which way was up and which was down, but I came hard. My legs shook, my body convulsed, and my pussy clamped down on his fingers. I'd never felt an orgasm like it, and I panted desperately as it went on and on.

"Such a naughty girl, soaking my fingers." He tutted. "But I fucking love it." I glanced back at him and watched him put his fingers into his mouth to lick my wetness from them. "Fucking delicious," he growled, and then he shuffled forward, lining himself up, ready to fuck me.

I didn't think I could take anymore, but when he thrust hard into me, I cried out, gripping the headboard.

He didn't hold back, and pounded into me, our bodies slapping together as he thrust so hard, I felt like he'd break the damn bed.

"That's it." He commanded. "Take it like a good girl."

He hammered into me hard and fast, and I was sure he'd leave me bruised in the morning, but I didn't care. I wanted him to.

"Harder," I begged, moving my hips in time with his. "Fuck me harder."

He clung to my hips, his fingers digging into my skin as he slammed into me, and as his piercings hit my G-spot at the most sublime angle, I felt my knees give way, and another orgasm was ripped out of me.

"Fuck, that's it. Milk my cock." He thrust a few more times, and then I felt him thicken and find his own release. I looked up at the window opposite to watch him come. In the reflection, I could see his head fall back, his mouth open in silent cries of ecstasy, and his body tense then relax as he came down from his high. As his head fell forward, he saw me watching and he climbed over me, pinning me to the bed with his chest to my back.

"Do you like to watch?" he asked. "Do you like watching me fuck you and seeing me come?"

"Hell yes," I answered honestly.

"Then you need to come back to the club. I have the most amazing thing to show you."

I tilted my head and glanced back at him, both of us panting. And the way he looked at me, in that moment, like I was his whole world, I knew I'd do anything he asked.

CHAPTER TWENTY-SIX
Shelley

When the realisation hits you that you might be falling for the one person you never even thought you'd like, it's surreal, to say the least. You don't see it coming until it's too late, and you've been pulled into the messy vortex, but at the same time, it feels… natural, beautiful, right. Nothing is forced because the connection you forged was created all on its own. It's an entity you had no control over.

It was always meant to be.

That's how I felt about Colton. Like I was powerless to stop this. The emotions took root, grew and blossomed despite ourselves. That old saying, 'There's a fine line between love and hate', had to originate from somewhere, or be inspired by someone's experiences. And we were living proof that it was true. Spiteful, hateful words became more loaded and cryptic.

Looks of fury morphed into a fire that burned differently. Time spent together created electric sparks that exploded in so many ways we couldn't keep up. Then we were thrown into a mayhem of feelings we were powerless to control. All we could do was go with it.

I had no idea where this journey would take us, and I'd be lying if I didn't say I was scared. That's right, the girl who'd killed more than once, who put on a front that nothing could faze her, was terrified. I didn't like handing control over to someone else, least of all someone who didn't have the best track record. Broken hearts and Colton King went hand in hand, or so the rumour mill told us. But if I took the advice my mother always gave me, it was to make my own judgments and not base my opinions on the gossip of others. I guess that's all I could do, trust in myself and hope for the best. After all, how well do any of us know another human being? How much can we really trust our future in the hands of another?

I was in the kitchen, putting a light lunch together and chatting to Bryony about the latest on Byers when I got the text.

"Do you think he'll go for it? Because I'm getting tired of this back and forth. I say we call his bluff. We can't go on like this, dancing to his tune. Colton's investigator still isn't any closer to getting an address," I whined as I chopped the tomatoes and held myself back from stabbing the knife into the wooden chopping board in anger.

"Let's give it a little longer. He doesn't like the terms I offered him, but we can work with that. I'll tell him he can have whatever he damn well wants if it gets us a face-to-face to finally end this fucker. Let's not forget, it isn't just about the blackmail.

He made Mum and Rosie's lives hell. He needs to pay."

She was right, of course. It did go deeper, but in my agitated state, I'd overreacted. We should continue playing the long game; it's what we were good at. I needed to stop acting like a cat on a bloody hot tin roof. Colton had me all wound up, and I needed to chill out.

"You're right. We deserve this. Our family deserves this."

Bryony grinned, then her smile morphed into a grimace. "Count yourself lucky I'm not taking Kate's advice. She thought we should send him a teaser… of us three. Something to entice him out of the woodwork."

"Hell no!" I almost choked on the slice of cucumber I'd just sneaked into my mouth. "That guy can kiss my ass, not drool over it."

My phone chimed on the kitchen table behind me, and I put the knife down, wiping my hands on the kitchen towel before picking it up. When I saw his name, I couldn't stop grinning.

"What's got you smiling like the Cheshire Cat?" Bryony asked.

"Nothing. Just Eric," I lied, tapping into my messages.

Colton: Check your doorstep.

Me: Why? Did you plant a bomb under the mat?

Colton: Finally! You unblocked my number. I thought this message would disappear into the ether of unread messages I've sent you over the past few

months.

Me: We're working together to find Byers. I thought it best to keep my line open.

Colton: Nothing to do with the multiple orgasms I've been giving you then?

Me: If you wanted a booty call, you've got the wrong number.

Colton: I've got the right number. And if I hear you call yourself a booty call again, I'll put you over my knee… ;)

Me: I hear you keep your promises…

Colton: I do. Doorstep… Now.

I wandered past a smugly grinning Bryony, who began to frown as I made my way out into the hallway. Before I opened the door, I looked through the peephole, but couldn't see anything. I'd expected to find Colton standing there, but there was no one. So, I opened the door with a sigh, kidding myself that I wasn't bothered, and when I glanced down, there was a large cardboard box on the mat.

I stepped onto our path and looked up and down the road, but I couldn't see him. So, I turned, picked up the box and walked back into the house, slamming the door shut behind me with my leg.

"What have you got there?" Bryony asked as I placed it on top of the kitchen table.

"No idea."

I took the knife I'd just used to chop the salad and ran it along the length of the tape on the top of the box. When I peeled it open, I felt the breath leave my lungs, my chest contracting with a mix of confusion and excitement. To anyone else, it would've looked like nothing, but to me it was everything. Inside were paints, brushes, pencils, palettes, and ink, all in the exact brands I used. All of it perfect, brand new, begging to be used, and I couldn't wait. It was the best gift I'd ever received.

I picked up a handful of pencils, and Bryony peered inside.

"Wow. Did you go a bit crazy with your online shopping this month?" she asked.

"No. It's a gift."

"From who?" I ignored her, but she wouldn't give up. "Whoever it is, can you tell them to have a word with Will Stokes about appropriate gifts. After the disastrous Halloween party, Will showed up at our door. When I opened it, he said, "Sorry I fucked up." and thrust a pair of swimming armbands at me. The guy thought taking the piss out of the fact we can't swim would win him points." She shrugged as I tried to stifle a laugh. "It's fine, though. I invited him in, made him a coffee. Might've added some of mum's laxatives, and funnily enough, he didn't stay for very long."

"There's so much about what you've just said that I need to unpick, but hold that thought. Let me send this text, then you're telling me everything. I need all the details."

Bryony and Will?

That was something I hadn't seen coming.

THE JOKER

"Nothing to tell," she replied nonchalantly. "He's a prick and I'm not interested." And with that, she waltzed out of the kitchen.

Yeah, right. I'd heard that before.

Me: This is amazing. Thank you.

Colton: I figured you weren't the flowers and chocolates kind of girl, although I can get those if you change your mind.

Me: I'd take these over any flowers and chocolates.

Colton: I knew you would. I'm glad you like them.

Me: How did you know what brands to get?

Colton: I saw them at your studio.

Me: And you remembered all of them?

Colton: I remember everything. I'm very observant.

I couldn't believe he'd done that. He was paying more attention than I'd ever given him credit for. And this gift was probably the nicest thing anyone had ever done for me.

Me: You certainly are. Now I need to find a way to say thank you.

Colton: You could let me see the art you're working on. I'd love to see your final collection, the zodiac one.

I wasn't ready for that. Not yet. As crazy as it sounded, I needed to keep that private, just for me, for a little longer.

Me: Nice try, but I'm not ready to share that.

I watched the three little dots appear and disappear as he typed his response.

Colton: Fair enough. Look in the bottom of the box then. Maybe that'll work.

I put my phone down, and with both hands, moved the art supplies to the side to find a black envelope at the bottom. Inside was a black credit card with The Sanctuary written on it. No note, just the card.

Me: You gave me a credit card?

Colton: It's a room card. Come to the club this Saturday, first floor, and I'll show you what it's for.

I turned the card over in my hand, expectation for what room it opened thrumming through my veins.

Me: I'll think about it.

Colton: You'll do more than think. Be there. Room eight. I'll be expecting you.

Like I could ever say no to him. But it wouldn't hurt to keep him guessing, so I didn't reply. Leave them wanting more, isn't that what they say? But the thought of Saturday night had butterflies going wild inside me.

What world would this card lead me into?

CHAPTER TWENTY-SEVEN
Shelley

Put me in an art studio, and I'm in my element. Place a knife in my hand, and I'll show you who's boss. Drop me into the middle of a heaving nightclub, with hundreds of people drinking and dancing, and nine times out of ten, I'll turn and walk right out. But it looked like tonight might be the one time I stayed. Actually, make that two. This was the second time Colton had got me to his Sanctuary. He really did have a way of persuading me lately.

I wandered over to the staircase that led to the first floor, holding my head high as I strutted with confidence I forced myself to feel. Each step I took felt heavy, not with dread, but a nervous expectation. Colton had a way of knocking me off my feet, obliterating all my expectations, and I knew tonight would be no different.

I'd chosen a little black dress, and I smoothed the skirt that'd ridden up my thighs back down as I reached the next floor. I fluffed my hair that hung loosely around my shoulders and painted a don't-fuck-with-me attitude on my face.

"Nice to see you again, Shelley," the security guy, I think his name was Gaz, said as I walked past him.

I let my mask slip slightly and gave him a quick, polite smile before righting myself.

"Are you looking for room eight?" he asked, then pointing down the corridor, he added, "It's just down there on the right. I believe you already have the key card."

"I do. Thanks." I gave him one last grin and headed in the direction he'd shown me.

This floor was a lot different to the main floor of the club. It was quieter, less crowded, and the vibe felt much more like my kind of scene. Colton was a social butterfly; I was a loner. Maybe that's what made things interesting. We were different, but that difference was what fascinated us.

The music up here was a slow, sensual beat, and I could feel my body reacting to it, my breath growing shallow and my heart racing the closer I got to room eight. The corridor became darker the further you went, like a rabbit hole leading you to the wonderland these men had created. I was Alice, all too eager to follow for the adventure that awaited.

Once I reached the matte black door with a brass number eight on it, I stopped and raised my fist to knock, then froze. Reaching into my purse, I pulled out the key card and placed it against the lock above the doorhandle. When the light flashed to show it'd opened, I pushed the handle down and walked in.

COLTON

I heard the click of the lock first, and my heart raced, knowing I was seconds away from seeing her. The door opened slowly, almost hesitantly, and then I saw her, standing in the doorway, wearing the tightest, sexiest black dress I'd ever seen. Her hair was a mass of curls tumbling over her shoulders, just the way I liked it, and her face was full of awe and wonder.

She glanced around in a daze of wonderment before her eyes rested on me, standing in the middle of the room with my arms folded and a shit-eating grin on my face.

"You came," I said, like a weirdo with no social skills.

"And you really brought it with this room." She sighed, taking another glance around. "I thought the hall of mirrors was a specialty of the funhouse?"

"This isn't a hall, it's a room of mirrors," I said, stating the obvious.

The mirror room had been my idea. Adam loved his dark room. Devon was all about the voyeur room, but the mirror room was mine. The walls were mirrored and angled so you could see anything from any perspective. The ceiling was mirrored too, and along the black floor, dancing under your feet, were twinkling star lights that added a hint of illumination so you could fully appreciate whatever happened in here. And, of course, in the middle of the room was a king-size bed, complete with black sheets, cuffs, and a side table filled with every toy you'd ever need.

We stared at each other. The air around us crackled with electricity as we both took a moment to brace ourselves, knowing what would happen in here tonight would be fucking amazing.

"I should've known you'd build a mirror room. You do love yourself." She smirked, pretending to insult me. Then she moved further into the room, and we began to circle each other like animals in the wild. Predator and prey. I did love a chase.

"It's not me I'll be looking at," I replied, and I think I saw her shiver before she turned to walk towards the mirrors and placed a finger against the glass, acting like I hadn't just said what I'd said.

"Are these two-way mirrors?" she asked, peering at the reflection of her fingertip for a clue.

"No." I took a step closer to where she stood. "Do you really think I'd share you with anyone else?"

I stood behind her, running my finger over her bare shoulder, and then I brushed her hair to the side.

"In some ways, we're so different," I told her on a whisper. "But in others, we're just the same."

I leaned down, my breath warming her neck as my fingers itched to explore and take what was mine.

She turned her head to the side and replied, "How so?"

I rested my chin on her shoulder, and we both looked ahead at the mirror in front of us as I snaked my arms around her waist and pulled her to me.

"I like to watch, and from what I saw in your bedroom, you like that too." I nuzzled into her neck and gave her a delicate kiss, inhaling her like she was a fucking drug. "I want to watch us fucking and see your face when I make you come. I want to watch every sigh, every cry, every moan, all of it. I want to live it, breath it, see it, feel it. Tonight, all that exists is you and me, us, getting lost in each other. A fuck like no other. Like nothing we've ever experienced before."

Slowly, she closed her eyes as I spoke, and I noticed the delicate rise and fall of her chest as she pictured every promise I whispered. As I pulled her closer to me, she sighed.

"I know there's mirrors, Colton, but why would it be different? Tell me."

I knew what she wanted. Shelley might project a certain image to the outside world, but she was human, like the rest of us. She wanted reassurance.

"Because it's you."

Our eyes met in the mirror, and I held her gaze as I said, "No one has ever made me feel like you do. Like life before was always leading to this. To you. You're all I want, Shelley. You're all I can think about."

"The sex is amazing. I feel that too," she replied, but her eyes said so much more.

"It's not about sex, Shelley. It's about the connection. You and me. Together, we don't just make fireworks, we implode our whole universe. I've never had that before. I never thought I'd ever have that."

"Me neither," she said breathlessly, her hands resting over mine at her waist.

I closed my eyes and held my breath as I prepared to leap off a cliff I never thought I'd fall from. "I only ever want you. It'll always be you."

Time stood still, and my heart flickered, hoping that the crack I'd opened to let her in wouldn't get ripped apart.

"Please don't say things in the heat of the moment," she replied. "Not if you don't really mean them."

I shook my head.

"I mean every word," I told her. "But maybe it's better if I show you. I've always been better with actions rather than words."

She huffed out a gentle laugh, and then her breath caught in her throat as I reached down to the hem of her dress and slowly pulled it up her thighs, over her ass, and then off. We stood in front of the mirror, looking at her gorgeous body in her black lace underwear. I ran my hands over her stomach, loving the feel of her velvet skin and how she sighed at my touch.

"Keep your eyes on me," I commanded, pulling my shirt over my head and then pulling my trousers, boxers and shoes off to stand behind her, totally naked.

Her eyes glowed in the mirror's reflection as she took in every inch of me.

I held her stomach and pulled her hips back to me as I grabbed her neck in my other hand and kissed her from behind. I couldn't get enough of tasting her, fucking her mouth with my tongue as I ground my hard cock into her ass. She reached up to grab the back of my head, her face twisted to kiss me back, her tongue eager as it swirled and danced with mine. Every movement of her lips made me harder, more desperate to be inside her. But I didn't want to rush this, and I didn't want to be selfish. She had to come first.

I kissed down her jaw to her neck then I looked up, watching us in the mirror as I held her neck and told her, "Eyes forward. I want you to watch everything I do to you. I need to see your face."

I kept my hand around her neck, but my other hand drifted over her stomach to tease over the top of her knickers. My fingers dipped below the lace, but it wasn't enough; we both wanted... *needed* more.

"Touch me," she pleaded quietly, and so I did, pushing my hand into her knickers and kicking her legs apart as I felt how wet she was.

I used a finger to stroke her, then I circled her clit, rubbing her the way she liked. Her head fell back onto my shoulder and her eyes drifted closed as she began to moan and rock her hips.

"Eyes open," I commanded. "Close them, and I'll stop."

She did as she was told, lifting her head slightly to watch where my hand was.

"So fucking sexy." I groaned as I watched her give up control to me. I'd never seen her look so beautiful, standing in her black heels and underwear, getting finger fucked in front of the mirror. Her legs open as I explored, her eyes hooded, and her mouth open as she sighed and moaned.

"Look how beautiful you are, how much you want me. I love seeing the need in your eyes," I said as I watched the way her eyes darkened the closer I took her to the edge.

Her chest began to rise and fall more rapidly now, and her hands gripped my arms like she was holding on for dear life. I kept my hand around her neck, whispering in her ear, "Let go for me. Show me how pretty my girl is when she comes."

She licked her lips and arched her back as she panted.

"More. I need more," she begged, and I pushed two fingers inside her roughly, filling her and feeling the warmth of her tight little pussy as she rode my hand.

Wetness coated my palm as she ground into it, and she reached down to cover my hand with her own, guiding me the way she wanted. As she came closer to orgasm, she trembled, and we both watched as I held her up, filled her, grasping her close to me because I wanted to feel everything.

I knew she was almost there, and I couldn't take my eyes off her face as she panted and cried, her hips rocking faster as my fingers curled inside her and my thumb pressed her clit, working her just the way she needed. I squeezed her neck tighter and growled in a low voice, "Watch yourself come. I want you to see what I'm doing to you. How fucking sexy you are. Look at yourself."

"I'm looking…" She gasped, keeping her head forward and her eyes on the mirror as she watched herself. I noticed her glance down to where my hand was fucking her, before looking back up at her face, pure lust reflecting back at her. I was painfully hard, and couldn't stop myself from thrusting my cock against her peachy ass, desperate for relief. But this wasn't about me; this was all for her, and seeing her reach her climax was un-fucking-believable. Worth every second of denying myself.

Her hands tightened their grip on me as she started to shake. I could feel her walls contracting, squeezing my fingers, and then she cried out, "I'm coming." And the way her face morphed into pure ecstasy as she came on my hand and soaked my fingers was the most amazing thing I'd ever seen. Her legs quivered and I held her steady. Her skin mottled a delicious pink hue as she cried and moaned, tilting her hips to milk every last drop of her orgasm.

"Oh, God." She sighed, and this time, when she closed her eyes and dropped her head on my shoulder, I let her.

"I just saw you at your most beautiful," I told her, giving her a gentle peck on her cheek as I reluctantly pulled my hand out of her knickers. "You're stunning when you come." I put my fingers into my mouth and sucked. "And you taste fucking delicious." I kept my fingers in my mouth as I stared at her in the mirror. Her pupils were dilated as she watched me lick my fingers clean. "Do you want to taste how good you are?" I asked her, and she nodded.

So, I pulled my fingers from my mouth, dipped them back into her knickers, and then took them out, lifting my hand to tease her lips with my fingertips, before slipping them into her mouth for her to suck. She sucked and swirled her tongue around my fingers like a fucking lollipop, making my already stiff cock leak precum on her ass.

I couldn't wait any longer. It was my turn to get off, and I couldn't fucking wait to fill her and fuck her until she could barely breathe.

"Are you ready for more?" I asked, and she smiled around my fingers. "Such a needy little thing. Now it's time for you to come on my cock."

I reached up to undo the clasp on her bra and let it fall down her arms to the floor. Kneeling behind her, I pulled her knickers down and off. But the heels? They were staying on.

"Are you going to be my good girl and let me fuck you against this mirror in your heels?" I lifted my brow in question, and she gave a little giggle. I'd never heard her giggle before. My tough cookie wasn't so tough, really.

"Only if you fuck me good and hard," she purred back, and I took my cue, pushing on her back to let her know she needed to bend forward.

"Hands on the glass and eyes on the mirror. I don't mind which angle you watch," I added, glancing at the mirrors either side of us that were tilted to give the perfect view of the side of her ass. "But I want your eyes on me."

I looked down at her perfect ass bent over for me. With my fingers, I teased her ass cheeks open to see her pussy glistening with her cum. I couldn't wait to see my own dripping down her leg, marking her as mine. I took my cock in my hand and ran the tip over her clit, then along her wetness, rubbing agonisingly slowly.

"Don't tease me, Colton. Fuck me," she begged.

I lined myself up and watched as my cock sunk into her, sighing as I felt her grip me with her tight, wet pussy. "I love watching my cock slide into you," I whispered, pulling out and then pushing back in slowly. "It's so fucking sexy." But when she reared back into me and moaned, "More. Faster," I chuckled. "Always so needy. You like it rough, baby, don't you."

Her smile turned wicked, and she purred, "Rough and hard, the way you always fuck me. I love it. Now, give it to me." And hearing her say that made the caveman in me turn feral.

"Yes, ma'am."

I gripped her hips in my hands, and started to thrust hard, fucking her roughly, watching the way her ass moved as I slammed into her.

"Do you like that, baby?" I moaned. "Do you like how I own your pussy?"

"Yes," she panted.

I looked ahead into the mirror as I rammed my cock into her harder and harder, faster and faster. Her ass clapping against my hips, her wet pussy leaking all over my balls, and her cries making my spine tingle as my orgasm built. She was watching me in the mirror, gasping as I rode her hard. Then she glanced to the side, and I looked too. Seeing our bodies together in this way, watching my cock piston into her was insanely sexy. I rolled my hips and moved to let my piercings work their magic, and she hung her head forward, then remembering what I said about stopping, she snapped her head back up and kept her eyes on me.

"Good girl," I praised her, and she moaned.

"Always for you."

I fucked her roughly against the mirror and she loved every minute of it. We both did. I knew she could take whatever I could give her. She was my girl in every sense of the word.

When I felt my balls tighten and my cock throb, I reached a hand down to circle her clit. Gathering the wetness on my thumb, I put my arm around her waist to hold her up and then, as I rammed my cock into her, I slipped my thumb into her ass, filling her the way I wanted to.

"Oh God. Oh fuck, yes." She groaned and circled her hips as I pounded into her. And then she came hard on my cock, squeezing my orgasm from me. My cock thickened and pulsed as I came inside her. And as I held her hips and rocked into her, taking everything I could get, I knew she was it for me. I'd never want anyone the way I wanted her. She was everything.

I stilled inside her, letting both of us get our breath back as she leaned against the mirror. Then, I pulled my cock out slowly and watched as my cum dripped out of her. My chest felt heavy, and a possessiveness unlike anything I'd ever felt before surged inside me. With my fingers, I followed the trail of cum, gathering it up and pushing it back into her. I wanted it to stay inside her. And yet, seeing it coat her pussy and trail down her legs made me want to fuck her all over again. I couldn't get enough. This girl was driving me crazy.

Shelley

I could feel him fingering me with his cum, pushing his fingers into my pussy. I felt sore, but I still wanted more. He made me crave more. I'd had two orgasms, I'd come on his fingers and dick, but it wasn't enough. I needed that connection he'd talked about. I needed to move this to the bed.

As if he could read my mind, Colton put his arms around me, lifting my quivering body off the mirror that was holding me up and said, "Let's try the bed out, shall we?"

I wasn't sure my legs would work, and was relieved when he picked me up and carried me over.

Gently, he lay me down in the middle of the bed, then came to lie next to me, stroking my hair as his leg entwined with mine.

"Do you know how special you are?" he whispered, kissing my neck and then manoeuvring himself to lie over me. He rested his elbow close to my head so he could look at me. "I knew that despite all the pushbacks this would be worth it."

I frowned. "What do you mean?"

"The pushbacks. You know, the road we took to get here. It wasn't easy, but it proves you were worth it. We're worth it."

My heart felt like it might burst, but my brain wouldn't let me speak. I was scared. Scared of getting hurt. I felt everything he was hinting at, but to say it out loud, that was something else entirely.

Maybe actions were better, like he'd said at the start?

So, instead of spilling words I was too afraid to reveal, I reached up and placed my hand on the back of his head, pulling him down to kiss me. With my kiss, I told him what I couldn't say.

I want you more than anything.

You make me feel all the things I never thought I'd feel.

Being with you makes me want a life I thought was out of reach.

A life that my father promised us but stole away.

I need you like I need my next breath.

It will always be you.

He kissed me the same way, his lips blending perfectly with mine, his tongue sliding against mine. Everything felt so right.

I opened my legs, and he settled his hips between them. His dick was hard, and I could feel it brushing over my pussy, so I tilted my hips, wanting to feel him again, but this time, it would be different, because we were lying together, our bodies as close as they could get. This was different because this wasn't fucking; it was making love.

He slid inside me, and I sighed into his mouth at the feel of him stretching me. I'd never get over how good it felt to have him inside me.

He groaned into my ear as he thrust on top of me and my legs wrapped tightly around his hips, urging him on.

"After tonight, your pussy will be moulded to my cock." He moaned. "You'll feel me for days."

"I hope so," I purred, digging my nails into his back and rolling my hips to mirror his thrusts.

We kissed and held each other as he thrust into me slow but hard. Then, he buried his head in my neck and swivelled his hips as he pounded me harder. I looked at the mirrored ceiling, watching his ass as he railed me, loving the way he moved and rolled his hips. I loved watching his body, watching him give me pleasure like this.

I couldn't take my eyes off the mirrored ceiling as I arched my back and came hard, wave after wave of ecstasy crashing through my body. My legs stayed wrapped around him as he grabbed onto my shoulders and thrust into me, chasing his own release. And then he let out an almighty roar as he came too.

Hearing him, seeing him, feeling what I did to him was everything, and I held him close as we both came down from our incredible high.

I'd always said Colton King would be the death of me as a joke to my sisters. But right now, lying in his arms with him buried deep inside me, I felt like not having Colton in my life *would* be the real death of me.

He was mine.

Every crazy, fucked-up part of him.

And even though it still scared me, I held onto him like I'd never let go.

I didn't want to let go.

Life had done a three-sixty on me and being with him was one heck of a rollercoaster ride.

Question was, would I survive?

Could I survive the man they all called The Joker?

Or would life come back to bite me in the ass?

CHAPTER TWENTY-EIGHT
Shelley

At some point, between my fifth and sixth orgasm, I must've passed out in the mirror room. But when I woke up, it wasn't mirrors that surrounded me, only black painted walls and the scent of Colton everywhere. He must've carried me back to his bedroom, and as I began to wake and become more lucid, I felt the weight of his arm around my waist and the gentle sound of him breathing as he slept behind me.

I felt conflicted.

On one hand, it felt right being here, immersed in Colton's world. Having him close soothed me. But on the other, I felt a nervous panic begin to set in.

Would it feel awkward in the morning?

Would I feel uncomfortable waking up here?

Would he even want me here in the light of day?

I did like my own space, I quietly mused, so maybe it'd be better if I left now? Keep the mystery alive and keep him on his toes.

The bed was warm and cosy, but my mind was a whirlwind of unrest. And so, blocking out the conflicting voices in my head, I gently lifted his arm off me and shuffled to the edge of the bed to sit up. I glanced back at him sleeping soundly, and it took my breath away how beautiful he looked. Eric called him interesting, but to me, he was so much more than that. He was perfect. I know it sounded silly to call a man beautiful, but he was, with his full lips, his high cheekbones and arched brows. Every tattoo was like another piece of the puzzle that made Colton who he was. They all told a story about the man he had become, and part of me wanted to wake him, ask him about every single one, but I didn't.

Instead, I saw my clothes on a chair by the door, and I stood up, slowly making my way over to them and putting them on in such a way so as not to wake him. He didn't stir, and I stood watching him sleep for a few minutes before sanity got the better of me. I turned to the door, opened it and stepped out into the coolness of the dark corridor, closing it quietly behind me.

I tiptoed away and got about halfway down the corridor before I heard a soft voice behind me.

"Shelley? Are you okay?"

I turned around, the darkness easing off a little to allow me to make out Liv's silhouette, with her silver-blonde hair glowing in the moonlight. She was carrying two bottles of water, and while I stood still, feeling a little dumbfounded, she walked tentatively toward me.

"Hey," I replied, breaking the dark silence.

"It's nice to formally meet you. I'm Liv."

She came to stand in front of me, and I felt a little uneasy, here in the corridor, trying to make my escape.

"I know who you are," I said, and inwardly cringed at how off that sounded. Liv didn't seem to notice though; her smile stayed firmly in place.

"Colton has told us so much about you. I've been dying to meet the famous Shelley."

"Infamous you mean." There I was again, on my guard. I needed to lighten up.

"Hardly. He thinks the light shines out of your ass, excuse my language." She smirked, glancing down at the floor and biting her lip, and then she added, "We've waited a long time for someone to come along and knock him off his feet."

I didn't know what to say to that, and as I took a moment to think and engage my brain before speaking, Liv beat me to it.

"You're leaving, aren't you? Does he know?"

"No. I think it's better this way." I hoped that she could see I was being sincere.

"You might think it's better now, and I'd never want to interfere, but when he wakes up and sees you've bailed, will it be better?"

Liv had known Colton for a lot longer than I had, and she was his friend. I couldn't argue with her for having his best interests at heart.

"Don't we all try and avoid the dreaded walk of shame? It's not the best start to your day," I replied, making light of the situation.

"It's only a walk of shame if you let it be." Liv sighed, and then stepping closer to me, she said quietly, "He is crazy about you. And he might not show it, but tomorrow, he'll be devastated that you left. Take it from someone who's been where you are. I know how you're feeling. The first time I came here to see Adam, I walked away. I thought I was running away from the dreaded walk of shame too, but I wasn't. I was hiding from my feelings, and I guess, what I'm trying to say is… are you doing the same? Hiding, that is."

I knew I was, and her words hit home as I thought about the things Colton had said and done, the way he'd always taken the first step and come to me. He was doing all the chasing.

"Shelley, if there's a chance that what's between you and Colton could be more than a one-night thing, then don't leave. And in my opinion, I think… no, I *know* he wants more. Don't turn your back on what could be the most amazing thing to ever happen to you. He might act like a joker to everyone else, but he's an amazing guy, the best. He'll always be there for you. He won't ever let you down. He's not made that way. None of these boys are. They're one of a kind. Diamonds in the rough. And if you find a guy like that, you hold on for dear life. I know he'll be holding on to you."

Fuck, her words were like a knife to my heart.

"I guess I'm just not comfortable putting myself out there," I said, by way of an explanation. But it felt so inadequate.

"None of us are." She smiled. "You're at a fork in the road. But which path do you choose? The pretty, rose-lined path with no adventure that goes on and on in a straight line? There's no surprises there because you can see where it leads, it's always the same journey. Or do you take the dark path with more bends and turns than you could ever imagine? The road might be bumpy, maybe a few thorny bushes to avoid here and there, and what lies at the end is a mystery; it could be heaven or hell. But isn't that path more exciting?"

My whole life had been the dark thorny path. It's what'd made me the person I was today. But in all honesty, would I want to choose the safer option?

Liv reached out her arm and patted the side of mine as she said, "I'll leave you to decide which path you're going to choose. No pressure. I'm always here if you need a friend. Good luck, Shelley." And she walked away, entering a room down the corridor and closing the door behind her.

I stood for a few moments, taking deep breaths, and then I strolled down the corridor.

I had made my choice.

CHAPTER TWENTY-NINE
Colton

"I always manage to come into the kitchen at the right time." I walked over to where Liv was standing over the oven, taking out two pain au chocolat for her and Adam's breakfast.

"The wrong time, you mean, depending on whose perspective we're talking about," Liv replied sarcastically. I watched her place them onto a plate and pour two coffees, and then she sighed and turned to me. "Do you want one?"

"Can I have two?" I looked at her under my lashes like I was begging, and she laughed.

"Don't give me that bullshit look. You can have them, on one condition."

"What?"

"You tell me if you're eating both or–"

"The other one's for Shelley."

She arched her brow and nodded with a hint of surprise.

"In that case, take the coffees too." She put the plate of croissants and two mugs onto a tray and slid it across the kitchen counter towards me.

"Thanks, by the way," I said, picking up the tray.

"It's fine. I'll just put two more in. Adam's still asleep anyway."

"I didn't mean for the breakfast. I meant for what you said last night to Shelley in the corridor."

Her eyes went wide.

"You heard that?"

"Yeah, and I appreciate you putting a good word in for me."

Her mouth was still hanging open as she nodded.

"Are you okay with... everything?" she asked.

I knew what she was getting at. Shelley had tried to bail, but I understood why. She had self-preservation down to a tee and she was a hard nut to crack, but I enjoyed getting her to open up. The sweetest things are always hardest to work for, and I loved a challenge. Besides, she was the only woman I wanted, and that was something that had never happened to me before. I never thought I'd be a one-woman man, but even the thought of talking to another girl made me nauseous. I guess Adam and Devon were right; when *the one* finally comes along, you know.

I knew.

I was like a horse with blinkers.

There was only Shelley.

"She stayed, didn't she? That's enough for me," I replied, trying to sound nonchalant. "But thank you for your kind words. It meant a lot."

Liv got busy making more coffee and fussing around the

oven.

"It's all good. I just want to see you happy," she told me as she fussed about.

"Seeing you in the morning, always makes my day." I laughed, and sauntered out of the kitchen towards my room, leaving Liv to her red face and embarrassment.

I walked in to find Shelley awake but still lying in the bed. When she saw me at the door, she smiled.

"Breakfast in bed? I never had you down as the domesticated type."

I chuckled, placing the tray on the bed as she shuffled to sit up.

"Don't get too excited. Its only croissants and coffee, courtesy of Liv. I stole Adam's breakfast."

Shelley picked up her coffee and blew on it before taking a sip.

"She seems really nice."

I sat down beside her on the bed, taking a croissant and stuffing it into my mouth.

"She is." I lay back against the headboard, unable to keep the smile off my face. "So, what are you up to today? Apart from being a slave to my bed."

Shelley rolled her eyes. "I have to go to the studio to finish my final piece, ready for the art gallery showing."

"The zodiac piece? Can I come too and watch you?"

She turned to put her coffee on the side table, stalling for time.

"You know the answer, Colton."

"But I won't get in the way," I argued.

"It's not that you'll be in the way, I just don't feel comfortable sharing my art with you yet."

I put my arm up behind my head, showing how relaxed I was. I was a cool guy. She didn't need to feel uncomfortable about me seeing anything. I had intimate knowledge of every other part of her life. Why was this so different?

"You seem to forget I've already seen your art," I informed her.

"Graffiti sprayed above a dead guy is not the same thing," she argued. "This is personal. Most artists like to keep their work private until they're ready to showcase it."

"Leah May is an artist," I countered. "And she plays new music to me all the time."

"Maybe she's more outgoing in that respect than I am."

I wasn't giving up that easily.

"And Liv has started writing poetry too. She lets me read all her notes and ideas."

"Really?" she asked, her face glowing inquisitively.

"No. But if she did start writing poetry, I know she'd let me read it."

Shelley huffed and gave me a playful slap on the chest.

"You're ridiculous." Then she frowned. "By the way, what's with all the black card and paper birds in your drawer? Are you a secret artist too?"

The little minx had been going through my stuff while I was out of the room. It didn't make me mad, though. I liked that she was curious about me.

"Now that–" I leaned forward and tapped my finger on the end of her nose. "–Is a secret you need to keep."

"Why? Are you afraid to show people your creative side?"

"On the contrary, I love getting creative... in the right

environment." I winked. "But that is a promise I made to someone else. It's something I was asked to do for Leah May, by her father."

Shelley sat quietly for a moment, and then she asked, "Why you? Why didn't her dad ask Devon to keep whatever promise it is you made?"

"Because he didn't want to ask Devon to keep secrets from his girl. That, and he knew I was the man for the job. He loves me. What can I say? I change people's lives."

Her mobile phone chimed from her bag on the chair, and I got up and went to fetch it, dropping the bag onto the bed between us before I lay back down.

Shelley grabbed her phone from her bag, and when she tapped the screen open and read the message, her face went pale.

"Kenny Byers is meeting us on Tuesday evening. He's given us an address in Sandland."

"Send me that address," I said, my body snapping to attention as I sat upright.

"You don't need to come. We can do the rest ourselves." I couldn't believe she'd pull the independent bullshit on me, and I shook my head.

"No fucking way. I have history with that man too. I need to be there. I won't take the kill away from you, but I want to see it."

The way she sighed told me she wasn't happy, but this wasn't up for negotiation.

"We'll all be there," I added. "You can try and stop us but it's happening."

"Fine," she replied, forwarding the message from her phone to mine. "But his final breath? That's all mine."

"I wouldn't have it any other way, baby."

CHAPTER THIRTY
Shelley

I should've been more open to him. He had as much right to revenge as we did. Kenny Byers had done wicked things in his life, and Colton's dad had been a part of it. Growing up in a house like that mustn't have been easy. But when all was said and done, I had to think about my mum and Aunt Rosie. They were the real victims here. It wasn't about the blackmail, or the threats Byers had sent us. It was more than that. We had to do this for every victim of his twisted crimes. The ones that had no voice back then. Today, we had to be that voice. We had to make him pay for what he'd put them all through.

***

The following Tuesday, Bryony, Kate, and I met the soldiers

a few hours before the meet-up with Byers, ready to stake out the house he'd given us as the venue. There was nothing special about it. It was a small, detached house in a quiet area of Sandland. The road it stood on was empty, just a few parked cars along the street, with the sounds of distant traffic, bird song, and the wind rustling through the trees. The neighbouring houses didn't appear to pose any threat, although we knew to stay on our guard, so we kept to the same formation we'd had at the last stakeout. Kate was going to join Tyler around the back of the house, Will and Bryony would scope things out over the street, and Adam and Devon were checking out the neighbouring properties. Colton and I were the lucky ones. We got to head inside to see if he'd set any traps, or better yet, find out if he was already in there.

Colton wittered away as we walked down the path, but I couldn't concentrate on what he was saying. I was too focused on what was going to happen today. I knew the soldiers had weapons in the van they'd parked a street away. We'd also come tooled up, and I had my knife on me.

Adrenaline, like nothing else, coursed through me. There was no feeling quite like a hit. The tension, thoughts of the unknown, the fire that stoked inside you, warming your belly and preparing you for the fight. It was primal. Feral. There was nothing like it, and after you'd made that kill, a righteous kill, the high was insane.

Before tapping into the soldiers' line of work, trying to get our own form of payback all those months ago, we hadn't ever imagined we'd do anything like this. But when someone threatens your family, it's incredible the lengths you'll go to to protect them.

"Are you ready for this?" Colton asked me as we stood at the front door. He reached into the inside of his jacket and pulled out a hammer.

"I'm always ready." I gave him a direct stare, a glare that told him not to question me today of all days.

"Our first kill together," he mused. "I've never had a partner in crime before."

"You work with four other men." I reminded him.

"That's different. We're a unit. With you–" he leaned down to whisper, "–It's much more special. It's us."

"Bonnie and Clyde mark two," I deadpanned.

"Only we won't get caught."

He glanced around, then smashed the hammer against the glass in the door, sticking his hand through to open the lock and then darting inside.

"If he didn't see us coming before, he'll know we're here now," Colton joked, creeping further into the hallway.

I rolled my eyes, hoping Tyler and Kate had a good hold on the rear in case he bailed out the back door.

The house was clean and smart but didn't look lived in. There was no dust or smells that might indicate anyone had been here. Not even a buzz from an electrical appliance.

Each room we checked downstairs was empty. So, we climbed the stairs slowly, listening for anything that might indicate an inhabitant was here, but there was no one. One room after another showed nothing. Byers wasn't here... yet. And when he realised we were alone, Colton turned to me, his eyes twinkling with wicked intent.

"All alone and ready for the ambush." He smiled and then sidestepped, reaching for a door and opening it to reveal an empty airing cupboard. "Shall we wait in here? Give him a real surprise when he turns up?"

I scoffed. In a house full of rooms, he wanted to squeeze us into the airing cupboard.

"Wouldn't a seat on the sofa with a gun pointed at the door when he walks in be better?"

Colton backed further into the tiny, enclosed space, shaking his head.

"But where's the fun in that? Besides, we don't do guns. It's too easy."

I'd heard that about the soldiers. They preferred weapons they could use to intimidate, torture, and terminate. Guns weren't their M.O. They never took the easy road.

I checked my phone, then sent a text to the others to let them know the house was clear, and then I followed him in, shutting the door behind me. As soon as I did, he shrugged his jacket off, letting it fall to the floor, then threw the hammer on top of it and put his arms around my waist, pulling me closer. Not that we were far apart to begin with. This cupboard could barely fit both of us.

"What are you doing?" I hissed as he began kissing my neck.

"You're tense. I'm trying to help you."

"I'm not tense, I'm preparing myself," I said, trying to sound serious but stifling a giggle at the way he was nuzzling into me.

He moved his lips from my neck to my ear, nibbling as he said, "You are tense, I can feel it in your shoulders. You need to relax. Being on your guard is one thing but being uptight will only stress you out more."

"And being too relaxed will get me killed," I reminded him.

He pulled his head back and frowned down at me.

"You won't get killed. I'd never let that happen. You're working with me now. Chill." He was always so positive, so breezy about everything.

I couldn't be that way.

Not today.

"This has to go right, Colton. There's no chill about it."

He sighed and gave me a solemn look.

"Whatever happens, happens. But take it from someone who's been doing this for a long time, going into a kill with stress and tension in your head is a recipe for disaster. You can't control everything. Sometimes, you have to go with the flow. Death isn't pretty and murder isn't perfect." He cocked his head and smiled. "You've just gotta go with it. Ride the wave. Enjoy the experience, whatever comes your way."

"I like your sunny attitude to murder." I scoffed. "It's really refreshing. But I can guarantee your friends don't have the same outlook."

He shrugged like he couldn't care less.

"I know Adam doesn't go with the flow," I went on. "And Devon? He's probably written a lesson plan for the attack. And don't even get me started on Tyler."

Colton threw his head back and laughed, then nuzzling back into my neck, he sighed.

"It takes all sorts," he said. "That's why we work so well."

And I couldn't help but think he meant that about me too. We were like chalk and cheese. I was uptight, and he was chilled. I was reactive, and he was, well… Colton. The Joker. The one that made everything seem lighter.

So, I let him take the lead.

I wrapped my arms around him as he kissed from my neck, up my jaw, and then found my mouth. As the urge to let go slowly swept over me, I let his lips work their magic, pulling me from the moment and taking me away to a place where all that mattered was how he made me feel. The tension he'd noticed in my shoulders ebbed away, replaced by fluttering in my heart and stomach. My fingertips roamed over his skin, my nails scraping delicately on the back of his head as he deepened our kiss. I guess this was what I needed.

The walls of the cupboard kept us tightly cocooned, but I was able to lift my leg, and hook it behind his hips as I tilted mine forward. I was desperate to feel friction in any way possible.

"We'll have to be quick," he whispered. "But sometimes quickies are the best. I'll make sure I hit the spot."

He winked, and I pulled him to me, fusing our mouths as I grappled with the buttons on his jeans, yanking them open as he fought with the elastic of my leggings, pulling and forcing them down my legs. Frantic to get to each other, we managed to free ourselves of the offending clothes that were getting in our way. His jeans were now around his ankles, and my leggings were on the floor. But we didn't care. We were desperate.

I ran my hand down the length of his hard dick and cupped his balls, teasing him and moaning into his mouth as I explored. He did the same, reaching between my legs and running his finger along my wet pussy and groaning in appreciation.

"You're so ready for me." He moaned and grabbed the backs of my thighs as he hoisted me up against the wall.

"Then fuck me," I commanded, and the way he growled, I knew I was in for a hard, fast ride.

He lined his cock up and thrust into me, and I cried out at

being filled so hard and fast.

"That's it, baby," he said, banging his hips into me as he pounded me against the wall. "Ride my cock. Use me. I want to feel you come hard for me."

I clung to his shoulders and squeezed my eyes shut as I felt every thrust, every slam of his hips. The piercings grazed my G-spot, and his dick stretched me in the most amazing way. I ground my hips in time with him, my clit rubbing against him until that spark of electricity crackled within me. The orgasm building as hard and fast as his thrusts.

"Faster," I urged him, wrapping my legs tighter around him. "Harder."

He grabbed my ass and pounded me, grunting in my ear and sending me over the edge. As my body slid against him and the wall, relentless thrusts turned to explosions, and I came, my walls squeezing and contracting around him.

"Fuck, yes. That's it," he cried. "Look at you, my beautiful girl, coming so hard for me. You're stunning." His words made me cling to him tighter, and then I heard him groan as he found his release too, his dick throbbing and pulsing inside me.

We stayed fused together as we panted in ragged, satisfied breaths, clinging to each other, neither of us wanting to let go. I buried my head in his neck and breathed him in, desperate to savour the moment. I don't know why, but something deep inside told me I had to make the most of fleeting moments like this. I had to grasp them tightly before they disappeared, floating away like a feather on the breeze.

Turns out I was right, as I jumped at the sound of a pounding fist on the door we were hiding behind. Then a familiar voice told us we needed to get out of there. Heaven was over, and it was time to take our place in the waiting room for hell.

I sighed as Colton pulled away from me, and we quickly attempted to clean ourselves up. He pulled his jeans back on, and I fussed over my leggings. And once we were somewhat respectable, Colton opened the door and stepped out.

The rest of the soldiers and my sisters were all standing on the landing, and I guessed they'd heard everything, but they didn't care. Adam had a face like thunder and held out his phone for Colton to see.

"I think we're too late," Adam announced, indicating for Colton to take his phone to read whatever message was on there.

"But he's not here yet," Colton replied. "Did he see us and bail?"

My stomach dropped as he said that, and I felt sick. I fisted my hands by my sides, hoping the pain of my nails digging into my skin would ease the nausea.

"Worse." Adam nodded at the phone. "Read it."

I moved to stand closer to Colton, so I could read the message over his shoulder.

This one's for you, Colton. A little thank you from me for everything you've done for our town. Byers didn't deserve to live. So, I've killed him… for you.

Until next time.

"What the fuck is that?" I stepped away. The bile rising in my throat made it difficult to speak, to breathe even.

"It's that creepy fucker, isn't it? The one who did Ross and Clive?" Colton stated, staring at Adam and then looking around the group.

"Obviously," Adam replied. "He's left us messages before."

"But not on our phones, he hasn't. What the fuck is this guy playing at?" Colton held the phone out for Adam to take.

"At least we know one thing, it's not Byers who's been killing them," Tyler added like that made any difference.

"So where is Byers?" Colton asked.

"I don't know, but did you check up there?" Adam pointed above him to where the hatch for the loft was slightly ajar.

We'd checked every room when we got here, but the one place we hadn't looked was the loft space.

My heart was in my throat and my hands were shaking as I watched Adam reach up and pull the small chain that hung from the loft door. As it opened, he pulled at the folding ladder attached to the door and set it on the floor so we could climb up.

Colton turned to me and put his arm around me, and for a moment, I let his warmth soothe me. But as I climbed the stairs behind the others, making my way up to the roof, a chill ran down my spine.

There was a single lightbulb hanging from the rafters, illuminating the space above. What I saw when I got to the last step made me feel like all the air in my lungs had been sucked out. My heart dropped to the floor, and my head screamed in protest. Kenny Byers' naked body was strung up from the rafters. There was a noose around his neck, and his body was a vile, filthy mess. A deep cut ran from his chest to his abdomen, spilling his guts onto the floor below him. He'd been hung, gutted, and left here for us to find. I should've been elated that he was dead, wiped off the face of this earth to never bring harm to anyone ever again.

But I wasn't.

I was devastated.

CHAPTER THIRTY-ONE
Colton

"**N**o,**"** I heard her whisper helplessly into the darkness of the loft. "No."

She shook her head like she couldn't believe what she was seeing, and then I felt the change. Bewilderment turned to anger, and she was moments away from losing it.

"He's gone, Shelley. It's over," I said, trying to offer some comfort.

"Over for you, maybe," she snapped, whipping her head around to glare at us.

"Hardly," Tyler added, totally misreading the room. "We still have a serial killer on the loose,"

"Good for you," Shelley hissed. "Meanwhile, we get nothing. No vengeance, no payback. But that's okay. You go and play vigilantes with your new target. It's not like this meant anything to you anyway." She gestured at Byers' body and turned away in disgust.

"He's dead, sis. We can't change what's happened," Kate tried to reason with her.

"It sucks, but it is what it is," Bryony added, stepping towards Shelley and holding out her hand to try and calm her, but Shelley was having none of it.

"This was our kill!" she shouted. "Ours. I wanted our faces to be the last thing he saw. He owed us that. But this?" She turned back round to point at the body. "This is a fucking joke."

She stormed over to where he hung and reached into her jacket pocket. Cursing under her breath, she pulled out her knife, the one she'd pulled on me when I first met her, the one she always carried, and she plunged it into his bloody chest. Then, leaving the knife lodged into his ribs, she stood back to admire her handiwork.

"That knife was meant for you," She spat in disgust. "So, take it with you into hell. You were given the easy way out. But if we'd gotten hold of you, they'd have needed dental records to identify you." Her words didn't help to ease her troubled mind though, and she charged back over to the ladder. "This is fucked up," she cried, throwing her hands up. "It's all fucking fucked up."

"Shelley, remember what I said about death..." I wanted to help her. Seeing her like this was tearing me apart. But when she heard my voice, she turned towards me, and the look of anger I saw made me stop in my tracks, hesitant to say another word.

"I shouldn't have let you distract me. I knew I needed to stay focused today." She wasn't making any sense.

"Look at him!" I gestured to the mess of a man swinging in

THE JOKER

front of us. "He's been up here for hours. A day maybe. There's no way we could've stopped this. It was out of our hands."

"I should've known something would go wrong." She half shouted, half cried.

"How? How could you possibly foresee this?" I argued.

"Because everything goes wrong when I'm…" She went to say something else but stopped herself. Tears were pooling in her eyes, and I waited, wanting her to finish her sentence, but she never did.

Instead, she turned and headed back down the ladder. I strode forward, having every intention of following her, but Kate ran down after her, and Bryony came to stand in front of me, putting her hand up to rest on my heaving chest.

"Leave her," Bryony told me with empathy in her eyes. "Let her calm down. When she's ready, she'll come to you."

I didn't like that idea. I didn't like the thought of her leaving without me, feeling so hurt, but I nodded and let Bryony turn her back on me and leave too.

Once we heard the front door close, I faced the others and asked, "Why does it feel like my heart's just been ripped out?"

Devon sighed, and Adam took a step closer to me.

"Because you love her," he said. "And when she hurts, you hurt a million times more. That's how it goes."

I couldn't speak.

All I could do was let Adam's words sink in.

I loved her.

I did love Shelley, and the thought of her being in pain was crippling me.

I stared at the ground in front of me, trying to find the right words, but there were none.

"Now you know," Devon added knowingly, and I sighed.

"What do I do now?" I asked.

"You give her time," Adam replied. "And when she's ready, you talk."

Five men gathered in a loft space talking feelings next to a gutted corpse swinging from the rafters. I'd laugh if it wasn't so fucking tragic.

"What if she never comes back?" I said, letting a rare moment of pessimism creep in.

"She will." I looked up at Adam as he spoke. "She loves you too. She's just pissed at the world right now, but she'll get over it. She wanted revenge for her family, and she didn't get it. We of all people can understand how that feels."

At that moment, Adam's phone went off, and when he scrolled to read whatever had been sent, he gritted his teeth. "Fuck, he's done another one."

We gathered around to read the message.

Adam, I've left you a little gift back at your warehouse. A thank you for all your hard work. I am enjoying giving back to you soldiers, the ones who do so much for us. But who will be next?

"Who the fuck are we going to find at the warehouse?" Will asked, and then, turning to Tyler, he added, "And why didn't your CCTV alert go off? I thought you set it up so we'd know if anyone broke in?"

"I did." Tyler took out his phone and started tapping. "I swear, after all this, I'm updating all my systems, because this is fucked up."

When we got to the warehouse, the door was unlocked, and as we pulled it open and walked inside, we could smell fresh blood. Whoever was here hadn't been here for long. That metallic scent that hung in the air was all too familiar.

In the middle of the room, chained to our chair that was bolted to the floor, was a body. The arms and legs were locked into the restraints, but the head was covered with a black plastic bag. The jeans were soaked with blood, and as we got closer, we could see that the nails on their hands were bloody and broken. Whoever this was, they'd died in this chair, gripping the wood and clawing to get out.

"He said this one's for you, Adam," Will said. "So, let's see who it is."

Adam took the lead, stepping forward to pull the bag from the head.

"Holy fuck," Adam said under his breath as he stood back. And there, in the chair, sat Chase Lockwood.

We'd never had much to do with the guy. We knew his dad was wealthy and they lived in one of the posher estates in Sandland. But our paths had never really crossed.

"What the fuck did Lockwood do to you?" Tyler asked, frowning at Adam.

Adam ran his hands over his face in exasperation.

"He bad-mouthed Olivia, remember? I stabbed his hand last year and pinned him to a fence."

"Fuck, yes. I remember that," I said and waited for him to add something else, but he just shook his head.

"Olivia is going to be gutted when she finds out. She didn't like the dude, but she didn't want this."

Through the mutters and sighs, Devon cleared his throat. "Whoever did this killed Chase as a gift for you. Something to say thank you, and yet all Chase did was say some shit that upset you and Liv?"

We all turned to look at Devon, who'd gone paler than he usually was.

"What if it's me next? What if…" He trailed off and then realisation hit. "What if he targets Leah May's dad?"

Devon and Leah May's dad hadn't always gotten along, to put it mildly. But I doubted this nutter saw through the nuances of human relationships when it came to his killing spree. And if he were going to choose someone to kill for Devon as a thank you, her dad would be a prime target. Anyone else who'd upset Devon was already dead.

"Go home," Adam told him, clicking back into business mode. "Get Leah May and go to her dad's house. I'll call Gaz and get him to sort the clean up here and at the Byers house."

"I'll come with you," Tyler added, following Devon as he charged for the door.

"You can both go," Adam said, looking at Will and me. "I've got this covered. Chase isn't going anywhere."

Will nodded and headed off too, but something held me back.

"I'll stay with you. Soldiers don't work alone."

Adam went to argue, but I walked over to where Chase sat and got busy unlocking the cuffs. Gaz might be clean up, but I wasn't about to stand around and do nothing. Besides, being here would hopefully take my mind off Shelley and what she was feeling. Death had a way of distracting you from life. That's what I hoped, anyway.

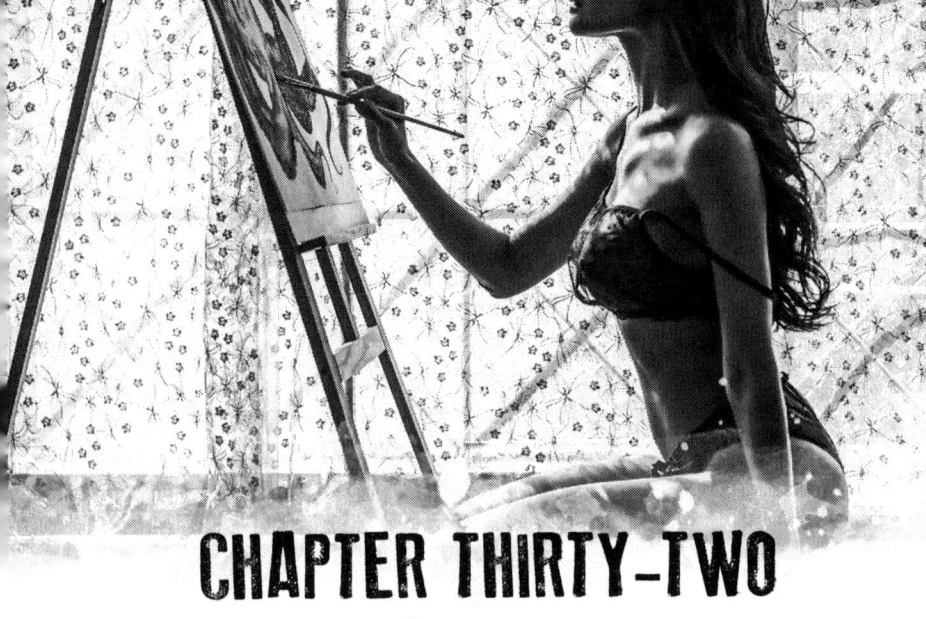

CHAPTER THIRTY-TWO
Shelley

I flew into my house like a bat out of hell, slamming the front door, then instantly regretting it when my mum came into the hallway asking where the fire was.

"What the hell is going on, Shelley?"

"It's nothing. I'm fine," I said, like a sulky teenager.

"It's not fine. One look at your face tells me you're angry. Come into the living room and tell me what's going on."

"I just need to go to my room." I tried to bypass her and head for the stairs, but she was having none of it.

"I don't think so, lady. Living room. Now."

I huffed but did as she asked. I was wound up like a coiled spring. Maybe I did need to offload?

"Where are your sisters?" Mum asked, sinking into the sofa next to me.

"They knew I needed to be alone, so they dropped me off

and went to Kate's." Truth was, they didn't want to be around me when I was like this. I knew that much.

"So, what is it this time?" Mum asked, eyeing me from her side of the sofa. "Because it can't be a fight at school, we're finally past that phase, but lord knows I fought your corner more times than I care to remember. How you managed to get to art college, and not get expelled still baffles me."

I wasn't the best pupil at school. All the hurt from my father's abandonment had been channelled into the bullies back then. It felt better to take it out on them.

"I never fought anyone that didn't deserve it," I replied, remembering the days of sitting in the cooler, waiting for them to ring my mum and tell her how much I'd fucked up that day. I usually got a stern talking to once I got home, a reminder not to throw away my education. And on the rare occasion they called her into school for a meeting, a grounding and loss of privileges. But she knew why I did it, why I was the way I was.

"Who are you fighting with now?" she asked, folding her arms and sighing, then her face dropped. "Is it Colton?" I swallowed, feeling my heart twist at hearing his name. "I know you've been seeing him. I'm not blind."

"I shouldn't have. I made a mistake." The words spilled out and I didn't even know if I meant them. I just felt so confused.

"What mistake? I don't understand." She frowned at me, leaning forward to show she wanted to know everything.

I considered giving my mum the watered-down version, or worse still, lying to her. But I was tired, and everything had become too much for me to bear. So, I opened up to her about the emails from Byers. I told her how we'd gotten involved with the soldiers and how they were helping us, leaving out the part about our own kills, and then I told her about Colton.

"But I was a fool to think it could work. It never works," I whispered to myself more than her.

My mum shuffled closer to me and placed her hand on my knee.

"Why wouldn't it work? Because of your father and me?" She squeezed my knee. "Are you going to base your whole outlook on life on my failed relationship with your father?"

"It wasn't only you that failed though, was it." I couldn't bring myself to look at her as I spoke.

"Oh, I know that." Mum scoffed. "He failed big time. He left us for another woman."

"No, I mean *we* failed. I did."

I chanced a glance in my mum's direction from under my curls and I saw her frowning.

"It had nothing to do with you. You didn't fail," she argued, shaking her head.

"Didn't we? If we'd been better, he'd have stayed."

Another sigh, and she squeezed my knee again, then shook it to force me to look at her properly.

"There's nothing you could have done to change what happened. He was selfish. We were better off without him." She took another breath, then added. "You really thought that? All this time, you thought you could have done something to stop it? Shelley… you're your own woman now. You're old enough to know that what happened to me won't necessarily happen to you. You do know that, right? Not all men are like that."

I nodded but didn't speak. How could I with a golf ball-sized pain in my throat?

"Answer me," my mum insisted.

"It wasn't a theory I wanted to test out... before now," I managed to say. "I preferred being on my own."

My mum fell back into the sofa, groaning under her breath, and slapping her hands onto her thighs.

"We fucked you up," she stated, going right for the jugular. "And that's why you're always so angry. You blamed yourself. And even now, at twenty-two, you think living a half-life is better than what you could have." My mum hung her head for a moment and then looked back up at me. "This stops today."

"What?"

"This wallowing," she said angrily. "The pity party. All the anger. You hear me? It stops. Today."

"I'm not having a pity party–"

"Aren't you? Because from where I'm sitting, you need to snap out of it. Start living your life and not wallowing in the failures of mine. My relationship was a shitshow. I get that. And I'm not saying you weren't affected when you were kids, we all were. But that's the past. You can't live there any longer, Shelley. No good can come from it."

"But don't we learn from the past?"

"Yes! I did! I learned not to trust a fraud who promises me the world. To do my homework before letting a guy into my life. But you? You need to make your own mistakes, and you can't do that if you're forever guarding yourself against pitfalls that might never happen."

"Again, isn't that the whole point? To avoid the pitfalls? Because they will be there eventually."

"Pitfalls like Byers or your dad maybe, yes. But Colton?" She gave me a sad smile. "He's not a pitfall, Shelley, he's a rollercoaster ride."

"Maybe I don't like rollercoasters."

I was lying and arguing for the sake of arguing now.

"Then he's a rainbow after the storm," she said, gazing into the distance with a dreamy look.

"That's a really shit analogy," I replied, bringing her back down to earth.

"I never said I was any good at those, but I'm right. He's not Byers. He's not your father. He's not his father. He's different."

I didn't know what the history was between Mum and Colton. I guessed she knew him through his dad, but did she really know him?

"He kills people, Mum. He's not a good guy." I felt guilty telling her so bluntly. That, and the fact that I'd killed too felt like a cop-out.

"I know what he does," she replied without batting an eyelid. "I also know where he's been and what other things he's done."

She closed her eyes, and taking a moment to think, she added, "I really shouldn't be saying this, and it goes against every promise I've made, but I think you need to know the truth."

"Go on," I urged, wanting to know everything she had to say. I needed to know it all.

"Colton might be a King, but he is nothing like his father. I first met Colton when he was thirteen years old. His father sent him to me for some… errand, and the boy I met that day was a far cry from the man he is now.

"He was timid, weak, broken down by his father and the burden of what they did in that house. When I met him, I told him he needed to be stronger, to fight back. And he did. It wasn't overnight. He had to find and build that strength, but don't you see, Shelley? He overcame the obstacles thrown at him. He came out the other end a better man. He didn't let what his father did tether him to a life he didn't want. He made his own life."

"So, I should be more like Colton and shrug off the shit my father left me with?" I said sarcastically.

"I'm not saying shrug it off, I'm saying fight it. Make something beautiful out of your life. Live it. Win, despite him." She took another breath. "There's something else I need to tell you, but this one has to stay between us."

I nodded.

What the hell was she going to hit me with now?

"I mean it, Shelley. You can't tell anyone, not your sisters, not your friends, and definitely not Colton."

"Okay, I won't say a word. What is it?" I leant forward. This I really needed to hear.

"When his father died, Colton sold their house and used every penny from the estate to pay back what his father had done. He sent a share of the money to every person that'd ever been hurt by the Kings, and that included us. If it weren't for Colton King, we wouldn't have a home to live in.

"When your father left, he left us with more than broken hearts. I was up to my eyeballs in debt. I had bailiffs knocking at the door and we were threatened with eviction. The day that cheque came to us, I was able to pay all of that off. We kept our house, and with the money leftover I could afford to go back to college and get some qualifications. Your Aunt Rosie did the same. She paid for her teacher training course, and I did my English literature degree. We made a better life for ourselves, for you, because of Colton King. And yet, that boy put a clause in every contract. He made us swear to never tell anyone that he'd gifted us that money. He didn't want recognition. He did it because he's a good man."

My heart was beating tenfold.

My mind a whirl of confusion.

I was speechless.

Months ago, I'd blamed everything that'd ever gone wrong for my family, for my mum and aunt, on Colton King. And now, I felt a burning guilt, because it'd been the opposite. He'd saved us.

"I feel like a dick," I cried suddenly, staring blindly at the carpet.

"You're not a dick," my mum said, but I shook my head.

"I am. I blamed him for so much."

How was I ever going to make this up to him?

"And yet he still pursued you," Mum added with a knowing tone to her voice. "I guess he wanted to prove himself in his own way."

"I fucked it up. I always fuck it up."

"You haven't. You just need to sort a few things out, talk it out with him. Life isn't always black and white, Shelley. Things go wrong. People make mistakes, but you work through them. You can't quit just because things get a little bumpy. That's not how life works. Not for us, anyway. Your dad was like that. One pothole and he'd bail, but that's not you, is it? You're a fighter, like me."

I was a fighter, but I'd been fighting the wrong battles.

"What should I do?" I turned to ask my mum.

"You cut the crap and go to him. You tell him how you feel. Be honest. Not all hearts are destined for heartbreak. Some do find their home in another." I heard the crack in her voice as she spoke. "No one deserves to hear that they're loved more than he does. And you do love him, don't you?"

I couldn't stop a stray tear from falling as I nodded.

"And no one deserves to feel that love more than you, my girl. You're made for each other. One with a heart that's open and full of love, and the other that's closed off and scared, frightened to feel the power of what it's like to love unconditionally. Please don't live like that, Shelley. I know I'm an old romantic with an unhealthy obsession with poetry, but I want all the happiness in the world for you. You deserve this. You both do. I'm not saying it won't be hard. You'll have days when he'll drive you crazy. You'll drive him crazy. Hell, I'm your mother and I find you infuriating most of the time. But putting that all to one side, you have to focus on the good times, the moments when there's no one else in the world, only the two of you. When he looks at you like his whole reason for being is you, that's what it's all about. The magic. Do you feel the magic?"

"Always."

"Then what are you waiting for? Go and tell that beautiful man that you love him. Or better yet, just look at him. Stand there and look in his eyes and wait for him to say it to you. Because he will. Go and get your happily ever after."

I felt a surge of adrenaline rush through me.

Yes, the day had started as a fuck up of epic proportions. Byers was gone and nothing had ended as I wanted it to. But that didn't mean this thing we had, my blossoming relationship with Colton, had to end.

It was still early days, but I didn't want to walk away. I needed to go to him and see if I could salvage something from this day. Because the thought of never seeing him or being with him made me feel a damn sight worse than I had done when I'd seen Byers. The thought of losing Colton was more painful than any knife, any wound. It was something that I might never come back from.

CHAPTER THIRTY-THREE
Shelley

Driving to The Sanctuary, I replayed every possible conversation over in my head, tailoring my responses and second-guessing his. But as I pulled up at the side of the building and saw him loading up their van with Adam and one of their security guys, everything I'd rehearsed fell away. All I could do was sit in the car and breathe.

I could do this.

I just had to stay true to myself and be honest.

We both needed to know where we stood.

Nerves that I never knew I had fluttered inside me, and with a hesitant hand, I opened the car door and stepped out. He heard the door slamming shut and turned to look my way. Catching the heat of his glare sent a fire through me, and I started to walk slowly towards him, but his strides were longer, and soon he was right in front of me, looking grateful to see me, and yet the uncertainty in his eyes told me he was probably feeling the exact same way I was.

"I didn't know whether to follow you, but your sisters told me you needed space," he said, trying to gauge my mood. "Are you okay? I'm sorry about what happened earlier, back at the house."

I'd never heard Colton apologise. In all the time I'd known him, I'd never heard him sound so contrite. He was always the cocky, confident one, but right now he seemed anything but.

"I overreacted. I'm sorry." I had to apologise too. Although I thought my outburst was justified at the time, it wasn't. I acted like a brat. And after finding out what my mum had told me, he had more right than anyone to feel betrayed.

"You don't have to apologise to me," he said gracefully, making my guilt multiply. "You felt pissed off, and I get it. He treated your family like shit, and you deserved payback on your terms."

"But we don't always get what we want, do we?"

He stared at me, his throat bobbing as he swallowed and stayed silent.

"I was a bitch today." I sighed. "And I shouldn't have been. He's gone and it's over. That has to be enough, it's out of my hands. I can't control everything."

"I get it. Control is important to you. But you're right, sometimes you need to let go."

I tensed at his words. It was my turn to fall silent and take a moment.

"What is this, Colton?"

He dropped his head, appearing to search amongst the dirt

and rubble for his answer. The fact that he couldn't look me in the eyes felt like a stab to my heart, but I carried on.

"Is it just sex? Is that all you want from me? Because if it is..."

His face shot up; his brow furrowed in confusion as he looked at me with apprehension.

"No." He took a step closer to me, but I folded my arms and took a protective step back. Seeing me retreat, he rubbed his hands over his face and sighed. "I know I have no right to get pissed at you for asking that. I haven't got the best family history and my reputation was kind of... dubious before I met you. What can I say–" He threw his arms up in the air in exasperation. "–I like sex. But that's not all this is."

I didn't reply. I wanted to hear everything he had to say before I responded.

"What I want," he carried on. "Is for you to judge me for me. Don't base your opinion on what you've heard. Let me show you, prove to you what sort of man I am."

"Okay."

He moved a step closer, and this time, I let him. I kept my arms folded, but I stayed put, looking directly at him as he spoke to me.

"I'm not the best with words; I prefer actions. But what I can say is, I don't want anyone else, and I've already told you that. I wish you'd believe me. I'll do anything to prove myself to you.

"When I see you, I get this craving, this need to be as close to you as I can get." He shook his head like he couldn't believe what he was saying. "I never thought I'd be the kind of guy to settle down, but then everyone kept telling me I hadn't met the one. That when the one came along, I'd know, and everything would change. I told them it was all bullshit. And then... there was you."

My heart flickered, but I stayed silent. Stunned by the beauty of his words.

"I don't even have to question if you're the one," he said, "because I know. I know because every morning when I wake up, you're the first thing I think about. All through the day, I wonder what you're doing and think of ways I can message you or see you. At night, even when I'm working a shift at the club, I miss you, and it's like physical pain. I probably sound like a psycho nutcase because we haven't known each other for that long, but time doesn't mean anything to me.

"From the moment I saw you on the dance floor months ago, before we'd even met and you were watching me, I was intrigued. Seeing you for the first time, arguing and sparring with you, that was the most alive I've felt, ever. I want to spend more time with you, get to know everything about you. Even your sarcastic, moody shit turns me on. I love that you keep me on my toes and make me work for it."

I had to smile at that part, and seeing me soften slightly, he took another step toward me.

"I don't know what's going to happen in the future, but I can promise you one thing—" He closed his eyes, then when he opened them, I saw the genuine, loving side of Colton he rarely showed anyone else. "—I'm in this for the long haul. No games. No bullshit. If we argue, and we will argue... you're a bomb and I'm the detonator, and that's never going to change, but when we fight, there's only three things you need to do; either kiss me, fuck me, or fight back, but you can't walk away. I'm going nowhere and neither are you."

He came right into my space, and with his thumb and forefinger under my chin, he lifted my face to look at him. "We don't hide from the fireworks, we embrace them. If it gets tough, we can't run, we have to stay and work it out. Because building something together is worth it, right?" He waited for me to reply and then, when my speechless, dumbass just stood there open-mouthed, he added, "We're worth fighting for, aren't we?"

I felt a tear well up in my eyes. I didn't like showing emotion, and it was taking everything in me to keep it where it was and not let it escape and fall down my cheek, giving away the fact that I was feeling something so big, so powerful that it scared me. But he reached up and stroked my cheek with his warm hand, and as I leaned my head into him, the tear fell free, and he wiped it away.

He'd got me.

He'd always got me.

"You don't ever need to be something else with me, only yourself," he whispered, and I hiccupped, listening to his words. Words that touched my heart, bringing it back to life.

"I know I'm not always open with you–" I started to say.

"You're trying though, and that's all that matters. We both are," he replied, putting me at ease even though I felt like I was continually giving excuses. "We learn to crawl, then walk, and after that we run. Small steps. It won't always be easy, but it'll be us. Fire and ice, fury and fear, heaven and hell; two parts of the same whole."

I put my hand over his as he caressed my face.

"I've never felt like this before," I said, opening my heart to him.

He smiled.

"Me neither."

I swallowed, unsure whether to say the words lodged in my throat, trying but failing to force them down or deny they existed.

"I think I might be f–"

But he butted in.

"I've already fallen."

I never thought I'd ever hear words like that from Colton. And hearing them right now made my head swim. I didn't want to hold back anymore. I wanted to jump in with both feet like he had. I wanted to experience every part of being with Colton King, from the fights and the days I wanted to pull my hair out, to all the love and memories, the future we could have together.

So, I did what both of us did best, I let actions speak louder than words and reached up and grabbed the back of his head, pulling him down to me for a kiss. The minute his lips met mine, I poured every ounce of love I felt into him. I said everything with my kiss, showing him I was right there with him. Loving him back, whether it was easy or hard, sunny days or ugly ones, calm or storm, I was there. I didn't want to be anywhere else.

We stayed in each other's arms, kissing, hugging, holding each other as we stood at the side of the building, not caring where we were. Eventually, I pulled away, but he kept his forehead pressed against mine.

"You always deserve the best." He sighed and then, with a smirk, he added, "That's why you got me. You hit the jackpot." And I couldn't help but smile at the old Colton shining through. "I hate doing this, but I have to go somewhere," he added, frowning with regret. "We've got soldier business that needs taking care of. But would you wait in my room for me? Liv's upstairs. You could chat to her, or you can stay by yourself in my room, whatever you want. But will you wait for me so we can talk some more when I get back?"

I nodded and smiled, lifting my hand to touch his lips, and he grinned and kissed my fingertips.

"Of course I'll wait for you," I told him. "Let me get my handbag from my car and I'll come up."

"Thank you," he replied. "I just need to finish loading up the van with Adam and Gaz, then I'll walk you up."

Reluctantly, I stepped out of his arms and turned towards the car. Glancing over my shoulder, I saw him heading back to the open door of The Sanctuary, but he turned his head to look at me, and when he caught me watching, he smiled and winked, and my whole body prickled and glowed from that one glance. I was caught in his spell; this complicated, mysterious, secretive man who never really let anyone in to see the real him. But he'd opened the door to me, and I knew more than I'd ever let on. I knew that he was one in a million.

A diamond in the rough.

My soldier.

My Colton.

CHAPTER THIRTY-FOUR
Colton

"Everything okay?" Adam asked as I strolled back into the chapel to help load the last few weapons into the van. We figured we'd join Devon and the others at Leah May's dad's vicarage. I wouldn't stay long, though. I wanted to come back and be with Shelley.

"Yeah, it's all good. She's going to wait here with Liv while we do our thing. I think we're gonna be okay. She loves me." I shrugged. "She might not have said it, but I know. How could she not?"

I smirked and glanced around to find most of the stuff was packed away. All that was needed now was for us to get in the van and go. Just then, Gaz wandered in, rubbing his hands together and whistling without a care in the world.

"Do you want me to come to the vicarage with you?" he

asked, eager to get in on the action.

"No, you head to the warehouse for the clean-up. We've got it covered," Adam told him, and he nodded.

"No problem, boss. I'll get the Chase mess sorted. You've got nothing to worry about."

My back went up, and so did Adam's. Adam froze and turned slowly to face Gaz.

"I didn't say who was there. I just told you we needed a clean-up." Adam's face was stone and his eyes bore into Gaz, waiting for his answer.

"You must've done." Gaz laughed it off like it was nothing, but there was a nervousness about him, and his smile was quivering, anxious and edgy. "I swear you sent me a text about it. Or maybe you mentioned it just now." He shrugged, avoiding eye contact.

But Adam shook his head. He didn't make mistakes like that. He knew what he'd said.

"It's you, isnt it?" Adam stated, his jaw tense as he gritted his teeth.

"What's me?" Gaz looked up, trying to show his innocence by staring us both in the face.

"I had a feeling it was you." Adam stepped forward, his fists clenched by his sides and his face contorted with fury. "But I was hoping I was wrong, because what you've done is fucked up. So un-fucking-believably fucked up." He stopped and took a few deep breaths. "I was praying you had more about you than to shit all over the ones who've given you a chance."

Suddenly, the innocent act Gaz was playing fell away, and his face went from exasperated shock to one of vicious anger, aimed right at us. He narrowed his eyes as he stepped forward, and I could see the tick of his jaw as he chose to fight back.

"Gave me a chance?" He scoffed, knowing his time was up but still fighting anyway. "You never gave me a fucking chance. All the years I've served you, done whatever shit you've thrown my way, and not once have you used me the way I should've been used. The way I wanted to be used." He bared his teeth like a feral animal, spit flying as he growled, "I clean up your shit, do the stakeouts you can't be arsed to do. Night after night, I stand on that staircase, watching over your fucking empire. And what do I get in return? Nothing. You've always seen me as a joke. But not anymore."

I wasn't fucking having this. He'd disrespected the wrong people.

"So, you repay us by leaving a dirty fucking killing spree across town?" I snapped. "A messy one that could've gotten any one of us arrested and sent down for life. You're a fucking liability." I moved forward, meeting Adam where he stood, but Gaz got spooked and reached into his jacket, pulling out a gun. Clear evidence that he was never soldier material.

"I proved to you I was a soldier," he said, waving the gun in the air haphazardly. "I was a better one than you'll ever be, because I worked alone." He held the gun up a little steadier and aimed it at Adam and then me. "Every kill I left was a gift for you, but nothing's ever good enough, is it? I'm never good enough."

We could've overpowered him. We had more strength behind us than he did, and every part of me was itching to barrel into him and knock the gun out of his traitorous hand. But when a familiar voice echoed from the open doorway, we froze. Everything seemed to happen in slow motion as Gaz preempted our impending ambush, and on seeing Shelley walk through the door and come up behind him, he grabbed her and held the gun to her head. He was taking the coward's way out. But he'd chosen the wrong target. I was going to tear him apart for putting his hands on her.

"Not so cocky now, hey?" he sneered. "One wrong move and I'll put a bullet in her." He pressed the gun into her temple as he held her tightly against him.

My heart thumped a rapid beat in my chest; adrenaline and fear warped with anger and fury to create a screech of white noise in my brain. No one touched her. He'd just signed his death warrant, and that death would be the most painful, drawn-out killing anyone had ever seen.

Shelley's eyes were wide, and she looked right at me like she was waiting for me to give her instructions on what to do. But as she struggled to break free of his grasp, he held her tighter. She didn't stand a chance. We were her only hope.

"Get the fuck off me," she hissed as she struggled, but nothing would deter him. When he put the gun right in her face and pulled a set of handcuffs from his pocket, ordering her to put them on, I tried to calm her with my voice. Let her know this was only temporary. We would fucking annihilate this motherfucker. But we had to be smart. Make him think we were playing along. Lull him into a false sense of security before we could strike.

"Just do what he says, baby," I told her calmly, then glared my warning at Gaz. "I'll have you out of here soon. And when we make him pay, I'll let you take the final blow."

It was a promise I intended to keep, and even though she didn't like it, she kept the fire burning in her eyes as she let him cuff her. She made sure he knew the score, though.

"You're a fucking dead man," she snarled. My girl would never give up. She was a born fighter.

Gaz just laughed back at her like the fucker he was. "We're all dead anyway, every one of us in this room. You just don't know it yet."

To try and distract him, Adam and I held our hands up in a fake show of surrender. We knew we had to play this the right way. The chapel was empty, and all our weapons were loaded into the van. The knife that Shelley always carried was still lodged in Byers' chest back at that house. We had nothing but ourselves and our wits. I'd have given anything for one of Devon's throwing knives to fall into my hand. A clean stab right between his eyes would've done the trick, and I was an ace shot. But wishes were pointless. This was real life.

"You don't need to hurt her," I told him, a growing desperation to act bubbling under the surface. It was like watching a bad movie play out, and I couldn't stop this. I hated that I couldn't stop it. "She's got nothing to do with this and she's done nothing wrong. If you want to hurt someone, hurt me."

But Adam hit the nail on the head when he added, "He doesn't care. He hasn't got the same code that we have. He kills for fun. None of the people, except Byers, deserved to die at his hands. But I promise you this," he hissed, pointing at Gaz. "You're gonna wish you'd never met the soldiers of Brinton when we're finished with you. I'll make sure you regret the day you ever crossed us."

"I didn't set out to cross you." Gaz held his chin up, as if he was righteous, shuffling back towards the door with Shelley held awkwardly in his arms as she fought against him. We struggled with our decision on whether to barrel into him and set off a chain reaction that could end in disaster, or keep our cool and see how this played out. Shelley's safety had to come first.

"Just let her go and let's settle this like real men," I urged, but Gaz wasn't a real man. He had no intention of surrendering to us. He wanted to take this to the bitter end.

"Sorry." Gaz shook his head. "No can do. This is going to end the way I want, not you." And with that, he dragged Shelley out of the back door.

We shot forward, running to stop him, but he shoved the gun into her mouth as he dragged her across the gravel over to the car.

"Stay where you are or I'll blow her brains all over this place." He threatened, and then he opened the back door of the car and threw her in.

The minute the gun was off her, we lurched forward, but we were too late. In a flash, he was in the car too with the doors locked and the engine revving. Instantly, she sat up, trying to open the door and bang on the window, but it was no use. She couldn't get out.

"See you in hell." Gaz cackled through the window at us, then sped down the path and out onto the road.

"Van. Now!" Adam shouted, running to the loaded van, jumping in and revving the engine.

Gaz might've had a head start, but it wasn't over yet.

We were coming for him.

And once we got to him, he was in for a lifetime of pain.

No one crossed the soldiers and lived to tell the tale.

And no one hurt my girl and got away with it.

He'd pulled off a double whammy, and for that, he'd get

double the payback. Hell on acid.

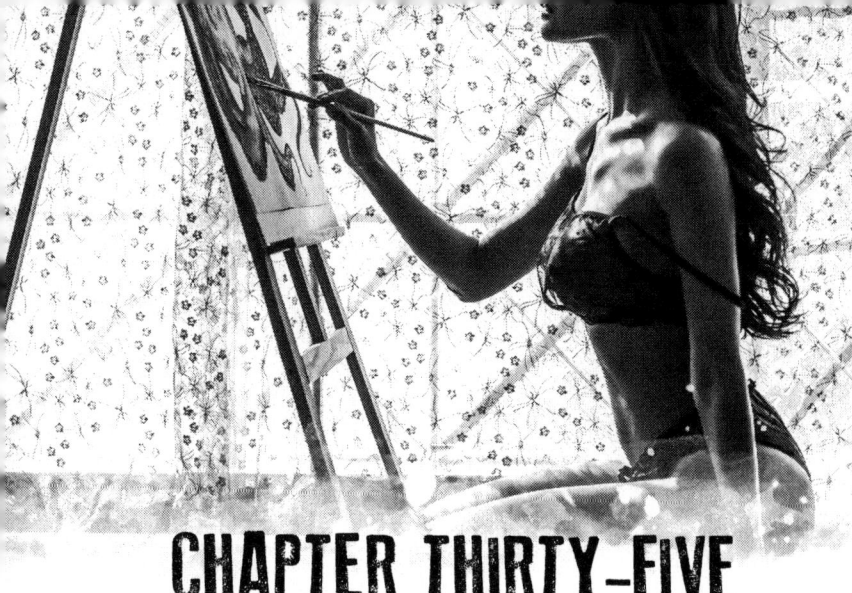

CHAPTER THIRTY-FIVE
Shelley

"You do know this isn't going to end well for you," I sneered from the backseat as I yanked and pulled at the cuffs restraining me, kicking out at the doors, the seats, anything I could reach to fight back.

"It's already over," he replied with a hint of amusement as he drove us through the dark streets of Brinton.

I knew he didn't give a fuck, and if I didn't do something soon, he'd take me somewhere and kill me. He had the gun rested in his lap, and I thought about grabbing it, but he must've second guessed my plans because he placed it on the dashboard in front of him, far out of my reach.

"When they find you, you'll be begging to die. They're going to make you suffer," I added, trying to keep him talking so I could formulate a plan.

I glanced out of the rear window, but couldn't see headlights behind us. It was pitch black on this stretch of road, and the hope that Colton was following with Adam was fading rapidly. I had to do this myself. I had to think fast.

"He won't find us," Gaz taunted me. "By the time he finds you, it'll be in pieces. Or better yet, I might mail you back to him piece by piece. He'd like that. Colton always has been a twisted fucker and now I'm going to turn the tables."

"You've got to catch me first," I hissed back, my hair falling in my face as I rammed my feet forward and thrashed in my seat.

But Gaz just laughed.

"I've already caught you. Where the hell do you think you're going to go tied up in my car?"

He huffed a laugh then added, "You know, I followed you once. Late at night, as you left your art campus. I trailed you down the dark streets of Merivale because I wanted to teach you a lesson. You thought you could come into our club and disrespect us. I didn't like the way you talked to Colton, and I wanted you to pay for that. But you shouted at me, do you remember?"

I ignored him.

Of course I remembered that night. I'd thought it was Byers following me. And now, hearing that it was him, I wished I'd stopped in that street and fought back. Hunted him down and made him pay for what he'd done.

"You stood there trembling in the dark, acting like you weren't scared, but you were, weren't you?"

I still ignored him.

"I thought about coming out of the shadows, challenging you, showing you what I was capable of, but something stopped me. Maybe I was saving you for this moment, I don't know. But you got lucky that night. Tonight, that won't be the case."

He took a sharp turn, and ignoring his idle threats, I glanced around at the trees looming over the road, enclosing us in as he sped down the lane. All my efforts to try and escape had been pointless so far. The only thing I'd achieved was breathlessness and a hopeless acceptance of what was to come. But I wasn't going to be another statistic. A notch on this fuckers' kill post. I'd rather take us both out than let him do whatever fucked-up stuff he was going to do. I wouldn't go down like that. That wasn't how my story ended.

Without a second thought, I lurched forward and using my hands that were cuffed in front of me, I put them over his head, pulling him back into the headrest as I tried to strangle him. He was strong and fought back, taking his hands off the wheel to grapple with me, making the car swerve and bump as we left the road and headed down an embankment. And all the time we struggled, fighting to gain control, neither one of us willing to give up.

"You fucking bitch," he shouted as he wrestled with my hands, pulling them over his head. But I wasn't going to give in, and I swung with as much force as I could and smacked him in the side of the head with my fists, sending him crashing into the window to the side of him. I shot forward, trying to get to the gun, but he saw my intentions and knocked it to the floor.

"You're gonna pay for that," he hissed as he tried to gain control of the car that was careering down the embankment. With one hand, he pushed me into the backseat as he wrestled with the steering wheel with the other. But it was no use. As we struggled, the uneven terrain the car was speeding across changed, and I heard an almighty whoosh as we hit something.

It wasn't solid ground.

It was water.

I hated water and I couldn't swim.

Panic hit me like a freight train. We were going down and there wasn't anything either of us could do about it. I was cuffed in the back. The gun was somewhere on the floor, hidden by the murky water that'd already started rushing around our feet. As the car bobbed on the surface, Gaz continued to fight with me, grabbing me as I moved backwards and tried to yank the door open, kick at the windows and try anything I could to escape.

The water was icy cold, creeping from our ankles to our calves and then up to our thighs. As realisation set in, Gaz turned his attention from me to his own survival, yanking on his door in a desperate bid for freedom, but the pressure of the water outside made it impossible. He couldn't get it open. In a panic, he tried the electric windows, but there was no power. The engine had ingested the water and hydrolocked. Nothing was working.

This was it.

This was how I was going to die.

Locked and cuffed in a car with a serial killer.

The water gushed in around us, and I pushed myself up to the roof of the car to get the last breaths of oxygen. Panting in deep breaths, I tried to stay calm and focus on the images flashing through my mind. Anything to make these last moments special.

I thought about my mum and dad in happier times, watching us at Christmas as we opened our presents around the tree. My sisters and I, playing in the yard, riding our bikes and scooters and drinking water from the garden hose pipe in Summer without a care. My Aunty Rosie reading me bedtime stories and sharing beauty tips as she did my makeup and told me I was the prettiest girl in Merivale.

And then, there was him.

Colton.

The soulmate I never saw coming.

The man I thought I hated more than anyone, but I didn't.

He'd saved me.

He'd saved all of us in so many ways.

And now, I was leaving him. And that thought broke my heart completely.

I'd never see him throw his head back and laugh like he didn't have a care in the world.

I'd never hear his silly one-liners or stupid comebacks.

I wouldn't get to feel his strong arms or taste his kiss, and lose myself in how he made me feel… like I was the only girl in the world. Like I was made for him.

His face was all I could see, and his voice echoed in my brain, telling me to be strong, to fight and never give up. I'd take that face and those words along with me into the next life and cherish them until we could meet again.

The man I loved, and yet, I'd never told him.

Why hadn't I told him?

My Colton. My world.

Eventually, the dark, chilly water took me like a black veil of hopelessness, covering my face and pulling me down into the murky depths. I let my body go limp as I fell back, taking one last gulp of air as the cold darkness dragged me away. The words I never got to say flooded my brain, scorched my heart, and stayed locked up inside, never to pass my lips.

Goodnight, Colton.
I'll wait for you.
I'll always wait for you.
You were it for me.
You were the one.
But now it's over.
And...
I love you.

CHAPTER THIRTY-SIX
Colton

We tried to catch up with the car, but our van wasn't as fast as the hatchback. All we could do was use the tracking system Tyler set up to watch where they were heading. We'd had all our vehicles fitted with trackers, and I was thanking my lucky stars that Tyler had instigated that. I couldn't see her, but I knew where she was, and we were minutes away.

Adam drove like a bat out of hell as I sat forward, watching the red dot on the screen that showed their route.

"He thinks he's so fucking clever," Adam cursed. "But he's fucking clueless. Did he really think he'd drive away and we wouldn't find him?"

"He doesn't know about the tracker, and I'm fucking thankful for it," I replied, wringing my hands together. "Some things are better kept between the five of us. We've always known that."

Adam kept one eye on the tracker and one on the road as he flew through Brinton Manor.

"We need to ring the others, let them know what's happening," he said, but at that moment, the red dot on the screen showed they'd veered off the road and were heading over unknown land. She was fighting back. I knew it.

"No time," I snapped, pointing at the screen and sitting forward. "They've gone off-road. We need to speed up."

"I'm going as fast as I can."

The engine roared as Adam drove full throttle, and I kept my arms planted on the dashboard, bracing myself against the roughness of the drive. But when I saw the expanse of blue on the screen, blue they were heading towards, I felt sickness wash over me.

"They're heading for the water," Adam said, and I wanted to reply, to tell him to fuck off for stating the obvious, but I couldn't speak.

She couldn't swim.

The red dot disappeared just as Adam came to a screeching halt in the middle of a country lane and flung the van door open.

"Fuck, we need to get to them," Adam shouted, pulling the side door of the van open and grabbing tools.

I opened my door and jumped out, running toward the dark embankment, desperate to get to her. There was no time to waste.

"Take this," Adam said, suddenly appearing at my side as we both ran, and he held out a hammer. "If they hit the water, they might not be able to get the windows open."

Hearing him say that and thinking about what it meant made bile rise in my throat. Nothing was going to happen to her. I'd made her a promise earlier today. She wouldn't die. She couldn't. She was mine to protect.

"She can't swim," I uttered helplessly.

"She won't need to," Adam replied. "We'll get there."

We ran through the undergrowth, following the tyre tracks as Adam used a torch he'd taken from the van to light the way.

"Don't hit the car window in the middle." He gasped. "You need to hit the corner to get the glass to shatter. Hitting the middle could just make the window flex and absorb the shock."

I didn't know how he knew all that, but I was so frantic I wasn't about to argue. Whatever was the fastest way to save Shelley was all that mattered.

We stumbled down the last part of the embankment, and when we came to the clearing where the river was, we saw the roof of the car on the surface of the water seconds before it disappeared, totally immersed and sinking with my whole world trapped inside.

I dived into the water, swimming down to where the car was. It was dark; I couldn't even see my hands in front of me, but then a streak of light shone from behind. Adam must've had a diving torch, and I'd never been so grateful in that moment for it. The two of us fought the current of the river as we pushed and swam with every ounce of strength we had, and then, we reached the car, and I could see the outline of her body lying lifeless on the backseat.

I tried to open the car door, but it wouldn't budge, so I lifted my hammer and began to smash the window, banging the corner until the pressure from inside and out worked in my favour, and the glass began to shatter. It wasn't fast enough, though, so I used my hands to pull and yank at the glass frame to try and get to her.

Seconds felt like hours, and when I managed to create a gap that I could reach through, I threw the hammer away and pushed forward, grabbing her cuffed arms and pulling her still and lifeless body through the window and into my arms. I had her, and needed to get her above water to give her a chance. She needed air. She needed me to be stronger and swim against an unforgiving current to get us back on land.

I was disorientated, but nature showed me the way, and after what felt like forever, I broke the surface of the river. With her in my arms, I managed to get to the edge and pull us both to safety.

I lay her on her side in the recovery position, unsure what to do at first, but then I rolled her onto her back and gave her mouth to mouth.

"Come on, Shelley," I begged between puffs. "Don't you fucking leave me."

I kept up the resuscitation, I'd never fucking stop, but it felt like I wasn't doing anything. But I wouldn't, couldn't accept that she'd gone. I had to keep going.

"Fucking breathe," I snapped, taking a gulp of air and covering her mouth with my own.

I was conscious of Adam falling onto the grass close by, but every part of me was focused on Shelley. Bringing her back was all that mattered.

"I swear to God, if you don't fucking breathe, I'll–"

My heart stilled in my chest as her body twisted and convulsed, and then the most glorious noise I'd ever heard filled the air… she was coughing.

I rolled her onto her side to let her cough up the water, and I rubbed her back, thanking God and anyone else who'd heard my pleas for bringing her back to me.

"You're okay," I repeated over and over. "It's going to be all right. You're okay. I've got you."

Her eyes slowly opened, and I couldn't stop my tears from falling.

"I should never have let him take you," I cried. "I'm so sorry."

She shook her head and tried to speak, but her voice was hoarse, and I shushed her, taking her in my arms and holding her.

"It all... happened... too fast," she whispered. "There was... nothing... we... could do."

I peeled my wet jacket off and wrapped it around her to give her some warmth. Then, I looked over Shelley's shoulder to where Adam sat, his chest heaving like he'd run a fucking marathon.

"He's gone," was all he said, and I knew he'd tell me later what'd happened. "We need to get her to the hospital," he added, taking his jacket off and throwing it over to me so that I could give her extra warmth, but Shelley started to protest.

"I don't... want... to... go." She shivered as she spoke, and even though I hated hospitals, I knew she wasn't out of the woods yet.

"You've got no choice," I told her forcefully. "You almost drowned and that river is fucking filthy. You need to get checked out by professionals. Please. For my sake."

She took a moment, then nodded. I picked her up in my arms, carrying her back up the embankment towards our van. She was as light as a feather, and yet the weight of what losing her would mean made me tremble against the cold night air. In

THE JOKER

all my life, even after everything my father had put me through, I'd never felt so helpless. This girl was my whole world. My future. The key to a life I never thought I'd have. And nothing and nobody was ever going to come between us again.

CHAPTER THIRTY-SEVEN
Colton

We drove to Sandland General, and I kept Shelley cradled in my arms all the way there. If she started to drift to sleep, I shook her awake. I didn't know if that was the right thing to do, but I felt happier having her fully conscious. Until a doctor checked her over and she was given the green light, I wasn't taking any chances.

As we drove, Adam did what I couldn't, ringing her mum and sisters to let them know briefly what'd happened but that she was okay and on her way to the hospital. He also rang Devon to fill him in on what had gone down. I half listened to him explaining that he felt cheated, Gaz had gotten off lightly. But Gaz wouldn't be resurfacing anytime soon. He was still in the car at the bottom of the river, his seatbelt holding him in place and one of Devon's hunting knives lodged in the side of his neck. He didn't get the ending we owed him, but he got the burial place that was fitting for scum like him; a dirty, filthy riverbed.

When we eventually pulled up outside the hospital, Adam headed straight for the emergency entrance. We didn't give two shits about parking rules, so we discarded the van on the pavement outside, jumped out and bolted toward the reception. I carried Shelley through the double doors and screamed like a mad man.

"Somebody, help me. We need a fucking doctor. Now!"

Everyone looked at us, standing there dripping wet in the foyer, but we didn't care. A passing nurse sprang into action, grabbing blankets before running over to us and covering Shelley to keep her warm. She tried to put one on me, but I shrugged it off. I didn't need help, Shelley did.

"She needs a fucking doctor," I hissed angrily.

"Don't be rude," Shelley scolded me, but the nurse didn't seem to mind.

"I can sort that out," the nurse said, ushering us down the corridor. "Bring her over here. I've got a wheelchair; you don't have to carry her."

"I'm not letting her go," I replied, holding her tightly.

"I don't need a wheelchair and I don't need to be carried," Shelley argued, wriggling and trying to break free so she could stand.

"It's me or the wheelchair," I stated, clinging even tighter.

"Fine. To save your back, I'll take the chair."

She was stubborn, but I wouldn't have it any other way. The fact she was arguing with me meant she was starting to feel herself again.

Adam stayed in reception, and I followed the nurse as I pushed Shelley in the wheelchair. They directed us to a private room, and reluctantly she got out of the chair and sat on the bed. I took the armchair next to it and put my hand on her knee.

"Once we're out of here, I'm taking you home and never letting you out of my sight."

She tried to hide her smile.

"I really hope you don't start treating me like some fragile doll."

"As if." I quirked my brow and gave her a sultry stare. "You're my little warrior, and I wouldn't have you any other way."

The doctor came in and did some preliminary tests. He said she'd be fine, but he wanted her to stay in overnight for observation. He was going to run some other tests, but all the words he was spouting flew over my head. The only ones that registered were, she was okay. After a night in the hospital, hopefully, she'd be allowed to go home tomorrow.

When he left us, I stood up and went over to her, kissing her head and telling her I was staying here too. There wasn't a chance in hell I'd leave her in the hospital on her own.

"Okay." She smiled, surprising me that she didn't argue. Then she asked, "Will you go and see if my mum's here?"

"Do you want me to get you anything?" The nurse was bringing her tea and toast, but I knew the tea would be dishwater and the toast probably as dry as fuck.

"A coffee and some chocolate would be nice. I don't really feel that hungry, but I'll try."

She'd try for me.

Fuck, I loved this girl.

I left her and went to the waiting area, glancing around to see if I could spot a coffee shop. I didn't want to buy some cheap crap from a vending machine. That's when I spotted Grace, and heard her cry of relief as Bryony and Kate hugged each other beside her.

"Oh my God," she sniffed, her hands over her mouth as she came towards me. Then she hugged me, and I put my arms around her, feeling a love I'd never felt before. Something akin to a parental kind of love, not that I could say what that felt like.

"She's okay, Grace. She's going to be fine," I said, stroking her back as she hiccupped through her tears.

Grace leaned back and then held my face in her hands.

"I swear to God, you're a guardian angel. Our guardian angel. Everything you've done for my family… I don't know what we'd do without you."

I shook my head, guilt weighing me down.

"She wouldn't be here if it wasn't for me, Grace. This is all my fault."

But Grace was having none of it.

"No. Don't say that. It's not true." I went to argue, but she shook her head. "I don't know exactly what's happened tonight, but I do know one thing; my daughter was coming to tell you she loved you. And that's all that matters, nothing else. She loves you, Colton. And you know what else?"

I stayed silent, words feeling pointless and unworthy of this moment.

"I love you too."

No one had ever told me they loved me. Not my mum before she died. Not my father throughout his miserable life. I knew my friends would do anything for me, but this… this was something else entirely. Someone loved me for me. Not because they had to, but because they wanted to. I didn't know how to react, so I hugged Grace, and in her ear, I gently whispered, "I love you too. Both of you."

"I know it's all so new, but I hope that one day, you'll see me as someone you can turn to. I might be Shelley's mum, but I'd like to be that someone for you."

And all of a sudden, years of pain I'd kept locked away began to seep into my pores, bringing fresh tears to my eyes.

"I want that too," I replied. A picture of a family, a real family with a mother who loved me and siblings who fought with me but had my back flickered in my mind.

I always thought it was enough to be a soldier. My brothers were my life, and I didn't need anyone else. I even remember saying it'd be a cold day in hell before I ever settled down. But why? Why had I fought so hard against something that could bring me so much happiness? Everything I wanted was mine for the taking. Mine because of her.

My Shelley.

I knew, in reality, it wasn't that kind of life I was rejecting, it was the fact that it was a life I never thought I'd get. One I didn't deserve. I pretended I was happy with the status quo because admitting the opposite would be like admitting defeat. I wanted a family of my own. I wanted to love and be loved. I wanted her.

"I'm going to stop here tonight, with Shelley. Make sure she's okay. Then tomorrow, if they agree to discharge her, I'll bring her home to you."

Grace smiled, and touching my face again, she said, "You're both welcome to stay. My home is your home."

I nodded and then led her to Shelley's room, opening the

THE JOKER

door for her but leaving the two of them alone. This was their time. I had the rest of my life to keep Shelley to myself.

Feeling a little lighter, I went in search of a coffee shop.

I thought my life was over when I saw the car in the water tonight. But now, it was only beginning.

There were four lessons I'd learned in life, or so I thought. Lesson one, everyone lies.

But I realised I'd been lying to myself the whole time. Thinking I didn't need anyone in my life. That I was okay as I was. I was a joker, a soldier, a brother in arms. But what is life without someone to love? A half-life, maybe?

Lesson two, I told myself to smile because it would fool everyone.

But who was it really fooling?

A mask will only work for so long. Eventually, life has a way of stripping you down. Adam had Liv, and Devon had Leah May. Our world was changing, and soon the others would find partners and want to build a life, have children, move on from where we were now. I didn't want to stand still and smile. I wanted to move forward too. I wanted to build my own life, with her.

The third lesson I taught myself was that friends are the family you choose for yourself, which still rang true.

But there was more to that lesson now.

As life evolved, I realised you could choose a family of your own, make a new life, and put right the wrongs of the past. I'd never treat my children the way I'd been treated. My children would grow up knowing they were loved, wanted, idolised, even, just like Grace had done with Shelley and her sisters. I could break the cycle and create something stronger, better.

And my last lesson; sometimes a lie is better than the truth. I'd been lying to myself for far too long. Now it was time to face the truth. I never used to believe in love, but now I did, and I felt excited for the future. For what lay ahead for me. It was time to be the man my father never was.

A man she deserved.

The man I deserved.

It was time to start living for her and for me.

COLTON'S EPILOGUE

Three Months Later

Life had been fucking amazing since Shelley had returned home from the hospital. She split her time between The Sanctuary and Grace's house, but most nights, she stayed with me. I loved having her around, and the more settled she became, the happier I was. Plus, she got on so well with Liv, Leah May, and all my brothers that it felt like we were one big happy family. The family I'd always dreamed of.

Gaz's overnight departure left some unanswered questions with the staff, but we told them he'd gone away to be with family, and they bought it. We made sure to keep the security team on side, but we vowed to do our own clean-up in future. We wouldn't trust anyone else with our business ever again. That shit was too important to risk.

And speaking of important shit, I was buzzing. Today was

the day of Shelley's final art presentation. The piece she'd been working on since I'd met her. The zodiac painting she still refused to show me, but right now, it was hanging somewhere in the art gallery I was crossing the main road to get to. I couldn't wait to see it. I couldn't wait to see her.

Feeling a strange nervous energy running through me, I pushed the glass door to the gallery open and stepped inside. As I did, a group of well-dressed, middle-aged women turned and stared at me. Actually, gawped would be a more accurate description of what they were doing as they looked me up and down. Okay, so I wasn't dressed in the obligatory office suit they seemed to favour. My black skinny jeans and black T-shirt weren't all that bad, but from the way they stared, it must've offended them pretty badly.

I really didn't fit in here.

I gave them a wink and a "Ladies," as I passed, which made them turn away in embarrassment. Then, I headed further into the gallery, taking a glass of champagne from the tray of a passing waiter as I ventured deeper into the artist's abyss.

But as I strolled further into the room, I only garnered more stares. I don't think these arty types appreciated me being in their space, but then I overheard one guy say, "It looks like him," and I smiled wide.

My reputation proceeded me.

I downed the champagne and when another waiter breezed past with a tray full of drinks, I swapped my empty glass for a full one. Glancing around, I tried to find Shelley, but I couldn't see her. The room was buzzing with people chattering and admiring the abstract art I didn't understand. Groups were gathered around discussing shades and tones like it was a fucking science. I felt a

THE JOKER

bit out of my depth. This was not my scene at all. But I was here for her, I was her support, and so I soldiered on, pushing my way through the crowds and turning the corner at the end of the room with a little extra swagger to boost my confidence.

And that's when I saw it, and my breath caught in my throat.

There, hanging high on the wall opposite and dominating the room, was a huge portrait of me.

Only it was more than that. Half was my natural face, but the other half was The Joker, with a sinister smile painted in a menacing yet curious way. A warning that nothing is quite as it seems. Don't ever judge a book by its cover.

I stopped and stared up at myself, marvelling at how Shelley had taken two sides of me and put them onto canvas for the rest of the world to see. I couldn't keep the smile off my face as I admired how the painting stared down at the room like a dystopian character from George Orwell's 1984.

Big Colton is watching.

Feeling dumbfounded, I moved closer to the painting, in awe of the attention to detail. It was breathtaking and I felt stunned into silence as I stood in front of it. The way she'd captured the twisted curve of my mouth as I smirked, the piercing stare in my eyes, every wave in my hair and freckle on my skin, it was perfect. She'd even included the Gemini tattoo on my shoulder. I was mesmerised.

"Do you like it?"

Her voice broke through my trance, and I turned to look at her standing beside me, biting her lip nervously as she waited for my verdict. This room was full of art, and yet she was the most beautiful thing in here, with her tumbling brown curls and her perfect, flawless face gazing back up at me.

"It's fucking perfect," I said, turning to her and taking her face in my hands.

There was nothing else I could say. One side was the cocky joker, but the other side was me–unfiltered, honest, just... me.

"I painted it from memory, but it wasn't difficult. Your face is etched up here." She tapped the side of her head, and I smiled, kissing her forehead. "This is how I saw you, when we first met. Hence the title–" She pointed at the plaque to the side of the painting. "–Two sides of the same story."

I took a step toward the plaque to read what was written.

Two Sides of The Same Story: My Gemini

Gemini is often misrepresented as being two-faced, but in reality, Gemini doesn't have a hidden agenda. Playful, curious, and quick-witted, they're the social butterfly of any group, and they brighten a room as soon as they enter.

They were sent to this world to mend differences and right wrongs. A true Gemini is always ready to give their life for their brother or their friend. Nothing is too much trouble for them. A Gemini can always be relied upon, they are the friends you make for life.

Throughout their lives, Geminis crave passion, excitement, and variety, but when they find the right person, a lover and a friend, they'll be faithful to them until the day they die.

When you're with a Gemini, one thing is certain; you'll never be bored. So hold on tight and enjoy the ride because Geminis live life to the full and always love unconditionally. To be loved by a Gemini is to know the true meaning of a soulmate forever.

Original Artwork by Shelley Masters

"I did research on the traits of a Gemini, and everything that's written there I pulled off the internet. It's funny–" she chuckled softly, "–because it describes you perfectly."

"I'm speechless." I glanced between her and the painting, and she laughed.

"Well, that's a first."

I put my arm around her and pulled her into me, needing to have her as close as I could.

"Is this why everyone was staring at me when I walked in?" I asked, cocking my brow in question.

"Probably."

"And there was me thinking it was because of my rugged good looks."

She pulled away slightly, smirking up at me.

"I'm sure it was that too."

At that moment, an older guy came over, stopping right behind us and patting Shelley on the shoulder. My back went up, so I pulled her further into me and glared at him.

"Excuse me, are you Shelley Masters, the one who painted this?" He gestured to her portrait, ignoring my warning stares.

"Yes." She blushed, and in that moment, I didn't want her to be shy, so I nudged her, wanting her to stand tall and proud. She'd made that art, and she needed to be fucking proud. I wanted to shout it from the rooftop.

The guy cleared his throat and reached into his jacket to pull out a business card.

"My name's Alistair Banks. I have a client that's very interested in purchasing this piece." He gave her the card, and she took it to be polite but shook her head.

"I'm sorry. This painting isn't for sale. I'm sure there's other pieces here that your client might be interested in—"

But he cut her off.

"No, I photographed this painting earlier and sent it to him. It has to be this one."

The guy wasn't giving up easily. Guess he had a thing for working-class heroes from the wrong side of the tracks.

"I'm very flattered he likes it—" Shelley went on, but he butted in again, pushing himself into her space to try and assert his power.

"He loves it! Jay's a massive DC fan. He needs this for his collection."

I didn't like the way he was bulldozing Shelley. His fake superiority pissed me off. Who wasn't a DC fan? DC was fucking awesome. But it didn't give him the right to come in and start throwing his weight around.

"But I already told you," Shelley said, standing firm and showing him she was no pushover. "It's not for sale."

"Everything has a price." He smiled smugly, and then turning to me, his smile grew wider. "And the muse is here too. Even better. Could I take your photo next to it?"

"No." I crossed my arms and stared him down, but he didn't care.

"I can offer you ten grand, cash," he stated proudly.

"No," Shelley countered.

"Okay." He tapped his finger on his chin and then announced, "Twenty. And maybe you could get the joker here to deliver it? Jay would love that."

This guy was getting on my last nerve. I wasn't a fucking puppet he could buy to perform tricks for him.

"I already said no," Shelley replied firmly before I could

give my response. A response that would've been a hell of a lot less polite than hers.

He rubbed his jaw like he was contemplating his next offer, and then he said, "I can go to thirty-five, but that's my absolute maximum. Final offer."

I faltered, and looking down at Shelley, I went to say something, but she beat me to it.

"There is nothing you can offer me that'll make me say yes. It could be thirty-five million and I'd still turn you down. This painting is important to me, and I won't sell it."

Fuck me, this girl didn't just own my heart; she'd ripped it from my chest and branded herself into my soul. She was perfect.

"How about another painting?" I suggested as I tried to tame the possessive beast inside me from breaking free and scaring this guy off. Today was about Shelley making connections that could benefit her career, and I wanted to help her with that, even if it meant aligning herself with this stuck-up twat. "A commission, maybe? You could do something similar, right?"

"Maybe." The guy gritted his teeth, and then smiling, he said, "I think we could work together. Give me a call, or better yet, I'll talk to the gallery and see what we can set up."

And then he spun on his heels, not even waiting for a response, and walked away with the same level of arrogance he'd greeted us with.

Shelley stood there watching him leave with her mouth hanging open. "So, that was…"

"Interesting and possibly very lucrative for you," I said, finishing her sentence. "But tell me one thing, why wouldn't you sell it? I mean, I think I get it, but I want to hear it from you.

He offered you a shit load of money, and you have the real thing standing right in front of you. So what held you back?"

She wound her arms around my waist and peered up at me, emotion swimming in her eyes as she tried to find the words to explain.

"Because some things are more important than money." She sighed. "This painting holds so many memoires for me. It's special. Every minute I spent on it brought me closer to you. It helped me to understand the man you are. I don't want to ever let that go. It's so much more than a painting. It's a journey. My journey to you."

I felt my heart melt at her words, and I leaned down, kissing the top of her head.

"Have I told you lately how much I love you?"

She rested her head on my chest.

"And have I told you that I love you more?"

SHELLEY'S EPILOGUE

Two Weeks Later

I was sitting in Colton's room, or rather our room at The Sanctuary, waiting for him to come home with what he told me was an epic surprise. He didn't know I had one of my own, though, and I could barely contain my nerves and excitement as I waited for him. I lay on the bed, twiddling my thumbs and clock-watching, willing him to come through the door.

Half an hour later, he burst into the room, like he always did, giving me a shit-eating grin and striding towards the bed, ready to dive on me and show me how much he'd missed me. But I was too fast, and I jumped up, motioning to the corner of the room where his surprise was. Instantly, his over-excited, puppy dog expression changed to one of awe when he saw what was there.

It was his painting, hanging on the wall.

The one I'd created just for him.

"Surprise," I said, without all the fanfare that usually followed that word. I didn't want to make a fuss. I just wanted him to know I was giving it to him because I wanted to say thank you. The painting was always going to be his.

"Fuck me." His eyes grew wide, and he walked slowly over to the wall where it hung, staring like it was the first time he'd seen it. "What is this doing here? Shouldn't it be in an art gallery or a millionaire's mansion somewhere?"

"No," I said, giving him a playful nudge. "It's yours. I want you to have it. It's my way of saying thank you."

"Thank you for what?" He turned towards me, peering down at me with that look in his eyes that made my stomach twist. The one that said he loved me. The look he only ever gave to me.

"For being you." I reached up on my tiptoes and kissed him, only a gentle whisper of a kiss, but it was enough to ignite a spark inside me. Being close to Colton always did that. It was like he held the key to every one of my emotions. My kinky, sexy little puppet master.

"I can think of other ways you could thank me," he whispered in that rumbling, sexy voice of his, sliding his arms around my waist and pulling me closer to him so he could nuzzle my neck. "And I'm looking forward to all those ways a little later but… thank you." He lifted his head to look at me with sincerity. "A thirty-five-thousand-pound painting is one hell of a way to tell me you love me."

I slapped his chest, and he laughed.

"It's not about the money." I scoffed.

"I know. I'm kidding." He placed a delicate peck on the end of my nose. "The fact you took the time to make such an amazing painting of me is priceless. I will treasure it forever, and when we get our own place and have kids and grandkids running wild, I'll tell them, Grandma Shelley was so insanely in love with me she couldn't even see straight. My face was all she saw; it sent her crazy. And so, she painted me to make sure I never aged. My image would be ingrained in her heart, mind, and the walls of her home for eternity. My ruggedly handsome face would live on forever."

"And I'll tell them you loved yourself so much I made you a portrait so you could worship yourself until the end of time."

"I wonder who they'll believe?" he mused. "Probably me, because let's be real, that face up there is the stuff of legends."

"You wish." I bumped against his side, and he hissed as if he was in pain and stepped back.

"Are you okay?" I asked, peering down at the sweats he was wearing, wondering why he wasn't in his signature black jeans.

"Yeah. I need to show you your surprise."

Tentatively, he took another step back and pulled his sweats down to his ankles with a self-satisfied smirk.

"For fuck's sake," I groaned. "Did you get more piercings?" Not that I'd complain about that. His piercings were fucking amazing.

"No." He twisted to the side and pulled up his T-shirt that was hiding the fact that he wasn't wearing any underwear, and on his left butt cheek was a small white bandage. "I got something else." He glanced up at me and said, "Take it off. Have a look."

I shook my head with a smile and knelt, pulling the tape that held the bandage with as much care as possible. When I saw what he'd done, I had to laugh. It was classic Colton.

There, in bold black letters across his butt, he'd had the

words 'Property of Shelley King' tattooed on him.

"Oh my God." I put my hands over my mouth as I kneeled on the floor. "What the hell, Colton?"

"I know I said I'd never get a girls' name tattooed on me, but you're not just any girl, are you? And I wanted to have you somewhere on my body."

Was he for real?

How could he make something so ridiculous and funny sound so sweet?

"But you put King, not Masters." I glanced up to see him holding a small, black velvet box in his hand.

"Now, don't freak out." He gave me a pointed stare, telling me to hold tight and listen, because I did have a history of popping off. "I know we're still new and its early days. But one, I didn't want to have to go through the ball ache of changing Masters to King when we do get married." He held his finger up as I tried to interrupt, making me hold my tongue so he could finish his speech. "Two, it's going to happen. You know as well as I do, we're meant to be, so don't even argue with me on that one. And three, I got you to kneel for the proposal so that makes it a win in my eyes." And there it was, that cheeky wink of his.

I wanted to slap his butt, but I knew it'd fucking kill after having the tattoo, so instead, I took the box he was offering, and opened it. Seeing the stunning solitaire diamond inside, I lost my breath.

"It's beautiful," I stammered, feeling tears well up. "I don't know what to say."

"Yes would be a start."

I grinned and stood up, wrapping my arms around his neck and kissing him.

"Yes."

He placed his forehead against mine.

"We don't have to rush into anything. We can take everything at your pace, but I didn't want to go another day without making it official. I want everyone to know you're mine. Always. And I'm yours."

"How did I get so lucky to find someone like you?" I asked, knowing he'd give me some crazy sarcastic response, but he didn't.

"Luck had nothing to do with it. But fate? I think that was working in our favour all along. You were brought into my world, and I was thrust into yours. But no one can deny that this, us, it was fate. It was meant to be. The Joker and the Queen. Forever. Now, it's time for our happily ever after."

I never thought I'd get one of those, so standing in his room, feeling like my heart might burst with how much I loved him, I did what I knew best. I showed him what he meant to me.

All night long.

A FINAL MESSAGE FROM COLTON

Dear Reader,

What a ride that was.

First, I want to thank you for sticking with me until the end. I know it got a bit crazy in parts, but it all turned out okay eventually, right?

I found her.

The one.

Who'd have thought it?

Not me, if you'd have asked me years ago. But now, I couldn't imagine my life without her. She's the Batman to my Joker. She's my everything.

I wanted to end my story by saying that my happily ever after will always be evolving; it'll never end. And maybe, when the other boys tell you their stories, you might catch a glimpse of what Shelley and I are up to in the future.

I know there's one burning question you're dying to know the answer to… who would I choose as my best man?

THE JOKER

Well, the answer is simple.

I have four best friends. Four brothers. So, when the time comes, and I manage to get Shelley down that aisle, I'll have four best men beside me.

Tyler is a people person, so he'll be right there at the door to the chapel, chatting to everyone and making them feel welcome.

Devon is good in a crisis, so I'll have him close at the altar to keep me in check. I might not show it, but nerves can get the better of me. And no one can pull me off the crazy ledge like he can.

As awesome as my jokes are, I can't do all my own speeches, so Will can be in charge there. I'm sure some of my sparkling wit has rubbed off on him over the years.

And Adam?

That man would die for us. We'd do the same for him. So, he'll be there by my side, ensuring I don't make a total tit of myself on the day.

I trust him with my life. I trust all of them.

I'm one lucky son of a bitch to have the best friends a guy could wish for and the most beautiful girl to share my life with. It just goes to show, not all jokers finish last.

I hope you enjoyed my story.

Until we meet again.

Colton x

THE END

Copyright @ Nikki J Summers 2022

AUTHOR ACKNOWLEDGEMENTS

What a whirlwind it's been, living in the mind of Colton King for so long. I must start by saying the biggest thank you to my husband and two children for living with a soldier obsessed, slightly… okay, a lot more than slightly, crazy wife and mum. I've spent most of my time writing this in a daze, living in Brinton Manor in my head, and occasionally coming back down to earth to visit reality. These boys have taken over my life. They've become real people. So, thank you for listening to me ramble on, for supporting me, and for cleaning out the guinea pig cage and doing the housework so I don't have to. You're the best. I love you. And I promise not to put you in any of my books.

To my best book buddy, my alpha reader, editor, and all-round awesome friend, Lindsey Powell. Thank for listening to me, supporting me, and letting me bounce my crazy ideas off you. You've pulled me off the ledge more times than I care to mention. I don't know what I'd do without you. Thank you so much for being you. I would be lost without you. If you haven't checked out her books yet, get on it!

Caroline Stainburn, what can I say? I'm so thankful to have met you. Thank you for your insights into Colton and for all the advice. You helped to make Colton who he is. I owe you so much for giving me the kick up the butt I needed to get this book out there. You helped me find my mojo and I'm forever grateful. Thank you.

To Lou J Stock, for taking a word document and creating pure magic. Your formatting always blows me away. Thank you so much for making my book the best it can be. You're awesome.

I'd also like to thank the brilliant people who created this amazing cover. Chris Davis, who answered my desperate plea for help, and persuaded the perfect Colton, The Joker, to be on the cover. After seeing Jord online, I couldn't have anyone else. You made my dreams come true, and the photographs you took were amazing.

To my perfect Joker, Jord Liddell. I can't tell you how honoured I was that you agreed to do the photoshoot. That smile, those eyes, every part of the photograph is stunning. You helped to bring my Joker to life, and for that, I will always be eternally grateful. Big shoutout to Rhiannon Carr for the messages and support. I agree, he's more than a ten. You two are awesome.

And finally, Lori Jackson, for adding the sparkle that brought this cover to life. Your designs are second to none. You killed it. Thank you so much.

To Candi Kane PR. Thank you for organising the cover reveal, release day, and all the promotion for this book. You made my life a million times easier, and I will be highly recommending you to everyone. You're amazing. Thank you!

To all the bloggers, bookstagrammers, booktokers, and everyone who takes the time to read, review, and make such brilliant edits on social media. I appreciate each and every one of you, from the bottom of my heart.

I'd like to say a massive thank you to Aelicia Greene, Suny Oliva (Bookslover09), Sandra Hearn (Sandralovesreading), Michelle Mastandrea (the_romance_reader_gal), My Darling Robin, Robyn (Books4days_with_robyn), Vesna Pringle (ves_gp_mua), Caroline (world_of_books65), Owella, I could go on forever! You guys are all amazing. I wish I could list all the bloggers, Tik Tokers, and everyone that shows support, but my book would be never ending because there are so many of you.

Special shoutout to Natalie at All I Read is Love and Angy at Collector of Book Boyfriends for making the official teasers for The Joker. You are amazing at what you do. Thank you so much! Go and check out their work. They rock.

To the indie author community, I love how encouraging, supportive, and utterly amazing you are. I feel proud to be a part of such a brilliant community. #indieauthorsrock

And finally, to you the reader. Thank you for taking a chance on my book. Thank you for reading Colton and Shelley's story. You make it all worthwhile.

Stay tuned, because Tyler and Will are up next, and you don't want to miss their stories. These boys won't know what's hit them when they meet their special partners.

Until next time,
Lots of love
Nikki x

For updates on my new releases and other news, follow me on the following platforms.

**INSTAGRAM
FACEBOOK
READER GROUP
TWITTER
TIKTOK
BOOKBUB**

Printed in Great Britain
by Amazon